QUIET ANGEL

By
Prescott Lane

TABLE OF CONTENTS

PART ONE

TWELVE YEARS AGO

CHAPTER ONE

IT'S THE SAME here every frickin' year. Gage spun a football and stared out at the pristine coastline. There were kite-surfers trying to stay up before the waves crashed down, and some fair-haired children building sandcastles while others splashed in tidal pools. He strained his blue eyes to the Atlantic horizon and thought he saw a dolphin jumping ahead of a shrimp boat.

Gage pulled his t-shirt over his sandy blond hair, exposing his chiseled abs and tan chest from cutting grass a few times a week. His parents were well-off, but they made him work for his money. He looked down at his toes in the sand, spotting a collection of seashells close by, the bright sun setting down on them.

He didn't know the first thing about seashells—no 18-year-old guy would know, or care, why they were all clustered near each other, why some sported radial ribs while others had ocher striations—but their different shapes and sizes held his interest for a moment. Then he looked out to the shrimp boat and tried to find the dolphin again, if there even was one out there.

It really didn't matter either way. He'd seen a dolphin before. He'd seen the whole island before. It was all the same as last summer and every summer before that. His family came here each year, to St. Simons Island off the Georgia coast. It was only a short drive from Atlanta and, as his parents told him, an escape from the hustle of everyday life.

When his family first started coming, their house was part of a quaint little village along the beach, and Gage liked his time on the island, a young boy building sandcastles and splashing around. But as the years passed and the island grew in popularity, it became more of a resort community for upper-crust snobs and their preppy kids who didn't have to cut grass.

It was a chance for the snobs to "summer" amongst each other in their three-story condos. Gage hated when they used the season as a verb. And he hated that there wasn't much for teenage boys to do, except, of course, to drink and smoke pot and chase girls. He didn't mind the occasional drink—he wasn't a boy scout—but not the rest.

He let out a sigh, knowing he was pouting, that he'd been pouting the whole car ride here, that he probably should just be grateful for being in such a majestic place. But he couldn't help it: he wanted to be anywhere else, preferably back in Atlanta celebrating high school graduation with his friends, spending time with them before heading off to the Naval Academy in a few months.

He tossed the ball above his head and caught it with both hands, as a group of fresh-faced guys—regulars from summers past—breezed past him, chatting about their new cars, the weed they stashed in suitcases, the Ivy League colleges they planned to attend. The guys looked like they were made in a Ralph Lauren outlet store, all looking spiffy in their plaid and yellow and blue hues. The guys stopped in their tracks, maybe 10 feet past Gage, seeing a new girl come out of a little cottage along the beach.

She had on a floppy white sunhat and a long periwinkle blue sundress. The guys apparently hadn't seen the girl in past summers, though one of them said he saw her a few days ago hanging around a woman who looked too old to be her mother. The girl curled up in a beach chair and opened a book. At that point, a different guy said the book worms always scream the loudest in bed, at least that's what he'd heard. When the laughing died down, the bets started as to who could screw her first.

Gage winced and gripped his ball. The girl appeared to be a bit younger than he was, but he couldn't be sure with the sunhat covering her face.

One guy moved away from the group, seemingly prodded on by the others, and began to approach the girl. The others followed a few steps behind, playfully, curiously, eager to see if the guy embarrassed himself or hear whatever smooth line may work on her. Gage moved a bit closer, too, spinning the ball in his hand, stroking the laces with his fingers, keeping his eyes fixed on the girl.

The guy reached the girl, and they exchanged a few words. Gage was too far away—probably about 30 feet—to hear what was being said. But he could plainly see her close the book and shake her head, as if she had no interest being on the same island with the guy, let alone talking to him. The guy looked to his friends for help, but they only egged him on, urging him to keep trying. A nervous smile on his face, the guy turned back to the girl.

She tilted up her head to look at him, and Gage caught her pure, porcelain skin under the sunhat. Suddenly nothing seemed the same anymore.

The guy reached down to stroke her arm, and the girl pulled away—a sad, scared look on her face. Gage could feel her tremble from a distance. He placed his hand firmly on the laces and cocked his right arm back. He fired forward, hurling a tight spinning spiral humming through the air, the ball landing just as intended. The guy grabbed his face in his hands, letting fly a string of curses, holding his nose as blood poured out.

Staring daggers at Gage, the guy stumbled back to his group, in no condition to do anything about what just happened. And his friends had no intention of doing anything for him, choosing instead to point and laugh at him. That was easier and more fun than locking horns with a guy with chiseled abs and a strong right arm, even if they outnumbered him.

The guy wiped some blood from his face and barked to Gage, "You could've just called 'dibs.'"

Gage rolled his eyes and jogged to get the ball. When he bent down to pick it up, a gust of wind kicked up and blew off the girl's hat. He grabbed the hat instead of the ball then stopped and stared at the girl, her chocolate brown hair tied in a braid, a silver pendant in the shape of wings hanging from a leather rope around her neck, her crystal blue eyes filled with caution.

"*Dibs*, huh?" she asked. "You hoping to score, too?"

"Um, no," Gage said quickly, his words falling out in a thick Southern accent. She raised her eyebrows, and he ran a hand through his sandy blond hair. "It's not that you're not hot." He looked away, embarrassed, wishing he was far out in the ocean with the dolphin. "I mean, you're beautiful, but I'm not looking for that. Just wanted to get my ball." She tilted her head to the side. "I'm sorry about that prick."

"Is he a friend of yours?"

"No."

"So why get involved?"

"I guess if you see someone in trouble, you try to help?"

She gave a slight smile. "So you make it a habit of saving young women?"

"Only girls in big hats."

She motioned to her hat in his hand. "Can I have it back?"

"Oh, yeah," he said and handed it to her.

"And don't forget about your ball."

"Right," he said and quickly scooped it up.

The girl looked away from him, down the beach at the preppy group, still hanging around and staring at her. Then she looked back at him—football in hand, hard body, a bit nervous, probably a year or two older than she. "Thanks for the save. I'm Layla."

"Gage," he said, a twinge of relief in his voice. "What are you reading?"

Layla looked at the spine of her book. "*History of Angels.*"

"Is this summer reading or something?" he asked and sat down beside her in the sand.

Layla bit her lip slightly and pulled her legs under her. "No, it's not for school. I just like to read about them."

"You still in high school?"

"Yeah," she said. "You?"

"I just finished." He played with some sand in his hands, trying to calm his nerves. "Who's your favorite?"

"*Favorite?*"

"Angel."

"Oh," she said, flashing a glorious smile, giving the sunset a run for its money, two huge dimples appearing on her cheeks. "There are so many great ones, but I guess my favorite is Layla."

"You're named after an angel? My parents named me after a tool. What's she the angel of?"

"Guardian angel of conception and childbirth. She brings the soul to the unborn baby in the mother's womb." Layla briefly looked into his blue eyes then out to the ocean, the sun barely visible on the horizon.

"Layla?" an elderly voice called out from the beach cottage.

Layla gave her a wave and smile then turned back to Gage. "My grandmother."

"Are you on vacation?"

"I'm staying with her for the summer, maybe longer."

"My family comes here every summer. Don't remember seeing you before."

"First time," she said.

"Where are you from?"

She paused for a moment. "Houston. You?"

"Atlanta," he said. "If you stay longer than the summer, I guess you're switching high schools?"

"I don't know my plans."

Her grandmother called out again. "Layla?"

"I better go see what she wants inside," she said and stood up. "It's getting dark, too."

Gage got up and brushed some sand off his shorts. When he looked up, she was already a few feet away, heading towards the cottage. His heart began to race: he didn't have her number and hadn't made plans to see her again. He wanted to but figured he didn't have a chance with her. He gripped his swim trunks for something— anything—to say.

"What's your last name?" he blurted out.

She gave a smile over her shoulder. "Baxter."

"Mine's Montgomery," he said, taking a deep breath. "Can we do something tomorrow?"

"Depends on what you have in mind." She opened the screen door and headed inside.

Everything has changed.

HER BEACH COTTAGE was a two-bedroom bungalow with a pair of Adirondack deck chairs facing the ocean. The harsh sun and salty air had left their mark, and so had a few tropical storms and a hurricane or two, all weathering the old wooden frame just slightly. But its pastel salmon exterior still carried a sparkle. Layla's grandmother made sure of that. She also made sure her cottage withstood the zoning changes allowing the creep of commercial and residential buildings seemingly everywhere but her property.

After lunch, with the sun high in the sky, Layla headed out to the deck and took a few steps in the hot sand, which quickly turned into cool wet mush. The salty breeze whipping her braid, she navigated the buckets of brown and green seaweed that came with the tide, keeping her feet in the mush, which felt good between her toes. Everything felt good here.

She lifted her long cotton sundress just slightly, as she made her way to the edge of the ocean, the churning waves washing her feet. She took a deep breath, taking in the salty air for all its worth, and looked out to the horizon, thinking back to three days ago, though it seemed like a lifetime, when she showed up, in a mad frenzy, to a place she'd never been before, to an island she'd barely heard of, to a sweet elderly grandmother she hadn't seen in years.

But here she was now, her feet in the ocean, still standing, her mind and body uncoiling a little each day. She walked along the edge of the water for about 30 yards, each step lighter than the last. Then she turned back to the cottage, and her blue eyes popped. Gage was sitting on her back steps kicking at some sand.

In between everything else, she couldn't stop thinking about him. He was the hottest boy she'd ever seen, blond hair kissed by the sun, tan skin, deep blue eyes, defined muscles. He seemed different than the other guys. But part of her wondered if he was part of the group of preppy guys, if this was still a game or bet. Her life was uncertain enough; she couldn't handle any more drama.

She watched him some more. It appeared his lips were moving and his hands were gesturing slightly. Then he shook his head and started again, appearing to practice whatever lines once more. After a few more tries, he lowered his head in his hands, defeated. Her stomach churned for him. No guy would try so hard—agonize like this on summer vacation—in a game he was so bad at.

She started walking to the cottage when he spotted her. She looked down at her sundress, slightly wet from her stroll, and tried to tuck a few loose strands from her braid behind her ears. But the ocean breeze made it impossible. Gage met her half-way with a broad smile on his face.

"I thought of something we could do," he said, his Southern accent jumbled in nerves, "but I didn't have your number."

"I don't have a cell phone," Layla said. "What did you come up with?"

"I could take you up in my dad's glider."

"*What?*"

His face turned pale. "You don't want to go?"

"I hate flying."

"You can't *hate* flying."

"Last time I threw up on the man in front of me," she said.

"No way."

"Sure did."

"I can't believe you hate flying. I was practically born on an airplane. My dad owns a commuter airline. I've been flying since before I could crawl."

"I've flown a lot, too, but I hate it."

"Angels fly," he said with a wry smile.

"They do," she said, returning the smile, "but people were made for land."

"You swim?"

"Well, yeah."

"Do you throw up on the fish?"

Layla laughed. "No."

"I promise you won't throw up in the glider."

"Not going to chance it," she said.

"I've been certified since I was 14."

She looked at him curiously, finding it oddly sweet he thought his teenage certification would somehow convince her, somehow comfort her enough to get on a "glider"—which sounded like some kind of flimsy paper airplane—when she's scared to death to fly on commercial aircraft operated by grizzled vets who'd logged thousands of hours of flight time. "Do you want to be a pilot?"

"Yeah, I'm going to the Naval Academy in the Fall."

Her grandmother called out from the screen door. "Layla?"

"Do you need to go?" Gage asked.

Layla looked to the cottage then back to Gage. She told herself to relax. There was no way this guy was playing her, no way she could be a bet. And the idea of hanging out with someone sweet, someone close to her own age, sounded pretty good, especially since she didn't know another soul on the island besides her grandmother. Plus, it could be fun to pretend, at least for a little while, that her life was normal.

"I'll catch up with you later, Grandma," Layla called back, keeping her eyes fixed on Gage.

"Does this mean we're going flying?"

"Maybe when you finish the Naval Academy."

"OK. I've got another idea. Let's head out to the recreation center."

Layla nodded. "I'll meet you there. I need to tell my grandmother."

GAGE WOULD'VE PREFERRED an aerial tour, but a leisurely bike trip would work fine, too. He rented two beach cruisers, a pink one for Layla with a white wicker basket upfront, and stocked it up with water bottles, surrounding them with a bouquet of wildflowers he picked along the way. He figured the flowers were a nice touch. But then he second-guessing himself, worrying the flowers were way too much, way too forward.

While he might consider this a first date, perhaps she just wanted a change of scenery, to get out of her cottage, wanting nothing more than a change of pace from her grandmother. He was about to ditch the flowers when he saw Layla walking towards him, her dimples on full display, so much so they appeared to have their own dimples. He breathed a sigh of relief and handed her a bike helmet. There was no way he was wearing one—he didn't want to look like a dork—but he wanted her safe. He helped her on the pink bike then began his little tour.

Gage started out along the shore, pointing out the beach shops brimming with new and returning vacationers, many just arriving for the Summer, some getting surfboards to head out to the ocean, some getting t-shirts with their names spray painted on, some swapping out old fishing poles for new ones. He'd gone by the shops a thousand times before, but it all seemed different now, the same sights and sounds that once bored him suddenly made new, given new life through her eyes.

They biked past a soda shop full of retro decor, vintage furniture, and soft pastels and pinstripes. He offered but she didn't want any ice cream, so they kept going. He took her along a few bike trails, blessed with shade, covered by stately oak trees. He shifted from one trail to another, along one particular path he thought he alone knew, until stopping in front of St. Simons Lighthouse, a popular tourist attraction on the island.

They parked their bikes against a tree, and he began to tell her about the place. He started by pointing out that it was a tall, white cylinder stretching high into the air, maybe a few hundred feet or so, with a flashing light up top.

"You should be a tour guide," Layla teased.

His face turned as red as the setting sun. He tried to think of something more to say, something beyond what their eyes could see, but there was nothing—not with her crystal blue eyes fixed on him. "I'm sure there is a brochure or something that could give you more detail."

She smiled. "I don't need more detail."

"Oh, OK."

"It's pretty to look at," she said, taking in his eyes. "That's enough for me."

Gage looked up at the lighthouse. "Sometimes my parents drag me to these jazz concerts they have out here."

"My grandmother has told me about those. She likes them, too," she said. "I played piano for about two seconds when I was little."

"My mom tried to get me to play piano, but I hated it, so I got her to let me play guitar. I wanted an electric one, but she told me Santa only brought acoustic guitars." He chuckled. "I've been playing since I was seven or so."

"You must be good. Do you write your own music? Or sing?"

Gage felt his face heat again. "I sing a little."

"Maybe you can play for me sometime?"

"Maybe," he said, blushing.

"And sing, too?"

"Maybe."

Layla smiled and looked away. "With the sun going down, I probably should check in back home." She walked to her bike and thought about what she said. *Home.* She wasn't sure why she used that word. She wasn't sure where that was anymore.

"We can go back along the beach," he said.

They hopped on their bikes, and Gage snaked around the lighthouse, finding an entrance to the white sand. They made their way past the herons and crabs and the last of the sun worshippers, heading all the way down to the water, the rushing of the ocean against their tires, the sand kicking up and swirling in the warm air, the rising tide whipping through the day's sandcastles.

They pulled into the recreation center. Gage lifted the flowers from the basket and handed them to Layla. She smelled them—some squished, some dirty, all wind-blown—and smiled. Then he walked her to her cottage along the beach.

"Do you need to go inside?" he asked.

"Not yet," she said and opened the screen door, yelling inside to her grandmother that she was back.

Layla took a seat on the sand, and Gage followed her lead, both looking up at the night sky twinkling above like diamonds. He looked over at her profile, the curve of her neck, her hair blowing slightly, wondering what she was thinking about. She had him thinking about everything he shouldn't be.

She suddenly looked over at him, catching him staring, but he didn't look away. To his surprise, she didn't, either. He felt his body leaning closer to hers, wanting to touch her, wanting to kiss her, both more than anything he ever wanted before. But she broke the moment, turning her head back up to the stars.

"The stars don't look like this in Houston," she said. "Too many bright city lights."

Gage groaned inside. "You miss it?"

"No," she said. "Things with my family there are, well, complicated. You miss Atlanta?"

"Not anymore," he said, seeing a dimple on her face. Layla exhaled and stretched out on the sand, looking directly up to the sky. Gage looked down at her, and his mind wandered to his body on top of her. He closed his eyes for a second, trying to stop the fantasy before it became obvious what he was thinking about.

"I used to sneak out into my backyard and sleep under the stars at home," she said. "Dream about being. . . ."

"Dream about what?"

"You know, the usual stuff," she said. "What's the meaning of life? Why am I here? What's my purpose? Why was the world created?" Layla saw a puzzled look on his face. *I sound like my grandmother.* "Of course, I made wishes, too."

"For what?"

She sat up. "That's between me and the angels."

"*Angels?*"

"Yeah, the stars are really angels."

"No, they're not. They're balls of gas and rock."

"Hardly."

"So which one is the Angel Layla?"

She pointed to the brightest star in the sky. "That one."

Her grandmother called out from inside. "Layla, did you call your parents today?"

"Yes, earlier."

"It's dark and cool," her grandmother said. "Come on inside, honey."

Layla stood up and brushed off some sand. "I'll see you tomorrow, Gage," she said and turned to go inside.

"Good night, Angel."

Layla smiled over her shoulder, her heart melting, before disappearing through the screen door.

CHAPTER TWO

LAYLA SUNK HER feet in the sand, just as the sun peeked through the clouds and the seagulls began their morning symphony. She adjusted her shorts and tank top then pushed her hands together in a prayer pose, taking a few deep breaths.

This was the third morning she tried the yoga meditation class. Her grandmother thought it would be good for her and encouraged her to keep at it, even though Layla thought she looked stupid, surrounded by toned and tanned women, and even a few men, all of whom seemed to know exactly what they were doing, having long ago mastered the strange art of reaching and posing and stretching their bodies.

The soothing voice of the instructor helped calm her nerves a little, its deep sound rolling in as gently as the morning waves. "Bring yourself to the present moment," he said.

Layla tried to do as he suggested, putting aside she was so young and uncoordinated, but her mind shifted once again—to the cute boy staying down the beach, their bike ride together, the lighthouse, the stars, his eyes, his perfect smile. The instructor told the class to move into a tree pose, and Layla shook her head to focus. She shifted her weight to one leg and moved her other foot to her inner thigh. Then, after a slight wobble, she lifted both arms over her head and pressed her palms together.

"This is a time to find peace and harmony," the instructor said.

But Layla's stomach didn't listen, churning around as a thousand butterflies whizzed inside, thinking back to last night, how he called her "Angel." A slow smile came over her lips. She thought to look towards his house down the beach, to see if he was out and get a glimpse of him, but she feared she'd fall down if she moved her head just the slightest. She chuckled at how much she sucked at yoga.

Her heart raced at the thought he might be waiting for her in front of her cottage. And if he wasn't, maybe she'd walk down to his house and knock on his door after class. She tried to tell herself that was a good idea—that he'd like that since he seemed to like her—but then her heart suddenly sank. Perhaps Gage didn't like her too much. Perhaps he just saw her as a friend, someone with whom to ride bikes. After all, he hadn't even held her hand, let alone tried to kiss her.

"If your mind starts to wander," the instructor said, "simply bring yourself back—gently."

She promised herself she wouldn't think about Gage anymore. She hadn't come all the way to Georgia to meet a boy. There were plenty back in Houston or wherever life would take her, wherever home might be. She was on the island to do exactly what she was trying to do—calm her mind, protect her soul, find some balance. There was no time or energy for boys, for love – especially since she had no idea how he felt about her.

She thought again to look down at his house, but the instructor's voice caught her. "Picture your whole body breathing in and out," he said. "Imagine all your energy, your love, as light flowing out into the universe."

Layla closed her eyes and let her chest rise and fall, taking deep breaths, the warm, salty air flowing through her. She tried to focus on his words, but it was hard with the voices in her head so loud. A few days at the beach couldn't take away what had happened, what was still happening. A few days with a perfect boy couldn't take away her fears. Still, the last few days had been good. She could feel a slight shift, at least some weight lifted.

"Listen to what the universe is telling you," the instructor said. "So often we talk, but now is the time to listen."

She focused on the seagulls, the crashing waves, her own breathing, far different sounds than the usual. She moved a strand of hair from her face, finding the usual chocolate brown a shade lighter, her normally pale hands, like the rest of her body, now slightly kissed by the sun.

The instructor continued on, "Everything is going to be OK."

Layla wasn't sure that was true, but his soothing tone was nice and continued to settle her. At least now she was safe. She could be a normal teenage girl. And maybe, if only for a few months here, she could send love into the world and hopefully get some back.

She moved into a downward dog position, her hips in the air, her hands in the increasingly hot sand, wishing she had a mat like the rest of her classmates. She once again told herself to focus; there was no reason to think about her classmates, let alone be jealous of them.

So she set upon a harder move to steady herself. From the downward dog position, Layla lifted one leg in the air and held it up, closing her eyes and focusing on her breathing, the seagulls, the waves – anything to steady her body.

But after a few seconds, her arms started to shake, and her bottom leg started to buckle. With the bright sun beating down, she let out a moan and began to feel dizzy, her mind and body on the verge of betraying her.

She opened her eyes. Everything appeared black, except for a golden hue which looked like sand. She squinted her eyes and found it wasn't sand at all. She was looking up, not down. She was looking at dirty blond hair—straight at Gage, her butt in his face. She popped to her feet.

"I was just looking, um. . . ." He stopped when Layla turned her attention to the instructor wrapping up the class. He wanted to bury himself in the sand—there couldn't be a worse stopping point—but there was no point in continuing if she wasn't listening. When the instructor finished up, Gage finished his thought. "What I was saying was, I mean, I wasn't looking at you. I was, um, looking for my dad."

"Your dad meditates?" she asked, dusting some sand from her hands.

"He comes to these when we're here in the summer."

"Was he in the class?"

"I guess not today." Gage gripped his messy hair. "He must've gone running."

"Why are you looking for him?"

"He and I were supposed to go flying later this morning, but it might rain, so my mom made other plans for them. She wanted me to tell him. I'm sure she'll find him."

Layla shrugged and picked up a thin round shell. She took in its smooth edges, with a few jagged spots, and held it out to him. Gage took it from her, his fingertips grazing her hand. "I used to call these mermaid coins."

They started down the beach together, and their steps soon fell into a rhythm, neither one of them knowing or saying where they were going. Grey clouds gathering and hours passing quickly, Layla pointed out other shells along the shore. Gage didn't know the first damn thing about sea shells but followed along with everything she said, listening as if his life depended on it.

He fixated on her every word, on her hands holding the shells, on her hair whipping across her face. If she wanted to talk about sea shells all day, he was fine with that. And he was fine keeping them in his pockets for her. But a part of him wanted to move things along. He wanted more. He wanted a chance with her. He didn't want to get stuck in the friend zone.

The clouds darkening some more, he looked down at her hand, mere inches from his own. He wanted to hold it, to massage it, to rub her sunburned knuckles with his fingers. But something told him not to. He didn't want her to pull her hand away. He didn't want to screw up things. He tried to tell himself there was no reason to worry. He'd held plenty of girls' hands before and kissed many of them, too.

But this girl was different, definitely smarter, more aware of herself and her surroundings. She was on a different level. She didn't seem to care about shit like makeup, clothes, impressions—like the island girls from summers past, always talking about an upcoming party or the latest gossip. Layla didn't seem to have time for that. It was hard to believe she was in high school. It was hard to believe she was 16.

Gage took a deep breath and gathered some courage. He inched his hand closer, slowly, carefully, his heart about to burst. He stretched his fingers out a bit, closing the gap even further, knowing he was so close, almost there, the promised land within reach as they moved stride for stride. He closed his hand, ready to feel her soft skin, to massage her sunburn, to change the world forever, but he only found air.

He looked to the side, and she wasn't there. He turned around to find her crouched down a few feet behind him, scooping up another shell from the slushy sand. *Crap.*

"This one is a marine mollusk," Layla said, handing him a brown and white shell. "Hang on to this one, too."

Gage could only smile and put it in his pocket with the others. "How do you know so much about shells? There's no beach in Houston, huh?"

"I don't know too much really. But Galveston is pretty close by. There's a beach there. My family would go sometimes."

"You still go there?"

She shook her head and looked in his eyes. No boy ever looked at her the way he did, sweetly, intently, like there was no one else on the beach but her. A drop of water touched her face. "Is that rain?"

They looked up at the dark clouds, spilling a few drops to the ground, turning into more, then more. "Come on!" Gage said and took her hand. "That's my house right there. We can make it." They ran about 50 yards then up a few steps to his back porch. He slid open the glass patio door and pulled Layla inside, closing the door behind them. "Let me get you a towel."

"You don't have to," she said, letting go of his hand and rubbing her bare arms, shivering. "I'll be OK."

Gage looked down at her, teeth chattering, rain drops sliding down her skin, her body up against the glass patio door. He began to rub her arms, pressing his body softly against hers, then took one hand and gently brushed a strand of wet hair behind her ear. He leaned in closer, setting his eyes squarely on her mouth.

Layla pushed her own hair from her face and stepped aside. "Aren't your parents home?"

"No," Gage said. "My mom made plans for them to go to lunch with some friends."

Layla shivered again, placing her hand on the doorknob behind her back and peeking out the window. "It's really coming down."

"It should pass pretty quick," he said. "Always get these quick showers in the afternoon. You hungry?"

"Starving," she said, keeping glued to her spot.

"I'll make us some sandwiches," he said. "Just let me go change out of these wet clothes." He pointed towards a hallway. "My room's just down the hall. Only bedroom on the first floor." He started towards the hallway then turned back. "And you don't need to stand by the door. You can walk around inside wherever. I'll be right back."

Gage raced to his bedroom, telling himself not to mess up this chance, not to make any more stupid comments like where his bedroom was. She looked nervous enough when he said his parents weren't home. He hoped they were having a very long lunch. They were always pretty strict with him: he wasn't supposed to be alone with a girl in the house, ever. And there were no exceptions for bad weather. He changed clothes as fast as he could, hoping she didn't bolt while he was gone, and grabbed a blanket from his bed on the way out.

Layla stood frozen at the door. She'd never been alone in a guy's place before and wasn't quite sure how to act, especially in a beach house worthy of the cover of *Coastal Living*. She didn't want to drip water all over the pine wood floors, or leave water spots on the slip-covered sofa and chairs. She scanned the large open space in front of her, the entire first floor decked out in different shades of white, with hints of pale blue in accent pillows, draperies, and vases, an open kitchen nestled on one side with stainless steel appliances and white and glass cabinetry. She glanced at a baby grand piano sitting in the far corner of the room, a guitar propped up on its bench. She started to take a step towards it but stopped upon hearing footsteps coming down the hallway.

Gage handed her one of his sweatshirts and pair of his high school gym shorts. "I'm sure these are ten sizes too big, but at least they're dry." He pointed to a door off the living room. "Bathroom's right through there." She took the clothes and left to change.

Gage tossed the blanket on the sofa and moved into the kitchen, keeping an eye on the bathroom door, his mind drifting to the hot girl dripping wet, wondering what she looked like naked, supple breasts, long flexible legs. He heard the doorknob and hustled towards the refrigerator, opening it to see what was available for lunch, the cool air blowing over his raging hormones.

He turned to find Layla walking gingerly to the kitchen. He tried not to stare, her chocolate brown hair cascading down the sweatshirt hanging to her knees, making it seem like that was all she was wearing. She put her wet clothes on a kitchen chair. "You can grab the blanket if you're still cold," Gage said.

Layla shook her head and strolled around the room, making her way to a white marble fireplace holding several framed photos. "Who are these guys?"

Gage looked over from the kitchen. "That's my sister, her husband, and my niece."

"Wow, she must be a lot older."

"Ten years," he said. "And she acts like she's my mother. You have any brothers or sisters?"

"Just a half-brother," she said. "He's much older, too."

Gage got back to the business of making lunch, but his mind stayed on Layla, roaming around in his clothes, likely without a bra. He finished up and made his way towards her when he realized he hadn't even asked what she wanted to eat. He thought to turn back to the kitchen, to start over, but then she turned around to find him holding two plates.

"I hope you like turkey," he said. "My mom hasn't stocked the fridge yet."

"That's fine," Layla said. "Can we eat in here?"

"Yeah." He put his plate down on the coffee table. Layla did the same and sat cross-legged on the white sofa. He sat down facing her then reached for the blanket. "You still look cold," he said and draped it around her shoulders.

Layla felt his warm breath on her neck, as he tucked the blanket around her shoulders. She glanced out the floor-to-ceiling windows to steady herself. "I think it stopped raining."

"You don't have to go, do you?"

"Not right this second," she said. "Is that your guitar?" Gage nodded. "Play something."

"Right now?"

"Sure. Play something for me."

Gage swallowed hard and felt like he could throw up. He got his guitar and sat down beside her again. He held it in his hands and strummed a few chords, thinking of a song to play. He scrolled through a variety of songs in his mind, wanting to land on something that would impress her, something that was unique, but wasn't too sappy or serious.

He cocked a smile and started to play—certain no one in the world would attempt to play hip hop, Shaggy's "Angel," on an acoustic guitar. Layla busted out into a cute little giggle, as Gage, grinning from ear to ear, kept on strumming and singing. She moved her body to the rhythm, keeping the beat he was playing, playfully waving her arms in the air.

Gage got to his favorite part—about the woman standing by her man during his incarceration—and was barely able to contain himself. He couldn't go on any longer, both of them laughing so hard, Layla doubled over on the sofa.

"I love that song," she said. "But I'm not into ex-cons."

"What kind of guys are you into?"

Layla bit her bottom lip and gave a little shrug. "Maybe guys named after tools."

He smiled and reached for her cheek, cupping it in his hand, and leaned forward slowly, his eyes focused on her mouth. Layla smiled, her dimples on full display, and leaned back just slightly, teasing him, making him come to her a bit more. Gage loved how playful she was, how sexy she was, all while wearing his clothes. He couldn't contain himself any more.

He moved quickly towards her. Layla fell all the way back on the sofa, with Gage landing firmly on top of her. He looked down at her, gazing into her crystal blue eyes, and ran his fingers through her wet hair. He leaned his head down to her, picking up a flowery scent as he got closer, something like lavender. He saw her eyes close and lips part, and he moved in for a kiss.

"Shit! My parents!"

LAYLA SAT ON the back patio, hoping his parents didn't call her grandmother. She couldn't blame them if they did. They'd walked inside, finding her dressed in their son's clothes, her own clothes on a chair, their son on top of her on the sofa. It looked so bad, such a horrible first impression.

They'd asked her to wait outside while they spoke with their son. She couldn't see his parents, but she could see Gage through the glass windows, the tension on his face, the concern in his blue eyes. And she could hear every word.

"It's very simple, Gage. You broke our rules," his father said. "So you're grounded for a week."

"Dad!"

"You aren't to step one foot off that back patio."

"Dad, nothing happened!"

"Because we came home," his father said. "Otherwise, we all know what would've happened."

"Layla's not like that."

"We don't know this girl," his father said.

"I do."

Layla smiled. *It's sweet that he thinks so.*

Gage looked to his mother for help. "This isn't fair! I'm 18!"

"I want to believe you, honey," his mother said, "but my goodness, her clothes were off."

"We got caught in the rain!" Gage said. "She was freezing, so I gave her some dry clothes. She changed in the bathroom, I swear!"

"She shouldn't have been in here in the first place," his father said.

Gage rolled his eyes and folded his arms across his chest. He'd never given his parents any reason not to trust him, but they continued to ride him hard. Maybe it was some kind of preparation for the Naval Academy. Or maybe it was because his parents, after having his sister, tried for 10 years to have him, so they were always protective of their "miracle baby," never wanting him to get in trouble.

"The sofa?" his mother asked.

"Nothing," Gage said, turning to look at Layla for a moment, waiting patiently on the porch for her release from prison. "I haven't even kissed her."

"You really like this girl?" his mother asked. Gage nodded his head.

"You're going off to school in a few months," his father said, and Gage nodded again. "You still broke our rules."

"I just want. . . ." Gage started then looked down.

"What do you want, honey?" his mother asked.

Gage could tell his mother was softening. She was his ticket to freedom. He mustered all of the sappy emotion he could, puppy dog eyes, quivering lip, a dramatic pause, to make his case. He had one chance, and this was it. "I just want to see her tomorrow," he said, pushing out a tear, "and everyday after until I have to leave. Please! I can't not see her for a whole week."

"Maybe we can. . . ." his mother started.

"Sorry, Gage," his father interjected. "Rules are rules. One week."

"This is ridiculous and so embarrassing," Gage said and looked out at Layla.

She offered him a tight, sad smile, kicking herself for putting Gage in this position. She never should've gone inside, never changed clothes, never teased him on the sofa. Perhaps it was penance she now had to watch this uncomfortable family drama. Perhaps it was penance for coming to St. Simons Island in the first place, bringing her hidden drama across the country, calling her grandmother just days before showing up, imposing herself on an elderly woman whose entire family—except for Layla—long ago decided to shut her out.

"What do I always tell you, Gage?" his father asked.

"Real men think with their hearts," Gage mumbled, "not their dicks."

"Right, and I just want to make sure you do."

Layla didn't like the conversation but thought his father's advice was solid. The man and his wife obviously loved their son and didn't want him to make bad choices. She couldn't fault them for that. Gage gave her a nod then walked to another room.

Layla couldn't see or hear anything. She thought for a moment that might be it, the last time she saw him for a week. She fiddled with the leather rope cord around her neck, suddenly worrying it could be even longer than that. Maybe his parents wouldn't let him see her ever again.

She thought to bolt back to her cottage, to talk to her grandmother before Gage's parents made a call. She couldn't risk her grandmother calling her parents back in Houston. Then she heard voices again.

"Five minutes, Gage," his father called out.

"Yes, sir," his son said with a hint of sarcasm. Gage came through the patio door, shaking his head, about to apologize when Layla sprang towards him.

"Are they calling my grandmother?" she cried.

"No," Gage said, handing her back her wet clothes. "I had to grovel, but they won't."

Layla exhaled. "I'm sorry you got in trouble. I knew it was a bad idea for me to be in your house when they weren't home."

"It's no big deal. They're strict and overprotective. They think I'm going to be president one day or some shit."

She shrugged and tied her wet hair into a messy bun. "I guess I should go."

"No way. I've got four minutes left."

"I don't want to get you into more trouble."

"It was worth it," he said, lightly taking her hand.

Layla felt her dimples explode, her heart fluttering, then remembered he was grounded. "Can you not ever see me again? Your parents must think I'm a slut."

"I told them you were a nice girl."

"I don't want them to think that I'm. . . ." The words got caught in her throat. "I'm not like that. I'm not."

"Of course not," he said and wrapped his arms around her, smiling slightly inside at how nervous he was to hold her hand a few hours ago. And here he was holding her as she clung to his shirt and buried her head. "No one thinks that, Angel."

"They must," she said, pulling away and wiping her face with the sleeve of his sweatshirt.

"Then we'll just have to prove them wrong."

"How?"

"My dad grounded me for the rest of the week, so. . . ."

"I thought he said for a whole week," she interrupted.

"You could hear?" Gage asked.

"Not everything."

"Good. He started off grounding me for a week, but I talked him down to three days."

"That's not so bad. Only three days."

"I'm a good negotiator. My dad and I are actually really close. He loves to fly as much as I do," Gage said. "But there's a catch. They said if I like you and want to spend time with you, then they need to get to know you. So you're grounded with me."

"Your parents grounded me?"

"Sort of," he said, flashing a smile. "They said we can see each other while I'm grounded, but only if you come hang out here with us."

"*Us?*"

Gage wrinkled his nose. "I know it's weird. They do strange shit sometimes. But will you?"

"Hang out with you and your parents?"

"Yeah," he said and took her hand again. "I know they're going to love you once they get to know you. It's going to be lame hanging out with them, but it'll only be for a few days."

Layla bit the inside of her mouth. This was the craziest punishment in the whole world—Gage's parents were punishing him by forcing him to spend time with them. It was actually kind of funny.

"Gage?" his father called out from inside.

"Time's up," Gage said. "I've got to get inside."

Layla took a step towards him, got on her tiptoes, and kissed him softly on the cheek. "I'll see you tomorrow."

FOR THE NEXT three days, Layla came to his beach house after yoga. She and Gage spent the mornings playing cards and boardgames with his parents and drinking ice cold lemonade and sweet tea. In the afternoons, she and Gage would watch a movie or listen to music together on the sofa in the middle of the living room, open to the rest of the house, without the comfort of a blanket. And at night, as if some reward, they'd sit out on the back patio and watch the sunset, where it was just them, together, alone—though under the eye of one parent or the other inside.

Gage thought the whole "grounding" thing sucked, but Layla didn't think it was so bad. She knew it could've been worse, much worse. His parents could've told her grandmother, and then her parents probably would've found out. That would've ruined everything. Her summer would've been over. But instead she got to hang around a cool guy and his cool parents, who quickly found her sweet and well-mannered and the smartest girl their son ever hung out with. He knew he had his parents' stamp of approval when his mother took a picture of them and put it in a frame next to his bed.

But Gage wanted some time alone with Layla. He needed it. The kiss on the cheek seemed a lifetime ago, and the high from her lips had long since worn off. Sure, it was great to sit with his arm around her in the living room or to hold her hand on the patio under the stars, but it was time for more—more touching, more kissing, and whatever else she'd let him get away with.

So when the "grounding" was over and the sun rose the next morning, Gage dashed to the kitchen, took the car keys off the counter, and hustled towards the front door. He placed a hand on the door knob, some long-awaited privacy in sight, when he heard his father's voice at the top of the stairs.

"Son, a word."

CHAPTER THREE

LAYLA GRIPPED THE golf club in her hands and wiggled her butt ever so slightly, getting ready to knock the ball through some metal posts then off a large triangle angled towards the final hole. Her preparation was solid, but she'd proven herself to be terrible at putt-putt. It took her at least 10 strokes to finish every hole, not to mention she twice hit her ball into a pool of water and once far off into the parking lot.

But she didn't care. And neither did Gage. He liked that she was terrible. The more strokes it took her, the more chances he had to see her stand over the ball in her sundress, bend over, and shake her ass a little. He was certain he had the best view in all of Georgia. Stone Mountain and Centennial Olympic Park had nothing on Layla preparing to hit a golf ball.

This time, Layla narrowed her eyes to line up her putt then jerked her hands forward—hard, fast, on the verge of sending the ball into orbit—but completely whiffed and spun around in a pirouette. When she stopped spinning, her whole face lit up, and she cracked up in a fit of laughter. Gage did the same.

"What's the score?" she asked.

He looked down at the score card. "It's close," he said, though he'd stopped recording numbers on the third hole.

"If I get a hole-in-one, then I win, OK?" She set herself for another swing.

"Sure," he said, "but I'm not too worried."

She raised an eyebrow towards him. "Let's not forget who the Scrabble queen is."

"Just putt," he said.

Layla lined up again and pulled her club back. When she came forward this time, the club flew out of her hands and onto an adjacent hole. "Oh God!" They looked at each other for a second before laughing together again. "I'm so bad."

"But you are so cute." He scooped up her club then took her hand. "Let's get out of here before you hurt someone." Gage led her to a little bench before returning their clubs to the front desk. He returned with a cold can of soda and found her twirling her angel wing pendant fixed to the leather cord.

"You wear that necklace everyday," Gage said, handing her the soda and taking a seat beside her.

"My father gave it to me years ago," Layla said and took a sip. "He told me it's bad luck to take it off unless you give it to someone you love, like he gave it to me."

"He's back in Houston with your mom and brother?"

"Half-brother," Layla said, placing the soda on the bench between them. "We don't really get along."

"Families can be a pain. I got a long lecture from my dad this morning."

"About?"

He smiled. "You."

"Me? I don't want to cause problems!"

"It's not that," he said. "They like you. It's just, uh, the usual stuff."

"What's that supposed to mean?"

His mouth suddenly dry, Gage eyed the soda between them. He didn't think he could take a sip, not after she had. He'd be fine with it, but she might not. He wasn't sure they were at that stage in their relationship yet. "I broke up with someone a month or so before graduation, and they don't want me getting attached before I have to go off to school."

"That was the big lecture?"

"Yeah, they don't get it at all."

Layla rolled her eyes. "They're just watching out for you."

"It's more than that. I'm about to go off to college, do exactly what my dad has wanted me to do. I won't know a single person. The work is going to be crazy—physically and mentally. The next 10 years of my life are planned out, and they want to talk about dating."

"How long were you with your girlfriend?"

"About a year," he said.

"Did you love her?"

"No," he said, running his hands through his hair. "I liked her, though."

"Then why did you break up?"

"Just wasn't working out."

"Sounds mysterious," she teased. "Did you cheat?"

"No, of course not."

"Did she?"

"No, there was no cheating," Gage said and looked down at his feet. "There wasn't much of *anything*." He closed his eyes after completing the sentence, wishing he could have it back.

"Not much of anything *physical*, you mean?"

"I don't want to talk about this."

"You broke up with the girl because she wouldn't have sex with you?" she asked, her tone not quite as playful as before.

"You make it sound so horrible."

"Because it is."

"It really wasn't like that. We dated for like a year. She was a fun, pretty girl. . . ."

"You aren't helping yourself."

Gage scanned the putt-putt course in front of him. Just ten minutes ago, he was having so much fun out there, looking at her ass and chasing her club and balls. He kicked himself for ever bringing up a past girlfriend then fumbling around about what did, and did not, happen between them. At this point, there was only one awful way out of this mess. "I'm a virgin," he whispered through gritted teeth.

Layla looked at him, confused. "And that's a bad thing?"

"If you're going off to the Naval Academy, I'd think so! They're going to eat me alive."

"Why do they have to know? Is there a box you had to check on the application?"

"You don't get it," he said and walked away.

Layla watched him leave, thinking it was sweet he apparently was inexperienced, and feeling bad for the inquisition. She wouldn't want someone questioning her past, her decisions. And she didn't know what it was like to be a teenage guy—especially a sensitive one about to become a midshipman, about to become part of a brigade, a battalion, or whatever the heck it's called. A slow rain began to fall, and she got to her feet.

"Gage!" she called out, but he kept going, through a lush garden of fruit trees and flowering bushes. She called out to him again but he still kept on, making his way towards the parking lot. She quickened her pace as the rain came down harder, finding some relief under a huge oak tree, its branches keeping her somewhat dry. "I'm sorry!"

He stopped in his tracks and walked a few steps back until he shared the safety of the tree. "I'm sorry, too," he said quietly. "You must think I'm a total asshole."

"Not a *total*," she said, giving a small smile.

"God, I hope you know that I'm not, well, that this thing between you and me isn't just. . . ."

"Well, aren't you?"

"No, I mean, no," he stumbled. "It would be great, but. . . ."

"*But?*" she teased.

"I'm not looking to use you. I wouldn't do that. I wouldn't do that to anyone," he said.

"I know. If you just wanted sex, I'm sure you wouldn't have a problem finding a willing girl."

Gage took a step towards her, and Layla stepped back against the tree trunk. The rain pattered the leaves above with a delicate rhythm, and the tree branches started to bend down, creating a little barrier between them and the rest of the island, the rest of the outside world. He caressed her face with his hand, wiping away a few wet hairs, then ran his hand under the cord of her necklace, his fingertips outlining the curve of her neck, her familiar lavender scent drawing him closer.

"My dad told me it would be a big mistake to fall in love this summer." His fingers followed the cord and came dangerously close to the curve of her breast. "I told him it was too late."

Layla gasped, and Gage moved in closer, taking advantage of her parted lips, kissing her gently, the warmth of his breath making her body roll. He slid his hand up to her neck and pulled her mouth to his. Their tongues moved slowly around each other—tasting, sucking, exploring, wanting. Gage suddenly pulled back, stunned at the raw heat between them. Layla felt it, too. This wasn't two teenagers stealing a kiss or some random make-out at a party.

"Layla, I. . . ." he started but couldn't finish.

She wrapped her arms around his neck. "Better do that again," she said and pulled him back to her lips.

OVER THE NEXT several weeks, they spent each day together, just hanging out on the island, talking about their dreams. Layla wanted to open a bookstore, and Gage wanted to be a pilot—though she teased he shouldn't discount singing in a nightclub. And whenever they had a hint of privacy—whether on the warm sand, on his parents' back patio, in his father's car, outside her grandmother's cottage, on the bike trails—they kissed like it could be their last. They both knew he'd soon be off to college, and she'd be wherever life took her.

His parents complained they'd hardly seen Gage all summer and insisted he spend the day with them on their friends' small yacht. It sounded like torture to Gage. But he thought he could manage if Layla came along. So he begged his parents to let her, and they did. It was an easy sell because they liked her so much. The best part of the day was jumping off the top deck with her, especially since she was wearing a navy blue bikini and occasionally lost a strap when she hit the water. Unfortunately for him, she quickly covered up each time before he could sneak a peek.

After an hour of jumping and swimming, they dried off on the bow. She stretched out on a towel, and he did the same beside her. He tried not to stare but couldn't help himself. She lowered her sunglasses to peek into his deep blue eyes, but they weren't focused on her face. He grazed his fingertips up her arms then gently ran his fingers across her collarbone, continuing on down the leather cord, leaving feather-light touches between her breasts, and sliding all the way down to her belly button. She felt her whole body heat up but tried not to squirm, not wanting him to know the effect he had on her, not wanting him to know how weak she was.

When he reached her face, he slid off her glasses and ran his thumb across her mouth. "I love that little indention on your lips."

"Cupid's bow."

"Huh?"

"The nickname for that little indention," she said. "Angels make it. They hush babies in the womb, placing one finger above the baby's mouth." She placed her index finger across his lips. "Leaves the little indention. And some religions believe babies know all the secrets of heaven, so angels have to erase the memories before birth."

Gage raised his eyebrows. "You're too smart for me, Angel." He brought her to his side and held her tight, rocking her to the rhythm of the ocean.

She nuzzled in close and looked up to the sky. Houston seemed so far away, like a bad dream starting to fade, seemingly replaced by a new one, one she'd read about many times before, usually involving a prince in a far away land, always involving a rescue and a fairy-tale love. "Tell me what it's like to fly."

"When I'm in the air, it's total freedom," he said, pulling her a little closer, his sweet Southern accent deepening, his hand grazing her back. "My favorite time to fly is right at sunset. I've got to get you to fly with me. I know you'd love it."

Layla didn't think so, but his sparkling eyes were somehow reassuring, somehow tempting. She wanted to freeze this moment, their past month on the island, to capture it in a bottle and hold it close to her heart. She needed something to hold onto. She felt her top come undone and quickly moved her hand to her chest.

"Tie that back!" she whispered firmly. "Your parents are inside— like 30 feet away!"

"No one's around."

Layla sat up and pushed him aside. She fumbled to tie it back herself, groaning in frustration as the straps slipped through her fingers.

Gage helped her. "Sorry," he said and lowered his head.

She tilted up his chin and smiled. "Later?"

THEIR BODIES WOBBLY from the day at sea, Gage held Layla on her grandmother's deck and looked down the beach at his house. They'd been "saying goodnight" for at least an hour. He leaned back down and gently kissed her neck. "You know, my bedroom's right off the front porch. I could leave my window open."

Her head darted up. "You want me to sneak in?"

"Or I can sneak inside here?"

"No way, it's too small."

"Well, my place then?"

"What about your parents?"

"Don't worry. They'll be in bed."

She hesitated. "Are you sure?"

"Just wait like 30 minutes to come over." He took her hand, swinging it to encourage her, sensing it was more than just his parents holding her back. He suddenly had a stroke of genius. "On second thought, I don't want you walking in the dark alone. I'll shine a flashlight towards your house so I can see you coming."

Layla lifted her eyes to his. "OK, 30 minutes."

"I'll be waiting."

CHAPTER FOUR

FOR TWO WEEKS, they kept the same routine. Gage kissed her "good-night" on her deck, waited 30 minutes, locked his bedroom door, and opened his window. Then he grabbed his flashlight to light the way for Layla to sneak over and into his room. With each passing night, their nerves got a little less, and their confidence grew they'd never get caught, two lovebirds sneaking around in the moonlight, making out in his bed right under his parents' noses.

Now it was time again. Gage grabbed his flashlight and turned it to the cottage. He flicked it on but didn't see her yet. He looked at his wristwatch. He was a minute early. He switched off the light and told himself not to get careless. That's how they'd get caught. He looked around his room, a few antique model airplanes scattered around. It seemed childish to still have them, especially the one on his nightstand near his phone and the photo his mother took when they were "grounded."

He was long past building model airplanes, now more interested in his model-looking girlfriend. But each night, Layla somehow seemed to hold him at bay, allowing him to explore the top half of her sundress, but nothing more. No matter how hard he tried, she managed to slow things down and snuggle into his side, a hint things weren't going further. And then they'd talk for hours, sharing silly stories, staring out the open window, dreaming about their future.

Gage turned back to the window and flicked the flashlight back on. He saw Layla's shadow on her grandmother's deck. He loved to watch her move, her soft features come into focus, stepping out of the darkness and into the light. Every step she took was a step closer to his arms, to his bed, and hopefully one time she'd stay the night. She hadn't yet, always slipping out the window after a few hours, never willing to fall asleep in his bed.

She reached his window, and he switched off his flashlight before helping her crawl inside. "It's cute you wore a sundress in the dark."

Layla rolled her eyes. "Are they asleep?"

Gage nodded then seized her in his arms and pressed his mouth against hers, letting his lips linger a few moments. Then he lowered her down until they were both sitting on his bed, their bodies pressed against each other. It wasn't long until they were stretched out, his hands sliding along the contours of her hips and ass, her hands in his sun-drenched hair.

He started to undo a few buttons on her dress, testing her boundary line. She gasped for breath, as his tongue traced around her neck. She tugged at his shirt and lifted it over his head, eyeing his tan skin and toned abs. Her hand went to his neck and urged his lips harder. She clutched his back, needing him closer.

He undid a few more buttons on her dress, and her smooth breasts spilled right out, the angel wing pendant between them. He loved she never bothered with a bra. His dick fully hard, he caressed her breasts. She let slip a quiet moan and arched her back. He wanted all of her, every inch of her. And it was getting harder and harder for him to stop.

He saw the usual caution in her eyes, her head overpowering the ache in her body. But there appeared to be somewhat less caution than other nights. Perhaps she was fighting a decision about how far she'd let him go. He moved to her lips again, hoping to persuade her, and decided to take the next step. He wanted to feel her.

He slid his hand under her sundress onto the bare skin of her thigh, letting it rest there for a moment. She stiffened, but he let out a light, little chuckle, then felt her body relax again. He kissed down her neck onto her collarbone and moved his mouth to her breast, his tongue slowly circling her nipple. She arched her back and slid her hands to his waist, their hips grinding together, finding just the right rhythm between them.

Then he pulled up her leg and pushed harder against her before reaching to yank down her panties.

"Wait! Slow down!" Layla whispered, pushing him back.

Gage pulled his hand away. "Slow down or stop?" He leaned on his elbow to catch his breath. She looked towards the open window, and he knew he had his answer. "OK," he breathed out. "Just give me a minute."

"I'm sorry," she said, pulled up her panties, and sat up. She fixed the buttons on her dress. "I feel like I'm teasing you, and I don't want to." She looked over at him, his face tight, his eyes closed, looking like he was in physical pain. "Are you mad?"

He took another deep breath. "I'm not mad." Then he pulled her to his side. "I love you."

Layla cupped his cheeks in her hands. "I love you, too." She pecked him on the lips. "I think we need to talk about this. What if we don't do it?"

Gage groaned. "How long are we talking about?"

"I don't know. I'm only 16," she said sweetly.

"I know. If you want to wait, then I'll wait for you. I won't like it, and. . . ."

"And what?"

"I'll have to whack off a lot."

Layla laughed. "You don't do it a lot already?"

"It'll be more now," he said. "But I'll wait for you."

"Now say we do it. Then what?"

"We do it some more," Gage said and tackled her back down to the bed.

"Then you leave for college." Layla lowered her head to his chest. "Then what?"

"Are you still thinking of staying here?" he asked and ran his fingers through her hair.

"That's my plan."

"We'll figure it out. I know I want you, and I know somehow we'll be together."

She looked out the window. "I need a little time. I don't want to do something I'd regret the next morning."

GAGE LAY AWAKE in bed, alone with nothing but her lavender scent. He so wanted to have her, and it seemed, at least for a minute, she felt the same way. Then things changed, just like the other nights. There'd be nothing below the waist, no sex, no sleepover. He crashed and burned again. He hated pushing too far, hated she told him to stop, hated to see her crawl out the window, then guiding her back to the cottage by flashlight.

But somewhere inside he understood what she was saying about her age, his college plans, the coming distance between them. He looked out the open window, hoping as always she'd come back. But she hadn't. It had been two hours. There was nothing except the roar of the night tide. He turned his eyes to their photo, the sun shimmering off her pale skin, her chocolate braid draped on her shoulder.

He let out a deep breath He knew he wasn't going to get any sleep with a raging hard-on. He had to find some relief, to release some tension, if he was going to get any sleep. And he didn't feel bad about it. It's not like he was jerking off behind her back; he told her he'd have to. Suddenly the phone rang. He ripped his hand out of his pants and grabbed it on the first ring.

"Gage?" Layla asked, her voice shaking.

"Yeah, what's wrong?" He sat up straight, and his dick went limp.

"I'm at the hospital."

"What? Are you OK?"

"My grandmother broke her hip."

"Jesus, I'm so sorry. When?"

"She fell getting out of bed to get some water. Like an hour ago."

"Do you need me? Is she going to be OK?"

"She's going to be fine," she said, her voice shakier than before. "It's actually not a big deal."

"That's good, right?"

"Yes, but. . . ." She fought back tears, thinking back to a few hours ago, their whole summer together, memorizing his muscles, how they first met.

"What is it?"

"Nothing," she said. "Just very scary."

"What hospital? I'll come over right now."

"No, it's late."

"Let me know what I can do."

"There's nothing. . . ." she began, her voice trailing off. "I guess I just wanted to hear your voice again."

"You sound weird, Angel. What's going on?"

"I've got to go."

"Um, OK. Please call me soon, and let me know how things are. And if your grandmother needs to stay in the hospital for a few days or whatever, you can stay at my house. I know my parents would be fine with that. They'd let you stay in my sister's old room. You shouldn't stay alone."

Layla hesitated. "I love you, Gage."

LAYLA RETURNED TO the beach alone, exhausted. The night had taken a toll—from starting and stopping with Gage, to bolting to the hospital, to leaving her grandmother and returning alone, to the consequences surely coming her way. She wasn't wearing a watch but knew it must be two or three in the morning.

It really didn't matter what time it was. Her time was up. Of all things, a broken hip had broken her plans, smashed them into grains of sand. It was over now. Of course, nothing good can ever last.

Her white cotton sundress dangled in the water, and she breathed in the salty air. She shuddered at the darkness around her—no moon, no stars, no flashlight—the blackness a signal of what would soon descend upon her. Her grandmother's cottage had withstood many storms, but Layla didn't think she'd be so lucky.

She stood at a point almost equidistant between the cottage and Gage's house. She hoped he'd flip on his bedroom light or power up his flashlight. But there was nothing, only more darkness. She kicked herself for leaving earlier. Maybe things would've been different. She looked towards her cottage. It was dark that way, too.

She looked back to his house and started that way, her heart pounding in her chest. She saw her footprints washed away by the tide, like she'd never even been there, like no one would remember her when the dawn came. She stroked her wings to calm herself. But it wasn't helping.

Maybe there were no angels on duty to help right now. Perhaps they'd long since gone to bed. Or maybe all the angels had fallen out of the sky tonight. After all, there wasn't a hint of light anywhere. Or maybe the problem was the same one as always—there are demons all around, too. And sometimes it's hard to tell the difference.

She tiptoed up his patio and saw his window still open. She lifted the bottom of her dress and crawled inside, hearing Gage breathe deeply, fast asleep. The room was just as she left it. She watched him sleep for a minute, his shirt pulled up just slightly, the covers at the foot of the bed. She stepped closer and bumped the bed. He groaned and turned his head towards her.

Gage opened his eyes, finding a vision in white standing over him, her crystal blue eyes fixed on him. Layla looked different than ever before. There was an urgency about her. She brought her hands to her dress and began to unfasten the buttons down the front. He rubbed his eyes, hoping more than anything he wasn't dreaming. He saw her hands start to tremble.

He stood up and took over for her, slowly undoing the buttons himself until he reached the last one. He stared at it for a moment, wondering if this was the right time—given their talk before she left, after whatever was going on at the hospital, how strange she sounded on the phone. He looked down at his dick poking through his boxers and unfastened the last button.

Layla slid her dress to the floor and stood before him, her angel wings dangling between her breasts. She expected him to take hold of her, but he appeared frozen, in awe, his whole body drinking in hers. She crawled into bed, as he locked his bedroom door. She reached for the covers, holding them up for Gage to join her. He slid under them and then on top of her, his body melting into hers.

THE MORNING LIGHT pouring in, Gage clenched his eyes and felt a cold metal on his chest and neck. He was too tired to care about the cold, too spent from his hot night, just needing a few more hours of sleep with Layla beside him. And he didn't give a shit if his parents found out. They'd get over it, and if they didn't, then that was their problem. He'd be off to college soon—and thankfully not a virgin anymore. It was great. She was great. He was glad he waited for the right girl.

He reached across the bed to pull her to him, but his hand landed on crumpled sheets. His eyes flashed open, and he sat up, naked. The cold metal hit him again. He looked down and slowly lifted her angel wings from his chest, dangling from her leather cord around his neck. He clutched the wings in his hand. *This means she really loves me.*

He smiled and looked around the room. The window was closed. The door was closed. Her panties and dress were gone. Something didn't feel right. She'd left other times but not like this. He wondered if she regretted what they'd done. She'd thought she might. He certainly didn't—not one bit. He looked over to his nightstand, seeing only his phone and model airplane. The photo was gone. He started to sweat, and the room began to spin.

He thought back to her shaky voice on the phone, the urgency in her eyes when she came to him. She'd come back to his room a different person. She'd come back with a purpose. He ran his hand along the sheets where she slept then touched the wings around his neck. He remembered how uncertain her plans were, how she didn't even know where she was going to school. Something must've happened to her. Maybe she went back to Houston. Maybe she went somewhere else.

He knew she wasn't coming back—not this morning, not tonight, not ever.

PART TWO

PRESENT DAY

TWELVE YEARS LATER

CHAPTER FIVE

LAYLA NEEDED TO get the hell out of Houston, its airport, any reference to the city. She didn't have a problem with the city itself, though it hadn't been home for years. And it's not like she was excited about getting on a plane. She just needed to get away from her family— from her mother, her half-brother, and her now dead father.

The taxi pulled up to the curb, and Layla hustled inside, boarding pass in hand. She decided not to run through the airport; she didn't want to make a scene. And she didn't think she'd be very fast in a black dress. But she walked as quickly as she could, weaving around other travelers, young and old alike, making her way through security.

She reached the gate. There was no line at the counter. She saw the flight was on-time. Feeling her fair skin flush, she caught her breath and breathed a sigh of relief. It would be good, she told herself, to get up in the air this time. It was clear sailing home now. She approached the counter to check in.

The clerk, a woman in her fifties with a sharp pencil poking through her hair bun, greeted Layla with the sincerity of an automated robot. She proceeded to explain the flight was overbooked, and a computer glitch had given away Layla's seat. The clerk said there was nothing she could do, except to offer a flight out tomorrow and a credit with no fewer than a dozen restrictions.

Layla tried to process the shitty news, all the hustling for nothing, regretting buying a ticket with Southern Wings. She couldn't stay in Houston another minute, let alone spend the night. She ran a hand through her chocolate brown hair. "Isn't there something you can do?" she pleaded, fidgeting with her useless boarding pass and plopping it on the counter.

"At this point, Miss Tanner," the clerk said, "another passenger has the right to the seat."

Layla squeezed her blue eyes shut, the clerk's words conjuring words from just hours earlier, words from her own mother, words that ran a chill down her spine and cut open her long-scarred soul. *He's got as much right to be here as you. Your father would've wanted him here.* Her father's funeral already had been awful, uncomfortable, cold. And her mother, as always, managed to make things even worse.

The clerk saw a line forming at the counter. "Miss Tanner, what would you like to do?"

Layla kept her eyes shut. She was never sure if her mother intended to be a bitch or if the woman was just so primitive, so backwards, that she just couldn't help but say stupid things. Either way, as far as Layla was concerned, there was nothing motherly about the woman, and there hadn't been for a very long time.

An earthy voice called out from the line, "Excuse me, ma'am, is there a problem?"

Layla popped open her eyes, all five senses recognizing the voice, one she hadn't heard in forever. She didn't dare turn around to face him. She hoped his question was for the autobot and not her, not wanting him to see her so frazzled, if he even remembered who she was. She heard footsteps coming up behind her, and suddenly he was standing next to her at the counter. Layla leaned her head down, letting her brown hair cover the side of her face.

The clerk shuffled her feet and stood a bit taller. "I'm sorry, sir, but we overbooked, and her seat was reassigned."

The man frowned and looked down at the boarding pass on the counter, recognizing the first name but not the last. He turned to the woman beside him. "Angel?" he asked softly, uncertainly.

Layla nodded slightly, the name tugging at her heart. *Only he calls me that.* "It's good to see you, Gage. It's been a long time."

They exchanged an awkward hug then stared at each other, both in shock. Layla took the chance to study him. She figured he must be about 30 now. His face looked the same as before—the same strong jaw, the same sandy blond hair, the same deep blue eyes. He was dressed in navy slacks and a white-collared shirt, and his body seemed even better now—broader, more intense. She chuckled inside thinking back to their summer, unable to recall Gage wearing anything other than swim trunks and t-shirts. Perhaps the biggest change was his voice; it retained only a hint of his sweet Southern accent, though she could still hear it loud and clear.

"What are you doing here?" he asked, a rush of memories flooding his mind.

She tucked her hair behind her ear. "I'm trying to get home to Savannah."

"That's where you live?" he asked. "I'm there a lot."

The clerk cleared her throat, and Gage flicked his eyes towards her. "Find her a seat," he ordered.

"Yes, sir," the clerk said and looked down at her computer.

"Gage, it's OK. I'll work something out."

"We'll get it fixed," he said.

Layla saw the clerk typing like her life depended on it. "You have some kind of pull around here?"

"If my airline makes a mistake, then we. . . ."

"*Your* airline?"

He pointed to the sign for Southern Wings. "Since my dad died a few years ago."

"You run the whole company?"

"I try to," he said with a chuckle. "It's not just a little commuter airline anymore." He flagged another clerk to open a second station behind the counter, and an army of weary travelers shifted to another line.

"So you became a pilot?"

"Just like we used to talk about," Gage said. "I went to the Naval Academy, became a pilot. When I got out, I took over for my dad, more of the business end. I'm licensed to fly commercially but don't do it very often."

"I'm sorry about your dad. I always liked him."

Gage offered a tight smile then turned to the clerk. "What do we have available for Miss. . . ." He stopped and looked at Layla, recalling the unfamiliar last name on the boarding pass. "Is it Miss or Mrs.?"

"Miss," Layla said. *He's still smooth.*

"But not Baxter anymore?"

"I changed it to Tanner."

"You got married?"

"No, I just changed it."

Gage nodded as if it made perfect sense, though he had no idea why she'd change her name if she wasn't married. He tried to steady his heart, remembering her in sundresses and now seeing her in a simple black dress. *She still looks like an Angel.* It was crazy to see her again, though he'd wanted to for years. He had so many questions—like whether she still had dimples and, more importantly, what the hell happened. As good as she still looked, a part of him wanted to yell and demand answers.

"How about you?" she asked. "Married? Kids?"

"No." He looked back at the clerk, her fingers moving at the speed of light. "What do we have available for Miss Layla Tanner?"

"Nothing in coach," the clerk said hesitantly.

"Then put her in first class," Gage instructed. "Charge it as a company expense."

"Yes, Mr. Montgomery," the clerk said quickly.

"Gage, I can't let you do that."

"You'd rather hang out in Houston another night?"

His question snapped her back to reality. "Charge it," Layla told the clerk, who nodded and printed a new boarding pass. Layla turned to Gage and thanked him.

"Not at all," he said and took the pass from the clerk. "I should be thanking you. You'll be keeping me company on the flight."

Layla's eyes bulged. "Wait, what?"

GAGE PEEKED INTO the cockpit with Layla by his side. "G-man!" the pilot cried, gripping his friend with a firm handshake.

"Dash, this is Layla," Gage said, placing a hand on the small of her back.

Layla trembled at his touch but managed a smile for the pilot, taking in his piercing brown eyes and long lashes. The man looked like he could be Denzel Washington's son. *Are all pilots hot?*

Dash looked Gage and Layla up and down. "No mile high club on my aircraft, OK?"

Layla turned a bright red, as Gage punched his friend in the shoulder. "You have to ignore him," he said, leading Layla to their seats. "That's why his call sign is Dash."

"Not because he's fast?" she wondered and took the window seat.

Gage chuckled and placed her bag in the overhead compartment. "It stands for Dumb As Shit."

"And you let him fly your planes?"

"It's the one thing he's good at. I can't take that away from him." Gage took a seat beside her. "Dash got so drunk one time at a party that he threw up on a captain's shoes."

"He's not drinking today, I hope?"

"Of course not."

She pulled down the window shade and buckled up. "Were you in Houston on business?"

"The Houston-Savannah flights have been running late," he said, rolling up his sleeves and undoing a button on his shirt. "I wanted to check it out, to see how we can improve things."

"Maybe Dash is to blame?"

"Too busy cracking jokes with the passengers."

"Or maybe the helpful clerk with the dagger in her hair?"

Gage sighed. "Sorry about that."

"It wasn't a big deal—at least not anymore," she said. "Don't you have people to check out the flights for you?"

"Yes, I have *people*," he said with a laugh, "a whole team of executives around the country, and they have their own personnel teams, too. But I don't want to lose touch with the hassles our customers have to put up with. And I really don't mind doing this particular run. My mom, sister, and her kids live in Savannah, so I'm there most weekends anyway. Nice change from running the company in Atlanta."

A flight attendant came over, as the plane started to taxi. "Can I get you anything pre-flight?" she asked.

Gage saw Layla gripping the armrest. "I forgot you hate to fly."

"Just the take-off," Layla said hopefully. "I'll be fine."

Gage turned to the attendant. "Can you bring one of those kits for uneasy flyers?"

"Yes, sir. Right away."

Layla turned to him. "There's a kit for people afraid to fly?"

"There is on *my* airline."

She relaxed her grip a little. "What's in it?"

"Chewing gum, earbuds, ginger tablets for nausea."

"You still like to go around saving women, huh?"

Gage gave her a polite smile, not wanting to remember "saving" the pretty girl in the floppy white sunhat and long periwinkle blue sundress—and then losing her, if that was even the right word. "What were you doing in Houston?"

"Flew in for my father's funeral this morning and now heading back," she said.

"Oh, I'm sorry to hear that," Gage said then waited for something more, perhaps a detail or two about how he died, when he died, whether it was sudden or not, why her trip was so short. But she gave him nothing, and her blank stare at the tray table indicated she wasn't about to. He knew so very little about her family. "Why such a quick trip?"

"It's better that way. I don't get along well with my mother and half-brother."

The flight attendant returned with the kit and raised an eyebrow at her boss. "We're about to take off, Mr. Montgomery."

"Of course," he said and reached for his seatbelt, brushing Layla's arm along the way, her fair skin as soft and smooth as before, her familiar lavender smell hitting him. *God help me! She even smells the same.* He quickly got the belt in his hand and moved to fasten it on the opposite side.

Dash greeted the passengers over the intercom. "We know you

have choices and want to thank you for choosing to fly Southern Wings today. There are clear skies to the East. We'll be flying at an altitude of 35,000 feet. And I'd be remiss if I didn't tell you we have the privilege of having the President and CEO of Southern Wings on our flight today, Mr. Gage Montgomery."

"I'm surprised he said 'remiss,'" Gage whispered to Layla. "That's a big word for him."

"G-man, excuse me, *Mr. Montgomery*," Dash continued, "has been a great leader for the company. He's a pilot himself, too. But I will have you know the best thing Mr. Montgomery does is make coffee, so he will be taking your drink orders during the flight."

Gage rolled his eyes, and the passengers laughed. Layla caught a glimpse of him out of the corner of her eye. It was amazing the charming guy who picked her flowers and kept his bedroom window open for her was now the head of a huge national company.

"And I'm happy to report that Mr. Montgomery will be taking *my* drink order, too," Dash said. "A little payback for the recent round of collective bargaining negotiations between the pilots union and Southern Wings. Got that, Gage? And folks, if he doesn't, I will regale you. . . ."

"'Regale'?" Gage whispered.

". . . with stories about G-man back when we were in flight school together. There are so many good ones. Ah, so many good times. I may just have to tell you some, whether or not he takes my drink order." Dash paused for a moment, as the passengers laughed again. "So, welcome aboard. We are expecting a smooth flight all the way to Savannah. And, Mr. Montgomery, cream and sugar, please."

Gage shook his head. "He's quite the character."

"I hope he tells some stories," Layla said. "Why'd he call you 'G-man'? Your name?"

"No. In flight school, they compared the number of G's we sustained in flight. Mine were always the best, even when they didn't have to be. So G-man stuck. My name was tame compared to most."

"Who had the worst?"

"Probably this guy Firecrotch. He was the horniest guy and a red head, so it fit."

Layla laughed. "Makes sense."

"We are clear for takeoff," Dash announced. "Enjoy the flight."

Gage saw Layla squeeze the armrests with her eyes closed, her mouth mumbling words in a whisper. "Which angel are you talking to today?"

Layla turned to face him, shocked he'd remember. "Just saying the Guardian Angel prayer."

"I've never met anyone who knows more about angels than you," he said with a smile. "You are like an angel encyclopedia. By the way, we're up."

Layla relaxed her hands then pulled up the window shade just slightly, seeing the plane climb into the late afternoon sky. "Thanks for distracting me."

"Probably the angels more than me," he said. "You live in Savannah?"

"Yeah, I own a bookstore in the Historic District."

"Just like you always wanted." His eyes caught hers, then he forced himself to look away.

"It's in this great old building we converted. My friend from college, Poppy, runs the adult side, and I run the children's side."

"*Adult* side?"

"Not like that." Layla rolled her eyes. "Fiction and non-fiction. Usual stuff. The two sides are connected in the middle by a cafe."

"What's it called?"

"Story Wings," she said and twisted her brown hair into a messy bun.

Gage couldn't help but smile, her bookstore with such a similar name to his airline. His eyes lingered on the curve of her neck. He shook his head to get hold of himself, remembering she once left him heartbroken. "I've got a little work to handle," he said, reaching for his phone. "You good now?"

"Sure, go ahead," Layla said, her heart squeezing a little. "I don't want to keep you from work." She turned her head towards the window and closed her eyes.

Gage stared at his phone. There were close to 50 emails he needed to answer, many from political consultants, some from his godfather, about the Georgia gubernatorial campaign. But he couldn't deal with any of that now.

He could only think back to his last night with Layla, not ready for the day to come, still wanting to savor the night—what they'd done, how they'd done it. To top it all off, she'd finally dared to fall asleep in his arms. He'd heard Layla drift off to sleep in his bed, and what a sweet sound that was.

He looked over at her beside him once again, this time sleeping next to him on his airplane, heading to the place where she lived and he so often visited. He wondered if the universe was trying to tell him something. She couldn't escape this time—not out of his plane. He urged himself to concentrate on work.

For the next two hours, Layla kept her eyes closed, pretending to rest or sleep, or at least keep her breathing steady. All of that was nearly impossible with visions of her father in a coffin, her mother's words echoing in her head, and her first love sitting beside her—the one guy she ever truly loved.

She thought about his hands, remembering the first time they held hers, and his arms, remembering the first time they held her. And his lips—she wondered if they still felt the same, or maybe even better. She wanted to turn and tell him everything, what she was dealing with back then, why she even came to St. Simons Island, why she left that night. But it didn't matter anymore.

She sensed he was done talking, done catching up. Saying he had work to do was just an excuse to cut off contact. The fact that he helped her with her ticket was just his Southern manners still intact or some customer relations ploy. And the fact that he briefly talked to her was probably just to get her in the air before she threw up and freaked out all the other passengers.

She couldn't blame him if he hated her. She wouldn't want anything to do with someone who'd done what she had. She didn't turn back to him until the plane came to a stop at the gate.

"I'm glad you were able to rest," Gage said.

"Me, too," she said, quickly unbuckling and standing up. "Thank you for the ticket. I'd like to pay you back. I'll send a check to your office in Atlanta."

Gage handed Layla her bag. "Please don't do that. My mother would skin me alive."

Layla smiled, hearing the slightest Southern accent dripping through, and instinctively reached for him. "Today was horrible, but you made it better." Gage looked down at her fingers grazing his arm. *Why am I touching him? Geez, Layla, take your hands off the man.* She blushed and moved her hand away. "I'm glad you're doing well, so successful. I'm really proud of you." She took her bag and walked past him off the plane, telling herself not to look back, to just leave like she'd done before, not wanting him to see the tears in her eyes.

Gage stood speechless. For a moment, he tried to catch up, wanting to call after her, to chase her down, to pick her up and kiss her. But his head wouldn't let him, screaming that she left him before, left him with so much pain. His heart still hers, always hers, his head won out this time, watching her leave again, disappearing into a crowd of travelers.

HE CALLED HIS mother from the airport. He said he couldn't stay the weekend. In fact, he had to catch the next flight back to Atlanta. Something had come up. It was business. It couldn't wait. He was sorry. He'd see her soon.

He didn't like lying to his mother, but he didn't see a way around it. He couldn't be in the same city as Layla, knowing where to find her—to yell at her, to kiss her. It was better not to think about her. That had worked pretty well for 12 years. It's why he kept himself so busy.

But there were times he just couldn't help himself. He looked up Story Wings on his phone and wrote the address on a small card, tucking it into his wallet. Then he looked at a flight monitor. The flight back to Atlanta couldn't come soon enough.

IT WAS ALMOST midnight, and Layla wasn't getting any sleep. She pulled herself out of bed and headed to her bookstore. Story Wings wouldn't open for hours, but the place always made her feel better, or at least helped her escape for a little while. After all, the bookstore seemed from a different era, an old antebellum post office she and Poppy renovated in the Historic District, an area of Savannah known for its distinctive grid plan, green spaces, and 18th and 19th century architecture.

They made it a point to maintain the vintage feel, with its creaking pine floors and distressed church pews, and historic front windows they kept filled with the latest books. Old world ceiling beams created a cozy little reading nook in the back, always a popular landing place for children's story time and teen and adult book clubs. And in the little cafe they built in the middle of the store—outfitted in all the modern conveniences along with an old brass cash register with a crank handle—they baked goodies each day.

Layla rubbed her eyes and put her key in the door, the wonderful smell of fresh scones hitting her right away.

Poppy stuck her head out from behind the counter. "What are you doing back now?"

Layla smiled as she walked to the cafe. She should've known Poppy would be there. She was always there. She eyed the purple locks of her friend's waist-length hair. "What color is this?"

"It's called Auburn Love," Poppy said and shrugged her shoulders. "It was supposed to turn out red."

"What happened this time?" Layla asked, plopping down on a big fluffy bean bag and crossing her legs. Her friend was notorious for abusing her hair whenever a relationship went south. In the past six months, Layla had seen every shade of the rainbow, cut or extended to every possible length.

Poppy sat down beside her. "His wife showed up at my apartment last night."

"*His wife?* The hottie firefighter was married?"

"Apparently so. I didn't know! We were having a late dinner, and she comes knocking on my door."

"Oh, Pop, I'm so sorry."

"He's got three kids, three little babies!" Poppy said, her eyes welling up, but only for a moment. "That bastard!"

"He didn't wear a ring?"

Poppy shook her head. "I thought his hours were strange because of his job, not because he was screwing me around the little league schedule."

Layla pulled her into a hug. Poppy never had a shortage of men, with her fun-loving personality, big breasts, and green eyes, but with always the worst luck. In the last year alone, she'd gone from the guy who couldn't make her orgasm, to another who needed some serious manscaping, to another who had a Call of Duty obsession. And now there was the adulterous firefighter juggling little league. "What happened with the wife?"

"She found a text he sent me," Poppy said. "She followed him to my place."

"Did you tell her you didn't know?"

"Of course! I felt horrible! I think she believed me."

"That's good, I guess," Layla said and released her friend. "Are you OK?"

"Except for suffering from fucker's remorse. What about you? Why are you back so soon?"

"The usual with my family. It's not worth getting into," Layla said flatly, then the corners of her mouth turned up. "But one part of the trip was interesting. I ran into Gage Montgomery in Houston."

"What?" Poppy cried. "How'd he know about the funeral?"

"Not at the funeral. I ran into him at the airport. He just came out of nowhere."

"Did you guys talk at the airport?"

"Not really."

"Any sex there?"

"No, you are so bad! He helped me with my ticket, and then it was time to get on the plane."

"What do you mean he helped you?"

"He *runs* Southern Wings."

"Holy shit! Jackpot!" Poppy shrieked. "Did you kiss him 'goodbye' before you got on?"

"He got on with me."

"*With you*? He came to Savannah?"

"He's apparently here a lot."

"Weird. How was the flight? Any sex there?"

"Will you stop?" Layla cried, giggling. "It was actually pretty awkward sitting next to him. One minute he seemed happy to see me, and the next he seemed angry. We actually didn't talk too much. But it was still good to see him and know he's doing well."

"Did you give him your number? Did he give you his? Did you guys make plans to see each other?"

"No, I left pretty quickly," Layla said and lowered her head.

"*Again*? I can dye your hair if you want."

WHEN GAGE LANDED in Atlanta, his first order of business was making sure his calendar was stocked with meetings. He found himself even hoping for a company crisis—maybe a flight attendant strike, or even a break room out of coffee. He wasn't about to let Layla occupy space in his mind.

His mother called during the week and could tell something was wrong. She could tell her son was exhausted, working himself to death, refusing to delegate even the slightest task. Gage half-listened each time she called, nodding along and telling her he understood and would try to do better.

But that wasn't good enough. She insisted he come to Savannah next weekend. She said he needed to relax, to get away. She didn't want his life cut short like his father's. She'd have a home-cooked meal waiting for him at her house. He let out a sigh. He'd do as his mother asked—and it had nothing to do with Layla.

He wouldn't go see her. He wouldn't think about her. He'd simply eat his mother's food, hang out at her house and see his niece and nephews, then head back to Atlanta when the weekend was over. That was it. There'd be nothing more—no wallowing over Layla, no thinking about her. And he'd quickly fall back into work. There was always so much to do.

But he couldn't fool himself.

CHAPTER SIX

HIS TEENAGE NIECE and young nephews by his side, Gage made his way through the Historic District. They'd only been walking a few minutes – along cobblestone and oyster-shell walkways – but he could sense the oppressive heat was taking a toll on the kids. He couldn't have them red-faced or drenched, or worst of all, cranky. That was not going to work. He steered them to walk under rows of oak trees dripping with Spanish moss, each offering a brief respite from the morning sun. But the shade only helped for a moment.

"Do we really have to go to a bookstore?" the middle child Jacob asked, surfing around on his phone. "I hate reading."

"I like reading but not paper books," the oldest Ava said. "I just like my e-reader. Bookstores are for old people—like libraries."

Gage frowned and looked at the youngest. "Well, I know Connor likes books. Don't you, buddy?"

Connor nodded and smiled wide, his blond curls bouncing, pleased as punch to have his uncle's attention.

"Because he's a little nerd," Jacob said.

"I am not!" Connor barked.

"Guys, guys, please don't fight," Gage begged. "I think we're getting close."

He took a deep breath then coughed a few times, nearly choking on a whiff of rotten eggs, the pungent odor from a nearby paper mill. The kids didn't flinch at all—their little bodies long ago acclimated to the one drawback in an otherwise magical city. Gage survived the odor then noticed the Olde Pink House across the street, a grand antebellum mansion and popular destination for Savannah ghost hunters. He thought to point it out to the kids but decided against it. The kids lived in Savannah, so they probably already knew about it. And if they didn't, they were probably too hot to care.

They turned the corner and came upon an old building with original wood and windows, full of natural light. Story Wings fit perfectly in the Historic District. He smiled to himself. It was obviously the kind of place Layla would love. "I need you all to behave yourselves," he said. "We won't be too long. Uncle G just has a little business to take care of." The kids shrugged in response.

They walked up a few steps and headed inside, the smell of books and bread and coffee hitting them right away. And Gage smelled something else, too – a distinct twinge of lavender. His heart jumped. She was close by. He looked down at the kids, wiggling around, poking and pinching each other. "Guys, please. . . ."

Gage stopped when his eyes landed on Layla, stepping out from between two bookshelves. She looked as good as ever, even better than in the airport. She looked how he remembered her on St. Simons Island, wearing a floral sundress. She put a book in the shelf then turned to face her new customers. She appeared as stunned as he was. He struggled for something to say, a reason to be in her store after so many years. No other woman got him so tongue-tied.

"Kids," he said, pushing them slightly forward, "this is Miss Layla."

Layla held her breath and walked towards them, smiling nervously. She had no idea what he was doing here. Maybe he was just curious about her shop, or maybe he'd come to demand answers. "Hi," she said.

"This is Ava," Gage said, "my niece."

Ava smirked up at her uncle. As the oldest, she was on to him. She could tell what the man's "business" was at Story Wings.

"These are my nephews, Connor and Jacob."

"I hate books," Jacob told Layla then dropped his head back to his phone.

Gage gave Jacob a menacing look and lightly smacked him on the head. "He's dyslexic," Gage said, "but that doesn't mean he can be rude."

"It's OK," Layla said. "Books aren't for everyone. Jacob, what do you like? Do you want to be a pilot like your uncle?"

"No, I'm too dumb," Jacob said.

Gage sighed. "You are not."

"Yeah, he is," Ava said, "but not because he can't read."

Jacob slapped his sister on the shoulder, and Connor started to cry. Gage looked over at Layla, his eyes apologizing for the horror he'd unleashed on her store. Layla shook her head that he had nothing to worry about then draped an arm around Jacob. The boy's cheeks flushed. At 12, any attention from a female—no matter how old—was a cause for total embarrassment.

"Jacob," she said, "I've got this huge Lego castle I need to put together for my front window display, but I can't seem to get it started. Could you help?" Jacob looked at his uncle for permission, and Gage nodded. Layla pointed Jacob to an enormous box, and the boy tore it open, starting to build without any directions.

"Ava likes to read," Gage told Layla, "but only on her e-reader."

"I have an e-reader. I like it, too," Layla said. "How old are you, Ava?"

"14."

"I thought so," Layla said, remembering seeing a photo of Ava as a toddler at the beach house. "Can I show you something that's good about books that you can't find on an e-reader?" Layla opened a glass case behind the counter and pulled out a hardback copy of a current tween bestseller that was soon to be a movie. She opened the cover of the book and showed Ava the inside jacket signed by the entire cast. "Does your e-reader have *this*?"

Ava jumped up and down. "OMG! Did you meet them? Were they here? They actually touched this book?" She ran her fingers across the jacket as if to transfer the actors' karma to herself.

Layla giggled. "Yeah, I met them all at a book signing."

"Uncle G, you have to buy this for me!" Ava begged.

Gage gave Layla a sideways smile. "How much is this going to cost me?"

"Nothing," Layla said and handed the book to Ava, who hustled to a chair to call her friends about this amazing discovery.

"I'll pay for that," Gage said.

"Not necessary. Consider it payback for helping with the flight," she said, offering a smile, a dimple popping out.

Gage felt his body drawn to hers. He always had a soft spot for her cute dimples. He reached for her hand and stroked her knuckles, remembering how nervous he was to hold her hand the first time. But now it felt natural—even after so many years.

"Uncle G," Connor said, pulling on Gage, forcing him to release her hand. "Tell her I'm five."

"He's five."

Layla bent down to Connor. "I'm 28. Do you like books?"

"I like books about airplanes," Connor said. "Uncle G, tell her about Petey!"

"We talked about this, buddy. No imaginary friend talk."

"He's not imaginary! He's close by," Connor said, "and he's going to bite you."

"He bites?" Layla wondered.

"Yeah, he's a crocodile and walks on two legs." Connor pouted his lip. "You can't see him, either?"

Layla took his little hand. "The thing is, only special children get to have friends like Petey. Adults can't see them, but I believe he's there."

Connor's face lit up. "He likes you."

"I like him," she said, feeling Gage's intense stare upon her. The man seemed different than the carefree boy in swim trunks, flying gliders, singing Shaggy on acoustic guitar. He was more serious, focused now. Perhaps that comes with running a huge national business. *Or did I long ago ruin who he was?* "Does Petey need a snack?"

"No, he just ate a sea turtle," Connor said. "Did you ever have a special friend? My sister and brother didn't, and they call me a baby."

"Well, that's not nice. I did have a friend like Petey when I was little. Her name was Aria, and she was an angel."

Gage tilted his head, his blue eyes soft, his heart warming. *She never told me about Aria. Maybe she didn't tell me a lot of things.*

"Wow!" Connor said. "Do you still see Aria?"

"Not in a long time," Layla said quietly.

"What does she look like?" the little boy asked, stepping closer to Layla as if they were members of a secret society.

"She was beautiful. She had blonde hair, and she glowed. Her wings were the purest white."

Connor hopped up and down. "Show her your wings, Uncle G!"

Gage picked up the boy. "You know I only wear my wings when I fly, buddy."

"Not those wings," the boy said and reached towards his uncle's shirt.

Gage nudged the boy's hand. "Active imagination."

"I like an active imagination," Layla said. "Connor, let's go check out some books."

Gage released a deep breath, happy to have a moment alone. As a pilot and businessman, he was always steady and secure, always one step ahead. But Layla had him in a tailspin, and he couldn't seem to maneuver out of it.

"Would you like some coffee?" a perky voice asked from behind.

Gage turned to find a purple-haired woman holding a coffee mug in the cafe. "No, but thanks anyway," he said, taking in her bright hair and face.

"I'm Poppy. I own the store with Layla." She smiled and poured herself a cup. "I'm guessing you're Gage."

He strolled up towards her. "How did you. . . ."

"Layla told me you two ran into each other. I assumed that was you with the kids over there."

"Those aren't *my* kids."

"I assumed that, too. I knew you'd show up sooner or later."

"I'm not here. . . ."

Poppy smacked his hand and leaned forward on the counter. "Stop lying to yourself. We both know why you're here. It's not for children's books. And why wouldn't you want her? She's beautiful, smart, talented."

"Sounds like *you* want her."

"I don't swing both ways. I prefer penis."

"Um, OK," Gage said nervously.

"She's not seeing anyone, you know."

"No, I didn't know," he replied, though that *was* good to know. Then he shook his head, knowing it didn't matter. There was no way he could ever be with Layla again. He couldn't trust her, no matter how much he might want her, the battle between his head and heart raging on.

"How do you run a whole airline?" Poppy asked. "I mean, you're so young! You're probably the youngest CEO in the whole world!"

"I don't think that's true. I'm not *that* young anyway."

Poppy pulled a mug from behind the counter. "The more I think about it, you do need a cup of coffee."

"I'm not a coffee drinker."

"That's the silliest thing I've ever heard. Coffee is a total non-negotiable. Got to have it. Like condoms and toilet paper. Can't live without it."

Gage bust out laughing. This purple-haired woman was as crazy as Dash. He looked away to find Layla and Connor coming his way. His nephew was holding a package of some kind. "What you got there, little man?"

Connor flew over to his uncle and leaped in his arms. "Look what Miss Layla made for me!"

"That's cool, buddy," Gage said, thumbing through a stack of airplane books tied together in an old-fashioned leather book strap. Connor hopped down and buzzed the books around like they were a 747. Gage looked over at Layla, emotions crashing over him again. It was time to go. *I'll walk away this time.* He yelled for Ava and Jacob. "We should probably get going," he told Layla.

"Sure," she said, a touch of sadness in her voice.

The kids gathered around and thanked Layla for helping them. Then Ava winked at her uncle and ushered her siblings out of the store, all the kids skipping together.

"Take care, Ang. . . ." Gage smiled. "Layla."

I'm not his angel anymore. "You, too," she said softly then thought to ask him to stay, but stopped before uttering a word. It wouldn't make a difference. Too much time had passed. And she'd caused too much pain.

"Gage, it was nice to meet you," Poppy said. "I'm sure I'll be seeing you."

GAGE GOT TO his sister's house and blew out a deep breath. The morning had been more stressful than any board meeting or union negotiation. Emerson greeted them at the door, her dark brown hair pulled in a ponytail, her black rim glasses atop her head. She looked at her baby brother's frazzled face and let a smile slip, impressed he returned the kids safe and sound, and most of all, happy.

Connor zoomed off with the book bundle, but Emerson grabbed it before he got away. "This is adorable," she said, putting her glasses on. "Who did this?"

"Just this little bookstore we happened across," Gage answered.

"This would be perfect for maternity gifts for employees."

"The flowers we send are fine, Emerson." His sister ran the marketing and public relations for Southern Wings, and her brain didn't have an "off" switch. She could be exhausting and—10 years older than Gage—very bossy.

"What was the name of the store? I'm going to call and see if they'd be interested."

"I don't remember."

"Story Wings," Ava said. "Uncle G was totally crushing on the owner."

Emerson lifted her eyebrows. "Oh, really?"

"It wasn't like that," Gage said.

"She liked Petey," Connor said.

"And she let me build this cool Lego castle," Jacob said.

"Sounds like a nice place," Emerson said. "Now, you kids go and get ready. Your dad will be here in a few minutes."

When the kids disappeared, Gage turned to his sister. "How'd the meeting go?"

Emerson shrugged. "How are divorces supposed to go? He doesn't want to talk except through lawyers. I think it's better now that he moved out. It was so tense before, and we kept trying to hide it from the kids. He'd wait for them to go to bed every night. Then he'd go and sleep in his office. He'd get up early so they didn't know."

"Do you want me to talk to him?" Gage offered. He always liked his brother-in-law. He wasn't sure what the hell happened.

"No, I'm the one who screwed up."

"*You?*"

Emerson nodded. "It will be fine. We will be fine. So tell me about this bookstore girl."

"Please don't try to make this into something it's not."

"A crush, huh? Mom will be thrilled."

CHAPTER SEVEN

GAGE STAYED THE weekend in Savannah then flew back to Atlanta. It was good to be home. He figured the distance from Layla would do him some good. He didn't like that Ava was on to him. And he didn't like Emerson needling him about a "crush." It wasn't true, and he wasn't a teenager anymore. He was the head of a national airline, and with his charm and good looks, he could get any woman he wanted.

But that wasn't really his style—at least not since college, when he nailed anything that moved. When he wasn't training at five hundred miles per hour, sex was another adrenaline rush, another thrill. It seemed the natural thing to do. But it got less thrilling over time, and in quiet moments, he knew there was something sad in what he was doing—screwing lots of women to get Layla off his mind. It wasn't entirely fair to them, though they never complained.

As he got older, he wanted something steadier and without a lot of drama. But the women seemed to always bring the drama with them. They were always falling in love with him, always wanting to get married, thinking he was the perfect guy to father their children. His most recent relationship, like many others, ended after about a year when the woman started hinting about rings and biological clocks.

Gage had no time for that. He was married to running Southern Wings, spending as much time as possible in the office. He put in the hours because he loved what he did and wanted to honor his father's company, and also because he was pretty young to be in charge. He wasn't about to give anyone any reason to believe he wasn't fully committed and fully capable of doing the job—and doing it better than anyone else could.

So his work ethic didn't help his dating life. It also didn't help that when he wasn't working, he was spending so much time in Savannah with his family, his mother now living alone, his sister and her kids going through a divorce. And perhaps most of all, it didn't help that he'd recently spent a lot of time thinking about Layla—how good she looked, how sweet she smelled, how sweet she was to the kids, how things ended between them.

He didn't like being so indecisive about her. It's not the way he operated. As an executive, he liked making decisions quickly and then going full throttle to execute them. He wished he could stop obsessing over her and figure out what to do. He needed a night out to clear his head, to get away from work, to decompress. He arranged to meet Dash at a downtown bar. As it turned out, Dash himself had a lot on his mind.

Before Gage could pop open his beer, Dash launched into an idea he'd been thinking about—that the FAA should require any baby who screams more than 10 seconds on a flight to be anesthetized before ever flying again. Dash said he wasn't trying to be mean—just thinking about crew safety and sanity—and didn't think there'd be any detrimental effects on the baby. Then he launched into another, suggesting changes in the way flight attendants dress.

"If they're in good shape, the FAA should require them to wear more revealing uniforms—shorter skirts, midriff tops," Dash said. "But if they've let themselves go, they should be required to cover up a bit. There would be a sliding scale in terms of fitness."

"What about male flight attendants?" Gage asked.

"It wouldn't apply to them, of course. I'm not sure we should even have male flight attendants."

Gage took a drink, spotting a group of women by a pool table. It occurred to him maybe he'd been thinking so much about Layla because he hadn't had sex in a while. Maybe his dick was getting in the way. It was time to rectify that.

Dash followed his friend's line of sight. "What ever happened with that hot piece a few weeks back?"

"Which one?" Gage joked.

"The one from the flight?"

"Layla? Been there, done that. I was just helping her out."

"She was pretty hot," Dash said. "Think I'd hit that a few times. Do you think she likes black guys?"

Gage narrowed his eyes. "Let's not talk about her."

"Seems like she's under your skin a little."

Gage looked back towards the pool table, renewing his search for the right woman. She needed to be hot and preferably with light hair. He didn't need any reminders of Layla. And she couldn't be looking for a commitment of any kind. He didn't need that, either.

"Maybe it's time to dust off your dick, G-man."

Gage downed his beer. "The easiest way to forget about one woman is to screw another." He headed towards the pool table, a platinum blonde with come-hither eyes waiting for him.

A NEW WORKDAY was just what Gage needed. It was time to focus, and not on women and their drama. He headed inside the eight-story corporate office of Southern Wings, greeting the receptionists and security guards by name. Built by his father years ago, the office was ahead of its time, with an open floor plan bearing the electric blue and white company colors, and glass windows and doors offering a team-oriented work environment, if not a particularly private one.

Gage rode up the elevator to the executive offices, chatting up some employees along the way. He loved talking to them, taking their pulse, getting their input. After all, there'd be no company to run without them, and he didn't want them to feel unappreciated. He reached the eighth floor and headed out, walking down a few hallways then through double glass doors into his corner office, pinching the bridge of his nose along the way.

His gray-haired secretary, Mary, greeted him with two aspirin. "Your father used to do the same thing when he had a headache coming on."

Gage politely thanked her. Mary was like a surrogate mother to him.

Having worked for his father, she'd known Gage since birth. He was certain she could run the entire airline by herself from her desk. He popped the pills in his mouth and took a stack of messages from her.

"And your godfather called confirming lunch with those political consultants," Mary said, "the ones you keep ignoring."

Half-listening, Gage flipped through the messages then wrinkled his nose, the slightest hint of lavender in the air. "Do you smell that?"

Mary crinkled her forehead. "What?"

Gage shook his head, apparently losing his mind. "Nothing."

"By the way," Mary said, "your sister wants to see you in her office first thing."

Gage rubbed his temples. "I can't handle any of her PR garbage right now. I mean. . . ." Then he caught himself and pushed out a smile. "I'll go see Emerson right now."

"Do you need more aspirin?" she teased.

Gage rolled his eyes and walked to his sister's office, the lavender scent getting stronger with every step. It was beyond aggravating. Layla was consuming his every waking moment, and now he was smelling her at work. He was clearly going crazy. Even the blonde from the bar couldn't help; he'd lost interest in her after one drink.

Gage flung open his sister's office door and discovered the reason for the lavender scent. The entire office was covered in book bundles from Layla's shop.

"Good morning, baby brother," Emerson said, sweetly lifting her glasses to her head.

"What the hell is all this? I thought I told you to stay out of it."

Emerson got to her feet. "I don't have to run these decisions by you."

"Is this shit why you wanted to see me?"

"It's not *shit*. And my job is just as important as yours."

"That's why you come into the office once a week."

"Just because I usually work from home doesn't mean what I'm doing is unimportant. Dad knew that."

Gage shook his head. "Look, I don't want her in my life. I don't want to do business with her."

"Then go tell her that yourself."

"*Go tell her?* What are you talking about?"

"She's getting coffee in the kitchen."

"Layla is *here?*" Gage slammed the door shut, his whole body trembling. "What the hell did you do, Emerson?"

"I went to her bookstore. I told her you were my brother, and I liked the bundle she put together for Connor."

"And now suddenly she's in Atlanta? In our offices? In our kitchen?"

"Yes. She brought me some book bundle samples. She had a layover on a flight to Houston. She's working up some prices for me."

"Jesus Christ!"

She reached for her brother's hand, but he pulled away. "I know she's the girl from that summer."

"You weren't even there."

"I didn't have to be," she said. "That was the only time you've ever been so tied up in knots over a girl—the same way you are now."

Gage flashed a look that his sister could go to hell. "It's none of your business, Emerson."

"I really like her if that helps," she said.

"It doesn't. And you shouldn't be talking to Layla—about me, or at all really!"

"*At all?* Two women can't talk business?"

"Come on, that's not what I meant! You're interfering in my life! Just because your love life is shit, you can't interfere in mine!"

LAYLA POURED HERSELF a cup of coffee. It was nerve-wracking being in the corporate headquarters. This was Gage's castle. He could pop into the kitchen at any moment or see her in the hall. She wondered if Emerson really cleared the idea with him like she said she did. Or maybe Gage was behind this whole book bundle thing. She smiled slightly thinking maybe this was his way of fixing things between them.

She saw some photos on a bulletin board, corporate officers and employees at various charity events, one of Gage at a Teach for America event sponsored by Southern Wings. She focused in on his eyes. He was a born leader. And he looked so good—as good as he did in her store. She spotted a photo of Emerson, a huge smile on her face, presenting a $10,000 check to an inner-city school.

Layla made her way back down the hall. Emerson's door was closed. She gently knocked and opened it, finding Gage and Emerson staring daggers at each other. "Oh, I'm sorry I interrupted."

"Not at all, Layla," Emerson said, faking a smile. "My brother was just leaving."

"Right," Gage huffed then snarked to Layla, "I don't want to intrude on your meeting with my sister."

"Um, I can see you're both busy," Layla said. "I've got to run anyway."

"Yeah, you're good at that," Gage said under his breath.

Layla bit her tongue, trying to stay professional, though it hurt to have someone she loved hate her in return. "It was wonderful to get to know you, Emerson. Take your time to think about the bundles. You can keep all the samples."

"That's very kind of you," Emerson said. "I'm quite sure the company will place an order. You do beautiful work."

"Thank you. Keep in touch," Layla said then walked out, careful not to look Gage in the eye.

Gage could feel Emerson looking at him with disgust. His sister had the "mother" look down pat. His heart yelled for him to stop Layla, to call the receptionist and security guards and have them shut down the elevators and lock her in the building. But his head reminded him of the heartbreak. He managed a few steps down the hall and saw her step into an elevator, their eyes finally meeting as a few silent tears rolled down her cheeks. He felt his weight shift towards her slightly, but then the door closed. *She's gone again.* He slumped back to his sister's office.

"God, you're an asshole," Emerson said.

"I'm sorry I said that about your love life," Gage said. "I'm really sorry."

"Not just that. You were an asshole to *her*."

He lowered his head. "I know."

"You're right that my love life is shit. It's been that way for years."

"No, you don't need to. . . ."

"For years, he just hasn't seemed real interested in me. He just stopped talking to me, really talking to me. We were all business and schedules and kids. The few times we'd go out, I'd always plan whatever we did. We only ever kissed when it was during sex, which frankly was only a handful of times a year."

"You don't have to tell me all this."

"I don't have anyone to talk to. I don't want Mom to worry, and my girlfriends all thought he was the best. He just showed no interest anymore. I mean, I've had three kids. I know I'm not as toned as I was. I know gravity hasn't been kind."

"I never saw him glance at another woman."

Emerson reached for a tissue. "That's what makes this so hard. He's a good man. He worked hard to give us a great life. I just don't think he enjoyed being with me anymore. It's like he didn't think of me at all except as the person he provided for and who took care of his house and kids. That's all I was."

"No, it's not."

"I tried everything to keep him interested. I watched sports, dressed nice, smelled good, waxed everything—and I mean *everything*." Gage stuck his fingers in his ears. "Lingerie, dates, trips, giving him space, snuggling with him. Nothing worked."

"Maybe there's still hope?"

She shook her head. "I screwed up bad. There was this guy in my bootcamp class I do a few mornings a week. He flirted with me. It made me feel good, pretty." She looked in her baby brother's eyes and saw her father's disappointment. "First it was just talking after class, then coffee, and then one day he walked me to my car—and kissed me."

"I don't want to hear this."

"I kissed him back. It wasn't just a peck."

"Jesus," he said softly.

"When I pulled back, I started to cry. I wanted it to be my husband kissing me like that." Emerson twirled her wedding ring. "It never went any further, but that was too far. I went home and told him everything."

"He must have gone ballistic."

"He did. The funny thing is, he thought we were happy, that I was happy." She patted her eyes. "I realized I'd rather be with him than anyone else. But he couldn't get past it."

Emerson tossed the tissue in the trash and pushed out a little smile. Gage always admired how his sister could pick herself up after a few moments of grief, put it in a box, and move forward. He, however, could pine over a woman for a decade and then act like a bastard and make things worse. He was going to have to settle things with Layla.

"I'm totally the wrong person to be giving advice," she said, "but this thing between you and Layla—whatever it is, whatever it may be—you don't want to lose it."

"Look, it was 12 years ago. It's over."

"I didn't get that sense from her," she said, a twinkle in her eye. "And I don't from you, either. I can see your head spinning."

"What am I supposed to do now? What am I supposed to say to her?"

"First thing is you need to get your head out of your ass, or she's going to disappear out of your life again."

"She's the one who left before!"

"Maybe it wasn't that simple. Women can be complicated. Maybe you should get over what happened. You know, you leave people, too! Always tossing women aside when things get serious. So don't be stupid now that you may have a chance again with this woman."

Gage gave his sister a hug. "Did Layla really fly all the way to Atlanta to deliver the bundles?"

Emerson nodded her head. "She has a connecting flight to Houston that leaves in a few hours. Her father's will reading is later today. Or maybe she had another reason for bringing them personally?"

Gage raised an eyebrow then reached across his sister's desk. He dialed his secretary. "Mary, I need you to get me on the next flight to Houston." He looked over at his sister smiling at him. "Sold out? How about the next one?" He looked at his watch and blew out a deep breath. "Sold out, too?" He pinched the bridge of his nose. "Then get the corporate jet ready. I need to leave in an hour. Please cancel that political lunch and clear the rest of my day."

CHAPTER EIGHT

LAYLA HEADED OUT her hotel room—drained from the flight, from the layover in Atlanta, from Gage snapping at her. It obviously meant nothing that he visited her bookstore. He was probably just trying to torture her. She obviously meant nothing to him anymore. He obviously had no intention of forgiving her.

She got to the lobby, feeling more and more tired, the impending doom coming closer. She told herself to buck up, that she'd survived her family before. But she couldn't help but worry about what could happen at the will reading, and about coming back alone to a lonely hotel room until her morning flight home. The quiet moments could often be the worst.

Layla started towards a cab then stopped in her tracks, finding Gage coming straight for her. She stood up straight, her stomach dropping, and braced herself for whatever he was doing here. He looked as serious as ever and a bit flustered, too. He was probably coming to deliver a few more biting comments, things he didn't want his sister to hear. "What are you doing here?"

Gage slid his arms around her and held her tightly, burying his head in her hair. "I'm sorry," he said quietly. "I'm sorry, Angel."

"No, I'm the one who's sorry," she said, gripping her hands along his back, tears falling down her cheeks.

Gage didn't want to let go. *This feels so right? God, help me. I want her back.* Holding her again, after so many years, felt like the first true thing since they ran into each other. After a few moments, they slowly pulled apart, and he dried her eyes with his fingers. "We should talk."

"Did you come here for me?" she asked. "How did you find me?"

"Emerson told me the flight. Poppy told me the hotel."

"You called Poppy?"

"I lost you before. I'm not about to let it happen again."

Layla lowered her head to his chest, crying again.

"I never really stopped looking for you," he said, one hand rubbing her back, the other stroking her hair. "I need some answers."

"I want to talk," she said, "but I can't right now."

"I know," Gage said. "We've got the will reading."

Layla's head darted up, and she stepped away from him. "*We?*"

"I'm going with you."

"No, Gage."

"This is going to be difficult. I just went through this with my dad. There wasn't a reading or anything, but there were all these lawyers and law stuff. The whole thing was uncomfortable. You need someone with you." He took her hand and intertwined their fingers. "Let me be there for you."

"You don't know what you're getting yourself into."

"Maybe not."

"Promise me no matter what is said, you'll stay calm."

"Don't worry about me," he said, feeling her hand tremble just slightly. "You need to keep yourself calm and strong."

AFTER A SHORT cab ride, they headed into a Houston skyscraper and up to a high floor. Gage opened the conference room door, bracing himself for whatever he was getting himself into, and followed Layla inside. The room was as big as an Olympic-size swimming pool, with one side of the room covered in glass overlooking downtown Houston. There was a long rectangular table made from fine mahogany and leather conference chairs for at least two dozen people. But there were only two in the room—a woman in her early 60's and a 40-something man, both seated together at the far end.

"Mother," Layla said coldly.

Her mother gave a sideways smile, eyeing the man standing behind

Layla. Gage kept his eyes on the man by Layla's mother. He had blond hair and a creepy grin. Gage grabbed her hand.

"Aren't you going to say 'hello' to your brother?" her mother asked.

"No," Layla said, "I don't have one."

"Still a little bitch," she said.

What the hell? Gage darted his eyes to her mother and made a move towards her. But Layla pulled him back, seeing her half-brother get to his feet. Gage looked the woman up and down, her strawberry-blonde hair and brown eyes, her hair and makeup flawless. She probably was beautiful in her time. He remembered briefly meeting her that summer after Layla disappeared, but wouldn't have recognized her on the street.

The half-brother came around the table towards them. Layla moved slightly behind Gage. He wrapped an arm around her and escorted her to the far side of the table.

The door opened, and a curly gray-haired attorney in a three-piece suit entered. The half-brother halted his approach and returned to his seat. Without saying a word, the attorney positioned himself at the head of the table next to Layla and Gage then surveyed the mother and half-brother sitting 50 feet away. "Would you like to come join us down here?" he said, his voice straining across the room.

"No," the mother said.

The attorney frowned. "Both of you, come sit down here. I'm not going to yell, and you will want to hear what I have to say."

"Whatever, man," the half-brother said then turned to his mother. "Let's slide down and get what's ours." They got up slowly, the half-brother coughing a little, his mother steadying him, and headed across the room. They sat down opposite Layla and Gage.

"I've been doing probate work for 30 years," the attorney began. "Just so you know, I've never done a will reading before, and I've never seen any other attorney do it. I thought it was something just in the movies or in books, a way to create a lot of drama and tension. There's actually no legal requirement that a will be read out loud to anyone. It's usually my job to decide which people are entitled to receive a copy of the will so that they can read it themselves."

"So what are we doing here?" the mother asked.

"Your late husband, Mr. Baxter, wanted to have a will reading," the attorney said. "He wanted all of you here—his wife, his stepson, his daughter—to hear his will."

"Who's this other guy?" the half-brother asked.

"I'm Gage Montgomery," he said, cool as ever, seeing a twinge of yellow in the man's blue eyes.

"Is that supposed to mean something to me?"

"Probably not," Gage replied.

"Do you have some business here?"

"Yes," Gage said and motioned for the attorney to continue.

"No," the mother said and eyed Gage. "This is family business."

"It's also *my* business," Layla said, "and Gage is here to assist me."

"Be quiet," her half-brother said.

Gage could feel Layla's legs shaking under the table. He glanced at her out of the corner of his eye. She looked like she could be sick. He gripped her hand and told the attorney to continue.

The attorney cleared his throat. "I believe Mr. Baxter made the right decision having a will reading because there is nothing standard about what he did in his will." He pulled out a five-page typed document from a file, lowered his glasses on his nose, and began to read for almost 20 minutes. He must have read 100 single-spaced paragraphs spelling out in excruciating detail that Layla's mother would, in essence, inherit all property of any kind that her husband, Mr. Baxter, ever owned.

As the attorney droned on, Gage rested his hand on Layla's shoulder. The worst seemed to be happening. What a dirty trick that Mr. Baxter would force his daughter to attend a meeting to hear she'd been cut out and to see her mother nodding along with each passing paragraph. He remembered Layla saying how complicated her family was. Things obviously hadn't gotten better since. He hated she came to Houston for this bullshit and hated he couldn't do a damn thing about it. The attorney finished up and took a long drink of water.

"Are we done here?" the mother asked.

"Not at all," the attorney said and took out another piece of paper. "The rest of Mr. Baxter's will is contained in this letter. Layla, it is a letter from your father to you."

Layla's mouth fell open, and Gage gave her shoulder a little squeeze. The attorney reset his glasses and began again.

"*My dearest Layla,*" he read, "*I can feel my time coming to an end. I'm not sick. In fact, the doctor says I'm in perfect health, but still something inside of me knows. Sometimes it takes the clarity of one's mortality to make other things crystallize in one's mind. All I keep thinking about lately is you, Layla, my only child. And in my heart, I know I've made a terrible mistake.*"

Layla gasped, and the attorney stopped reading for a moment.

"This is ridiculous," her mother snapped and stood up.

"I suggest you sit back down," the attorney said, and the woman did so.

"How do we even know he wrote this?" the half-brother asked.

The attorney lifted his glasses. "I can assure you Mr. Baxter did. He wrote it and signed it in my presence. There were also two other witnesses here, and they also signed it. When he was done and everyone had signed, I notarized it. I'll be glad to give you a copy when I'm through reading."

"We'll be wanting one," the mother said.

The attorney lowered his glasses and continued reading. "*I know it's too late. I know it's too much to ask for your forgiveness, but I was wrong. I know now that you were telling the truth. I'm sorry I didn't believe you. I don't have the courage to tell you while I'm alive. I know I will burn in hell for my part, my neglect, my stupidity, and I know some day you will rise to all the angels in heaven. So I will never look upon your face again. Do you remember when I gave you your wings?*"

Gage slid a hand to his chest, as Layla dropped her head to his shoulder, sobbing. He had no idea what was going on, but from the horrified looks across the table, it was obvious he was in the middle of a shit storm.

"*You probably don't remember, Layla. You were only three. It was right after the first time I caught you talking to Aria. We thought it was so cute that you had an imaginary friend that was an angel. I know now she was real, and she was protecting you when I wasn't. I'm sorry, my baby. I love you always, Daddy.*"

The attorney filed away the letter and handed Layla a box of tissues from a credenza.

"You can stop the acting now, Layla," her mother snapped. "No one is buying it."

"You can shut your mouth, bitch!" Gage said.

"Fuck you, man!" the half-brother barked. "Layla, I see you've found a man that deserves you."

Gage prepared to fire back, but Layla squeezed his hand. Her half-brother wasn't worth it. And she could hold her own. There was no sign her legs were shaking under the table anymore.

The attorney cleared his throat. "Shall I continue?" He didn't wait for an answer. "Layla, your father has left you a lump sum payment of $250,000."

Layla's head whipped around, and her mouth fell open. Her mother and half-brother nearly fell out of their chairs. "How much?" her mother cried.

"$250,000," the attorney said again and passed Layla a piece of paper. "The money is already in an account with your name, and only your name, on it. No one can touch it but you."

"We'll see about that," her mother spewed.

The attorney turned to her. "Your husband anticipated your reaction, so I have here a check for $50,000. It's blank. It's yours, Mrs. Baxter, so long as you sign this paper." He held it up. "It states you will not contest his will now or in the future, or in any way seek to obtain for yourself or anyone else the $250,000 he has left to Layla. If you refuse to sign, I've been instructed to make the check out to Layla. Then she can walk down the street and cash it."

Gage looked at Layla, her mouth still open, then glanced at her mother, seeing the manipulative wheels turning in her head.

"You've got two minutes," the attorney said, looking down at his watch.

"Two?" her mother asked.

"Your husband's requirement."

"What about me?" her half-brother asked.

"You get nothing," the attorney said. "All life insurance policies were cancelled, and all stocks and assets were sold or otherwise left to Mrs. Baxter and Layla. He wanted to make sure you didn't see a penny.

Now, if your mother chooses to take the $50,000, I can't control whether she gives some or all of it to you. Mr. Baxter understood that. He didn't like it, but he understood."

A slow smile came across Layla's face. Her father was finally protecting her. "Thank you, Daddy," she whispered.

"You have no idea what we're going through," her mother said, reaching for her son's hand.

"Can't be worse than what I went through," Layla said.

"Angel?" Gage asked.

"Who's 'angel'?" the half-brother wondered.

The attorney looked at his watch. "What's it going to be, Mrs. Baxter?" he asked and picked up the pen.

The woman whispered something to her son and patted his hand a few times. "Where do I sign?"

LAYLA LAUGHED OUT loud when she got outside. "I'm done, Gage! I don't ever have to deal with them ever again! I'm totally and completely free!" She flew into his arms and kissed him hard on the lips, running her hands wildly in his hair. Her feet left the pavement as he lifted her in the air, pulling her tighter to him.

Gage felt her smile and opened his eyes. He saw her half-brother staring at them from the curb and placed Layla down on the ground. "He's coming towards us," Gage said and moved Layla behind him.

"Layla, I need to talk to you," her half-brother called out.

"Stay away from me," she said, fidgeting with Gage's shirt sleeve. "It was bad enough I had to just sit in the same room with you – and stand across from you at my father's casket."

"He wanted me there. Mom told you that. He loved me."

Gage could feel her heart racing. "You should leave," he said. But the man didn't move a muscle. He just stood there, his eyes strangely yellow. Gage looked back at Layla. "Are you shaking? Let's go."

The man smirked. "She never could be still and quiet."

Layla reared back and spit straight in her half-brother's face. Then she lunged at him like a caged animal, flailing her arms, trying to claw and scratch his eyes out. Gage could hardly believe what was happening. He pulled her away and carried her a little ways down the street, hoping no one saw what just happened or recognized him as the head of Southern Wings.

Gage shoved her in a cab and looked back at her half-brother, a cold hardness on his face, the same creepy grin. He got in beside her and told the driver to head to the hotel. "What's up with your family? What's going on?" he asked and patted her knee. She moved her leg away. He reached out again, but she moved even further this time.

He could see her trembling. He held out an arm and waited for her to come to him. She looked over from under her lashes then slowly scooted towards him—until he could wrap his arm around her and stroke her hair. "Quiet, Angel, I've got you," he said, his stomach twisted in knots but sensing her calming just a bit. "I've got you."

CHAPTER NINE

AFTER SLEEPING 15 hours, Layla woke up to find Gage asleep on an uncomfortable chair, his feet propped on the hotel room desk. A slow smile came over her. She rested her head on her knees and studied his face, his strong jaw, the way his sandy blond hair fell just right, the slightest stubble on his face. He looked the same as the last time she saw him sleep.

Then something caught her eye under his shirt collar, and her breath caught. She leaned closer to get a better look. *Amazing*. It was impossible he'd still have the leather cord holding her wings, let alone be wearing them. She got up quietly and headed for the bathroom, needing some space before she started to cry.

"Sneaking out again?" Gage asked.

Layla kept walking and slammed the bathroom door. *Another snide comment*. The man apparently couldn't decide whether to be nice or a complete jerk, whether to avoid her or show up and apologize, whether to pull her into his arms or push her away. She was sick of it. She tore into her hair, combing out some tangles, then brushed her teeth like she was chiseling stone. She flew open the door and grabbed her suitcase.

Gage stretched and ran his hand through his hair. "Our flight's not for another six hours." Layla didn't respond. She placed the suitcase on the bed and began to pack. "What are you doing?"

"I've decided to rent a car and drive home."

"It's like a two-day drive from Houston to Savannah!"

"So?"

"Is this about what I said a minute ago? Sorry about that."

Layla finished up and slammed her suitcase shut. "If you hate me, I can handle that. I was always prepared for that, but the back and forth is driving me nuts. You fly all the way out here, stay with me all day and night, kiss me on the sidewalk. . . ."

"Wait a minute! You kissed *me* on the sidewalk."

Layla put her hand on her hip and held his eyes. "It was a mistake. It won't happen again."

"Layla, it doesn't have to be that way."

"Yes, Gage, it does. When you cut my heart out, I can't take it." She headed for the door.

Gage scooted in front of her. "Please don't run off," he whispered and lowered his head on hers, his dark blue eyes falling to her lips. "What if I kiss you?"

Layla threw down her suitcase. "That's exactly what I mean! Decide! Decide if you love me or hate me or like me or never want to see me again!"

"I don't know what to feel. I mean, you disappear into thin air without a word for 12 years and then suddenly there you are—looking exactly the same. You even smell the same. So I don't know what to feel."

"Seems to me like you're angry at me, and you have every right to be."

"Of course, I'm angry. Did you ever think what it was like for me, waking up after the best night of my life and finding you gone? Wondering if you regretted what we'd done, if I'd hurt you in some way? Wondering if I was terrible in bed?"

"I'm sorry."

"I deserve to know what possible reason you had to leave me like that."

Layla knew he was right. It was time to tell him what she couldn't before. It was time not to be quiet. She sat him down on the bed and took his hand. "My half-brother molested me on and off since I was three."

Gage's eyes shot to hers, then he headed towards the door. "I'm going to kill him!"

She jumped in front of him. "No, Gage!"

"Move!"

"No," she said calmly.

"Layla, move!"

"No."

"Where does he live? Here in Houston?"

"Please calm down."

"Tell me! Tell me where your mother lives! I'm going to deal with her, too. She didn't protect you."

"She didn't believe me. She thought she had to choose between her son and her daughter. She chose him."

"What the hell?"

Layla reached out and stroked his cheek, directing his eyes to hers. She could see him soften slightly. "I need you right now."

Gage pinched the bridge of his nose, trying to control himself, to steady his breathing. "Do you want to tell me about it?"

"Not in any detail."

"OK," he said, "whatever you feel you need to share."

Layla shook her head at his perfect answer. She told him it started when she was very little, around three, and her half-brother was 15. She spared him most all the details. He didn't need to know about how her half-brother would slip into her bed at night, telling her to keep quiet, how she cried herself to sleep, how she prayed she'd never wake up, how she worked through it all a long time ago.

"Did you ever tell anyone?"

"Not for a long time. When I was real young, he would mutilate my stuffed animals, decapitate them. He'd tell me he'd do the same to me if I ever told."

"Sick fucker."

"He actually told my parents I was the one ripping their heads off. And since he was older, they believed him. So my parents considered me 'troubled' from a very early age—and not just for the stuffed animals. For as long as I can remember, I was seeing my angel, Aria, and talking to her. It was cute at three, but my parents were concerned at eight. They had no idea what Aria was doing for me. When my half-brother came at me, came in my room, she would come, too, and wrap her wings around me, protect me in her own way. Aria saved me—or at least tried to."

"When did you tell your parents?"

"It was when my half-brother moved back in. He'd been gone a few years—out on his own somewhere—but he ran into some financial problems and came back. He was as crazy as ever. I was freaking out. I was so scared it would all start back up again. Thankfully, it didn't. But he reminded me not to tell. You know how he reminded me? He snapped my puppy Coco's neck right in front of me."

"Jesus Christ! When was this?"

"A few days before our summer."

"You told your parents anyway?"

Layla nodded. "They didn't believe me. I was the 'troubled' girl, remember? I had to get out of that house. I couldn't deal with my parents not believing me, or the fear he might hurt me again. He just killed my dog. So I ran off to my grandmother's place."

Gage looked into her eyes and felt the pieces coming together—her sudden arrival on the island without any family; her reluctance to talk about them; the uncertainty of her plans during and after the summer, not knowing if or when she'd leave, or where she'd finish high school.

"I took a bus from Houston in the middle of the night. My mother hadn't spoken to my grandmother in years—they had a huge falling out a long time ago—so I figured I'd be safe there. Every few days, I'd fake calls home so my grandmother wouldn't get suspicious. And I knew my mother wouldn't be calling my grandmother about me, even if I was 'missing.' My mother hated her. So I figured I was safe, at least for a little while. I planned on never going back home. But I never planned on you."

"I never planned on you, either," Gage said, placing a hand on her cheek. "My life was planned out for me for like 10 years, but I never saw you coming. Knocked me right on my ass."

"I remember," she said. "You were so adorable. I didn't want to leave you."

"Then why did you?"

She shook her head, recalling how everything fell apart. "My grandmother got hurt. When I went to see her in the hospital, she told me she called my parents—only because she didn't think she could care for me anymore. She said they were coming to get me, that they didn't know where I'd been. She tried to convince them to let me stay, that I was happy. But they wouldn't listen. I think deep down she knew something terrible was happening." Layla took his hand. "I couldn't go back there, Gage. I just couldn't. I knew I had to leave that night before they got there. I needed a head start, but I wanted to see you first."

"I'm glad you did."

"I wanted to know what it felt like to have someone treat my body with love, tenderness, to know sex could be beautiful and special, that someone would see me that way instead of taking and using me. I knew I had to leave, but I wanted, I needed, to take those memories—*your* memories—with me. I needed to know that was possible, something to keep me alive, hoping for."

"Why didn't you tell me what was going on? I could've helped you."

"I was 16. You were barely 18. There was nothing you could do."

"I would've gone with you. We could've gone off together."

"I knew if I told you, that would be your answer. I knew you wouldn't let me go. I couldn't let you throw away your future, hurt your family like that."

"Maybe my parents could've helped?"

"My own parents didn't believe me, Gage."

"*I* would've believed you."

"I know that."

"Are you OK now?"

"Yeah, as good as can be. I've done a lot of work in therapy, and I'm in a good place now. When I was old enough, I changed my last name to Tanner. It was my grandmother's maiden name. I prefer to look forward, not back. I won't let him—or my mother—take anything else from me. He took enough. They both did."

Gage paused for a few moments to take it all in. Of all the things he thought might've happened, he never considered anything like this. "Why didn't you say 'goodbye'?"

"I wasn't strong enough to do that. I was really messed up and scared. I'm sorry. If you'd done to me what I did to you, I would've died. I don't expect you can ever forgive me. Please know I'm truly sorry I hurt you. I wasn't trying to."

"I know that." Gage pulled out the leather cord and lifted up the wings. "I got your message."

Layla touched them with her hands. "I haven't felt them in so long. I can't believe you kept them."

"I always wear them. You told me it's bad luck to take them off—unless you give them to someone you love." He stepped towards her, his eyes focused on her mouth. "I haven't loved anyone since you."

"Me, neither. But we're not kids anymore."

"We're not. I know what I'm doing this time," he said, leaning in close, his breath tickling her neck.

She blushed and pulled away slightly. "You knew what you were doing then, too."

"I guess I did," he said with a crooked smile.

"If we're going to do this, it can't be based on what we had. It has to be about who we are now."

Gage placed a hand on her cheek, knowing she was right. "Will you have dinner with me tomorrow night?"

Layla's dimples exploded on her cheeks. "What about today?"

"Today, I'm helping a dear friend get home. Tomorrow, I'm seducing a beautiful woman. It'll be a fresh start."

"Can you really forgive me?"

"I already did."

CHAPTER TEN

A DOZEN CHILDREN huddled around her, Layla looked up from "Pokey Little Puppy" and saw Gage with a bundle of white calla lilies and purple lavender. Her heart skipped a beat. She straightened her hair just a little. She wanted to jump into his arms but settled for flashing a smile. He gave a slight wave and mouthed he was sorry for being early, for coming to her store instead of her house. She shook her head that it was fine and continued reading.

Gage couldn't remember the last time he was so excited for a date, so excited to get his hands on a woman. He was determined to get back what they lost, to make up for lost time and pick up where they left off, to have the life they should've had together. He couldn't wait to feel her soft pale skin, her chocolate hair—and this time hopefully without any clothes on.

He wandered into the little cafe, where a group of young mothers were chatting up each other while their kids were in Layla's hands. Each woman was more beautiful than the next—brunettes, blondes, blue eyes, brown eyes, all in perfect shape. They looked like sorority sisters from a Southern college, or models advertising Savannah's sweet charm. At once, they all stopped talking and greeted the tan, muscular man with open mouths and lustful thoughts.

"Ladies," Gage said with a smile.

He walked past them to Poppy's side of Story Wings and browsed a section of new releases, both fiction and non-fiction. He came upon rows of magazines and found a few on recent trends in aviation. He flipped through them to pass the time and, shockingly, found no mention of anesthetizing crying babies or flight attendants dressing like strippers. Dash would be so disappointed.

"Knew you'd be back," Poppy said, appearing out of nowhere.

Gage recognized the woman but not the hair. "What did you do to yourself?"

"You don't like blue?"

"Blue's fine, but wasn't it purple and long?"

"Yeah, that was last week. I cut it into a bob now."

"Do you do this a lot?"

"Do what?"

"Dye your hair and chop it all off?"

Poppy thought for a second. "I guess so."

"She changes her hair with each failed relationship," Layla said, coming around the corner. "One day I'm going to walk in, and she's going to have a shaved head." Gage handed Layla the flowers and kissed her on the cheek. She lifted them to her nose and smiled. *He brought me flowers again—and these aren't windblown.* "They're beautiful. Thank you."

"Sorry I'm early. I couldn't wait. 12 years is long enough."

"Damn, that's a good line," Poppy said. "I mean, panty-dropping good. You should marry him, Layla."

"Poppy!" Layla cried.

Gage chuckled. "I like Poppy's ideas."

"Which one?" Layla teased. "Me dropping my panties or us getting married?"

"Both." Gage pulled her hips to his. "Marry me?"

Layla laughed, though wondered if he was serious. "Not today."

"Tomorrow?"

"Not tomorrow, either."

"I'm going to keep asking," he said.

Layla rolled her eyes. "Let me finish a few things, and then we can go. But I need to go home and change."

"You look great," he said.

"Another reason to marry him," Poppy said.

"Not today," Layla said and walked to her side of the store.

Poppy turned to him. "Do you really not like my hair?"

"It's fine," he said. "I'm just wondering what's wrong with the real you."

She drooled. "Please tell me you have a brother."

LAYLA LIVED CLOSE to Story Wings. She loved walking to and from work, sometimes stopping off at one of the squares, or parks, in Savannah's elaborate grid. There was always another new monument or statute to check out, another gazebo or bench to sit amongst the azaleas and beautiful fountains. But it was nice right now just to walk straight home with Gage, holding her flowers in one hand, her other hand holding his.

"Here it is," Layla said. She opened a little white gate into a tiny front yard with perfectly-shaped blooms of white and pink camellias, extending all the way up to her small green cottage, with a porch and two rocking chairs. She led him inside. "Just let me change. There's cornbread on the counter and tea in the fridge. Make yourself at home." She bounded up the stairs.

Gage made a quick call for transportation then poked around the house. It was cute and quaint, and as small as it appeared from the street. There was a living room, with one wall holding a wood-burning fireplace and vintage white bookshelves holding a collection of first edition books. But there was no TV. He was certain a flatscreen would look perfect over the fireplace. He wandered into the galley kitchen and looked in the backyard. It resembled the front, full of bright-colored flowers. He pushed open a door to a guest bedroom, finding it was more of an office or workspace. There was no TV in there, either. He flicked on a light, and his eyes landed on an old photograph, its edges tattered. He slowly picked it up in his hands, his mind racing back to their "grounding," back to when Layla took it from his bedroom.

"I'm ready," Layla said from the doorway, wearing a light pink cotton sundress with ties for the straps, her brown hair flowing down her back.

"Me too," he said, putting down the photograph.

She came up beside him and rested her head on his shoulder. "We were so in love."

"I still feel the same way," he said, swooping her off her feet into his arms. "How is that even possible?"

"You still *love* me?"

"I tried not to," he said. "But it's hard to tell your mind to stop when your heart won't listen."

"There wasn't a day that went by that I didn't think about you," Layla said.

He looked into her crystal blue eyes. "I missed you, too, but you were never far." He touched his shirt with the wings inside. "You were always there."

Layla kissed his chest then looked up to his eyes, hungry with desire. She wiggled down, but he quickly pinned her against the wall. "Gage," she whispered, unsure if she was asking him to stop or keep going. He brushed his lips against her neck then moved up to her mouth. He parted her lips and slowly stroked her tongue with his. Her body got hotter with each stroke, until it was white hot and screaming to be touched. She clenched her muscles to get a grip; after all, the man was only kissing her. She placed a gentle hand on his chest. "A fresh start, remember? We aren't just picking up where we left off." *But God knows, I want to.*

He blew out a deep breath and took a step back. "OK."

"I've never had sex on a first date," she said, taking his hand, "and I'm not going to start now."

"It's hardly our first date."

"A little patience," Layla said. "You were so gentle and patient before."

"But now I know what I'm missing!" Gage gave her a little squeeze then saw a table with wire, stones, and shells. "What's all this?"

"I make crosses sometimes." She pointed to one on the wall made from white seashells. "It helps me relax." She held up another out of wire and turquoise stones.

He took it from her. "I've never seen anything like this."

"It's just a hobby."

"They're beautiful."

"You can have that one."

"I'll keep it in my office." Gage kissed the top of her head. "Do you sell them?"

"No, I donate them to Hope Cottage to auction off and sell. It's a small charity that helps girls that have been molested. They do great work," she said. "I'm giving them the money from my dad."

"Layla, that's generous, but. . . ."

"I'll pay off some bills first."

"Your dad wanted you to have that money. He wanted to finally take care of you."

"It was guilt money, Gage. The letter meant more. His belief in me meant more. His apology meant more."

"But. . . ."

"Enough about money."

"OK, but before you do anything, could you at least buy a TV for downstairs?" She laughed. "Please tell me you have a TV somewhere. Upstairs bedroom maybe?"

"The bedroom is made for a few things," she said, "and TV isn't one of them."

He raised his eyebrows. "No TV in the bedroom is fine with me."

SEVERAL TIMES LAYLA asked where they were going, but Gage would never tell. It was fun to keep it a surprise. And he knew if he told her, she'd be nervous or maybe not even go.

She knew right away what he was up to when the limo exited towards the airport. "It better not be a glider." He laughed and squeezed her hand. The limo made a few more turns then drove out through a private gate and onto the tarmac. Her eyes bulged at the four-seater plane about 50 feet away. "I don't think so."

"It's a short ride," he said. "It's perfectly safe. It's actually how I got here from Atlanta. The pilot is excellent, too. You'll like him."

"It's not that Dash guy, is it? Dumb As Shit doesn't inspire confidence."

An older man appeared from under the aircraft. "Everything checked out great. She's ready to go." Gage took a clipboard from the man and ran his eyes over it.

"You must be Miss Layla," the man said. "I'm Walter. I hear you hate to fly, but this little lady is in tip-top shape."

"It's so tiny," she said.

Gage handed the clipboard back to Walter then opened the cockpit door. He helped Layla inside and threw the seatbelt harness over her, buckling her in and pulling the straps securely.

"Wait!" Layla cried, looking for Walter, suddenly nowhere in sight. "Where's the pilot?"

"I'm the pilot," Gage said. "This is my plane."

"*You're* flying us? You own your *own* plane?" She looked around frantically, scared to death she was sitting in the co-pilot's seat of what seemed a paper airplane. "Where's the crew, the flight attendant, the peanuts?"

Gage hopped in and began fiddling with the instrument panel. "That would be on the company jet."

"Then I want the jet!"

"I'll take you on it soon, but this is such a short trip."

"You know, I could've just taken a commercial flight to Atlanta."

He smiled. "What makes you think we're going to Atlanta?"

GAGE LOOKED OVER at her—her hands gripping the armrest, her lips moving in prayer, her eyes closed tightly. "Open your eyes," he said.

But she shook her head violently. He reached over and touched her hand. Layla's eyes flew open, and she shooed her hands at him. "Both hands on the wheel!"

"It's not a car," he said. "Look, the sun is starting to set."

Layla looked out the side and put her hands against the window, leaning in close towards the fiery majestic orb painting the heavens. Gage took it all in. The sun's red and orange hues were nothing compared to her. He wanted this night to go perfectly. The plane dipped slightly, and Layla turned to him with nervous eyes.

"It's fine," he said. "You know how you hit a bump in the road? You get the same thing in the air."

"I thought you said it wasn't like a car."

He rolled his eyes. "You want to try?"

"Uh, no way." She leaned her head back and watched him. He was in total control. He looked young and happy. She was still trying to figure out the man, but she recognized this guy, the teenage boy she once knew. "You love flying, don't you?"

"Yeah, I don't get to do it enough. I'd fly everyday if I could." He caught her staring and gave a little wink. "You try." He reached for her hand and put it on the stick with his on top. "It's called a yoke, but it's pretty much like a steering wheel." She relaxed her grip, and Gage moved his hand.

"Don't let go!" she cried, but Gage put his hands behind his head. "Gage!"

"Just pretend you're driving. You probably eat and drive, talk on the phone and drive, put on makeup while driving." He ran his fingertips down her arms, her porcelain skin so soft and smooth, catching a glimpse of her cleavage, breathing in the lavender. He let his mind wander. The cockpit was small, but so was Layla. She could pull up her dress, straddle him, and make love to him with nothing around but the setting sun. *That would be pretty damn perfect—flying and fucking at the same time. Never done that.* He leaned over and slowly kissed her neck, seeing her breasts swell as she drew a deep breath.

"Mmm. Don't distract me." He pulled at the tie on her dress strap. "Gage."

"Yes," he groaned.

She took his hand, put it back on the stick, then scooted back. "Fly the plane."

"I'd rather. . . ."

"I know what you'd rather," she said, tying back her strap. "Be good."

"I like being bad." Gage opened a console and handed Layla a small blindfold. "Put this on."

"Now I know you're crazy! You want me to fly blindfolded?"

"Otherwise you'll know where we're going. We'll be on the ground in five minutes."

"Just so you know," she said and slipped on the blindfold, "this is officially the worst date ever."

AFTER A SHORT limo ride and walk, Gage let her take off the blindfold. He'd tortured her enough. When she did, her hands flew over her mouth in shock. She was standing on the patio of his parents' beach house on St. Simons Island, a small bistro table lit in candlelight set out for dinner.

"Is this still the worst date ever?" he asked, smiling.

"It's getting better. This is beautiful." Layla took in the ocean, the salty air, then remembered her last footsteps out on the beach, washed away, all alone. "I haven't been back since."

Gage adjusted the chairs so they faced the ocean. "I figured."

They ate under the twinkling stars, and Gage kept his hand on Layla the whole time, stroking her fingers, occasionally grazing her thigh. It seemed like only yesterday they were snuggled together on lounge chairs watching the sunset.

"How are we getting back to Savannah?" she asked.

"I thought we'd fly back. It's an hour and half by car."

"Is that tiny plane safe in the dark?"

"Of course, it's safe. I'd never take you up if it wasn't." He cocked his head to the side. "But if it makes you feel better, we could stay the night and fly back early in the morning."

Layla shook her head and smiled. *The man is relentless.*

"So I guess the question is," Gage asked, "do you trust me to fly you home in the dark, or do you trust me to sleep with you in the dark?"

"I might need to think about that," she said and turned to look inside the beach house through the huge windows off the patio. She saw the soft whites, the cool linens, and headed inside, with Gage following behind. The place looked exactly the same. She smiled spotting the guitar in the corner of the living room. "Do you ever play anymore?"

"Not really," he said, picking it up and strumming a few chords.

"Remember when you used to play and sing for me?"

"I don't remember that at all," he said, blushing.

"Sing for me," she said. "You always had a great voice."

Gage considered it for a moment but then put down the guitar. "Maybe some other time," he said. "By the way, I created an account for you with the airline, so you can fly whenever you want, and it will just be charged to me."

"You didn't have to do that."

"It will make things easier with you in Savannah and me in Atlanta during the week."

"You've got this all figured out, don't you?"

"I'll fly in every afternoon or evening and back to Atlanta in the morning. And if you ever have time, on your off days or whatever, you could fly to me. That's why I got the account for you."

"You really have given this a lot of thought."

"Of course, I have," he said. "I'm not going to lose you again. Some people have hour long commutes in a car. I'll just be doing it by air. And it's only 45 minutes." He tilted her chin up to look in her eyes. "What I don't have figured out is where I'll be sleeping when I'm visiting."

"Oh!"

"I usually stay with my mom in Savannah on the weekends. But maybe I can get a better offer from you?"

"I don't have an extra bed," she teased.

He squeezed her hand. "Layla, I'm serious. I'm not letting you go again."

"That's sweet, Gage, but it's a little fast. One of us has to be practical. If it were up to you, we'd be married already."

"OK, I'll give you a month, but then we should get married."

Layla laughed. It was funny the way he said it. But something told her that deep down, underneath all the charm and sexiness, the man was afraid. She lowered her head to his chest. As much as he wanted to be close to her, he was afraid to get *too* close without something more from her, something to make things secure. He was probably just half-serious about marriage—she could blame Poppy for mentioning it—but she obviously still had some making up to do.

CHAPTER ELEVEN

GAGE CLEANED UP the bistro table, still wondering whether they were flying back or staying the night. He came back inside to ask Layla but saw her disappear into his old bedroom. He watched her slide a hand across the comforter then pick up a pillow, lifting it to her nose. He took a step inside, the floor creaking beneath him, and Layla turned to face him.

"I'll never forget seeing you beside my bed in that white cotton sundress," he said, sitting down beside her on the bed. "You really looked like an angel. I thought I was just dreaming about you again."

"You dreamed about me?"

"I still do sometimes." He cleared his throat. "I could tell in your eyes that night that something was different. But then you started to unbutton your dress. I saw your hands trembling, and I thought you were just nervous."

Layla smiled. "So you sat up and undid the buttons yourself?"

"I was quicker," he said, flashing a naughty look.

"I could tell you were nervous, too. You got to the last button and hesitated."

Gage fiddled with the hem of her dress. "Then you slid your dress off your shoulders, and it fell to the floor. I remember telling myself I was supposed to look at your eyes, but you weren't wearing a bra." He reached up and outlined the top of her dress, his fingertips gently sliding just underneath the cotton. "I see you still hate bras."

Her dimples showed. "I saw you swallow hard as you got to your feet, your eyes slowly sliding over my body."

"I walked over to the door and locked it, watching you crawl into my bed. I kept thinking I should say something romantic, but I was so shocked."

"You got in bed and leaned over me, running your fingertips down my cheek."

"Your breasts pushed against my chest."

"You leaned down and kissed me softly," she said. "Then you ran your hand down to my breast, caressing me."

"Your eyes closed, and you inhaled a deep breath."

"I felt your tongue slide over my nipple. Your mouth was so warm."

Gage's eyes fell to her cleavage. "I could hear your breath growing ragged."

"I could feel you hard against me," she said. "I pulled you to my lips, and you kissed me gently, your tongue slowly stroking mine."

"Then you pulled away slightly. I thought you'd changed your mind. But then you reached down and tugged at my boxers. I couldn't believe it. I thought I was going to jump out of my skin."

"I slid them down and rolled over on top of you."

"I watched you kiss your way down my chest and stomach, your tongue darting in and out of your mouth, so wet, warm, smooth."

"I could feel you quivering beneath me," she said.

"When you slid your mouth over me, I thought I was going to ruin the rest of the night. I watched your mouth sliding me in and out, fighting the urge to finish."

"I got a little taste of you and knew I needed to stop, but I really didn't want to."

Gage shifted on the bed and adjusted his growing hard-on. "Really?"

"But you pulled me up to you, holding the back of my neck, and kissed me so hard. I lost my breath."

"I rolled you over and slid your panties down. I stopped for a second wanting to remember the way you looked naked before me—your breasts full, your eyes glistening, perfectly shaved."

Layla blushed. "You leaned over to kiss me again and slid one finger inside."

"You were so wet and warm." Gage gave her another naughty smile. "I had to know how you tasted."

"I remember the first outline your tongue made over me."

"Your back arched up."

"You slid your tongue inside me."

"Your muscles clenched begging for me," he said. "It was so sexy."

"I remember thinking you were a god."

Gage chuckled. "I had no idea what I was doing. I just listened to you, and when you moaned or tightened, I figured that was right."

"You were very attentive."

He leaned in close to her. "Watching you come for me that first time was such a high—the way your hips bucked, your muscles tightened, the way you bit your bottom lip to try to contain yourself. And the way you said my name—that was the first word either one of us said. I'll never forget the way your sweet voice sounded as you came panting my name."

"I was shocked how intense it was, how totally incredible you made me feel. That was the first orgasm I ever had."

"But not the last of the night."

"No, not the last," she said. "And you were so sweet after, holding me, kissing me gently. It was like you weren't in a hurry. You wanted me to enjoy my own pleasure. You were so unselfish even though you were hard as a rock."

"I think I was nervous, not sweet."

Layla elbowed him. "You were sweet. I was the nervous one. When you leaned over me, and I could feel you pressing against me, my heart was pounding so loud."

"I was waiting for you to change your mind," he said, "but when you took hold of me and glided me inside you, I almost lost it right then."

"You stroked my cheek and stayed very still, watching my eyes."

"You gave me the sweetest smile ever and pulled me into a kiss."

"Then you slowly started to move."

"You felt so warm, tight." Gage looked away for a second. "I can still remember it exactly. You were trusting me. I was afraid I was going to hurt you."

"I knew you wouldn't."

"Then you tightened yourself around me."

"You groaned so loudly I was afraid you'd wake your parents."

"I really didn't care at that point," he said. "You felt so damn good, and you kept clenching me tighter and tighter, drawing me deeper and deeper with each thrust."

"You started so slow and gentle, in and out, in and out."

"I wanted it to last forever," Gage said. "Making love to you was the best feeling in the world."

Layla smiled. "But then you moved faster and harder, and my whole body exploded again."

"That time you bit down on my pillow. Watching you come sent me over the edge."

"You yelled out my name!"

"And you kissed me hard on the mouth to shut me up."

"You pulled me to your chest and held me tight—like I was the most precious thing in the world."

"You were," he said. "You still are."

"You whispered that you loved me."

"I felt tears on your cheeks and started to panic."

"They were happy tears."

"You said they were the best tears you ever cried," Gage said.

"I saw a few tears in your eyes, too."

"No way," he said, but knew she was right. "You fell asleep in my arms. I watched you for a long time trying to figure out how to not leave for college, how we could be together. I planned on never leaving you." She stroked his cheek, and he shifted his head away. "I woke up the next morning and reached out for you. But you were gone."

"I woke up early. I thought about leaving you a letter but heard your parents walking around and knew I needed to go. I took off my angel wings and placed them around your neck. I ran my fingers through your hair one last time. I had tears running down my face. I grabbed the picture of us from your nightstand then went to the window. I turned around for one last look. I whispered 'I'm sorry' and left."

"I sat up thinking maybe you just went home worried about my parents, but then I felt the cord around my neck. I knew that meant you loved me, but my heart started racing. Something just didn't seem right. I threw on clothes and rushed to your grandmother's cottage, but when I got there, your parents were there. They told me you'd stolen your grandmother's car and runaway *again*."

"I took her car and drove to Maryland, crying the whole time."

"*Maryland?*"

"Annapolis," she said softly.

"What? Your parents thought I knew where you were! They were asking me all kinds of questions! I can't believe you went to where I was going!" Gage leaned back, stunned. "Annapolis, really?"

"I knew you'd probably hate me when you got to college in a month or so, but I wanted to see you and apologize. I hoped you'd forgive me. And by that time, I figured my parents wouldn't be looking at you anymore for clues about where I was."

Gage's eyes darted up. "You were protecting me by not telling me where you were?"

"I didn't want you to get in trouble! You were a legal adult. You could've gotten in a lot of trouble for helping me. That's why I never called you. I needed them to believe you didn't know where I was."

"I didn't!"

"I know," she said and touched his hand. "I just wasn't sure what they were capable of."

Gage stood up and looked out the window, the one she used to crawl through to see him, the same one she used to leave. He looked back at her, so sweet, so delicate. He couldn't imagine a 16-year-girl—abused and scared—all alone in a strange city. "You never came to me."

Layla drew a breath. "I only had a few hundred dollars saved up. A lot of that was used up on gas just getting there. I enrolled myself in high school with a post office box—more money. I thought I only needed to make it a year or so, and if I worked hard, I could graduate early and apply to college with loans. I was naive, but I was desperate. I never stole or did anything illegal ever—besides taking my grandmother's car."

"How'd you survive?"

"I moved the car around each night so no one got suspicious. But I never moved it too far. The school had free lunch. That was the one meal I ate a day. I spent the evenings in the car doing homework. I'd shower in the gym at school. I stayed to myself, and no one seemed to notice anything. It wasn't so bad. It was actually better than home. I was losing a ton of weight, but it was working. Then one day I was walking back to the car and saw it being towed away. I'd parked it illegally by mistake. Everything I had was in that car, all my clothes, most of my money. The only things I had were my ID, a few bucks, and that picture of us. That was 10 days before you were starting the Naval Academy."

"What did you do? Where'd you sleep?"

"I started going to shelters."

"Christ," he cried.

"I couldn't go to the same one too often because I looked so young. People started to ask questions. And sometimes they were full."

"Did you sleep on the streets?"

"Only once or twice," she lied, encouraging him to sit down again. "Then it was the night before you were coming. I was so excited. I knew you weren't going to be happy to see me, but I wanted to look my best. I went to a thrift store and spent five dollars on a new sundress and another five dollars at a fast food restaurant hoping to look healthier. That was the last of my money."

"But you never came," he said, lowering his head to hers.

"The shelter was full that night. They turned me away at the door. I started walking down the street. It was already getting dark. I needed to find a place for the night. I was cold and worried and not paying attention. Two guys followed me and came up behind me, one on each side." She looked up at Gage and shook her head. "I woke up in the hospital two days later, strapped down to the bed, with my parents standing over me."

Gage stood up. "What happened with the two guys?"

"They offered me money for sex."

"No, no, no!" he yelled, gripping the back of his neck.

"I would've starved to death before I did that. They said they were trying to be nice and pay me, but if I was going to be a bitch about it, they'd just take what they wanted."

"They raped you?"

"They tried—ripped my dress, tore off my panties. They beat me up pretty bad, but I fought them off."

"Two guys?"

"They had me in an alley on the ground. They hit and kicked me a few times. Then all of a sudden—and I know this is going to sound crazy—but when I was on the ground, Aria came to me." Gage raised his eyebrows. "Her light glistened, and something reflected on the ground. I reached out my hand and stretched out my fingers for whatever it was. I stretched with all my might. And I got it—a broken bottle with a jagged glass edge. I wrapped my hand around it—it cut me a little as I gripped it—and just started swinging at them."

"You stabbed those fuckers?"

"One of them. The glass went straight through his cheek. It was just hanging there in his face. The guy shrieked. There was blood squirting out everywhere, on him, on the other guy, on me. They hit me again and ran off. I crawled to the street. I was in bad shape. I remember being on the ground thinking about you, knowing I'd failed, that I wouldn't get to you. I'd been so close. I was just one night away, one night from seeing you again. My faith, my dreams, my hope were all gone at that point. I passed out. Someone must've helped me because I woke up in the hospital."

Gage closed his eyes and felt a pain in his chest. The thought of Layla abused by her half-brother, and then alone in an alley, beaten, was just too much. He hated he wasn't there to protect her. *No one will ever hurt you again.* "How'd your parents find you?"

"I had my ID on me. Didn't take the hospital long to figure out I was a runaway. They called my parents. They kept me tied to that bed the whole time I was in the hospital like I was a mental patient."

"You beat off two rapists, and they were dragging you home to live with one," he said. "Did he touch you again?"

She shook her head. "When we got back to Houston, my parents put me in a psychiatric hospital for teens. They thought I needed treatment. And maybe I did. At least my half-brother couldn't get to me there. I did what I was told and never said another word to anyone about him. I didn't see the point. It was months before I was allowed phone and letter privileges. I figured you'd moved on by then. You'd already started school. We were thousands of miles away from each other. I told myself these things have expiration dates and to let you be happy. I thought about looking for you, Googling you, but it would've been too painful to see what I gave up. So I never did."

"I tried a few times to find you over the years," he said. "I even went to your grandmother's cottage one summer wondering if she knew where you were. But some neighbors told me she'd died."

"My grandmother passed when I was in college."

"You have no idea how much I worried. So many sleepless nights the rest of the summer, at the Naval Academy, on and off my whole life really. I mean, my mind would go into overdrive and. . . ."

"*And?*"

"We didn't use any protection that night. I worried you got pregnant."

Layla reached for his hand. "I'm so sorry. I never considered you'd worry about that. I didn't get pregnant."

Gage blew out a long-held deep breath and sat down. "I just could never find you. I had no phone numbers, no address. It was like Layla Baxter didn't exist anymore."

"I guess she didn't," Layla said. "I told you I changed my name. That was after high school. I graduated early then went to college on loans and scholarships. And I never looked back. I used my inheritance from my grandmother to pay off the loans."

"Must have been a good bit of money?"

"Yeah, my mother actually fought me for it. My mother didn't speak to her for close to 20 years and then she claims to be entitled to an inheritance? I ended up just splitting it with her mainly because I didn't want to have any contact with her—not even through lawyers. But it was fine. Half was enough—got me debt-free for the time being and the rest helped get the bookstore off the ground."

"Seems like your life's on a better path now."

"You don't have to worry or save me anymore."

"Sounds like you saved yourself, Angel."

PAST MIDNIGHT, LAYLA wasn't about to get on an airplane, certainly not one so small. It just didn't look like it would work in the dark. They'd certainly crash into the Atlantic Ocean on takeoff. And even if the plane managed to work, she was sure she'd die of panic during the flight. No amount of blindfolding or tender touches could possibly keep her alive. And she didn't want the date to end talking about the sad, ugly parts of her past. Years ago, she'd put that behind her.

She stared at his bathroom mirror, wearing an old Naval Academy t-shirt from his dresser. It covered all the right places but could've been longer. She tugged on it a bit then resigned herself the shirt wasn't budging; it long ago had settled on its size. She told herself to relax, that she'd been through worse than sleeping next to a gorgeous guy. She breathed deeply and came out of the bathroom, finding Gage under the covers with his hands behind his head.

"Get that grin off your face," she said.

"Your fear of flying is useful," he said, getting a full view of her long, smooth legs, the tiniest hint of booty cheek. "Reminds me when you wore my clothes before." He patted the bed for her to take her spot next to him.

"Are you hoping to play boardgames now?" She slid under the covers beside him. "You're still dressed?"

"Would you prefer I wasn't?"

"No, I mean, I just thought you'd be. . . ." Layla paused. "Will you be able to sleep in jeans?"

"I think I'll get the best sleep I've gotten in a long time—now that you're back where you belong." Gage gave her a little squeeze. "And just for tonight, I'm promising to behave."

"Why?" Layla asked.

Gage chuckled. "I'm sure you feel a little trapped here, so I'm not going to take advantage. But when we get off the island tomorrow, you're fair game."

Layla placed her head on his chest. "We talked about 12 years ago. Tell me where you want to be 12 years from now."

Gage stroked her hair. "God, I'll be 42."

"OK, how about five years from now. We used to dream together all the time. Tell me where you'll be in five years."

"You want me to tell you a bedtime story?"

"Mmm," Layla moaned, relaxing into his heartbeat.

"In five years, I'll be with you. We'll be getting ready to celebrate our fifth wedding anniversary, and we'll have our first baby on the way. We'll. . . ."

Layla closed her eyes, letting his dreams, his desires, fill her heart. It obviously wasn't the first time he'd thought about a future together. He went on about where they'd live, how they'd manage work, who their friends would be, the kind of pet they'd have. His words like magic, she could believe everything he said, and could tell he believed it, too.

Gage felt her breathing slow to a crawl and looked down at her asleep in his bed—again. It had been a long time coming. He was confident she'd be staying through the night this time. "That's the story of us, Angel."

GAGE WOKE UP at peace. There was something strangely magical about sleeping next to the right woman, how she could make a man feel everything was right in the world. He stretched his arms across the bed, hoping—accidentally, of course—to graze Layla's breast or ass. That would be a perfect start to the morning. But his hands landed on cold sheets. His eyes flashed open.

He sat up straight and scanned the empty room. He leaped to the floor and darted into the bathroom. It was empty, too. He called out for her in the house, but there was no response. He looked at the clock. He was going to be late to work. He had to find her. *This can't be happening again.*

He sprinted out to the beach, still damp from the night tide, the morning sun nearly blinding him. He rubbed his eyes to focus. He looked out to the ocean, but no one was there. He looked up and down the beach, storm clouds forming all around, and made out a figure in the distance surrounded by light.

The figure was walking towards him. It looked like a woman. The clothing looked like a sundress. He couldn't make out a face, but it had to be her. He gnashed his teeth for a moment, pissed she'd left, slipped out of bed again. He jogged towards her and yelled out her name. "Layla!"

"Gage, what is it?" she called out. "What's wrong?"

He reached her and grabbed her by the arms. "You can't keep disappearing on me! You can't ever do that again!" He saw her eyes grow wide and let go. "Don't ever do that again, please."

She ran her hands through his hair. "I left you a note on the pillow."

"There was no note."

"Yes, there was, and I poured you a glass of water. It was on the kitchen counter next to some leftovers from last night. I made a plate for you."

Gage pinched the bridge of his nose. "What are you doing out here?"

"I just wanted to check out my grandmother's old cottage. Is that OK with you?"

"No."

She laughed. "*No?*"

"No."

"Are you serious?"

"Yes, I'm totally serious. I can't believe you'd leave. Our first morning together!"

"I didn't *leave!* I left you a note!"

"You left."

"I was coming right back! You make it seem like I crawled out the window again!"

"I guess I should be grateful."

She looked him up and down, her eyes narrow and hard. "F off!"

Gage nearly fell on his ass. He couldn't remember her talking like that ever before. Granted, she hadn't actually said the word, but it was close. A loud thunderbolt ripped through the sky. He looked out at the ocean, sheets of rain on the horizon.

"Last night was great, but you're being a real jerk now. I've tried to be completely open and honest with you. I can't change the past. I'm not looking for sympathy or pity. I can only tell you what happened. And it's up to you to do what you want. But I'm *not* going to put up with this. It's not going to work like this, not with you throwing a tantrum about when I get up in the morning."

"It just scared the shit out of me to wake up and not see you! All sorts of awful things started running through my mind."

"I'm not a scared teenager anymore. I'm not running away."

"*I* was scared, OK?"

She took his hand. "It's fine to be scared. But you need to handle it better than this. I mean, news flash! I might need to pee in the morning! I might not be there right when you wake up."

"Hold it."

"No," she said, grinning.

He saw the rain getting closer. "Let's go. I'll call the limo to drive us back to Savannah."

"We're not flying back?"

"Not in this weather. I'll take a commercial flight to Atlanta from there."

"Before we leave," she teased, "be sure to check for the note, the leftovers, the glass of water. It's all there."

"Oh, I will," he said and pulled her into a hug. "While I'm doing that, you should arrange for someone to cover the store for you. Since we're driving, I'm not sure I can have you back for opening."

"It's fine. I'm off today."

"Then I think I'll take off, too. Let's go to your place."

GAGE SHUT OFF the water and stepped out of her shower, bumping his head on the rod. It didn't hurt at all. It was actually more uncomfortable taking the shower, crouching below her low ceiling, squeezing in the space no bigger than a tiny closet. He reached for a towel and wiped off his face. The towel smelled like Layla, like sweet lavender.

His clothes in the wash, he wrapped the towel around his waist and ran his fingers through his hair. He wiped some steam off the mirror and rubbed the stubble on his face. He needed to shave, but it didn't matter. He wasn't going to the office today. It felt weird not to go. He couldn't remember the last time he missed a day.

He came out of her bathroom and looked in the backyard. Layla was sitting barefoot on the grass surrounded by her brightly colored flowers. Her eyes were closed, her head tilted towards the hot Savannah sun. Her damp hair was tied back in a braid—just as it often was 12 years ago. He smiled at her peaceful face and walked outside.

She felt him coming towards her. "Want to join me?"

"What are you doing?"

She took in his muscles, his abs, and bit her bottom lip. "I'm at church."

"I think the Pope would disagree," he said and sat down across from her. "Church is on your knees, sitting in hard pews."

"You're wrong about that," she said. "I still go to Mass on Sundays, but I feel closer to my angels, my God—or Goddess—outside in nature."

"I remember you doing those beach yoga services, the ones my dad did. Seemed like a bunch of hippies."

"When do you feel most at peace, most centered, most happy?"

"When I'm flying, I guess."

"Then that's your church," she said. "Want to try with me?"

"What am I supposed to do? Chant? *Um, Um, Um.*"

She laughed. "Are you judging me? You know what Mother Theresa used to say about judging people?"

"I don't recall. Am I in Sunday school?"

"She said if you judge people, you have no time to love them."

"Now you're making me feel bad. What do I do?"

Layla took his hands in hers. "Whatever you're comfortable doing. You can say the rosary, just talk to God, talk to your Guardian Angel."

"What do *you* do?"

"Different things. A minute ago, I was just saying a little prayer to send out light and love to the world."

He bit his tongue not to laugh. "*Light and love?* For real?"

"Close your eyes."

He did as she said and sat in silence for a minute. It seemed like an hour. Every few seconds, he'd peek at her, finding her eyes still closed, her pale skin growing a tad rosier. Then he'd close his eyes again. In between peeking, he said a little prayer for Layla, thankful she'd come back into his life, even if she apparently was some hybrid Catholic New Age freak. Maybe she always was. He didn't care. She was the same girl he used to know, the same girl he always loved. He kissed her gently on the lips and lowered her to the ground, his towel doing nothing to hide how much he wanted her.

Layla pushed him back with a smile. "Stop being in such a hurry. The 12 years are gone. We can't get them back."

"We can try," he said and put his hands on her hips, looking into her eyes. "I want you."

"I can tell," she said, looking at the bulging towel. *He's used to getting what he wants.* "I'm not going anywhere. So there's no need to rush."

Gage groaned and rolled on his back, staring up at the heavens. A butterfly landed on his head. He went to swat it away, but she grabbed his hand. "Layla, it's sitting right on my head."

"Wish I had a camera." The butterfly flew off and fluttered around them. "Butterflies are signs from angels. They mean change is coming—a transformation."

Gage smiled. "I love you."

"I love you, too."

GAGE SPENT THE rest of the day trying to work from her sofa. But more often that not, he just watched Layla mill around her place, whether making a perfect mess in her kitchen, paying some bills, doing her laundry, calling some customers about book orders. For so long he'd wondered what she was up to, how she spent her time. Now he had a front row seat.

This is what he'd been missing. *This is what my life with her will look like.* It sure was better than a life filled with back-to-back conference calls and constant emails, especially from the political operatives who always knew how to find him. He didn't want it to end. He pulled her to his lap on the sofa.

"I've had a good couple days with you," he said, stroking her chocolate hair, "but I've got to fly back to Atlanta in the morning."

"I figured," she said quietly.

"I hate to leave."

"I know. Me, too."

"I'll fly back here tomorrow evening."

"You can bring some things to leave here, if you want."

He smiled and searched her eyes. "Marry me? Marry me so I can hold you every day?"

"Not today."

"Tomorrow?"

"Not tomorrow, either," she said and pulled him into a kiss.

"One day you'll tell me 'yes.'"

CHAPTER TWELVE

OVER THE NEXT few weeks, Gage never missed a day in Savannah. Sometimes he'd sneak out of work and be at her shop by lunch. Sometimes he'd be waiting inside her house when she came home, then insist on taking her to the nicest restaurants or some show or festival going on around town. Other times he'd have to work late and show up at her house when Layla was already in bed. He'd slip under the sheets and wrap his arms around her until they fell asleep together.

Today he needed extra time to get to Savannah and set up a surprise at her house, so he snuck out of the office early. He worried a little he wasn't spending enough time in the office—even though no one ever complained or probably even noticed. Mary didn't care. She was happy he was happy. He told himself not to worry. He could miss a few days here and there. Plus, he was more than capable of running the company from his phone or laptop. He finished setting up just before Layla's key hit the door.

He heard her giggling when she walked in. "What did you do?" she cried.

"I went shopping," he said and greeted her with a kiss.

Layla picked up a teddy bear. "For stuffed animals?"

"I thought you could use some new ones."

She looked around her den—every piece of furniture, every nook and cranny, covered with stuffed bears, cats, dogs, ducks, elephants, lions, and every other animal on Noah's Ark. "You are totally insane! I love it!" She greeted each animal with a little hug then looked at him standing in the middle of the room, thinking her heart might burst that he remembered, that he thought to give her back—tenfold—something taken from her. "I don't deserve you. This is too much."

Gage wrapped his arms around her. "I'm glad you like it."

"I love it! I love you!" Her eye caught something above the fire-place, behind a row of stuffed animals on the mantle. It was a huge flatscreen TV. "You tried to cover it up, didn't you?"

"I was hoping you wouldn't notice."

She rolled her eyes. "You can keep it there. I presume it's for you anyway."

"Well, you're not having sex with me, so I need something to do," he said. "I have one more gift for you. And I'm a little worried about this one."

Layla watched him disappear into the guest bedroom. She couldn't imagine what else he had. She didn't need anything else. He came out holding a small dog, a brown and white Cavalier King Charles Spaniel with big brown eyes, decked out in a pink rhinestone collar. Layla threw her hands over her mouth and almost melted to the floor. "Oh my God! She's adorable!"

"Her name is Pippa," Gage said, gently handing her to Layla. "She's four."

"Where'd you get her?"

"A rescue place in Atlanta," Gage said. "She's totally healthy, house-trained. She was found on the side of the road. She had an infection, and they had to fix her. They think she was probably used for breeding in a puppy mill. And when she got sick, they just threw her out."

"I love her," Layla said and snuggled into Pippa, wagging her tail.

"I thought she could go to the store with you. And she was good on the plane coming here, so you can bring her with you if I ever get you to Atlanta."

"I'll get there soon. The store has just been crazy." Pippa licked Layla's face. "She's just the cutest dog I've ever seen!"

Gage pointed to the back door. "I installed a doggie door before you got home."

"Good thing I like her."

"My back-up plan was to drop her in Emerson's backyard. The kids would go nuts."

Layla carried her new friend to the sofa, and Gage sat down beside them. He patted Pippa then let his fingers slide onto her long legs, then under her shirt onto the small of her back. "Just snuggle with me," she said.

He moved his hands to the dog's ears. "I'm tired of snuggling."

"Poppy calls this the 'snuggle screw.'"

"Huh?"

"When a guy tries to turn snuggling into screwing."

"The whole point of snuggling is to get to the screwing."

"Pig," she said and let out a huge yawn. "And don't talk like that in front of Pippa."

"My Angel is tired."

"I'm sorry. This is all so wonderful what you've done. It's just my period. I get really bad cramps."

"Have you seen a doctor?"

"I have some pain pills, but I don't like to take them."

"Can I do anything?"

She shook her head and scanned all the animals in the room. "Can you stay a little later in the morning?" Gage nodded. "Good, because I have an idea for some of my other pets."

GAGE FIDGETED WITH his phone then shoved his hands in his pockets, hoping to calm his nerves or at least stop fidgeting. He was growing a bit stir crazy without sex, and nothing was going to happen with Layla on her period. And now he was in the last place he ever thought he'd be—the lobby of Hope Cottage. He didn't know what to say or do, whether to make eye contact with the girls coming in and out. He decided it was best to just keep his head down. They all probably hated men anyway.

It was sweet Layla was donating the stuffed animals to the girls. But she needed to finish soon. He had a plane to catch back to Atlanta. He picked up a few brochures. Hope Cottage touted itself as one of the most successful centers in the country, treating patients from nearly every state with outpatient services; individual therapy; art, music, and movement therapies; and an inpatient program for girls suffering from eating disorders or cutting behavior. The strand connecting them all was that the girls were sexually assaulted or molested.

An office door opened, and a lady with curly gray hair came out. "You must be Gage? I'm Sarah. I'm the Director here. This is so generous what you and Layla are doing."

"Layla gets all the credit."

"I hope you understand why you can't go back. Some of our girls are, well, in a sensitive place."

"It's no problem," Gage said then pointed to a picture on the wall of a young nun.

"That's me," Sarah said. "I wasted my hot years in the convent."

"So you're not a nun anymore?"

"No, I renounced my vows after the abuse scandal in the Church."

"I know Layla has a hard time reconciling being Catholic and an abuse survivor."

"Layla's a special woman. She gives so much to the center."

"Layla has a huge heart. She always thinks of others before herself. Sometimes, I wish she'd take care of herself first."

Sarah smiled. "From what I see, she's doing a pretty good job taking care of herself."

Gage wasn't going to argue with an ex-nun doing God's work. "How many girls do you treat?"

"Inpatient about 50. Sadly, I turn girls away every week. The money Layla recently gave us was stunning and will help tremendously. But we will still have to turn girls away. Hopefully not as many, but some."

"Don't turn them away. Call me, and I'll cover the cost."

Sarah looked him up and down. "You're not fooling an old lady, are you?"

"No, and I'll sponsor flights for any girls traveling to the center who can't afford it."

"Flights?"

Gage pulled out his business card. "I own Southern Wings."

Sarah leaped into his arms. "Oh my goodness! Really? That's so generous! You have no idea how much this will help our families!"

"I'm happy to do it. Just let me know," he said. "I'll leave word with my secretary, Mary, if you can't get me."

Sarah released her grip then dried her eyes. "You know, we only have so much space. I sometimes turn girls away because of space. If we accept everyone, we'll have space issues."

"Well, you call me if you need anything. And let's just keep this between you and me. There's no reason for Layla to know."

LAYLA SPENT ANOTHER 30 minutes at Hope Cottage, which made it impossible for Gage to make his flight back to Atlanta. He had a lot of work to do, conference calls and virtual meetings throughout the morning that he couldn't take in the air. Layla assured him Story Wings had a good wireless connection, so if he wanted, he could set up shop there.

Gage went about handling his calls and meetings from the cafe area. He didn't know, but Layla would sometimes peek in to make sure he was fine. She didn't want to disturb him. She'd listen from behind a bookshelf. She had no idea what he was talking about but loved just hearing the direct way he spoke, the cool and confident sound of his voice, like nothing ever rattled him. But one time she was startled hearing him pound away on his computer and bark on his phone.

"Mary," Gage said, "I know they want to talk to me. Tell them the offer is generous. But tell them I haven't made a decision yet." He pinched the bridge of his nose. "Yes, I know, Mary. I'm looking at their emails now. I've been looking at them for weeks. Put them off!" He paused and dropped his head in his hands. "I'm sorry if I'm taking this out on you, Mary. They're just driving me crazy. I'll be back in the office tomorrow."

He looked up to find Layla in front of him, her arms crossed, her foot tapping, and quickly hung up. "You're scaring my petite-sized customers," she said.

"I'm sorry."

"You can walk over to my place if you need more privacy."

"It's not that."

"I think he's on his period!" Poppy called out from behind the counter.

"Maybe so," Layla wondered.

Gage laughed. "Man period?"

"Yeah, symptoms include irritability," Poppy said.

"Check," Layla said.

"Inconsiderate and childish behavior," Poppy added.

"Check," Layla said.

"Not interested in sex," Poppy wondered.

"*No* check," Gage said quickly.

"Right, I think that symptom only applies for the female period," Poppy said. "During the man period, guys still want sex—rough, hard sex."

"Poppy, keep your voice down!" Layla cried, looking for customers in earshot. "We're at work!" But Poppy just laughed a hearty laugh and walked to her side of the store.

"I'm not having a man period or whatever," Gage said.

"You did seem a bit snappish on the phone," Layla said. "What's all the fuss about?"

"Oh, just work stuff," he said. "Some political folks trying to meet with me. They're very persistent."

"What about?"

"I'd rather not talk about it. It stresses me out." Gage pointed to his laptop and phone. "Actually *all* of this stresses me out."

Layla nodded she understood and took his hand, wondering if the confident, measured Gage was just an act. Maybe so, but there was no doubt the man was good at his job—and consumed by it, too. *I don't like seeing him this way.*

"I mean, it's my dad's company," he said. "I've got to take care of it, build it."

"Your dad wanted you happy."

"I'm happy *here*."

"Me, too," she said and pecked him on the cheek. "Maybe you should try to fly more often. I mean, fly a plane yourself. I know that helps you relax."

"I've been doing that a lot—many hours flying back and forth to see you. Getting to fly so much has been part of the fun of being with you again."

"That's good. I don't want all the back and forth to be a burden."

"Not at all," he said. "Have you ever thought about how we both love to fly?"

"You, planes. Me, angels," she said. "You know, you should try to break away from work today. Have some fun."

He looked over his calendar full of calls and meetings. "What did you have in mind?"

FORSYTH PARK WAS Layla's favorite spot in the Historic District. She loved the large Parisian-inspired fountain at the north end, a famous destination for both tourists and locals alike, and wasted many afternoons there lost in a book. And now she was walking there with Gage and Pippa, the dog darting around like she'd never seen grass before. It was nice the kids came along, too, though Ava and Jacob had their heads buried in their phones.

Layla looked up at Gage, holding a picnic basket and a bag and bracing Connor on his shoulders. The man had a big smile on his face, and she couldn't help but smile herself. He'd replaced the weight of work for another kind, a better kind, and she could tell he loved it. *He'll be a good dad.* They reached a good spot, and Gage dropped the basket and bag and lowered Connor to the ground. Then he plucked the phones from Ava and Jacob.

"Hey!" Ava groaned.

"I was about to beat the game!" Jacob cried, as Gage turned off the phone and put it in his pocket.

Gage ignored him and went to turn off Ava's phone. "Who's Justin?" he asked and began to scroll through her text messages.

"Don't read those," Ava begged. "That's private."

"You shouldn't be texting a boy anything that's private," he said. "It should only be related to homework."

"It's summer, Uncle G," Ava said.

"Then there's no reason to be texting a boy." He put her phone in his other pocket. "Does Emerson know about this boy?" Ava looked down.

"You are so busted," Jacob said, laughing.

"Shut up!" Ava barked.

"I heard her giggling with her friends about him," Jacob piled on.

"I hate you," Ava said.

"Don't fight!" Connor said. "Why does everyone fight all the time?"

Layla bent down to Connor. She found a pink feather on the ground and tickled his arm. "Whenever you find a feather, it means an angel is near."

Connor smiled. "Do you thinks it's Aria?"

"Maybe," she said.

He took the feather from her fingers. "I've never seen a pink feather."

"The angels leave different colors," she said. "They each mean something different. Pink means the angels are joining in on our fun. White means they are near. Black means there's something bad happening, and your angel is helping you."

"Wow," Connor said. "That's cool."

"You know what else is cool?" Layla dug in the bag. "I brought bubbles. And they come in different colors." Connor's face lit up, and she handed him the bottle. They went off with Pippa to blow bubbles by the fountain.

"Uncle G," Ava said quietly, "are you going to tell Mom about the texts? There's nothing bad."

"I'm not sure," Gage said with a smile.

"Oh, come on!" Jacob moaned. "The first time Miss Perfect Ava does anything wrong, and you're not going to rat on her!" Gage pulled out Jacob's phone. "Hey, what are you doing?"

"I'm looking at your texts," Gage said. "Any girls?" He scrolled a bit. "You're probably too smart to leave them up. You probably delete them." Gage pressed another button.

"What are you doing now?" Jacob asked nervously.

"Checking your search history. If it's clean, then I'll tell on Ava. If it's not, then I won't."

"OK, OK," Jacob cried and reached for his phone. "Please don't. . . ."

Gage raised his eyebrows. "I think I found something here. In fact, I think I found a whole lot of somethings." He looked down at his nephew, beet red and scared.

"What's Jacob been doing on there?" Ava asked.

"How about we let this all go?" Gage suggested. "No one gets in trouble?" Ava hugged her uncle tightly, and Gage put an arm around his nephew. "No more boys, Ava. And Jacob, call me instead of using the internet, OK? You can always talk to me." Jacob nodded but was too embarrassed to make eye contact.

"Look! That bubble's about to hit Uncle G!" Connor said. "There's another one! And Pippa is trying to eat it!" The three kids laughed at Pippa then ran off a few feet, taking turns blowing bubbles at her, torturing the poor crazy dog chomping away in the air.

Layla spread out the blanket and sat on Gage's lap. "What was on his phone?" she whispered.

"He's almost 13," Gage said. "You can imagine."

"Porn?"

Gage laughed. "Thank God, not yet. It was stuff about how to, um. . . ."

"Kiss?"

Gage laughed again. "He was searching how to hide an erection, and whether jerking off is normal."

"I hope I never have a boy," she said. "The kids really love you."

"I worry about them. They're going through a lot with the divorce. When you and I get married. . . ."

"*When?*"

"Absolutely. When we get married, divorce is not an option, OK? No matter what, we stick it out." Layla kissed him slowly on the lips in agreement.

"Gross!" Connor yelled. "You could get sick that way."

"Uncle G, maybe we'll tell Mom you're sucking face in front of us," Jacob said.

Gage sprang to his feet and wrestled Jacob to the ground. "Ava and Connor, come help me beat up your brother!"

CHAPTER THIRTEEN

LAYLA PLACED PIPPA at her feet and buckled up, the seat belt pinching her butterflies just a little. It was more than the usual nerves for take off. It was where she was heading—to his turf, to his city. And she fully expected he'd want sex. She did, too. So she couldn't blame him really. They'd been together about a month and done less than they had as teenagers.

Not that Gage hadn't tried. She just didn't think she was ready. Or maybe she was ready and just scared, fearing that if they did it, he wouldn't think it was as good as their first time. Or maybe she wouldn't measure up to the other women he'd been with. She certainly didn't want to disappoint him.

Her phone buzzed. *Have a safe flight. See you at the gate in 44 minutes.* She hadn't expected Gage to pick her up in the airport. But then again, she didn't know what to expect for the weekend. All she knew was there was some party or event he wanted her to attend tomorrow night. So Layla packed the only cocktail dress she owned but worried it wasn't nice enough.

Poppy wasn't worried about what she was going to wear. She was just happy to be going. Out of the blue, Gage invited her to come along and offered to fly her in tomorrow. Poppy jumped at the chance and for several days talked Layla's ear off about what to do with her hair.

The plane accelerated down the runway, into the great unknown. Layla looked down at Pippa underneath the seat in front, hoping for some support, some reassurance. But the dog didn't have a care in the world. She just licked her paw and plopped down to sleep.

GAGE PACED IN front of the gate. He looked at his watch, the clock on his phone, the one on the wall. Any minute she'd be back in his arms where she belonged.

"G man," Dash called out. "Waiting on your lady?"

Gage couldn't help but grin. "Yeah, where you off to?"

"Tampa," Dash said. "I'll be back for tomorrow night." Gage nodded then looked back to the gate, his foot tapping on the floor. "You do know only ticketed passengers are supposed to be beyond the security checkpoint?"

"I can go wherever the hell I want."

"Just saying you might get a cavity search. Or maybe you'd like that? Or maybe you want to get all up in Layla's cavity?" Dash laughed so hard he hunched over, his hands on his knees.

Gage looked down at his friend with amusement. Dash was one of the finest pilots in the country, his flight training second to none, his safety record impeccable. But to hear him talk, to see him bent over, one would think he was a crazy person who put on his Halloween costume several months too early.

"'In the butt, no babies' was always your motto," Gage joked.

"And 'bang 'em like you bought 'em' was always yours," Dash said. "Wonder if Layla knows that?" He gave a little nod towards the gangway.

Gage turned to find Layla walking towards him, holding a dog carrier and a bag. He could see her dimples. He lifted her up off the floor and buried his head in her hair. "I missed you," he whispered.

Layla wrapped her entire body around him and pressed her mouth against his. Then she heard clapping and whistling and suddenly remembered they were in the middle of the Atlanta airport. Blushing, she pulled away, and Gage put her down. She looked up to see Dash leading the applause.

"Get a room!" the handsome pilot yelled out. "Security!"

"Layla, I'm sure you remember Dash."

"Of course she does," Dash said. "I've been told I'm unforgettable."

"With shit in your name," she said, "how could I forget?"

Dash wrapped his arm around her shoulder. "I like you."

"Good," Gage said, "because I'm keeping her."

"Always knew you were a family man at heart, Gage. All those years chasing ass never suited you." Gage closed his eyes in horror. "Sorry, Layla. I didn't mean any disrespect."

"It's OK," Layla said and took Gage's hand. "I benefit from his *mad* bedroom skills."

Dash busted into another hearty laugh and headed towards his gate. "See you guys tomorrow."

"Layla, I'm so sorry. Dash embellishes. I. . . ."

She kissed him gently on the lips. "You still love me?" Gage nodded. "I'm still the only woman you ever loved?" He nodded again. "That's all I need to know." She started to walk from the gate, and Gage quickly picked up the carrier and bag and fell in line with her. "So Dash is coming to the party tomorrow?"

"Yeah, unless I kill him first."

LAYLA STARED UP at a sleek glass building reaching into the night sky. "This is where you live? It's a hotel!"

"Yeah, but there are private residences on the top floors," Gage said. "That's what makes it great. You get the benefits of a hotel at your house. There's a fitness center, 24-hour concierge service, a small convenience store, pet care for Pippa. The best part is the rooftop helicopter pad."

A doorman met them in the lobby. "Good evening, Mr. Montgomery. Here's the extra key you requested." Gage handed it to Layla. "Do you need assistance with your bag or carrier?"

"No, I can manage," he said, "but thank you."

"Is there anything else I can do for you this evening, Mr. Montgomery?"

"No, that's it." Gage led Layla through the lobby, with its glitzy chandeliers and polished marble floors, towards the wood-paneled elevator. The door opened, and Layla moved to put the key away. "Don't do that. You need it to get up to my place." Gage showed her how to use the key to access the higher floors.

A little elevator voice called out where they were headed. *25th floor penthouse.*

"How rich are you?" Layla asked, as the door closed. "You must be mortified by my little house."

He gave her tight ass a little squeeze. "I love being wherever you are."

"I bet you do," she said. The elevator voice announced their arrival to the top floor. "That's pretty cool how it talks to you." They stepped out and took a few steps along a hallway leading to double doors. "You have the whole floor?"

"Yeah," he said, smiling, and opened up. "Make yourself at home." He let Pippa out of the carrier, and she darted towards a sofa in the den.

"Pippa!" Layla cried, as the dog curled up in a ball between two pillows.

"It's fine. She should make herself at home, too."

"I probably should've taken her to pee before coming up."

"If she pees, it's fine. We'll clean it up." He took her bag and headed towards his bedroom, disappearing for a moment.

Layla grabbed Pippa from the sofa and took a minute to wander around the penthouse, taking in the open floor plan, fine furniture, wood floors. The kitchen had stainless steel appliances, but it looked like they'd never been used. There were at least two huge flatscreen TVs, one over the fireplace in the living area, and another in a room she wasn't sure of, a room full of rich mahogany wood and lined with rows and rows of old books. It could've been an office or a library.

Gage came out of his bedroom. "What do you think?"

"I knew you had money, but. . . ."

"It's just a house," he said. "Come see the balconies."

He led her outside and pointed down to the street. She followed his hand, her stomach in knots. She could hear some noise coming from the cars and people below. A Friday night in downtown Atlanta was on the verge of getting cranked up. For once she wished she were in the confines of an airplane, not simply held up by a thin sheet of concrete poured by construction workers who may not have had any idea what they were doing.

Gage put an arm around her and motioned towards the skyline. He pointed out the CNN Center, the aquarium, and World of Coca-Cola. She'd seen all those places before, though never with Gage, and certainly not from the heavens. "The best part is I can walk to work." He directed her eyes to another spot. "The Southern Wings corporate office is just down the street, right between those two buildings."

HER HAIR DRIPPING wet, Layla wrapped herself in a bath towel and headed to her suitcase in his bedroom. She stubbed her toe on his briefcase. "Ouch!"

"Sorry," he said, looking up from his laptop. "Guess I shouldn't leave that on the floor." Layla rifled through her bag, and Gage eyed her half-naked body. He felt his dick press against his pants, knowing he was being ruled by only one part of his anatomy. "What do you need?"

"I forgot my blow dryer. Do you have one?"

"Guys don't blow dry their hair."

"Then I guess I'm going to dinner with a wet head."

"Let me check," he said, and she followed him back to the bathroom. He opened a few drawers in the vanity and encouraged her to do the same. "If I don't have one, I'll head down and buy you one. They probably have one in the store in the lobby." He moved to the linen closet while Layla continued looking in the vanity.

Her eyes popped. "Um," she said, clearing her throat.

Gage stuck his head out of the closet and saw Layla holding an unopened, wrapped tampon, dangling it with two fingers like it was the end of a rat's tail. "Why are you showing me that? Are you still on your period?"

Layla threw it at his head. "It's not mine!"

A look of terror washed over his face. He searched his mind for what could've happened, for what to say or do. First, he made a mental note to fire his housekeeper. It had been months since a woman had been to his place, so there was no reason a tampon should be hanging around. Second, he had no idea whose it was. He hadn't been in a relationship for a long time and couldn't imagine one of the girls he periodically saw would ever store a tampon at his place. Third, he knew the tampon obliterated any chance of sex tonight. A girlfriend doesn't want to be reminded of another girl. *Fucking tampon ruined my night.*

"I really don't know who it belongs to. Emerson, maybe?"

Layla busted out laughing. "Your sister uses the bathroom in the master suite? And she leaves tampons here?"

"It might be from my last girlfriend. I don't know. But I don't want you to be uncomfortable here," he said hurriedly. "I mean, I can remodel the bathroom. My bed is actually new. So are the sheets. No one's been in them but me. But we could always sleep in the spare bedroom if. . . ."

"We don't need to get into all that, Gage. It's not like I don't know you've been with other women. It's been 12 years."

He released a deep breath and wrapped his arms around her. "OK, but I want you to know I've only ever made love to one woman."

Her eyes welled up a bit. "That's sweet of you to say."

"It's true," he said. "And I woke up every morning loving you."

THEY ATE IN an exclusive dining club. Gage knew it was beyond what Layla expected, but he wanted to celebrate their first night together in Atlanta. And he also hoped that after some good food and wine, she might be ready to take the next step in their relationship. God knows, he was ready.

And for a good while, everything was going according to plan, both of them laughing like teenagers, holding hands across the table, feeding each other fine foods that were impossible to pronounce. But just as the second bottle of wine came, the night turned upside down. Gage got an urgent message.

A Southern Wings aircraft en route from Denver to Chicago was experiencing mechanical failure. It would be making an emergency landing in Des Moines in the next hour. So, while Layla picked at dessert, Gage was on his cell phone. His executive team seemed to have everything under control. But he knew more was required.

He'd been out of the office so much lately. This wasn't a time to work remotely. He couldn't be wining and dining his girlfriend during a company crisis. He had to get to corporate headquarters. He apologized to Layla and called her a cab. Then he called his doorman, instructing him to take care of whatever she needed when she returned.

IT WAS THE middle of the night when Gage began the short walk home from the office. Over the years, there'd been plenty of midnight walks home, but he couldn't remember ever one at this hour. There wasn't a soul around. The streets were eerily quiet. Atlanta had shut down for the night. His mind was starting to shut down, too.

The hours and hours of dealing with the FAA, the media, his executive team had taken a toll. So had ensuring the pilots had whatever resources they needed to safely land the plane, which they did. But there was still so much to do. He drafted a few emails—some to himself, others to his team—on ways to improve maintenance and customer service in emergency situations.

He quickened his pace, wondering if Layla had waited up for him. It would be so nice to come home to her each night. Then his mind wandered a bit more. It would be so nice if Layla waited up for him donning a bustier with a garter belt, or a g-string, or perhaps she kept it simple and was just naked. Any of those would be fine.

He reached his building and waved to the doorman. "Good morning, Mr. Montgomery," he said. "Before it got too late, I made sure Miss Tanner was doing fine. And I walked the dog, too."

Gage thanked him and got in the elevator. He accessed his floor and watched the numbers tick up, as slowly as their relationship was moving. The elevator announced his arrival, and he made his way down the hall, saying a quick prayer Layla had waited up and was scantily clad. He opened the door quietly, not wanting Pippa to bark.

He saw a tiny light coming from his bedroom. He hoped that meant she was still awake. He gently pushed open the door, a small grin forming. She was sound asleep in his bed, in one of his old t-shirts, a book across her chest. He turned off a lamp and lifted the book from her. Pippa raised her head. He hadn't even seen the dog snuggled in beside her.

Pippa yawned and stretched and made her way to Gage's pillow. She spun around three times before plopping down on it. Then she let out a deep breath to let him know she was satisfied with her spot. Gage rolled his eyes. The dog certainly had made herself at home. And so had Layla. He stroked her face and gave her a quick kiss on the cheek.

Then he reached in his pocket for what he'd been carrying all night.

LAYLA ARCHED HER back, stretching, and reached for Gage. But her hand landed on Pippa. She looked at the clock. It was late morning. She couldn't remember the last time she'd slept so late. Pippa hadn't been out in like 10 hours. She hoped there wasn't a little present on the floor somewhere. And she hoped Gage wasn't still at the office. She rubbed her eyes then let out a high pitch scream.

Wet from the shower, Gage walked in wearing only boxer briefs and the leather angel wing cord around his neck. "Everything OK?" he asked, smiling mischievously.

Layla held up her hand. "What's this?"

"A diamond ring."

"I see that!"

"A four-carat cushion-cut diamond ring in a halo setting, if you want to be specific."

"I'm wondering how it got on my finger?"

"I put it on there last night."

"What?" she cried. "I don't remember that."

"You were asleep."

"You put an engagement ring on my finger while I was sleeping?"

"No," he said and took a seat on the bed. "I put a diamond ring on your finger. You called it an engagement ring, which is fine if that's what you think."

"It's on *that* finger, Gage, and it's a huge diamond. What else am I supposed to call it?"

"A gift, a token of my love, a. . . ."

"You are insane! This isn't how you propose!"

"I've asked you like 15 times."

"You counted?"

"Of course, Dash bet me it would take 40, but. . . ."

"You bet Dash?"

Gage tensed up for a moment, kicking himself for bringing up Dash. "I don't know why you're so surprised. I told you I'd give you a month. A month was yesterday." Layla got up off the bed and let out a little huff. Gage captured her hand and dropped to one knee. "Marry me, Angel."

Layla looked away. She couldn't look down at him. If she did, she'd scream "yes" so loud the doorman and all of Atlanta would hear. She released his hand, and he stood up and walked away. She fixed her eyes on the huge rock twinkling on her finger and smiled brightly inside at the halo setting. *Because he calls me Angel.* She heard a few chords and turned to find him with a guitar.

Gage smiled at her and blew out some nerves. He hadn't done this in a long time. But here he was sitting on his bed, about to sing to the girl from his past, the girl of his dreams, with her cute dog beside him. He knew full well the song was cheesy, but Train's "Marry Me" was perfect. The first lyric said it all: forever would never be long enough with Layla.

Layla's hand flew over her heart. She watched him, vulnerable, exposed, half-naked with her wings. Her heart melted with every word. He looked like the teenage boy she knew. And now a man, he still wanted her, needed her, vowed to protect her—even after everything she'd been through.

She looked down at the ring. Gage seemed to have everything in the world—but only wanted her. She wasn't sure what she was waiting for, what else she wanted or needed in life or in a man. "Stop," Layla said.

Gage put down the guitar and got on one knee. "I've wanted to marry you since I was 18. Don't make me wait another second."

Layla drew a deep breath and pulled herself together. "Ask me 25 more times." He looked up at her, his eyes wide. "We should let Dash win the bet."

"Why?"

"Because you've already won my heart."

He swooped her down to the bed. "Marry me?" he asked again and again, tickling her each time.

"Yes!" she screamed. "Yes!"

Gage stopped, both of them breathless. "*Yes?*"

"Yes," Layla said, smiling. Gage leaned over and trailed kisses down her neck, his hands grazing her panties. "Maybe we should wait until the wedding night?"

Gage's head darted up. "You have got to be kidding me."

"It might be romantic."

"Are you marrying me *tonight?*"

"Wait!" Layla sat up in bed. "There's not some surprise wedding happening tonight, is there? There *is* actually some kind of event, right?"

Gage chuckled. "Yes, but that's a good idea."

"Gage!"

"I'm kidding. I want to give you everything you want. But we can't have a long engagement if you're serious about the sex part."

GAGE WALKED TO his bedroom, hearing Layla spreading the news. She flashed him a smile and hung up.

"We need to change our plans a little bit," he said. "We need to fly to Savannah tomorrow."

"Is everything OK?"

"Yeah, I need to see my mom."

"You told her about the engagement?"

"Yeah, she's happy," he said. "It's just that I haven't seen her, well, since we got back together. She's used to seeing me once a week or so since Dad died. She gave me the mother guilt trip and everything."

Layla looked down at her feet and the huge diamond on her hand. She hadn't given any real thought to Mrs. Montgomery in years, the sweet Southern lady who once "grounded" her and Gage. The woman obviously had been through a lot lately—losing her husband, her daughter on the verge of divorce, worried about her grandkids' family life. "You think she just wants to see *you*? Don't be foolish. She wants to size me up."

"She knows you, Layla. She knows we started dating again a month ago. It's fine."

"It doesn't matter if she knows me or not. She's freaking out her son got engaged to someone he's been dating a month." Layla pointed to herself. "The same woman who left her son without a trace."

"Sounds like you're the one freaking out."

"Well, yeah! She probably hates me!"

"She's not like that. I told her that you told me why you left, and it was a good reason. And now that I know everything, I understand why you did what you did."

"She didn't press you?"

"No, I told her I wished you'd let me help you back then, help you make a different choice, but I know why you didn't." He gave her a little squeeze. "Look, Emerson and the kids will be there. They will take the spotlight off of us, I promise."

"OK." Layla looked at the clock. "What time do I need to be ready tonight?"

"Not until around six."

"What is this thing anyway? You've been so secretive. I don't even know if my dress is appropriate."

"It's a surprise," Gage said. "I'm wearing a tux, so. . . ."

"Great, my dress isn't going to work." She playfully swatted him. "You could've told me."

"I can take you shopping for a dress. I'm giving a little speech and. . . ."

"You are? Why don't you tell me these things?" She pulled him towards the door. "We better get shopping. I can't believe you're giving a speech. Your fiancée can't look like crap."

"It's impossible for you to look bad."

"I don't think I even packed a strapless bra. Oh God, what if the dress is backless? I'll need one of those crazy bras. Do you know how hard those are to find?"

"I vote for no bra—and no panties."

"Deal."

Gage's deep blue eyes lit up. "What?"

"Until we got back together, I slept nude."

"What? You've been holding out on me."

Layla laughed then turned serious. "I used to sleep in layers of clothes as a child, as if that would stop him. When I got older and started therapy, I started to embrace my body, not hate it." She shrugged. "So I found power sleeping nude."

"My fiancée is a nudist. That should break the ice with Mom."

"I guess I'll have to sleep in pajamas until we get married."

"A month."

"A *month*?"

"If you really want to wait until we're married, then the wedding should be in a month."

"You can't plan a wedding in a month!"

"You can when you have lots of money."

"The bride pays for the wedding!"

"Not this one."

Layla flipped over and straddled him, pinning his hands down. "So you expect me to marry you in a month and let you pay for the whole thing?"

"Basically," he said. "And just so you know, no matter when the wedding is, I'm open to sex beforehand."

"You're *open* to it?"

"I'm open to anything with you, Angel."

"Well," Layla said, tilting her head as if in deep thought, "I'm a pretty open-minded girl."

CHAPTER FOURTEEN

GAGE COULDN'T HOLD back any longer. It had been way too long, 30 days. And now there was nothing between Layla and her ice blue dress. He lunged at her in the back of the limo and pinned her to the seat. He climbed on top of her, kissing her mouth, her neck, their tongues stroking each other.

"My dress, my hair, the event!" she protested softly.

Gage hit the intercom button. "Circle the block," he told the driver then looked down at her panting below. "I won't make it through the night knowing you don't have on panties." He brushed her breasts with his hands and gave her hip a little squeeze, his dick bulging through his tux, pressing against her body. He slid a hand down her upper thigh and inched it slowly up her dress.

Her breath ragged, Layla moved his hand away. She sat up and straightened her dress. "Not like this. There's plenty of time for hot, fast sex in the back of limos."

"I'll take my time," he promised.

"No," she said, her voice no more than a whisper. "There's something I want to do first, something I've waited years to do." She hiked up her dress a little and got on top of him, straddling him. She gently kissed his neck and slid down his body until she was on her knees. She looked up at him as she undid the button and zipper on his pants. Her eyes grew large when his hard dick came out right away.

"I decided no underwear should go both ways," he said.

She smiled at the surprise and licked her lips, moving his pants down to his ankles. She rubbed his inner thighs then took his balls in her hands and stroked them softly. His body trembled under her fingertips, the beautiful diamond accenting them.

Gage wanted her mouth on him so badly, to feel her tongue, her wet warmth surrounding him. He looked down at her, almost begging, his body tingling in anticipation. She moved closer to him. He could feel her warm breath. But just when he thought she'd slide him, she lowered her head and ran her tongue across his balls, lightly sucking. "Yes," he groaned loudly. Layla stopped and raised her head just slightly. His eyes shot open and locked on hers. He held her gaze as her mouth slid over him, her pink lips and warm tongue magically working him up and down.

He leaned his head back and closed his eyes. Her mouth still felt familiar. He felt himself grow longer and harder in her mouth, and he could feel himself starting to build. He told himself not to finish yet. She'd just started. It felt so good. He strained to hold back. But when she slid up and down again and flicked her tongue across his tip, he came hard, long, shooting into her mouth without warning. Panting, he looked down at her continuing to suck, making sure she captured all of him.

She kissed his semi-hard dick and lifted up his pants, fastening back the button and zipper. She sat beside him, and he fell into her arms, resting his head on her chest. Gage slid his hand under her dress. "I want to watch you come for me now." Layla spread her legs slightly as he slid down her body.

A loud ring stopped his progress. He took out his phone to turn it off but saw he needed to answer. "Yes. . . ." He looked at his watch. "I didn't realize. . . . OK, five minutes." Gage hung up and reached under her dress and slid a finger inside her.

"God," she moaned and arched her back.

Gage leaned over her, as he moved his finger in and out. "This isn't how I wanted to do this. I wanted to bury my tongue in you until you begged me to let you come."

Layla dug her hands into his back. "Please, oh please! It's been forever!"

Gage liked hearing that. He wondered just how long it had been. And he liked she was growing wider and wetter each time he slipped his finger in and out. His dick grew hard again. "Fuck it," he said and threw her dress up higher. He leaned in and gave her a hard suck, tasting her, swallowing her, while still working her with his fingers. She released a hand from his back and gripped the seat, thrusting against his mouth and fingers. "Just lie back and let me make you come," he growled, sucking and stroking her, breathing in her sweet scent.

Layla spread her legs wider and buried his head between her legs. She ran her hands through his hair, as he brought her to the point of no return. Her entire body trembling under his mouth, she screamed his name when she came, so loud she was sure the limo driver heard. Gage slid out his finger, and she moaned at the loss of contact. She looked down at him on his knees, her dress around her stomach, and let out a sexy smile.

He was sure five minutes were up, but he sensed she wasn't done yet. She still had more to give him. And he couldn't resist trying. He wasn't going to leave her unsatisfied. He went down and licked her again. Her legs tightened together, and he knew he was right. He flicked his tongue in her, and her hips bucked up, as if begging for more. He blew out a warm breath and watched her body roll.

His hard dick poked against her leg, and Layla reached for him. "I want you!" she said. "Now!"

"Thank God!" Gage said and quickly unzipped his pants. His phone vibrated against the floor of the limo. "Shit." Layla scooted back, trying to calm her hair as Gage answered. "What? . . . Bad traffic! . . . We're close." He hung up and groaned, seeing Layla adjusting her dress, knowing the moment was over. He ordered the driver to step on it.

Layla looked at him from under her lashes, and her dimples blossomed. She scooted towards him, fixing his hair with her fingers, adjusting his jacket and tie. He tucked in his shirt and zipped up. Then she looked down at herself. "Help me! I don't even have a mirror!"

Gage leaned close to her lips. "You look amazing. Your eyes are sparkling. Your lips are the perfect shade of red. Your cheeks have just the right blush."

"I need a bathroom, a toothbrush, a mint!"

"I like the idea of you wet all night with the taste of me in your mouth," he said. "I definitely like the taste of you in mine."

The limo came to a quick stop in front of a hotel. Gage didn't wait for the driver to come around. He hopped out and took Layla by the hand. She straightened her dress as she got out, making sure the spaghetti straps were up and the right places covered. She heard someone calling out and looked over to find Sarah rushing towards them.

Layla looked to Gage. "What's going on?"

"Sorry, we're so late, Sarah," Gage said. "Bad traffic on 285. Nothing we could do about it."

"I'm willing to overlook it," Sarah said and gave them both a hug. "You look beautiful, Layla." Sarah quickly ushered them along a red carpet. "We've got to get you inside. Everyone's waiting for your speech, Mr. Montgomery."

"The charity is Hope Cottage?" Layla asked.

Sarah smiled. "He didn't tell you, Layla? He and his sister organized this whole thing. So many rich and powerful people inside. Southern Wings is getting us a new building."

"A new building?" Layla cried, stunned, her mind racing. *OMG! An ex-nun was calling us in the limo!*

Sarah led them up some stairs and through a back entrance and into a huge ballroom, all white except for lavender floral arrangements atop dozens and dozens of round banquet tables. There were at least 1,000 people in black tie waiting for the guest of honor. Sarah pointed Layla to her table.

"Got to give a speech, babe," Gage said, winking at her, and waited to be introduced on stage.

Layla made her way to her table. It was incredible Gage and Emerson orchestrated all this, that Gage even knew Sarah or was even involved with Hope Cottage. Layla had no idea. She simply couldn't believe where she was, what was happening. And she was happy to see some familiar faces at her table—Poppy, Emerson, Dash—among some others she didn't know. She took a seat next to Poppy.

"Did you get a little post*boned*?" Poppy whispered.

"No! Hush!" Layla said. A waiter put an entree in front of her. She looked around, seeing everyone else was onto dessert and coffee.

"Tell that to your hair," Poppy said, fidgeting with her own, now its natural dirty blonde color and cut in a pixie. "It's sexafuckalicious!" She took Layla's hand and took in the ring. "Jesus, that's huge! I can't believe you're getting married."

Emerson flashed Layla a smile. "I'm so happy for you."

Layla gave a little wave, showing off her finger, just as Gage took the stage to a round of applause.

"Good evening," Gage began. "I want to thank everyone for coming." He gave Layla a subtle smile, as cameras flashed all around him.

"Just how many times did you come?" Poppy whispered. Layla kicked her under the table.

"Right now, a child is being sexually molested," Gage said. "Is it your child? I know what you're thinking. It can't happen to your child. Things like that don't happen in your family. But sexual predators don't care if you're rich, poor, white, or black. They don't care which religion you are or which political party you belong to. This is not a problem of 'other' people. And this is not a woman's issue. I don't need to tell you all the good things Hope Cottage is doing for girls who've been sexually assaulted or molested—the inpatient and outpatient services; the individual therapy; the art, music, and movement programs. They treat girls in Savannah and the rest of Georgia, and most every other state, too. They are treating our girls." He paused. "Let me say that again— they are treating *our* girls. And nobody does it better."

An older gentleman sitting one seat from Layla leaned towards her. "He looks very polished—almost presidential." Layla gave him a confused look and smiled politely. The man looked slightly familiar, but she couldn't place him.

"Every man in this room has a daughter, mother, sister, niece, and, yes, maybe even a son," Gage said. "They're all potential survivors. We are here tonight to give a voice to those who've had theirs stolen— silenced. We are here to speak for them, to them. On each table is an envelope with a letter. The brave girls at Hope Cottage took the time to write down some of their feelings, thoughts, stories. There are no names on the letters. And that's the point. These letters could be written by any child, even yours. Before you leave tonight, I'd ask that you read the letters—word for word." He motioned to a side door and waved someone up. "One brave young woman asked to come tonight to read her letter in person."

Gage stepped away from the podium, and a ginger-haired, freckled-faced girl took the stage, her eyes fixed straight down. She couldn't have been more than 20. The crowd greeted her with polite applause, somewhat nervous about what was coming. The girl opened a folded sheet of paper and took a deep breath.

"The title of my letter is 'Why I'm Fucked Up.'" The girl looked over at Sarah who gave her a little nod. "My first memory is of my grandparents taking me to Disneyland. I remember them letting me drink soda for the first time, and that I screamed my head off in fear of Donald Duck." The crowd laughed. "Not bad for a first memory, but you haven't heard my second." She stopped to gather herself, the letter rustling in her shaking hands.

"My second memory, the one that haunts me to this day, the one that has shaped my life, is being naked under the gaze of that same grandfather. I wasn't more than three. I still wore footed pajamas. When he was done, when my pajamas were on the floor, he told me I was bad. He told me it was my fault. He told me I made him do it. And I believed him. He was the adult. He was family. That's the moment I became fucked up." An old photo of her—in pigtails and pajamas— flashed on a huge screen behind her. She looked back at it. "That's me at three. I was cute, huh?"

She turned back to her paper, her hands steadier now. "But I know the dark parts of her soul, the broken and fragmented spirit, the feelings of loathing and self-hatred. To hate yourself before you even have a word for it. He told me if I said anything, I'd be punished for being bad. So I kept my mouth shut. I stayed silent. Silence became my best friend, my armor. There were members of my family that didn't know what my voice sounded like. I cried myself to sleep every night for years, begging God for the next day to feel better. I wished myself dead more times than I care to admit. I'm sure I was suicidal by the time I was five."

She stopped for a moment, folded her paper, and looked out to the crowd. "It's really hard for me to admit that. I started to grow up, develop, get tall. It was horrible. I was so uncomfortable in my body. My body was the enemy, the very thing that pained me. I blamed my body for what happened, believing there was something about me, about my body, my soul, my very existence, that made these things happen to me. It's crazy, I know. But this letter to you, to no one in particular," she said, holding up the folded paper, holding back her tears, "is my fight back. No more silence."

Another picture flashed on the screen. "That's my little sister, Katie. Turns out our grandfather had been molesting her, too. And turns out that Katie wrote a note, too. She wrote everything down. Everything he did to her—year after year after year. The letter was several pages long. It went on and on and on. Her letter was her suicide note. Katie killed herself 457 days ago. Hung herself from a tree in the backyard. She was 14." The girl wiped a few tears from her face. "I was silent too long. I'm sorry, Katie."

Gage stepped back to the podium, and the girl buried her head in his chest, sobbing. Layla got to her feet and held up her glass. "For Katie!" she said. The crowd followed her lead, and so did Gage. "For Katie!" they called out together.

The girl started off the stage, and Gage stepped back to the podium. "Thank you for sharing your story with us. And thank you for being so brave." Then he turned to the crowd. "As you know, Hope Cottage needs another building. There are girls who need help, girls who have nowhere else to go. I know girls like this."

Gage paused for a moment, catching Layla's eye, then gathered himself. Poppy placed a hand on her arm, and Layla gave it a little pat.

"He's really good," the older gentleman at the table whispered to no one in particular.

"If these young girls can open up their souls in letters and in person," Gage continued, "the least we can do is open up our wallets." He smiled. "Of course, I could just write the check myself! But I'd be doing you all a disservice. I know you want to help. You wouldn't have come tonight if you didn't want to help. And these girls need your help. They need your support."

Gage found Sarah in the crowd and pointed to her. "Sarah, I know we talked about raising $2 million tonight. I know that's what Hope Cottage needs. But we're going to do better than that. We're going to raise $5 million tonight." Sarah nearly fell over in shock. "There are good folks here tonight, Sarah. They're going to help. They're not going to let you down. I mean, I know who they are. I know where they live. I know their travel habits. I can make life very difficult for them with airport security!" The audience roared.

"So tonight, Hope Cottage will get every cent it needs and more. And if for some reason we come up a little short of $5 million to-night—which is not going to happen—Sarah, you give me a call. I'll make up the difference—and then I'll call TSA!" Gage walked off the stage to loud applause and headed straight for Sarah, giving her a big hug, camera lights popping all around.

Emerson took the stage to go over the plans for the evening, and the different rooms for the silent and live auction, for singing and dancing. As his sister spoke, Gage shook a few hands then sat next to Layla, stroking her cheek. Emerson wrapped up with a final announce-ment. "If we reach $5 million," she said, "I'll have my baby brother sing for you!"

"I thought you only sing for me," Layla whispered to him.

"I didn't know anything about that," he groaned then spotted Em-erson coming back to the table. "What the hell did you do?"

"Oh, loosen up, Gage!" she said. "When's the wedding?"

"A month," he said before Layla could respond.

"That's fast. Are you preggo?" Poppy asked, seeing Dash staring at her.

"No!" Gage and Layla said at the same time.

"A month is so quick," Emerson said.

"If you can pull off this event in two weeks," Gage said, "then you can plan our wedding in a month."

Emerson about fell over. "You want me to plan your wedding?"

"It would make us both so happy if you would," Layla said.

"I'll help!" Poppy said. "I could help with styling."

"Sure. I'll call you," Emerson said.

"Poppy, your hair looks great—very natural," Layla said.

"You think? I'm not so sure. I was thinking maybe I should. . . ."

"Leave it alone," Gage said. "It's the real you for a change."

"Were you fake before?" Dash asked.

"Nope, I'm real—boobs and all," Poppy said. "I know you were wondering." She flashed a smile, downed her drink, and sashayed off, with Dash following behind like a puppy.

Gage took Layla's hand and gave her a little twirl. "You OK? I know I sprang this on you, but I wanted it to be a surprise."

"It's a beautiful surprise," she said, leaning in close, her eyes on his lips.

Emerson yanked on her brother's tux. "You have to play host, remember? Need a few photos for the press coverage for Hope Cottage."

He kissed Layla on the cheek. "Go check everything out. I'll catch up with you."

Layla took a minute to settle herself, to process everything, running her hands along the flowers on the table. Gage and Emerson—probably mostly Emerson—had thought of every last detail, even including Poppy. Layla looked around at the crowd. They could've been anywhere else tonight, doing whatever else, but here they were making their way through the ballroom to the auction room, the casino area, the makeshift dance hall, all in support of Hope Cottage, for young girls who needed help. She wished she'd known people cared so much when she was a child. *I might not have been quiet for so long.* She picked at her dinner a little then cut through the crowd to the silent auction room, surveying some items on display.

Poppy barged in and cornered her. "Tell me what you know about Dash! He said he likes my breasts!"

"He just came right out and said that?"

"Yes! It was wonderful. He said he liked my hair, too. So what do you know? Tell me! Tell me!"

"Not much. I know he's not married. He's a pilot—supposed to be a real good one."

"And?"

"He has no verbal filter, which you already know."

"And?"

"He's a man-whore."

"God, I love everything about him! He's totally humpalicious! What should I do? I know he's just looking for a little booty."

"Are you OK with that?"

"Absolutely."

"A little smash and dash?"

"I'm rubbing off on you," Poppy said and skipped out of the room.

Layla smiled. It was good to see her friend so happy—after all the failed relationships, all the hair-cutting episodes—even if it was a bit strange Poppy was falling hard for Gage's handsome friend. Layla turned back to the auction, and her eyes popped at the current bids—tens of thousands of dollars for bottles of wine, for trips to Caribbean islands, for sporting events, for roundtrip private flights on Southern Wings to anywhere in the world. Then she saw one of her handmade crosses on an easel.

"What do you think of it?" a husky voice asked, coming up beside her.

Layla looked into the dark brown eyes of a dashing hottie. "Well, since I made it, I think it's beautiful."

He chuckled. "You're the artist?"

"It's just a hobby, really."

"I see more than that," he said, writing down a $15,000 bid. "I better win."

"That's very generous."

"Any chance I could get a dance with the artist?"

Layla looked away, embarrassed, just as Gage slipped his hand in hers and kissed it, making sure her ring caught the light. She loved how smooth Gage was—the way he'd show up out of nowhere, the way he'd be just jealous enough to let her know he cared, the way he'd stake his claim without all the chest-bumping bullshit. She gave the brown-eyed hottie an apologetic smile, and he walked away.

"See something you like, Angel?" Gage asked.

"Not at all," Layla said.

Gage kissed her softly. "Did I tell you how stunningly beautiful you are? I can't wait to get you alone later."

His warm blue eyes slid over her body, hungrily. The heat coming off him caused her heart to beat rapidly. She didn't know how just his eyes could make her so needy, so completely hot. "Do we have to wait until later? Isn't this a hotel?"

"I like your thinking. Give me five minutes. I'll meet you on the balcony." He pointed to a set of doors.

Layla walked outside, a mixture of nerves and excitement washing over her. She looked down at her hand. It was strange to be wearing a ring, to suddenly be engaged. She usually was more cautious and would think things through. But this felt right. It felt good. And she couldn't wait to start planning the wedding with Emerson and Poppy. She wondered if Gage would want a big or small wedding, where it would be, who they'd invite. It didn't matter to her.

"This event tonight, it's perfect!" a voice bellowed from behind. "It's getting a ton of press."

Layla turned to find the older gentleman from her table nursing a drink. "It's been a good night."

"Damn near genius." He extended his hand. "Governor Clements."

Layla shook it, kicking herself she hadn't earlier recognized the former governor of Georgia. "Layla Tanner."

"I know," he said. "Gage speaks highly of you. Congratulations on your engagement."

"Thank you. How do you know Gage?"

"His father and I were close friends."

"His father was a good man."

"I didn't realize you knew his father," Governor Clements said.

"Gage and I dated as teenagers."

"His father wanted the best for Gage."

"Me, too."

The governor sipped his drink and leaned in close. "Gage might think he fooled everyone tonight, but we both know better, don't we?"

"I'm not sure what you mean."

"This sudden interest in women's issues!"

"I still don't understand."

He leaned in closer, a twinkle in his eye. "Hope Cottage is about *you*. Am I right?"

"Excuse me?"

"That was rude of me. I apologize. It's just that you live in Savannah, and Hope Cottage is in Savannah, and out of nowhere Gage is suddenly supporting the charity. And I'm very happy he is—don't misunderstand me." He clasped his hands in prayer. "Please forgive me if I've misread the situation."

Layla relaxed a little. "I guess there's nothing to really hide. I brought Gage to Hope Cottage a few weeks ago."

"I knew it!" Governor Clements said, smiling brightly. "You don't get to my position without drawing some connections, without knowing a little about human behavior!"

"I had no idea he was *this* interested in Hope Cottage." She pointed towards the ballroom. "I had no idea about any of this. It was a complete surprise."

"It was a surprise to me, too. Gage is a good man. I've known him since he was a little boy, and he still manages to surprise me." The governor took another sip, and his face turned serious. "You're going to need to be ready to answer questions about Hope Cottage. You know that, right?"

"Now I'm back to being confused. What questions?"

"People might wonder why you're so interested in that place."

Layla held his eyes. "I care about the well-being of abused girls. Is there a problem with that?"

"Of course not, Layla. I'm sorry if I'm upsetting you. I don't mean any harm."

"I have no idea what you're getting at."

He took a deep breath. "I think you care about the well-being of those girls because, at one time or another in your past, you were abused yourself."

"*What?*"

"Am I right?"

Her instinct to run, she looked towards the door. She couldn't believe the former governor of Georgia was talking to her about her past, let alone making correct assumptions about it. *Where is Gage?* She calmed herself then stiffened her spine. "My past—whatever it may be—is none of your business."

"I agree with you!" he said. "It's just that the press—they don't! They think it's *their* business, or at least the public's business, to know. So they'll dig into everything—what's happened to candidates and their families in the past, what motivates them now, what they. . . ."

"Did you say *candidates*?"

"Layla, has Gage not told you he's considering a run for governor of Georgia?"

"For governor? Are you kidding me? Gage runs Southern Wings. He loves flying. You've got the wrong guy."

"I'm surprised he hasn't told you. He's been groomed his whole life for this! Military service, good grades, successful businessman! The last piece of the puzzle was you, Layla. The timing couldn't have been more perfect if I'd planned it."

Her head began to spin. She walked to the balcony ledge and looked up at the stars, trying to make sense of what Governor Clements was saying. She wondered whether this was really happening, whether what Governor Clements was saying was true. *Why wouldn't Gage tell me?* She thought about the timing of the engagement and wedding. *A month.* For a moment she wondered whether Gage was planning their life around some upcoming deadline to announce his candidacy. But that couldn't be true. She trusted the man loved her—had loved her for 12 years—and that she wasn't some pawn in a political game. Still, she was pissed he proposed without saying a word and scared what awaited her if he threw his hat in the ring.

"Are you saying Gage is using me to get elected? Because I don't believe that for a second."

He met her at the ledge. "Not at all. I'm simply saying it doesn't hurt to have a pretty girl on his arm. I mean, do you know how hard it is to get elected as a single man? Especially in the South? It's virtually impossible. People would think he's gay or should be a priest or is just plain defective in some way. With you at his side, he's going to be terrific."

"Not that I care," she said, "but you seem to have some real concerns about me."

"I'm always concerned about everything, Layla. That's how I got elected governor many years ago. That's how I got re-elected, too, many years ago." He patted her hand. "I just want you to be ready for the questions that will come. I want to make sure you'll be ready with answers."

Gage appeared in the balcony doorway and wrapped an arm around her waist. "I see you met my godfather."

"Sure did, *Governor* Montgomery," Layla said, smiling through gritted teeth.

Gage laughed. "What craziness has he been saying to you?"

"Not craziness!" Governor Clements said. "We need to strike while the iron's hot! Georgia is split down the middle. This state is hungry for a third party candidate. You'd be strong, Gage. I know it!"

"Not tonight," Gage said and motioned the governor back to the party. "Go spend some money." The old man nodded and gave Layla one last look before heading inside.

Layla pushed Gage's hand off her. "You want to be governor? Since when?" Gage closed the balcony door. "Don't you think you should tell me something like that? Is this why you want to get married so quickly?"

"Angel," he said calmly, "I've been approached to run. Governor Clements—my godfather—and a few others ask me like everyday. I haven't given them an answer."

"But it looks better if you're married."

"How can you say something like that?"

"Your godfather pointed it out to me! Trust me, it wasn't anything I was thinking about. Are you using Hoping Cottage in some way?"

"No! Did he say that?" *What a disaster. I guess we're not getting a hotel room.*

"Not exactly. But he did say he knew tonight was about me!"

"He said that? It's not just for you. It's for all of Hope Cottage, the girls, Sarah. I'm really sorry he said that. He gets excited."

"And he said I'll need to answer questions about my past on the campaign trail! Gage, did you tell him what happened to me?"

"No! I would never! How could you think that?"

"Because he said he knew about it!"

"I didn't tell him anything. He doesn't know anything. He's just very, um, perceptive."

She threw a hand on her hip. "Oh, so I give off some signal that I was molested?"

"No! Jesus! That's not what I meant! He just reads situations. He makes connections. He figures things out. He's always thinking three steps ahead. I'm so sorry. I'll talk to him."

"You need to talk to *me*! You're thinking about running for public office. That's something I should know—before asking me to marry you!" She turned the ring on her finger as reality sunk in. "I just don't know about this. There are so many things we haven't talked about— things to work out, things we don't know about each other."

His stomach dropped. "Like?"

"What about my store? Where are we going to live? Do you expect me to move to Atlanta? Do you want kids? When? How many? We almost had sex in that limo, and you don't even know if I'm on birth control."

Gage exhaled. "You can do whatever you want with the store. We can live in Savannah or Atlanta. I can commute if that's what you want. I want kids in a few years but want to enjoy you first. I'd like either two or four, an even number. And I assume you're on birth control." He smiled at her. "How'd I do?"

"Bad," Layla said. "Saying we can do whatever I want is a cop-out. You have to have a feeling one way or another. The kids thing is fine, but only two. And guess what, buddy, I'm not on birth control, so we could've started the kids thing way earlier."

"Well, I guess since we're getting married in a month," he said, "it really doesn't matter when we start." Layla threw up her hands and started towards the door. He grabbed her before she reached it. "Hey, I was kidding. We'll figure it all out. We'll make those decisions together."

"And the decision on running for governor?"

"That, too," Gage said, nuzzling her nose. "If I really was sure, I would've already announced. But I'm not sure. We can and will talk about it. Maybe I should have talked to you before. I just hadn't figured things out in my own mind yet."

Layla offered a slight smile. "I need a little time." She stepped away from him towards the balcony door. "I can't marry you in a month." She opened the door and disappeared into the ballroom.

Gage felt like he could throw up. He thought to run after her but figured she needed space. His godfather was a good man—like a second father—but he could come on strong. The old man must've really done a number on her. Gage kicked himself for not telling her everything weeks ago. He searched his mind for what to do. He looked up to the night sky and offered a few words to Layla's angels. It was worth a shot. Maybe they were out there somewhere. Maybe one of them was on call. He waited a few minutes for a response, but there were no butterflies, no feathers—nothing.

"$5.5 million!" Emerson shouted over a microphone. "Come on up to the stage, baby brother! I've got your guitar waiting!"

Gage shook his fists at the heavens. "Shit!"

THE CROWD GATHERED, as Gage walked to the stage. Layla could tell his stride wasn't as crisp as before, that he didn't want to be up there. He was pushing out a smile. She wondered what he'd be singing this time. It would be different than what he sang this morning. Gage started by thanking everyone for an incredible night, for the incredible donations, and assured everyone the money would be put to good use.

"I can see it on your face," Poppy whispered to Layla. "Do you want to tell me what's going on?"

"No," Layla whispered back. "Dash, have you had a good night?"

"Yeah," he said, "and I've been trying to tell Poppy it will be even better in a hotel room later."

Layla raised her eyebrows. "What do you think about that, Poppy? Are you up for that?"

"The man's got dick confidence," Poppy said. "I'll give him that."

"I assure you I've earned it," Dash said.

Gage picked up his guitar. Amidst an array of flashing cameras, he slung the strap over his shoulder and took a seat on a stool.

Dash winced at the first chord, sensing some country song. "What the hell is this crap?"

Layla didn't respond, though she'd heard Blake Shelton and Christina Aguilera's "Just a Fool" a hundred times before. She looked down at her feet, sensing his eyes were on her.

Poppy wrapped an arm around Layla. "I'm so glad you're marrying him."

Layla looked at the diamond on her finger, and a single tear rolled down her cheek. She looked up at the stage. His eyes, as she suspected, were locked on her. And she sensed everyone else was looking at her, too, as he sang about waiting for a long-lost love to come back. She heard the pain in his voice, the pain she'd left him with 12 years ago, the pain she'd left him with 10 minutes ago. *I don't want to hurt him again.*

But what Governor Clements had said was just too much, and the fact that Gage had kept everything from her was just as bad. She felt a little cry sneak out.

CHAPTER FIFTEEN

GAGE UNDID HIS tie and tossed it on the floor. The best day of his life, the best night of his life, had turned to shit. Layla reached for his hand, as he reached for Pippa. He put the dog on her leash and went downstairs for a walk. He needed some space, a moment of calm, to think through what she said, and everything leading up to it. *I can't marry you.* . . .

He took Pippa to a small area of grass and watched her piss all over it. It seemed fitting. The rest of what Layla said—*in a month*—didn't matter. The first four words were what mattered. Her doubts were what mattered. In a few hours, they were supposed to fly out to see his mother, so he could introduce Layla as his fiancée. Now he wasn't even sure she was anymore.

Layla approached quietly from behind. "If it's not because of the campaign, why are you in such a hurry to marry me?"

He turned to face her, still in the ice blue dress, her feet bare. "It has nothing to do with the campaign. I told you that. I just want to be with you, to start our life together."

"Is it because you're scared? Don't rush to marry me because you're scared."

"You think I want to marry you because I'm *scared?*"

"Yes, I think you're scared of losing me. If you're honest with yourself, you'll admit that's part of it."

"No, it's not!" he barked. "Besides, you promised you wouldn't run off again."

"I'm not. I'm right here."

"Bullshit. You are fighting this, us, at every turn—like there's some rulebook about how long a couple has to date, how long an engagement should be. I hope that when we're 90 years old, I'm still learning things about you. I hope you can still surprise me."

"I didn't say I didn't want to marry you," she said, a few tears beginning to fall. "It's just that girl tonight, the one who spoke. She had so much courage. I could *never* do that."

"No one is asking you to."

She curled her toes in the grass. "If you run for office, I might have to."

"That's what this is about?"

"Gage, you have no idea what it was like to talk to your godfather. It made me scared."

He threw his arms around her. "Then I won't run. Decision made."

"But if your dream. . . ."

"No dream I have is bigger than the one I have for us."

"But if this is something you want, then I don't want to be the reason you don't do it. I just can't give speeches about what happened to me. I can't be some new face of child sexual abuse."

"You don't have to be."

"I don't want some reporters or opponents digging into my past."

"I'll protect you as much as I can. I'll probably punch anyone who brings it up."

"My past could hurt you. It's dark and ugly and. . . ."

"Stop," he said, cupping her cheeks in his hands. "Running for office was my dad's dream for me. It holds some appeal, but I'm not sure it's the right time. I'm not sure it'll ever be the right time. We have our babies to consider, too."

"Our two babies," she said, smiling.

"Angel, if you don't want to ever publicly talk about your abuse, that's fine. I understand that. I will do everything in my power to protect you, even if that means I don't run."

"But I don't want to be the reason. I don't want you to regret not. . . ."

"I know regret," he said. "Regret is not looking for you longer. Regret is not kissing you that day in the Houston airport. Regret is not making love to you in the limo tonight. You are what's important to me. The kids we'll have one day are what's important to me."

Layla melted into his body, a sense of security returning. "29 days. It's two a.m. now. 29 days until we get married."

LAYLA STARED UP at the red-brick mansion with white dormers and columns and black shutters framing the windows. There was a square park across the street. She'd walked the park many times, never realizing how close she was to Gage or his mother. He led her through the wrought iron fence enclosing the house and two oak trees.

"Is this a good idea?" Layla asked.

"Everything will be. . . ."

"Uncle G!" Connor came out of nowhere and blindsided Gage, pretending he was crushed by an NFL linebacker. Gage dusted himself off and seized the boy, tossing him in the air, catching him just before he hit the ground. "Fly me back to the house!" Gage lifted Connor on one shoulder, and the boy began to make buzzing sounds, holding out his arms and legs. "Come on, Miss Layla!"

"She doesn't like to fly," Gage teased.

"We won't let anything happen," Connor said and reached out to her. "Will we, Uncle G?" Layla smiled and took his little hand.

"Nothing that she doesn't want to happen," Gage said with a wink.

"Can Petey ride, too?" Connor asked.

Gage rolled his eyes then pretended to throw the walking crocodile on top of Connor. Without saying a word, the boy wiggled to get down, and Gage placed him on the ground. Gage and Layla squatted on the grass so they were eye level with Connor.

"Did Petey bite you?" Layla asked.

"No," Connor said, his lip in a pout. "Ava and Jacob call me a baby all the time. I forgot I'm trying not to play with Petey anymore. I don't want to be a baby."

"You are my little man," Gage said.

"No, I'm not! I know you don't think he's real, Uncle G!" Connor threw himself into Layla's arms. "Miss Layla's the only one who believes Petey's real."

She patted his head. "Then everyone else is stupid."

"That's a bad word," Connor said.

"I know."

Gage watched the way Layla held Connor and stroked his hair. The two had some connection, no doubt forged out of imaginary things. To them, Aria and Petey were as real as the Savannah heat and as necessary to life as sweet tea. Gage poked Connor in the side. "I'm sorry, buddy. I know Petey is your friend. I should've believed in him before. Sometimes I can be stupid, too—but not anymore. Maybe we can all play together later."

"That would be the most awesome, best thing ever!" Connor jumped up and ran towards the front door. "Uncle G wants to play with Petey! Ava and Jacob are stupid!"

Gage wrinkled his nose. "Emerson is going to be pissed. We taught him a bad word and bought into his delusion."

"I think it was sweet what you did," Layla said and pecked his cheek. Gage leaned in for more, his eyes fixated on her mouth, and she placed her hand on his chest. "Not in your mother's front yard. I'm nervous enough." He took her around the side of the house, and they came upon a little arbor covered in vines. He pinned her against the house and kissed her hard, pressing his body against her. "Gage, what are you doing?"

"You said not in the front yard."

"I meant the whole area," she said, kissing his neck.

He grabbed her hips and locked eyes with her. He bit his bottom lip, and his eyes fell to her lips again. His hand ran to the back of her neck, and he pulled her to his mouth, running a hand to her breast, caressing her. Layla gave a little moan then saw two eyes staring from behind an oak tree. She pushed Gage away so hard he lost his balance and stumbled backwards. Gage steadied himself and saw Jacob peering from behind the tree, his young nephew's mouth wide open.

"You had your hand on her. . . ."

"Jacob!" Gage yelled, holding up his finger. "Stay right there." He turned back to Layla, who was beyond red. "No need to worry."

"What?" she cried. "This was like a porno for him."

"I suspect he's seen worse," Gage said. "Go on ahead, and I'll make sure Jacob doesn't say anything."

"You want me to go into your mother's house alone? I haven't seen her in 12 years."

"Would you rather stay here and have Jacob stare at your rack?"

"Oh my God!" Layla nudged him towards the boy. "Go make sure we didn't scar him for life. I'll wait here."

Gage headed over to Jacob, still behind the tree. "You shouldn't spy on people."

Jacob smirked at him. "Well, you shouldn't grope your girlfriend in Grandma's yard."

"Good point. But I thought we were alone."

"Outside? And I thought you were only supposed to do that stuff when you're married!"

"That's right!" Gage said through gritted teeth. "Now what's this going to cost me?"

Jacob looked around his uncle at Layla leaning against the house. "Tell me how you got her to let you do that?"

Gage thumped Jacob in the head. "Eyes on me." Jacob turned them back to Gage. "Girls your age don't even have boobs, so don't worry about it."

"Older girls do."

Gage rolled his eyes. "$50, and we don't discuss this again."

"100!"

"$75."

"100!"

Gage pulled out his wallet and shoved a crisp $100 bill in his nephew's hand. "Gage, are you giving him money?" Layla called out.

Gage didn't respond. "Hush money," he whispered to his nephew and pushed the boy in her direction. "Now go tell her how sorry you are for sneaking up on us."

Jacob stuffed the bill in his sock and walked towards Layla, his eyes straight ahead. "Miss Layla, I'm sorry. . . ." Gage smacked his head before he got out another word. "Hey, what was that for?"

"Keep your eyes on her feet or her face!"

Jacob quickly looked down. "I'm sorry I snuck up on you, Miss Layla."

"Now scram!" Gage said.

Jacob darted towards the backyard, a huge grin on his face. "Keep your hands to yourself, Uncle G!"

"How much did you give him?" Layla asked.

"Enough to keep him quiet."

"You can't just pay off children!"

"Gage?" a sweet old melody called out from the backyard. "Are you here, Darlin'?"

"Yes, ma'am." Gage kissed the top of Layla's head and intertwined their fingers. He led Layla towards the back of the house, seeing his mother come around the side.

His mother's face brightened. "There's my baby boy." She cupped his cheeks in her hands. It didn't matter how old her son got, or what he did—piloting planes, military, running Southern Wings—he'd forever be the baby and be treated accordingly.

"Good to see you, Mom."

Layla smiled seeing Gage blush. His mother had the same petite frame Layla remembered, and the same kind and loving face. Though her once long brown hair was now gray and cut in a bob, she looked far too young to be a widow.

His mother lightly slapped his face. "I haven't seen you in over a month."

"Sorry, Mom, I've been a little busy." He squeezed Layla's hand.

"Nice to see you, Mrs. Montgomery," Layla said.

His mother frowned and began to look around. "Don't tell me my mother-in-law is haunting me from the grave. I wouldn't put it past that crazy old loon! She's the only Mrs. Montgomery I know. I'm Helen."

"Mom, you remember Layla."

"Well, I guess I better since she's going to be my daughter." She pulled Layla into a huge hug. "I guess you should call me 'Mom,' not Helen." She stepped back and grabbed Layla's hand. "The ring is beautiful."

Layla smiled. "Gage has good taste."

"I'd hope so! I raised him!" Helen put her arm around Layla and led her to the backyard. "So I hear we only have a month to get this wedding put together."

"Damn!" Gage said. "Emerson has a big mouth."

"Language," his mother scolded. "The kids are around here some-where."

Layla looked over at Gage, his head hanging low like a school boy. "Sorry," he mumbled.

A brick walkway led to a grassy area in the backyard, with the focal point a large white square gazebo trellised in budding rose bushes. Actually, the entire yard was outlined in rose bushes. Helen walked them to the back porch and a circular table holding a pitcher of iced tea.

"So, Layla, what are you thinking about colors, food, venue?" his mother asked, pouring a couple glasses. "I can tell Emerson is stressing out already. She has a portfolio together for you and Gage to look at today."

"Already?"

"Of course, we have to get crackin'."

"Right," Layla said, her eyes wide to Gage. "Something small, I think." He gave her an approving nod. "Quaint."

"Lavender," he said, both women turning to him. "Lavender in the flowers."

Helen smiled. "I look fabulous in purple, so that works. Layla, Emerson's been raving about your store, the book bundles, the wedding, how beautiful your dress was last night."

"Don't forget about the singing!" Emerson said, coming out of the house.

"Singing?" his mother asked.

Emerson pulled out her phone. "You have to see this, Mom. You're going to flip. Gage sang to Layla. It was so sweet. Every woman in the place was crying, and every man in the place was jealous."

Gage reached for the phone. "We don't need to watch that."

His mother swatted his hand and took the phone. She turned her back to watch. When she turned around, her eyes were misty. "Gage, you haven't sung in front of anyone since before college."

It didn't take Layla long to figure out why. She hated Gage gave up something he loved because she hurt him. She felt her own eyes water. "Restroom?"

"Down the hall, third door on the left," Emerson said.

Layla headed inside and found the hallway. She began to count the doors and reached the third one when Connor popped out of the bathroom, wiping his hands on his shirt. "Let's hide from Petey," he said and pulled Layla into the living room. They crouched behind a chair together.

"Do you think Petey can see me?" Layla asked. "I think my arm is showing."

"No, he's not looking for you. He's looking for me." Relieved, Layla sat down cross-legged. Connor giggled and flopped in her lap, his blond curls bouncing. "Mommy says you will be my aunt soon."

"Is that OK with you?"

"It's the best. But do I call you Aunt, or Layla, or Aunt Layla, or Aunt L?"

"Whatever you want." They heard some laughing, and Layla stuck her head out, finding Gage grinning.

Connor hopped up. "You gave away our spot, Uncle G." Gage held up his hands in surrender. "Auntie Layla, when you marry Uncle G, will you be able to punish him?"

"Absolutely," Layla said. "Since it's so close to the wedding, I can start punishing him now. What'd you have in mind?"

"A spanking! He's been really bad."

Gage laughed so hard he fell on the sofa. Connor launched himself on top of his uncle, his knee striking Gage in the balls. "Shit!"

Connor's blue eyes got huge. "That's worse than stupid."

Layla picked up the boy. "I think you just took care of the punishment."

"Jacob says that's crackin' nuts!" Connor said.

Helen walked into the living room. "What's so funny?"

"I cracked Uncle. . . ."

Gage put his hand over the boy's mouth. "Nothing, Mom."

"Connor," Layla said, "Uncle G and I need to ask you something really important."

"Hey, buddy," Gage said, "when I marry Layla, we are going to need some help at the wedding."

"I want to help!"

"Good. Because we have a special job for you—the most important job. We need you to carry our wedding rings for us. Do you think you can do that?"

"Wow, I can do that."

"Thanks, little man. You'll walk down the aisle carrying a little pillow. . . ."

Connor stuck out his tongue. "That's girly. That's what Cinderella's slipper was on."

"That's the way it's done, dude," Gage said.

"Maybe Connor has a better idea?" Layla wondered.

"I could attach them to my remote control airplane and parachute them in. That would be cool."

Layla tapped her fingers on her leg. "What if the rings miss their target?"

"Hmm," Connor said. "I know!" He ran to a pile of toys and came back with a pilot figurine. He lifted the pilot's arms in the air. "I can put a ring on each of his arms and carry him down the aisle."

Layla took off her ring and handed it to the boy. "Go to the other side of the room, and show me how you'll do it."

Emerson came in the living room, finding her son marching with his pilot man, Layla's diamond ring hanging from its arm. "It works!" Connor said and started jumping up and down.

Emerson grabbed the ring before it flew off and handed it to Layla. "What's going on?"

"Mom, I'm going to carry the rings for Uncle G and Auntie Layla!" Connor said. "The pillow is girly. The remote airplane is tricky. So I'm using my pilot guy. I have the hardest job!" Emerson raised an eyebrow. "I'm going to tell Ava and Jacob."

Gage swooped up his nephew. "Have Ava and Jacob come see us. We need to give them jobs, too." Connor scurried out of the room as Emerson sat down.

"I can work with him about the pillow," Emerson said.

"Don't you dare," Layla said. "He's precious. Pilot man will work just fine."

Emerson pulled out a binder and placed her glasses on her nose. "Let's get started. Layla, are you thinking of having the wedding in Atlanta, Savannah, or back with your family in Houston?"

"Atlanta or Savannah would be easier," Gage said, rescuing Layla from having to answer.

Helen chimed in, "The cathedral in Atlanta where your father and I got married is beautiful."

"We really want something small," Gage said.

"You have to be married in the church," his mother said. "Layla, I remember you're Catholic, right?"

"I was raised Catholic."

"Well, there's that little church down on. . . ." Helen tapped her head. "What's the name of that street?"

"Actually, Mom, I was thinking it might be nice to get married outside somewhere."

"You must be married in a church," Helen said.

"Oh shit!" Emerson mouthed to Gage.

Gage cleared his throat. "Actually, Mom, I talked to the bishop this morning. He said that if he gives his blessing, then a priest can marry you outside at an appropriate venue."

Layla looked up at him. "You called the bishop?"

Ava and Jacob barged in the living room, slapping each other. "Stop it!"

"You stop it!"

"Guys!" Gage called out. "Both of you stop it!" He took Ava's hand and sat her down.

Ava saw Layla's ring. "Wow, is that real? Can I try it on?" Layla handed it to Ava. The girl put it on and held her hand to the light.

"Ava, I was hoping you'd be a bridesmaid," Layla said.

"I'd love to!" Ava threw her arms around Layla and shrieked so loud her whole family covered their ears. "Mom, can I wear a strapless dress? Can I wear high heels and makeup, too?"

"We'll see," Emerson said. "Maybe low heels and a little makeup."

"Yes!" Ava said. "Uncle G, does this mean I'm going to finally get a cousin—hopefully a girl?"

"Eventually," Gage said taking the ring off Ava and slipping it back on Layla.

Jacob snickered from the floor, "Uncle G, you have to wait until *after* the wedding for that, right?"

"Jacob!" his grandmother cried.

"Sorry, Grandma." Layla turned bright red, and Gage thumped him in the head. "I'm happy for you, Uncle G, but I don't want to be in the wedding."

"Jacob," Emerson said.

"Mom, are you going to make me?" Jacob asked. "Ground me again?"

"I'm not going to make you," Emerson said.

Gage sat on the floor beside him. "Why are you grounded this time?"

"Got an F on a book report in English," Jacob said.

"He can do a makeup report," Emerson said, "but he won't do it."

"Because I'm stupid. Because I can't read. Connor can read better than I can!"

Ava got up. "I'm sick of this. I'm going to look up dresses on the computer."

"You are not stupid," Helen said. "You are very bright."

Jacob held in tears. "Please don't make me try to read another book."

"What about an audio book?" Layla asked.

"We do that sometimes," Emerson said, "but we can't find all the books in audio."

"I'll find them," Layla said. "Give me the list. I'll find them." She took a seat on the floor by Jacob and patted his hand. "And if I can't find them, we can make them ourselves."

"Why didn't I think of that?" Emerson wondered.

"Thank you, Miss Layla," Jacob said.

"Sure," Layla said. "But you have to do something for me now. You have to work really hard and do the reading at our wedding."

"I'll ruin everything," Jacob said.

"We'll pick an easy one," Layla said. "First Corinthians. *Love is patient; love is kind.* You've heard that one, right?"

"Yeah," Jacob said. "But what if I mess up?"

"What if I trip going down the aisle?"

"I'll catch you," Gage said. "And we'll catch you, Jacob." The boy sat quietly for a moment, terror on his face.

Layla wondered if she'd pushed too far. "You know, there are some really famous smart people with dyslexia. Einstein, Edison, da Vinci, Picasso, Spielberg. And those are just the ones I can remember."

"Why didn't I look that up?" Emerson asked. "God, I'm not winning mother of the year."

Jacob hopped up. "I'm going to kick Ava off the computer and look up more famous guys with dyslexia." He started to run out of the room then turned back. "Miss Layla, I'll do the reading at your wedding."

"Thank you," Gage and Layla said.

"That's sweet of you, Layla," Emerson said.

"I'm happy to," Layla said.

"The kids are totally exhausting," Gage said. "Emerson, I don't know how you aren't totally insane by now."

"Jack Daniels," his sister said. "Jack is my best friend." She looked down at her binder and began to scribble some notes. "OK, back to work. Dash is your only groomsman?"

"Yep," he said.

"You really need more friends."

"He has multiple personalities, so it works."

"Ava is a bridesmaid," Emerson said. "Anyone else?"

"You," Layla said.

"That's nice. Thank you. Poppy, too?"

"No, Poppy's not a bridesmaid."

"I thought she was your best friend?" Emerson asked.

"Since my father's passed, Poppy is walking me down the aisle."

Helen wrinkled her brow and scooted forward in her chair. "Let me get this straight. My grandson is going to carry the rings on a toy man? My other grandson with dyslexia is doing the reading? And some woman is walking Layla down the aisle?"

Layla smiled proudly. "Yes, ma'am."

"The rings may end up in the gutter. Jacob may vomit all over us. And you will look like a lesbian coming down the aisle," Helen said, laughing. "It all sounds like the perfect Savannah wedding."

Gage looked sweetly into Layla's blue eyes. "Savannah it is then."

LAYLA LEFT GAGE to manage his mother and sister on color schemes, flowers, and music. She didn't care about any of that—neither did he— but Gage at least had to pretend he did with his family so involved. She slipped out to the backyard and took off her shoes. The blades of grass felt good on her feet. She walked out to the gazebo, taking in the greenery, the rosebushes, all around the white lattice. She sat down on a wicker sofa and leaned her head back on some pillows. She closed her eyes, the gazebo reminding her of the time it rained after she and Gage played golf on the island, when they took cover under a tree, its branches bending down to create a little barrier between them and the rest of the world.

"Dear?"

Layla felt a hand on her shoulder and popped up her head. "I'm so sorry. I'm just taking a minute to recharge."

"I like to do that myself," Helen said and sat down beside her. "You must be exhausted with the party and engagement."

"A little," she said, embarrassed, "but Gage isn't outside almost falling asleep."

"Gage goes full throttle—especially when he wants something."

"I'm learning that."

Helen smiled. "You know what I remember most about you? How

happy Gage was that summer. His father, bless his soul, was a wonderful, loving man. But he put a lot of pressure on Gage—his legacy and all."

"Gage wanted to make him proud."

"He's a good son, but I used to worry if Gage was making *himself* happy. I remember how the two of you would snuggle up on that old lounge chair every night and watch the sunset over the ocean. I thought it was such an odd thing for two kids to do together every night. My husband used to tease me and say it's because we didn't know what was happening underneath that blanket." Helen chuckled. "But I knew better."

"You did?" Layla asked, a lump in her throat.

"I saw Gage always had his hands on top of the blanket." She winked at Layla. "I knew I liked you. Any girl who'd make a boy keep his hands above the blanket was a good girl in my book."

"Gage was always respectful. He still is."

"He better be! I remember sitting out one morning drinking coffee, and his father came walking up, having just come from one of those spiritual services they hold on the beach each morning—yoga meditation or something. He went every morning except Sundays when we went to church as a family. Anyway, this one morning he came up the patio. He told me he saw you at the meditation."

"I saw him there almost every morning," Layla said.

"He couldn't believe a 16-year-old girl was watching the sunset at night with his son, then getting up at the crack of dawn to meditate. We couldn't get Gage up before 10—unless, of course, he was seeing you." Layla smiled. "For some reason, that's what I remember about you most. The way my husband looked on the patio that morning, telling me our son was in love with a girl who went to sunrise yoga meditation on the beach. Of course, I remember your cute sundresses, too."

"I still wear them."

Helen ran her hand along a rose petal. "As a parent, you just know when your son has found the love of his life. Our son just happened to find you when he was 18."

"I was only 16."

"Did Gage ever tell you his father and I got married when we were 18, right before he went into the military?"

"No."

"We were such babies. We had no idea what we were doing. But we were so happy. We thought Gage was going to use that to plead his case not to leave you."

"And not go to the Naval Academy?"

"My husband was preparing for Gage not to go."

"Gage and I never talked about that back then."

"We knew it was coming."

"I wouldn't have let him give up his dreams for me."

"His father had a spot reserved for him at the University of Georgia just in case. That was going to be our compromise. Go to school *somewhere*. And it was only a few hours from your grandmother's place, so he could see you every weekend if you were living there."

"But then I left."

"No need to relive it, dear. Gage said you had a good reason for doing what you did, but please be sure this time. It took a toll on him. Not knowing what happened was the worst part. I'm not sure he'd survive losing you a second time."

"Me neither," Layla said. "I almost died the first time." Layla figured Helen probably thought she was just being dramatic. "Your roses are lovely."

"My late husband planted them for me. He knew he was sick then but didn't tell me. He didn't want to burden us. It wasn't until he had to tell us that he finally did. He told me before he died that he wanted to make sure I was surrounded by his love when he was gone. That's why he planted the roses." Helen kissed her fingertips and held her hand to the sky.

"Could Gage and I get married here in the backyard?" Layla asked. "I'm sure Gage would want to be by his father's love when he marries me."

Helen pulled Layla into a hug. "That is so sweet and thoughtful. Of course, you can."

Layla wrapped her arms around Helen, feeling tears run down the woman's face. Layla closed her eyes—trying to remember if her own mother ever held her like this. It felt new, a little uncomfortable, but she could certainly get used to it.

LAYLA DROVE GAGE to the airport hanger in the early morning. She hated that he had to leave every day, that they were living in different cities. She pulled up to his tiny death trap. "Is this how it's going to be when we get married?"

"If I'm commuting from Savannah," he said, "I guess there's no way around it."

They took a few steps to the plane, and he tilted up her chin, lowering his lips to hers. Her tongue gently met his, and her body softened against him. He pinned her against the plane and pressed his body into her. He opened the door and lifted her into the back. There was just enough room to crawl on top of her.

Layla spread her legs just slightly and released a little moan. He slid his hand under her sundress, feeling her smooth warm skin. He saw her nipples peaking against the thin fabric. She pulled off his shirt, and he ripped her dress over her head, her breasts smashing against his chest. His tongue lingered on her neck.

"I love your body on top of mine," she whispered.

"Good, because I plan on burying myself deep inside you." He kissed down her neck and twirled his tongue around her nipple. Then he glided a hand to her thigh and lifted her leg to his hip, growing harder as she moved against him. He slid a finger through the side of her lace panties and grazed her slick wetness. "I can feel how much you want me." Panting, Layla arched her back.

Bang! Bang! Bang!

"What's that?" Layla threw him off her, thinking the plane was exploding. She knew this day would eventually come. She just didn't expect it to happen in a plane resting in a hanger. And she didn't expect to be topless, either. She scrambled to put her dress back on before she died.

Gage put on his shirt and looked out the window, his lips tightened in a line. "Walter is checking the plane."

"Did he see us?"

"I don't think so."

Layla leaned her head on the seat. "You commuting is not working."

"It'll work. I'll move to Savannah. I can commute."

"Let's talk about it. Not you make an executive decision."

"Just tell me what you want, and I'll make it happen."

Layla smiled and shook her head. "That easy, huh?"

His phone rang. "I'm turning it off." He shoved it in his pocket. "Where do you want to live?"

"My store is here in Savannah."

"My family is here, too."

"But your career is in Atlanta."

Gage nodded then added quietly, "The Governor's Mansion is there, too."

Her stomach dropped, but she kept her face neutral. She got the feeling he was testing the waters, vetting her in some way. "So you've decided to run?"

"I haven't decided anything,"

"When do you have to decide?"

"Few months or so." Walter banged on the window and gave a thumbs up, which Gage ignored. "We'll figure this all out."

"Can you tell me why you want to be governor?"

"It's a chance to help people, mostly. I see so many problems, people in trouble and I. . . ."

"You said something similar that first day we met." *When you see someone in trouble, you should try to help.*

Gage pulled her closer. "I think I could do a lot of good."

"I think so, too. But you do a lot of good now."

"I try. I'm not sure about the whole thing. I know it's what my dad wanted for me. I think they were grooming me from preschool. But I'm not sure I want to open myself up, my family up, to that kind of life."

"*Or me?*"

He gave her a little squeeze and held up her ring finger. "You're my family now." Walter banged on the window again, and Gage gave him a little wave. "We'll figure it all out."

"Seems there's a lot to figure out. And one of us is always coming or going. It's like we don't even have time to talk."

We never have time for sex, either! If it wasn't her period, it was a tampon or his godfather, or he was buried under work. But he knew she was right. Things had been crazy lately. She moved to get out of the plane, and he captured her hand. "We'll make time. What do you want to talk about?"

"I don't know. So many things."

"No, tell me," he said and poked her in the side. "What?"

"Whether you run, where we live, things like that." Walter banged on the window again and gave another thumbs up. "We obviously don't have time now."

"I promise we'll make time to talk about those things," he said. "Anything else? Anything I can answer quickly?"

"Why did you stop playing guitar and singing?"

He looked her square in the eye. "Because for a long time, I didn't have anybody worth playing for."

CHAPTER SIXTEEN

LAYLA SCOOPED UP the newspaper on Story Wings' front steps, still wet from the morning dew. She unlocked the entrance and saw a few lights on. "Pop?" She tossed the paper and her purse on the check-out counter. Poppy peeked out from the cafe. "No shaved head? I guess things went well with Dash."

"He's so hot!"

"I know! And his eyes—I would kill for his long, full lashes."

"I don't care about his lashes!" Poppy said. "It's his long, full. . . ."

"You did not!"

"Yes, I did! Several times! It was a total sexpalooza! I just got back from Atlanta this morning."

"You spent all weekend with him?"

Poppy nodded excitedly. "Well, he spent all weekend inside me. But that counts, right? He's so huge. I wasn't even sure if it would fit. But we worked it out."

"I'm glad you managed. Did you do anything but bang each other?"

"No, why would we? He banged me up against a wall. You know that's my favorite. I'm addicted. He's so strong, and I'm so petite. He just throws me around and screws me anyway he wants. It was total porn."

Layla held up her hands. "Filter, please."

"I think he really likes me. He asked me to dinner."

"When are you going?"

"That's what I asked him," Poppy said, swooning. "He said that he wanted to every night for the rest of my life." They started to scream and screech like schoolgirls. "You don't think that was a line, do you?"

"It totally was," Layla said, "but a darn good one." She heard her phone ring and saw it was Gage. She didn't answer, not wanting to miss any juicy details.

"Dash already called to make sure I got back OK," Poppy said.

Layla hugged her friend. "This is all such great news!"

Poppy pulled away a little and lowered her head. "I've got something I need to talk to you about. I should've said something before."

Layla's phone rang again—it was Gage—and she ignored it once more. "What is it, Pop?"

"I have to sell my side of the store or close it down."

"What? Why? I can't afford all the rent on this place alone!"

"I know, and I'm so sorry. I tried to find a buyer, but once they looked at my financials, they backed out. I haven't pulled a profit in almost a year. I'm barely keeping afloat. Everyone has an e-reader now. Adults don't buy books anymore. You don't have that problem because little kids still like to hold a book and drool on it and eat it and all that shit."

"What are you going to do?"

"Get a real job, I guess."

"How long?" Layla asked, hearing her phone yet again.

"By the end of the month," Poppy said. "It's actually good timing, I mean, with you getting married and all. I figured you'd be moving to Atlanta and. . . ."

"Gage and I haven't decided what we're doing."

"Layla, be serious. The man is a millionaire like 50 times over. He runs one of the most successful airlines in the country. You honestly think he can do that from Savannah, or by commuting everyday?"

Layla sat down, her head swimming. *This was the last thing I needed.*

The store phone rang, and Poppy reached to answer. "Yeah, Gage, she's right here. . . Stop yelling!" Layla took the phone. "Warning—he's pissed off about something."

"Gage, what's going on?" Layla asked.

"Why didn't you pick up your damn phone?" he barked.

Layla hung up. Poppy nodded at her friend, impressed. "He's not going to speak to either one of us that way." The phone rang again, and

Layla hit speaker. "Poppy's with me. You can apologize now."

Gage exhaled. "Layla, there's no time for this shit." Layla hung up again.

"He's going to go ape-shit crazy," Poppy said with a laugh and unfolded the morning paper.

The phone rang again. "Maybe I shouldn't answer this time," Layla said.

Poppy scanned the paper, and her eyes exploded. "Answer the phone! You're on the front page!"

"What?" Layla swiped the paper, seeing a photo of Gage singing to her at the Hope Cottage event, right below the headline: *Will There Be a Wedding in the Governor's Mansion?* She hit speaker on the phone. "Gage, we're on the front page!"

"I know," Gage said.

"How did this happen?" Layla cried.

Poppy searched her phone. "It's all over the internet, too!"

"What?" Layla cried, as Gage began to mumble a string of curse words. "Just local, right?"

"No," Poppy said. "Atlanta, too. It's all over Georgia. Wait, here's one on a national site! And here's a YouTube video of Gage singing to you!"

"Shut up, Poppy!" Gage barked.

"Stop yelling at her!" Layla said.

"I'm sorry," he said. "Layla, listen to me. Emerson is on her way to get you. Go with her. The corporate jet will bring you to Atlanta."

"Now?" Layla asked.

"Poppy," he said, "will you please have someone cover for Layla today and tomorrow?"

"Sure," she said. "I'll watch Pippa, too."

"Thank you," Gage said. "Angel?"

"I'm here."

"Emerson should be out front in a minute or two," Gage said. "She's in a black town car."

Layla looked out the window. "It just pulled up. I see her. Gage, how did this happen?"

"We can talk when you get here. I'll see you in a little over an hour. Everything will be fine." He hung up.

Poppy wrapped her arms around Layla. "I guess this wasn't the greatest time to tell you about the store."

Layla didn't respond. Her problems were well beyond paying rent. She grabbed her purse and walked to the car. Emerson was in the backseat with a phone to her ear. She gave a tiny smile and mouthed she was talking to Gage.

"Stop yelling!" Emerson shouted then told the driver to hit the gas.

Layla was barely buckled when the car sped off. She kept quiet as they headed to the airport, listening to bits and pieces of Emerson talking to Gage. She couldn't hear what he was saying, but by what his sister was saying, and how she was fidgeting with her hands and glasses, they were both a nervous wreck. The story was more than they expected.

The driver pulled into the airport, and Emerson ended the call. She threw her phone in her purse and took out a mini bottle of whiskey. "You want one, Layla? I think I have another one in here somewhere." Layla politely declined. "I take them with me off the planes. I keep them in my purse." Emerson unscrewed the cap and took a swig. She glanced over at Layla, who looked like she just got thrown in the deep end of the pool. "You need to prepare yourself."

"For what?"

"Gage," Emerson said. "You're about to see a very different side of him."

"I already heard it this morning," Layla said. "What happened? I thought the press was focusing on Hope Cottage, not me and Gage."

"They were. I took care of it myself. Gage and I decided not to even mention the engagement because he didn't want to draw attention to anything other than those girls."

"So someone leaked the engagement?"

Emerson took another swig. "Maybe someone did. But you had a ring on, so anyone would know. Maybe he should've waited until after the party to ask you. But I guess he was tired of waiting."

"What about Gage considering a run for governor? I didn't think that was public knowledge. Now it's splashed on the front page!"

"I don't know." Emerson finished the bottle and opened another. "But maybe I shouldn't be complaining right now—all the stories are positive, planting Gage as the next great governor."

"Then what's Gage so upset about?"

"You," Emerson said. "That you've been thrust into the limelight with him. He hasn't made a decision and wasn't expecting this kind of attention so soon."

"So he's going to try to smother me in protection?"

"Just try to play nice and understand it's coming from a place of love," Emerson said. "And don't hang up on him again." She lowered her glasses and pulled out a stack of papers. "This is every article run so far."

Layla flipped through them all, scanning the headlines: *Sorry, Ladies, He's Taken. Steamy Serenade to Georgia Beauty. Georgia Governor Hopeful Engaged. Teenage Romance Blooms into Engagement. Southern Wings Exec Building Hope Cottage—and New Life with Layla Tanner.*

Emerson took a drink. "Maybe the Democrats or Republicans told the press Gage might be running?"

"Why would they do that? And how would they know Gage and I dated as teenagers?"

"I don't know. Maybe they're trying to scare Gage off? They know he's the full package. They don't want a third party jumping in the race."

"But all the stories are positive, like you said?"

"They are *now*," Emerson said. "I work in PR, so I know how the press operates. Gage does, too. This is day one. The public and the press are eating it up. It's like you and Gage are the next Prince William and Kate. But the digging will start soon. The press will do some digging on its own. The political creeps will do some digging, too. They feed stuff to the press, and the press then takes it a step further, does the dirty work. For now, I don't know what's going on exactly. Maybe the Democrats or Republicans know they can get to Gage through his new fiancée? Just sending a little message that you will be fair game."

Layla swallowed hard, remembering what Governor Clements told her, how perceptive he was, the connections he drew, the correct assumptions he made. And if it was all so clear and obvious to him, it probably was to others, too. There surely were other political folks thinking three steps ahead, eager to expose her and tear her apart, all to torpedo Gage.

Emerson straightened her glasses and saw the fear on Layla's face. "Who knows, honey? I don't mean to scare you. I'm just spitballing. It's part of my job."

Layla and Emerson landed in Atlanta, and a black town car with tinted windows whisked them to the corporate office. The car navigated through a sea of reporters and camera crews and pulled into an attached parking garage. Emerson swiped an access card to get in and at several other checkpoints before pointing the driver towards a private parking area. Then she took Layla to a secure elevator bank, and they headed up away from the chaos below.

Layla stepped onto the executive floor and found chaos of another kind. Employees were shuffling papers, moving quickly down the halls, barking on their phones. A few employees glared at Layla as she walked by, clearly recognizing her from the news coverage. They were not shy about letting her know that she – whoever the hell she was – was the cause of their stress and Gage's horrible mood.

"If I didn't know better," Layla whispered, "I'd think a plane crashed."

"Gage would be calmer during that," Emerson said, leading Layla through heavy glass doors. "Hi, Mary. How bad is he?

The secretary gave Layla a small smile. "Maybe he'll calm down now that you're here. Congrats on your engagement."

"Where the hell are they?" Gage barked, stomping out of his office.

"Traffic," Emerson said.

Gage stopped in his tracks, his eyes bitterly cold. "I need five minutes in my office with Layla," he said and reached out a hand to her. "Emerson, I'll see you in the boardroom in five minutes."

Layla took his hand, and he pulled her inside. "Five minutes, Mary. No interruptions." He slammed the door behind them.

The office was huge and dark. The shades were drawn. Gage sat down on a sofa and pulled Layla onto his lap, burying his head in her neck.

"Gage, what's going on? How did this happen?"

"Just let me hold you, Angel."

Layla stroked his back and ran her fingers through his hair. She wasn't sure what else to do, or what exactly he needed.

"I'm so sorry," he said.

"It's not your fault."

"No running, right?"

"Only to your arms."

He picked up his head and kissed her softly on the lips. "Wait in here for me." He got to his feet.

"For how long?"

"I don't know. Mary will get you whatever you need. Don't go out. Don't open the shades. There are cameras everywhere outside. There's a bathroom through that door." He pointed to the side of his office.

She stood up. "You made me fly all the way to Atlanta to stay trapped in your office?"

"I needed you close. We can talk about stuff when I'm done with Emerson."

"No, I want to hear everything going on." Gage shook his head, left the office, and slammed the door behind him.

Layla walked around for a moment, seeing the morning papers spread across his desk, next to her cross holding down a few business letters. Layla ran her fingers across it. She walked out of the office and heard Gage yelling down the hall. She made her way past Mary and followed his voice. She came upon the boardroom—one of the few private spots in the building without any glass or windows—and stood outside. She couldn't see Gage or his sister but could hear everything loud and clear.

"You are not my sister today!" Gage hollered. "You are just another employee who fucked up."

"This is not my fault!" Emerson shouted back.

"You are in charge of PR, Emerson! You are in charge of what's in the papers and on the news! How is this not your responsibility?"

"I did my job! This is totally out of my control."

"Maybe if you spent less time at home crying about your divorce, you'd do a better job here at work!"

Layla winced, wanting to reach through the door and kick Gage in the balls. She hoped Emerson kicked him herself.

"Go to hell, Gage!" Emerson barked.

"*You* messed this up, Emerson. Did it ever occur to you Layla might have things going on, things she doesn't want reported?"

"I'm frankly not thinking about Layla when I do my job, Gage. I'm thinking about the company! This company is just as important to me as it is to you!"

"The *company*? I'm concerned about Layla right now! Her life is now on full display! I have crazies emailing my corporate address asking for her autograph, a picture, a lock of her hair! Do you think I want perverts emailing me at work, obsessed with my wife?"

"Gage, I really think you're overreacting. Layla's strong. We can get her security if we need to. But I think she'll be fine. She can handle the attention."

"Emerson," he said quietly, "you really have no idea what you're talking about."

"Want to tell me?"

The question hung in the air. Layla's whole body shivered. She thought to barge in the boardroom but knew Gage would keep his mouth shut.

"Never," he answered. "I just can't deal with this—on top of trying to run the company."

"Then maybe you should consider one of the dozen offers you've had to sell it," Emerson said. "Can't run for office and run Southern Wings."

He shook his head and pulled at his hair. "This is just one big cluster fuck. Everything's out of control. Emerson, you're fired."

Layla gasped and burst inside, her eyes on fire, like a laser on Gage.

He opened his mouth to speak, but she raised her hand that he better not. She put an arm around Emerson. "Take it back and apologize."

"What? Were you listening out there?"

"Take it back and apologize."

"Her job is to control this stuff, and she didn't do her job."

"You're not being fair. You're not thinking clearly."

"I need someone who can handle these things, someone who's focused."

"Gage, I really don't like you right now. Don't you think she's been through enough?"

Emerson wiped a tear from her eyes. "It's fine, Layla." She started to leave, but a knock on the boardroom door kept her inside.

Mary peeked her head in. "Mr. Montgomery, I'm sorry to interrupt, but your mother is on the line. It's the fifth time she's called in the last 10 minutes."

Gage pinched the bridge of his nose, another emotional woman in the mix. "This can't be happening," he muttered a few times.

"I'm sure she's seen the paper or turned on the news," Emerson said.

"Would you like me to say something to her, or should I put her through to you?" Mary asked. "Otherwise, I believe she'll just keep calling."

Emerson looked at her brother, talking to himself, scrunching his face. "You know, Gage, I could handle Mom—that is, if I still worked here."

"What?" Mary cried. "What happened?"

"Gage just fired me," Emerson said.

"For what?" Mary asked, staring daggers at her boss. "What did you do?"

Gage shook his head. "No, no, no, it was just a misunderstanding. . . ." he said then stopped, surveying the three women before him. He couldn't bullshit his way out of this. He was no match for them. He'd been an asshole—he knew it—and lashed out. He loved his sister. The last thing he wanted to do was mess up her life even more. And the thought of calling his mother to explain the recent headlines and to say he'd just fired her daughter was too much to bear. "Call her."

Emerson adjusted her glasses. "I'll need an apology and some manners."

Gage rolled his eyes then looked at Layla, a tight-lipped grin on her face. "I'm sorry, Emerson, for what I said. Can you please handle Mom?"

"Sure," Emerson said.

"And thank you for bringing Layla here."

Emerson left with a spring in her step, giving Layla a wink along the way, with Mary following behind. Gage pulled Layla into a hug. "I'm sorry I lost my mind a little."

"*A little?*"

"OK, a lot. Everything's just happening too fast," he said and began to pace.

"What's going on? Who leaked this?"

"I'm trying to find out. These stories—as positive as they are now—are like a warning shot from them, that they'll one day use you to get to me."

"Who's *they?*"

"I'm going to find out."

"Aren't you being a little paranoid?"

"No. Where you're concerned, I can't be careful enough."

"Do you know anything?"

"I've made a few calls and am waiting to hear back. But my main focus has been you, getting you here, making sure you're OK." Gage sunk down in a chair.

Layla walked up behind him and massaged his shoulders. "I need to go back to Savannah tonight."

"No, not tonight. I need a few more days to. . . ."

"There's some stuff going on with Poppy."

"I need you to spend the week here."

"I can't. Poppy can't pay her share of the rent, and I can't cover the whole thing. It looks like we have to close Story Wings."

"I'll buy the building," Gage said.

"That's sweet, but no."

"I'll cover Poppy's share."

"It just won't be the same without her. We built that place together. I don't want to do it alone or with someone else."

Gage offered another option but treaded lightly. "I guess that frees you up to move to Atlanta. You could start a new career here."

"I don't know what I want to do. The store was always my dream."

"What's Poppy going to do?" he asked.

"She doesn't know. The money from selling will buy her a little time."

Gage nodded. "Give me tonight and tomorrow. I'll fly back with you tomorrow night." Layla stopped the massage, and he looked up at her behind him. "That's the best offer I got, Angel."

CHAPTER SEVENTEEN

LAYLA HAD NO idea what she was doing in Atlanta. She'd spent the entire afternoon trapped in Gage's office, worrying about the media down below and what they had in store for her. If she didn't get out soon, she'd have to steal one of Emerson's bottles of whiskey. She needed a distraction. Her mind raced about whether to move to Atlanta. Now that she'd have to sell her store, there was really no reason she couldn't. She hated to leave her little house in Savannah. She loved it there. She'd made her home there. But she knew it was time to make a new one with Gage.

She moved to his lap. "I've been thinking. With the store closing, I think it's best to move here with you. I don't want you commuting everyday."

"If that's what you want, then great. What about your house?"

"I guess I'll sell it."

"Are you sure? You love that house. You love Savannah."

"I'm sure."

He smiled and kissed her lips. "OK. Do you want to open a new store here? I can help you."

"I'm counting on being the First Lady of Georgia," she joked.

He laughed. "That could be good, or I could knock you up? Then you'd have a lot to do."

"We said we'd wait a little while," she said.

Mary came over the intercom. "Mr. Montgomery, everything has been arranged."

"Thank you," he said and looked at his watch.

"What's been *arranged*?" Layla asked.

"A surprise for you," Gage said.

"*For me?* Haven't we had enough surprises already today?"

"This is a good one," he said. "We just have to get out of the building."

MARY ARRANGED FOR a car to pick them up from the parking garage and slip out a secure side exit away from the throngs of media. She instructed the driver he wouldn't be taking Gage and Layla very far. But despite the careful planning, when the car came out, a few reporters signaled Gage and Layla were likely in it. Other reporters soon swarmed the car, all of them following closely behind, moving in and out of traffic, some on foot, others in vans, taking pictures, waving for the car to stop. The driver made the few blocks and pulled in front of Gage's sleek glass building.

"We're going to your place?" Layla asked.

"Not exactly," he said. "Now, when we get out, don't say a word. Just hold my hand. You'll remember it's just a few steps to the door. The doorman will be waiting for us. He knows we're coming. We'll get inside, and he'll keep these assholes out. OK?" The driver opened their door, and Gage and Layla got out amidst camera lights popping and reporters shouting questions.

"Will you wait and have the wedding in the Governor's Mansion?" one reporter asked.

"Are you two living together here, Mr. Montgomery?" another reporter wondered.

"Miss Tanner, Mr. Montgomery has made sexual abuse charities one of his top priorities. Will you continue that work during the campaign and as First Lady of Georgia?" another reporter asked, sticking the microphone in Layla's face.

Gage put his arm in front of Layla and forced the microphone back. "Hey, give my lady some space."

They reached the front entrance, and the doorman pulled them inside, locking the door, keeping the animals outside. "Is everything ready?" Gage asked him, as Layla headed towards the elevator.

"Yes, sir," the doorman said.

Gage captured her hand. "We aren't going up." He turned to the doorman. "We'll have complete privacy, right?"

"Yes, sir. No windows."

"Gage, why do we need privacy?" she asked.

He smiled. "You'll see."

"This way, ma'am." The doorman led them down a hallway.

"Gage, tell me what's going on," she said.

He shook his head and smiled. "It's more fun to keep you in the dark."

She smirked at him, whispering, "At least I'm not blindfolded this time, although that could be fun."

"It could be," he whispered back, "and we better find time soon, blindfolded or not!"

The doorman took them to a set of double doors. As he unlocked them, Gage lifted her hand to his lips, and her dimples popped out. The doors opened wide, and Layla's mouth hit the floor, looking into a conference room holding a sea of white gowns and bridesmaid dresses. The doorman closed the doors behind them and disappeared.

A bridal consultant dressed in black approached them. "Mr. Montgomery, we've been expecting you."

Gage nudged Layla forward, and the woman stuck out her hand. "I assume you're the bride, Miss Tanner."

"Layla," she said. "Gage, we're dress shopping? Now? After today?"

"I know it was on your 'to do' list."

"Only have a month, sweetie," the consultant said.

"Less than that," he said and kissed Layla on top of the head. "I'll pick you up in a few hours."

"Wait!" Layla cried. "You aren't staying?"

"I thought that was bad luck or something," he said.

"I don't care about that."

Gage cupped her cheeks. "Well, you don't need my opinion. You'll have plenty."

Another door opened, and Ava ran into Layla's arms. "Uncle G flew us in on the corporate jet!"

"*Us?*"

Emerson, Helen, and Poppy walked inside. Layla greeted them with tears flowing down her cheeks. She looked back at Gage. "With everything going on today, you arranged this? You had all these dresses sent here?"

He wiped her tears away. "I'm not going to let anything get in the way of us—our plans, our future."

Ava took her hand. "Aunt Layla, I found the most perfect brides-maid dress! It's strapless and flowing, and it comes in lavender. Mom said I could try it on if you liked it. Oh, I hope you like it, but if not, there's this other one that's a little short. Mom thinks it will be too tight, but I like it."

"Ava?" Emerson said, laughing. "Layla is here to look for dresses for her, not anyone else."

"Nonsense," Layla said. "Ava, show me your picks first."

GAGE HEADED TO the penthouse, needing some peace and quiet. And he wasn't about to ruin it by turning on the television or powering up his laptop. He didn't want to see himself or Layla or, worse, some asshole reporter speculating about them. He downed a glass of water then peered out a window at the media camped out in make-shift tents, waiting like vultures. He heard the scene was the same outside Story Wings in Savannah.

He cursed under his breath, drew the shades, and collapsed on the sofa. Since the sun rose, he'd flown back to Atlanta, saw their lives splashed on the front page, flown Layla to Atlanta, fired and re-hired his sister, and arranged for wedding dress shopping. It was actually Mary who arranged that, getting the finest boutique to deliver wedding dresses to his building in a matter of hours, and having his family fly out, too. He hoped it would take her mind off the media circus.

His phone buzzed in his pocket. He looked at the name and quickly answered. "What took you so long to call me back?"

"I was playing golf," Governor Clements said, his voice cheery. "And nothing interrupts that."

"Have you seen the papers today?"

"Yep, it's great! The State of Georgia is in love with you! Layla looks like the perfect Georgia peach, and you don't look too shabby yourself!"

"I don't care how we look! How did this happen? Who leaked that I was considering running?"

"Well, that's an easy one," he said, chuckling. "I did."

"What? Why'd you do that?"

"Because you're dragging your feet," Governor Clements said. "I thought you could use a little nudge in the right direction."

"It wasn't your job to do that!"

"Gage, I simply couldn't let that charity event go to waste. That's not the right word, of course. The event was great—everything about it—all the money that was raised, and everybody's heart in the right place. But it was a great opportunity—a great backdrop for a potential campaign!"

"What?" His godfather was like a father figure—good-intentioned but impossible.

"All the coverage is hearts and rainbows at this point," Governor Clements continued. "I made sure of that. The press loves the idea of a young couple in the mansion—a wedding, babies playing on the lawn. It all reminds them of JFK."

"JFK got shot!"

The old man laughed. "I'm sorry you're upset. You shouldn't be. I was just trying to help."

"You put Layla at risk!"

"Oh Gage, if that's true—and what I did was so bad—then I'm sure Layla has now told you she wants no part of this and has told you not to run."

Gage paused, the question hanging in the air. "No."

"Of course not. That's because Layla's a strong woman. I could tell from the moment I met her."

"You scared the shit out of her!"

"I didn't mean to. I'm sorry if I did. She's been through a lot—well, I don't know it for a fact, but I could sense it. We don't need to discuss it. We both know she'll be good for women, good for Georgia. And I trust you can keep her safe and protected throughout the whole process."

Gage shook his head. "How am I supposed to tell her you're the one that caused all this news coverage, that you're the reason all these assholes are camped outside my house? I mean, you are like family!"

"Simple," Governor Clements said. "Don't tell her."

Gage hung up, wishing Mary was around with some aspirin. It didn't seem right not to tell Layla. But the damage was done. And she was dealing with her own mess right now—closing the store, a wedding, a move to Atlanta, unwanted fame. He didn't want to add to all that. His job, like his godfather said, was to protect her and keep her safe. He called in a reinforcement.

"Have you seen the news?" he asked Dash.

"Nope. Recovering from a sex hangover."

"I heard you spent the weekend with Poppy."

"She's a little hottie."

"You going to see her again?" Gage asked.

"Do you think Layla's OK with that? I don't want trouble for you and your lady."

"Layla doesn't care. I need to know if you like Poppy enough to see her again."

"Yeah, I planned on taking her to dinner soon. What's going on?"

"I need you to do me a favor," Gage said. "I need to change your route."

GAGE DIDN'T SAY a word to the media for days and corralled his godfather to keep his mouth shut. He didn't want to add fuel to the fire. If they could just lay low and keep quiet, he figured the media storm about a third party run, and what impact "the handsome aviator with fresh ideas" might have in the Governor's Mansion, would run its course.

And he was right. The coverage slowly died down over a couple of news cycles. Sure, there was still the occasional poll showing he'd defeat any Republican or Democrat, and an occasional puff piece about his time at the Naval Academy and growing Southern Wings. There wasn't much else. It seemed they were in the clear.

But the coverage soon shifted to Layla—the children's bookstore owner who'd captured his heart. She was originally from Houston and now lived in Savannah. In her spare time, she was involved with Hope Cottage and made crosses that were auctioned off for charity. She was perfect for Gage, and no one had a bad word to say about her.

The media love affair didn't last long.

CHAPTER EIGHTEEN

IT STARTED INNOCENTLY enough, the press excited about a possible wedding in the Governor's Mansion. There were interviews with bridal consultants, fashion designers, caterers, and more to get perspective on planning such a huge event. Gage and Layla had a good laugh watching all the coverage. None of the idiots had any idea they were getting married in two weeks in his mother's backyard.

After the wedding speculation ran its course, some in the media thought Layla might be pregnant. There was no "baby bump," but a pregnancy could explain the quick engagement. The media was unsure how the public would take the news of a baby out of wedlock. It likely might have an impact on Gage's decision whether to run. He and Layla laughed at this story, too.

Then things turned dark. News broke that "Layla Tanner" wasn't her real name. That led to a series of news articles wondering why Layla would change her name, and hours of talk from so-called "experts" about why a person would ever do that. The reasons usually aren't good. There is usually some complication about the person. The person usually has something to hide, that she's running away from and wants to forget.

Today news broke that a "Layla Baxter" once lived in a homeless shelter in Annapolis. The media suggested it probably was the same woman since Gage was in college there at the same time. They wondered how he came to "associate" with her, and what a young girl with family in Houston was doing in a shelter. One possibility was that Layla, despite the sweet façade, was "troubled" and could be "difficult," so much so that she once ran away from home for a summer.

HIS BLOOD BOILING, Gage switched off the television in his office. A fury of pain was heading her way if he didn't do something quickly. "I'm sick of this shit," he barked. "I'm going to put a stop to it."

"How do you propose to do that?" Emerson asked.

"I'm going to tell them to stop."

"That won't work," she said. "That's a terrible idea."

"Have to say I agree with her," Governor Clements said. "You're too emotionally involved."

"You'll only make things worse," she said.

"Emerson, I'm not going to sit around and do nothing when they're attacking my future wife!"

"You're not going to help things, Gage."

"I want them to hear from me, Emerson!"

"The goal is to *help* things. You talking doesn't accomplish that."

"I don't see you helping things! I'm going to talk to them. You can't stop me. There's always one or two of them hanging around outside on the street like cockroaches."

Emerson shook her head and lowered her glasses. "Can I convince you not to do this?"

"No."

"Can I?" Governor Clements asked.

"No."

"OK," Emerson said. "Then let's draft a statement together— something we can control."

"I'm not reading a statement!"

"You don't have to read it," Governor Clements said. "It's just a few talking points. We just want you to be under control if you say something. It will only take one reporter making a snide comment, and you're liable to bash his head in. That wouldn't be good for you, the company, Layla. Your sister is right. Let us help put something together."

LAYLA WANTED TO be strong. She didn't want to be intimidated. She could bear a story every few days, but now the drips about her past were coming quicker—all the "questions" the media had, as if they had the right to ask them, and all the "answers" they wanted, as if they had a right to those, too. She wiped a few tears from her eyes.

Poppy walked in the break room. "You going to hide in here all day?"

"Are the reporters still outside the store?"

"Yeah, a handful. I just flipped them the bird when I put up the "Going Out of Business" sign."

"All the digging the press is doing—it's horrible," Layla said. "They make me seem terrible."

Dash stuck his head in. "Sorry to interrupt, but someone's here to see you, Layla."

"Move it!" Helen said, swatting Dash's shoulder. "Let me see my future daughter-in-law."

Layla smoothed her sundress as Helen shooed Poppy and Dash away. "I can't imagine what you must think of me."

"Honey, I know who you are," Helen said.

"I appreciate that," Layla said. "I wasn't expecting to see you."

"One of my own has been attacked!" Helen said. "Where the hell else would I be? Sorry for the language. I save my curses for extreme situations."

"Me, too."

"Well, let's hear it then."

"I'm not sure I should."

"Give me your best curse at those damn reporters!"

"There are a few children in the store."

"I'm sure it's nothing they haven't heard before. You hear the way my grandkids talk. Now, make me proud! Just don't use G.D. We are fine Southern women. We don't go there."

Layla took a deep breath and shook out her hands to prepare.

"Shit!" she said with a laugh.

"You can do better." Helen pulled out two mini bottles of scotch from her purse. "This might help. Emerson gets them for me from the planes."

Layla looked down at the bottle. "Damn, shit!"

"Come on!" Helen said, shooting back her bottle. "Those assholes invaded your privacy! Made up all kinds of shit! Let them have it!"

"Fucking bastards!" Layla screamed and took a sip, choking slightly.

Helen cheered. "Fucking cunt bastards!"

Layla took a big slug and channeled her inner Poppy. "Fucking cunt, son of a bitch, damn mother fucking bastards! And bitches, too!"

"Feel better, dear?"

"We should've done this days ago," Layla said.

"Gage asked me not to interfere," Helen said. "He didn't want your privacy invaded even more."

"Do you want Gage to run for governor?"

"My opinion doesn't mean squat anymore," Helen said. "What do you want, Layla? It's you they're ripping apart."

"I told Gage I don't want them to win. He needs to make the decision that's best for him."

Poppy rushed in. "Layla, turn on the TV!"

"What are they saying about me now?" Layla asked. Poppy reached for the remote and turned it on. "Oh my God! What's he doing?"

GAGE WALKED OUTSIDE the Southern Wings corporate office, and three reporters swooped down on him. For once, he stopped and let them gather around, even giving them a moment to set up their equipment. He rubbed the wings under his shirt and took a deep breath, reminding himself to stick to the talking points – without any cursing or potshots. When the reporters and cameramen were all set, Gage picked one of the cameras and looked straight into it.

"For the past week," he began, "the best person I know—the most important person in the world to me—has been the subject of relentless media coverage and rampant speculation. It's as if there is nothing else going on in Georgia—and the rest of the country—but her. Of course, I'm talking about Layla Tanner. She didn't ask me to speak here today. And she's probably mortified that I am. I just couldn't take it any longer."

Layla's hand flew to her chest, her heart melting. Gage was standing in front of the whole world defending her, loving her.

Helen placed a hand on Layla's shoulder. "I love my baby boy."

"The last thing Layla wants is attention," Gage said. "She hasn't asked for it. She doesn't deserve all the negativity. She's a sweetheart, a private person, a strong woman. She owns a children's bookstore in Savannah. She does charity work. And yes, at one point in her life, she changed her last name. To those in the media wondering why, and any folks at home who are curious, I want you to listen up—because I have an answer for you: *It's none of your damn business.*" Gage paused for a moment and let out a smile.

Watching on her office laptop, Emerson flashed a look to Governor Clements. "Thirty seconds in, and he's already gone off script." She wiped a little sweat from her forehead.

"Maybe," Governor Clements replied, "but his approval rating with women just shot up 50 points. He's a natural. I just wish he knew it."

"As for the other reports," Gage said, "they are packs of lies, distortions, and misinformation. I don't know where this trash is coming from, but this is exactly what's wrong with the media—and our politics today, for that matter. You can turn a person's private life upside down in a news cycle. Then after a little while, you reporters move on to another story, someone else, and poke around there for a bit. And you move on again. One thing you never do is look back at the dust in your wake, the mess you made."

"I love how he's shaming these parasites," Helen said.

"Layla, I'm in love with your man," Poppy said.

"I love him more," Layla said dreamily. *He'll protect me no matter what, no matter the cost.*

"Go ahead and talk about me and my company all you want," Gage said. "But I'd ask that you stop with Layla. I don't expect you'll be hearing from her on any of the issues you think are newsworthy. As far as I'm concerned, you folks in the media are not worth her time. She doesn't owe you anything. And anyone watching at home who has questions about Layla, she doesn't owe you anything, either. She has better things to do. And you can save your breath because I'm not going to take any questions. I've said enough." He turned and walked back inside Southern Wings.

Emerson let out a deep breath. "A bit of a harsh ending, but at least he kept his cool."

"I think he did great," Governor Clements said. "But let's hope she's not more of a target now."

LAYLA'S PHONE RANG 30 seconds later. "I saw it."

"I probably should've warned. . . ."

Poppy ripped the phone from Layla's hand. "Should've told them to fuck themselves! Without lube!"

Gage chuckled. "Poppy, put Layla back on the phone."

"OK, but I wanted to tell you I loved it," Poppy said.

"I loved it, too!" Helen screamed.

"*Mom?* Hello?"

Layla laughed. "I've got two crazy women with me."

"Was that my mom?"

"Yeah, she came over to teach me how to curse." Layla smiled as Helen and Poppy walked out. "They just left."

"My mom came to teach you how to curse?"

"Yeah, and how to drink whiskey," Layla said. "I love her."

"I guess you handled the latest stories better than I did."

"I'm trying." She tucked her knees under her. "Gage, I can't believe what you did. I didn't think it was possible to love you more, but then you go and do something like that."

"Angel," he said softly, "I told you I'd protect you—or at least try to."

"It meant so much to me."

"Let's just hope it worked. If I don't run, this will all go away."

"I've told you before—you need to make this decision because of what *you* want. I can handle this, especially after what I saw you do today. I just don't understand why they're so fascinated with me, why they won't stop digging around."

"We need to have some fun and not think about this for a little while."

"Poppy's been bothering me to hang out with her and Dash."

"Good, invite them over. I'll fly in this afternoon."

"I love you, Gage."

"I love you, too," he said. "One more thing—I want to hear you curse. I usually only hear it when you're mad at me."

She smiled into the phone. "Fuck."

GAGE LOWERED THE top of the grill, and Layla flashed him a smile. She looked great holding a glass of sweet tea, in tight cut-off jeans and a white cami with just a hint of lace at the top. Her hair was pulled up in a high ponytail—very simple, very sexy. He set the glass on a little picnic table and pulled her hips to his, gripped her ass, forcing her to hike up her leg. He pulled a cube of ice from the glass and gently placed it on her neck, slowly gliding it across her skin and trailing kisses behind the ice.

"Gage," Layla said, pushing away slightly. "There could be reporters lurking around."

Gage stopped for a moment and cocked a half-smile. "Let 'em watch." He slid the ice in his mouth, seeing her eyes darken with desire, her breath heavy. He cupped a breast and pushed it out of her cami. He ran his cold tongue over her nipple, licking it, circling it. Layla tossed her head back and released a little moan as he lowered her onto the picnic table and pushed himself against her. He reached for the button and zipper on her shorts then slid them down to her ankles. He ran his fingertips under her white lace panties, planting a kiss between her legs. "God, I love how wet and ready you get for me."

Layla reached for his shorts and stroked him gently. "I love how hard you get for me." Pippa began to bark and claw at the back gate. "Poppy and Dash?" She pulled up her shorts.

"Shit! They're early!" Gage adjusted Layla's shirt and hustled over to the grill.

"I've got margaritas!" Poppy yelled, coming through the gate.

Layla checked herself one more time. "Great!" she called out, turning to greet their guests.

"I've got beer!" Dash said. "Gage, you cooking? She's got you on husband duty already?"

"Shut up and toss me a beer."

"Gage, you leave Dash alone," Layla said. "I'm glad you changed his route. He's been so helpful at the store—carries stuff, gets us lunch everyday, pushes back reporters." Dash and Gage locked eyes for a moment.

"Don't forget he keeps me flexible," Poppy added.

"Thanks for that, Poppy," Layla said. "Let's go in and get some margarita glasses."

POPPY BEGAN RIFLING through cabinets in search of glasses. "It's the next one over," Layla said, watching Gage through the kitchen window.

"He's totally husband-cute."

"I know," Layla said with a little giggle. "Less than two weeks."

"The wedding's coming so fast."

"I can't believe it," Layla said and poured them each a drink.

"So much still to do to get ready. Emerson's been great to work with," Poppy said. "And Gage is such a good guy. It was so nice he changed Dash's route so he could spend more time with me. Dash likes doing just the Savannah-Atlanta route."

"Too bad he's always here during the day. I wonder why Gage didn't make it so he's here overnight?" Layla nudged Poppy in the side. "I'm sure you'd rather have him here at night."

"We're managing," Poppy said. "The timing's been good, too, hav-

196 | PRESCOTT LANE

ing a strong guy around to help pack up around the store."

"Maybe Dash is husband material, too?"

Poppy shrugged. "He's a stud, but it's early yet."

"Pop, not every guy is a jerk."

"I'm just saying it's too early to tell if he has 'hot guy syndrome.' You know, they're all sweet and helpful in the beginning then suddenly they turn into total fucktards." They walked back outside, drinks in hand. "You just wait a few weeks, and then Mr. Husband of the Year over there will royally screw up something."

Gage looked up from the grill. "Thanks for the vote of confidence."

Poppy smiled. "You know I love you."

"Hey, Poppy, where's my love?" Dash asked.

"She's trying to decide if you're going to turn into a fucktard," Layla said.

Gage pulled Layla to him and slid a hand in her back pocket. "I love it when you say 'fuck,'" he whispered. She rested her red face on his chest, her dimples in full bloom.

"Well," Dash said, "I'm trying to decide if I'm just a chocolate novelty."

"Poppy's taste in men is as colorful as her hair," Layla said. "Black, white, Asian, Native American, Latino. And wasn't there an Eskimo in there somewhere?"

"I never did an Eskimo!" Poppy said. "Besides, we all can't marry the guy we gave our v-card to."

"Poppy!" Layla cried.

"What? Did I go too far?" Poppy took a drink. "Fine, Layla, you can say something about me that's a secret."

Layla bit her lip and walked a little circle around Poppy. There were so many things to choose from. She stopped in front of her friend and flashed a satisfied look. "She's a beauty queen."

"You bitch!" Poppy barked.

"A beauty queen?" Dash wondered. "I mean, you're hot enough, but. . . ."

"She was in the Miss Georgia Pageant," Layla said.

"What color was your hair, Poppy?" Gage asked.

"Shut the hell up!" Poppy said. "My mother was a Miss Georgia. She had me in pageants before I could walk."

"Did you win?" Gage asked.

Poppy shook her head. "I screwed a judge and got kicked out."

"I don't believe that," Dash said. "I've screwed you, and you would've won for sure."

"OK, OK, I'll tell you what really happened," Poppy said. "I got fat."

"You weren't fat," Layla said.

Dash took Poppy in his arms. "I like women with a little size. I bet you were a cute little plumper."

"I was," Poppy said. "I thought fat sex would be gross, but sex is sex. It didn't really matter. I was *awesome* no matter what."

"Wait! I'm confused," Gage said. "You're so thin now, Poppy. Why'd you gain the weight?" Layla threw Gage a nasty look. "What? She can talk about our virginity, but I can't ask about a few extra pounds?"

"Dude, don't you know shit?" Dash asked. "You never ask about a girl's weight."

"It's OK," Poppy said, laughing. "I had a bad breakup around the time of the Miss Georgia Pageant and ate my way out of it."

"I gained five sympathy pounds with her," Layla said.

"Layla's a good friend," Poppy said. "She kneed the bastard in the balls—and told everyone in his frat he had a needle dick."

"He deserved it," Layla said.

"Dash, I guess you better treat Poppy right," Gage said, "or Layla will be coming for you."

"What did he do?" Dash asked. "I don't want to make the same mistake."

"You tell him, Layla," Poppy said. "I'm going to refill my drink."

Layla waited until Poppy went inside. "They'd been dating for six months or so, and Poppy told him that she loved him. It was the first and only time she's ever said that to a guy. And you know what he said back? He told her he loved *fucking* her, but not her."

"Asshole," Dash said.

"She dyed her long blonde hair red the next day and chopped it all off." Layla turned to Dash. "So don't play with her. She acts all casual and whatever about guys, but it's all an act. I'm not saying you have to be in love or anything, but you better be honest. If it's just sex, she can handle that as long as she knows from the start. Just don't act like it's something that it's not."

GAGE WIPED DOWN the grill while Layla went in to get ready for bed. He felt good about how the day turned out. And he felt good about how he handled the media. He dreaded going back to the office in the morning. There'd be reporters all over the place. And there'd be piles of work to go through. He'd been so distracted lately. His in-box was the size of a small child, and his list of unread emails spanned a football field. The thought of digging through it all sucked.

He finished outside then turned on the flatscreen above her mantle. They were rerunning his press conference, with a photo of Layla on the side of the screen, and the headline *Continuing Coverage* splashed across the bottom. *Obviously they didn't listen.* But he had no illusions they would. He wondered if this was more than just the press digging around, if there was something else going on. Perhaps someone was trying to convince him not to run.

His cell phone rang. "You did a good job this morning," the former governor of Georgia said, "but you know they're not going to stop."

Gage shut off the television. "I know. What's going on?"

"I've been doing a little digging. Probably overstepped my role as godfather, political consultant, or whatever I am. But I needed to know exactly what we're up against, so I can protect you and deal with it."

"*And?*"

"How much do you know about Layla?"

"Everything."

"I can't imagine that's true," Governor Clements said then launched into Layla's entire life from birth to present, everything from her grammar school grades to tax returns she filed five years ago. He moved to the details of her abuse and time on the street.

"I know all this!"

"You know she was hospitalized for depression in Texas? On suicide watch? Considered a danger to herself and others?"

"Yes, but how the hell did you find out about that? Those are private medical records!"

"Got in touch with a few friends of friends. Some folks owed me a few favors. Not hard when you've been around as long as I have and know the right people."

"I can't have the press getting their hands on that stuff!"

"Of course not. I'll work on burying the records. But this other issue may be a little tricky. Did you know she stabbed someone?"

"Jesus Christ! She was attacked!"

"The press, other candidates, could speculate it was a trick gone bad."

"That is insane! I can't have all this come out. Pull the plug on this political shit!"

"Son. . . ."

"No, I won't do it. I won't run."

"Son, just listen. Every candidate has secrets. Their families do, too. I think I can help. But I needed to make sure you knew everything first."

"What are you talking about? How can you help?"

"It's probably better if you don't know the details."

"I don't know about any of this anymore. Maybe it's not the right time. I think it's best. . . ."

"You're running, Son. Don't let the good people of Georgia down. Hell, don't let your father down." His godfather exhaled. "Look, just give me some time. Let me see if I can figure out who's leaking things. Pay them off if I have to. Get some records buried."

"You think these stories are being *leaked*? I thought this was just the press digging around, that this was politics as usual."

"No, it's more than that. This is a smear campaign against you and Layla."

"Why? Who's doing this?"

"I'm trying to find out. No one's giving me names."

"What's your best guess?" Gage asked.

"Who's Layla close to? It's somebody she's close to."

"Not her family. That removes them."

"Friends?" Governor Clements asked.

"Poppy. But she wouldn't do this."

"Doctors?"

"From a decade ago? I doubt it, but I don't know."

"Ex-boyfriends?"

"Layla hasn't mentioned any." Gage pinched the bridge of his nose. "Look, please just figure it out. Protecting her is the most important thing."

"I'm surprised you don't have a guard on her."

"I've got it handled."

"Good. I think you can protect her *and* run for office. Just leave this to me. Enjoy your wedding, your bride, your honeymoon. Give me that long."

Gage exhaled. "OK, but you've got to keep me in the loop. Don't go behind my back again."

He hung up and walked to her kitchen window, looking out at the stars. He searched around, finding the right one, the one she showed him on the beach 12 years ago. *The Angel Layla star.* He'd looked at it so many times over the years, missing her, wishing for one more second, one more kiss.

Now he needed to be close to her, to hold her. He'd promised to protect her. He had to trust his godfather could make everything disappear. And he wasn't about to go to tell Layla what the old man found out—and how easy it was. He was a little afraid if she knew, she'd run away again. She'd done it before. He couldn't let it happen again.

GAGE STOOD IN the doorway and watched her sleep, all curled up in white sheets. She looked like an angel, peaceful, sweet, beautiful. He slipped off his clothes and nudged Pippa to the foot of the bed.

The soft warmth of her body greeted him. He brushed a strand of hair from her face and breathed in her lavender scent. She gently rolled over, and her blue eyes fluttered open. "Sorry I woke you," he said before her lips fell to his mouth.

He wound her hair in his hand and pulled her deeper into their kiss, their tongues slowly massaging. He slipped the covers away, and she sat up slightly. She pulled her t-shirt over her head, locked eyes with him, and slipped off her panties.

He grew hard at the sight of her simple beauty, her sexiness, all laid out for him. He hadn't seen her this way in 12 years. He slid his fingers along her curves and cut a path down her smooth, milky flesh, tracing her breasts and down her flat stomach, grazing her inner thighs.

She reached for the old leather rope around his neck and pulled him to her lips, circling her tongue with his, melting into him, a deep ache building between her legs. Then she wrapped her body around his.

He ran his fingers down her spine and kissed his way to her neck, gently caressing her nipple. "I missed every inch of you," he said, sucking and nibbling, slipping a finger inside. Layla moaned, and he let out a sexy chuckle. "You missed me, too." She dug her fingers into his shoulders and pulled him tighter.

Gage took her breasts in his hands and slid down her body, feeling her shiver beneath his tongue. Her legs dropped open, welcoming him, and his warm breath came over her. He outlined her folds with his tongue, and she melted into his mouth. "I could stay here all night."

"More," she begged.

He loved hearing that, as much as he loved tasting her, watching her, stroking her. He grabbed her ass and pushed her tighter against his mouth, sucking her hard, his tongue slipping in and out of her.

Her muscles clenched, begging for more. "Don't stop."

He watched her arch her back. It was better than going Mach speed in a fighter jet. She was so raw, so free, and all for him. Her body started to quiver, and he could tell she was almost there. He slid a hand to her breast.

She tightened her legs and gripped his hair. "Gage!"

He brought her down slowly, enjoying the last of her tremors, planting light kisses between her legs. Her body quivered, coming alive again. He knew she wasn't done, that she was building back up. He slid up her body and stared deeply in her eyes. She flashed him a sexy smile and widened her legs.

"I'll be here in the morning," she said and slid off his boxers.

"You better be," he said and slipped himself inside.

She suddenly stopped. "Condom?"

"No," he groaned, thrusting slowly in and out of her.

"You don't have a condom?"

"Like this," he said. "Just like this, like our first time." He brushed his fingers on her cheek, and their eyes locked on each other. "Just this once." Their bodies began to move together, remembering each other. He rolled his hips into her, and she pressed hers against him.

He pulled out slightly then firmly pushed back in. He did it again, totally filling her. He lifted her leg to his hip and gripped her ass, going deeper inside. They settled into a delicious rocking motion, slow but hard. "You like that?"

"Mmm," she moaned sweetly.

As much as he wanted to speed up, he held back and watched Layla build beneath him. "Angel," he whispered, "I love you."

"I love you, too," she said, holding his face in her hands. He hit just the right spot, and her mouth dropped open, her breasts rising and falling.

"Tell me you're mine," he said.

"I'm yours," she said, going crazy from his dirty talk, his dick slipping in and out of her, his breath warm on her neck. She arched her back and tossed her hands in his hair. She moved them wildly, struggling for something to grip.

This was intense, raw heat like nothing she'd experienced before, and far different than their first time, both of them full of nerves back then. The man had learned a thing or two since he was 18. She rolled her hips and thrust hard against him.

"Finish with me," he groaned. "I need you to finish with me."

She moved her hips quickly, wanting to do as he said, desperate to come again. She slid her nails down his back and grabbed his ass as she pushed against him. Her body began to shake. "Oh my God!" Then Gage let himself go.

Breathless, he held her to his chest and brushed a strand of chocolate hair behind her ear. "God, you are so damn good. Exactly how I remember."

Layla sat up and straddled him. "Tell me you're mine."

Gage looked up at her naked body, a halo of moonlight around her. "You own me, Angel."

THE STAYED TANGLED up all night, barely sleeping. When the morning came, she flashed a coy smile. "You're still here?"

"You, too?" He ran a hand down the curve of her hips. "Couldn't think of a more beautiful way to start my day."

She stretched out her naked body. "We finally got it right."

"I don't want to leave you. I want to stay in bed all day."

"Then stay," Layla said, hooking a leg around his hip.

"I can't. I have lots to do still back at the office—still playing catch-up. And I need to get things in good shape before the honeymoon."

"Speaking of, where are we going?"

"You'll find out soon enough."

"Can I get a hint?"

"No."

"How long will we be gone?"

"A month."

Her eyes popped. "A *month*?"

"Is there a problem with that?"

"No. I mean, I've just never heard of a honeymoon lasting a month!"

"We're doing things a little different. Our whole relationship has been a little different, hasn't it?"

"I guess it has."

"And I want you to myself for a little while."

"I'd like that. No reporters, no newspapers," she said. "Have you decided anything?"

He swallowed hard, the things Governor Clements found out swimming in his mind. "Do you think I should run?"

"It's not up to me," she said. "If you think you can help people, maybe you should?"

"I'm not sure it's worth it."

"So is that a *no*?"

"Not yet. I just hate what they're doing to you. Hopefully it dies down soon."

"It's hard," she said. "But I'm not going to let them control my life. They can dig around if they want, but they're not going to control me. I've never let anyone control my life—despite everything I've been through." Layla sat up and kissed him gently. "How about I fly back with you this morning? I could use a day off. I've got everyone working, and Dash will be there helping Poppy, so I can play hooky."

"I don't know if I'll be able to sneak away. I'm pretty busy today."

"Hire me for the day!"

"For what position?"

"I'm flexible for *all* positions."

"Can I have my way with you in-between meetings?"

"What about during them? I'll wear a dress for easy access."

"You're hired."

CHAPTER NINETEEN

THE WEDDING WAS a week away. But Layla had another event to deal with—some business-political alliance reception that Gage was going to. Reporters would be there. Cameras would be there. It was like going into the lion's den. She didn't want to go. But it'd raise questions if she didn't. It might even be "breaking news." So she decided it was best to show up. After all, the reception was in a nice place—a historic mansion in the Low Country nestled around a salt marsh and towering oak trees, complete with stables and a riding corral.

Gage stopped on a path to the mansion and pulled her into a little kiss. "Mostly a bunch of snobs and assholes here, but I promise everything will be fine."

"Do I look OK?" Layla asked, smoothing the bottom of her blue and white sundress.

"It depends. Do you have on panties?"

"Of course."

"Well, if I run and get elected, I'm going to write something in the Constitution about going commando. It should be a state holiday."

He took her hand and led her inside. He seemed to know every-one—federal and state politicians, executives across every industry. This was the elite of the elite, standing in little circles with glasses of wine, congratulating each other.

Layla didn't know a soul. She tried to make small talk but didn't have much to say about the rising cost of jet fuel and the latest economic regulations. And she sensed everyone was sizing her up, judging her, probably waiting for the next shoe to drop on the evening news.

When a sleek political type suggested a walk to the stables, she saw her exit. She planted a kiss on Gage's cheek and excused herself to get a drink. She found a bar down by the water in the backyard.

"What can I get for you?" a familiar voice asked.

Layla smiled. "You're the bartender?"

"They don't put in enough whiskey, so I make my own." Governor Clements tossed a piece of ice in his glass, and Layla got some sweet tea. "Have you been down to the water yet?" Layla shook her head. "Let me show you." She took her glass and followed along a wooden deck to a porch swing hanging from an oak tree. "I'm sorry about what the press is doing. I told you to expect it, though."

"They seem to know everything about me," she said and sat down.

Governor Clements knew that wasn't true—so did Layla—but he wasn't about to say so. "You have my sympathy."

"Thanks, but that's not necessary."

"So true. You're a strong independent woman. Gage tells me how hard you worked in college, building the store, all the volunteer work. Your work with Hope Cottage is inspiring. You're good for Gage."

"I feel like this is leading somewhere."

Governor Clements laughed. "You're reading *me* now? Well, you're absolutely right. I'm leading somewhere. I usually do have a purpose when I talk. The fact of the matter is, Layla, Georgia needs Gage to run."

"I haven't told him not to."

"I'm hoping you can do more than that. I want you to convince him *to* run because he's wavering."

"Because he thinks I can't handle the coverage?"

He shook his head. "He's wavering because he thinks *he* won't be able to handle it if the coverage gets any worse."

"You think it might get *worse?*"

"Anything's possible." He took a drink. "I mean, you and I talked some before. There's more that could come out, isn't there?"

Layla wasn't in the mood to play games. "It seems we both know there is. Just be honest with me."

"Since we're being honest, it's probably best you talk to Gage about this."

Her heart pounded. "You talked to Gage about this?"

"Yes, and you should, too," he said. "And when you do, convince him he can handle whatever may come." Governor Clements patted her shoulder before walking off. "I know you'll be a good politician's wife."

Her hands shaking, Layla gripped her glass like her life depended on it and set off towards the stables, a strong smell of horse manure leading the way. It seemed fitting. She made her way past a collection of flies and found Gage at the far end standing next to a man and a horse. She could tell Gage didn't care about what the man was saying. He was just smiling and playing along. Gage would be a great politician. He flashed her a smile that she didn't return. He waved her to come over, but she shook her head. There was horse manure lining the path. She was going through enough shit. She wasn't going to walk through more. *He can walk back through the crap to me.*

Gage excused himself and made his way to her. "You need more sunscreen. I don't want you to burn."

"Maybe your godfather can get it for me," she said. "We just had a very interesting talk. I always learn a lot from our little chats. Stuff you don't see fit to tell me. You've been talking to him about me behind my back."

"Yeah, I talked to him about the press conference. Is that OK?"

"You've talked to him *way more* than that," she snapped. "What exactly does he know about me? Did you tell him things about me?"

"Of course not. Now's not the place for this, Layla. At least give me the chance to explain before you get so worked up."

"*Worked up?* I'm not worked up. I'm down right ticked off!" Gage moved to speak, but she held up a finger. "Why didn't you tell me?"

"I didn't see the point. He's trying to help keep things hidden, buried."

"Right. He's been such a great help so far."

"Oh, come on!" Gage said, his Southern accent dripping.

She looked away. "I'm ready to leave."

LAYLA STARTED BACK up before the limo made it out of the driveway. "I hate secrets. I lived with one for too long. They destroy. You can't keep secrets from me."

"I don't keep secrets from you," Gage said. "But I'm not going to burden you with details about my work, my career, or. . . ."

"You aren't single anymore. We're getting married next weekend. I'm not asking for secret Navy codes or the hidden agenda of the FAA. This affects me, too. This is about me. This has everything to do with me."

"I'm just trying to protect you. Please trust me to handle it."

"That's not good enough. Why are you keeping things from me? You think I'll run?"

"No. . . ." Gage stopped himself. "Well, it's crossed my mind."

She looked in his eyes. *Finally an honest answer.* "You know what makes me want to run? Secrets. They scare me more than the press ever could."

He looked away. "My godfather leaked that first story about our engagement and me thinking about running for governor."

"Why would he do that?"

"He knew it would create a buzz. He controlled the stories so they were romantic. He knew it would up public opinion and hoped it would give me a little push to run. He's a manipulative old goat."

"And now he's digging into my past?"

Gage nodded. "I'm sorry he's doing that."

"Don't apologize for *him.*"

"I'm sorry I didn't tell you. I'm sorry all this impacts you. It burns me up."

"That's better."

"It's just that he found out everything so easily, Angel. It scares me. He's trying to bury things. It won't take long for the press, opponents, to find out everything. I hate I can't totally protect you."

"If the press digs up more things," she said, "I can handle it."

He felt her tremble a little. "I don't know what to do. There's so much pressure from all sides. I can't seem to figure out what the right decision is."

"Maybe you should fly on it?"

Gage chuckled. "Don't you mean pray on it?"

"Same thing for you."

OVER THE NEXT few days, the reports came hard and fast. There was new information about Layla's whereabouts the summer she ran away. It was 12 years ago. She went to her grandmother's house on St. Simons Island. Shockingly, Gage was there, too. His family spent time on the island every summer.

He and Layla hung out together. The exact details of the relationship were not fully known, though the press was working hard to figure it all out, to find anyone who may remember them from that summer. But it was a long time ago, and no one seemed to remember anything about two teenagers.

There were many questions that needed answers: whether Gage knew Layla was a runaway that summer, and what made Layla end up in a homeless shelter in Maryland after leaving the island. One theory was that Gage got her pregnant. Layla couldn't tell her parents—she'd already run from them—so she followed Gage to Maryland.

As a college student with no money, he couldn't afford to care for her. So she stayed in a shelter. He should've done more for her. She probably got a back-alley abortion. There were reports she checked into a Maryland hospital, probably to clean up the mess. Or maybe she gave up the child for adoption. Gage probably covered it up. None of this was good for a future politician.

Gage and Layla could only watch it all unfold. "None of this is true," she said.

"They do it for ratings, to make money," he said. "It doesn't matter if it's true."

"But where do they come up with this stuff? I mean, there are no sources for anything they say."

We need to figure out who's doing this. "They just spin things out and splash it on TV, newspapers, magazines."

"This is so ridiculous, shameful. Should we issue a denial? I don't want people to think I had an abortion or had a child, or that you were kind enough to let me stay at a homeless shelter in Annapolis."

"I'll have Emerson handle all that," he said. "Maybe we should sue?"

"And then they'd take my deposition—force me to talk about my past under oath. Nope."

"Should I make another statement, tell them to stop?"

"The first one didn't matter—but I loved it. Maybe I should talk to the press? Release a statement? Emerson could help me. I wouldn't have to say anything specific. I could keep things vague."

"They won't be satisfied with that."

"Well, I guess your godfather needs to step up whatever he's trying to do."

CHAPTER TWENTY

WITH THE NEWS swirling and the bookstore closing tomorrow, it was a good time for an impromptu bachelorette party. Poppy had several ideas. She offered to round up some really good male strippers—the kind that do "nasty things." Emerson was intrigued, but Layla nixed the idea. Poppy also suggested they fly out to Las Vegas on the corporate jet, but Emerson nixed that one, and Layla wasn't too keen on flying across the country.

So they settled for after-hours cocktails and girl talk in the Story Wings cafe. And it wasn't long until they were on their third bottle of wine.

"Dash and I have crossed several things off my sex bucket list," Poppy said.

"A sex bucket list?" Emerson asked.

"Yeah, every girl has one," Poppy said.

"I must have lost my list somewhere between Ava and Connor," Emerson said, pouring herself another glass. "Layla, don't tell me you have a sex list for my baby brother." Layla locked up her mouth with her hand.

"Oh, she's got a list," Poppy said. "She just doesn't share. I bet there's lots of role playing, Gage playing the politician, and Layla the naughty little mistress."

"I cannot hear this!" Emerson said and threw her hands over her ears.

Dash popped in, and the ladies clammed up. "We're closed! What are you doing here?" Poppy cried. "Get out! We're having girl talk!"

"I can do girl talk," Dash said. "Besides, it's one of the few nights I haven't had to fly back to Atlanta."

"I don't care," Poppy said, marching him out. "It's one of Layla's last nights before she becomes Gage's old lady. I'll see you later." She locked the door.

"I see Dash more than I see Gage," Layla said. "He's always hanging around here."

"It's because I'm good in bed," Poppy said. "Emerson, I think you need to start a sex bucket list. I think you have a case of mono-penis. You've been with the same one too long."

"Filter," Layla said, as Poppy handed Emerson a pen and paper.

"You want me to write it down?" Emerson downed her wine. "I'm not sure where to start."

Poppy pulled out her phone. "I've got 50 things on my list and only about a dozen left to go." She began to scroll through. "How about sex in a public place? That's a good one."

Emerson adjusted her glasses. "It's been a while but done that."

"How about sex in a car?"

"Done it."

"Sex in a plane?"

"Done it."

Poppy clapped her hands. "Good for you! You're kinkier than I thought. Give a rim job?"

"Oh, Poppy!" Layla cried. "Please tell me you haven't done that!"

"I don't even know what that is," Emerson said.

"If you have to ask," Layla said, "then it shouldn't be on your list."

"Prude," Poppy said. "How about rough sex? Like getting a spanking or using a whip."

"Who am I supposed to do that with?" Emerson wondered.

"Look, Emerson, you're still hot," Poppy said. "There's something kinky about those glasses you wear. Just find a hot guy. Let him tie you up. And then let him bend you over the kitchen sink."

Emerson wrinkled her nose. "I'd have to suck in my stomach for that."

"You're in better shape than I am," Poppy said.

"Standing upright everything looks like it's supposed to," Emerson said. "But when you get to 40, you don't want to tempt gravity. Trust me on this one."

Poppy frowned. "I really think you'd feel better if you just found some young stud to ride you hard."

"Emerson, you don't have to listen to Poppy," Layla said. "She once handed a complete stranger her panties at a bar."

"That was number 10 on my list," Poppy said. "And then I had bar bathroom sex with him. That took care of number 39."

"Don't brag," Emerson said. "I can't even remember the last time."

"You poor thing," Poppy said. "You need B.O.B. Battery-operated boyfriend."

"I've got that!" Emerson said. "These days I'm replacing my batteries all the time!" The ladies busted into a huge laugh before Emerson turned serious, leaning in and motioning for Layla and Poppy to do the same. This information was top secret. "I need you two to promise me something."

"Anything for you, bitch," Poppy slurred.

"One of the biggest fears I have is that I will die suddenly and my mother will come to pack up my things and find my B.O.B." Emerson grabbed their hands like they were swearing their lives to each other. "So promise me if I die, you will come get him and dispose of him before my mother finds him."

"Promise," Layla said.

"Me, too," Poppy said. "You both have to do the same for me."

"We'll need several large trash sacks," Layla said.

"Seriously though, Emerson, you need to get back out there," Poppy said. "I've got an idea! We should go out dancing. It will be so much fun—Layla's last night out as a single gal. And Emerson, it will be good for you to dust the cobwebs off your vagina."

Layla pulled out her phone and sent a text to Gage. *Going out with the girls. CU later. Love.*

IT WAS AFTER 10 at night when Gage landed in Savannah. He walked outside the airport and powered on his phone. Layla's text popped up, and his heart rate jumped. Sure, it was nice she was hanging out with friends, but unless Dash was keeping an eye on her, they were out alone, unprotected, where any crazy or reporter could ambush her. *Someone's leaking things to hurt her. Or me? Who?* He thought to call or text her but didn't want to interrupt her night or sound possessive. He fired off a text to Dash: "Where is she?"

He thought about who could be leaking things. His godfather said it was someone close to Layla. She never mentioned any bitter employees or bad break-ups. And if it was someone close to her, that would rule out any business rival from a competing airline or a disgruntled Southern Wings employee. And that would rule out a potential political opponent, or even a bitter ex-girlfriend pissed he's finally marrying when he wouldn't before. None of them made sense.

He hopped in a cab, and the driver asked where he was heading. He stared at his phone, willing a reply. Finally an address came, and Gage relayed it to the driver. The place wasn't far. Gage texted back: "Are you with her?" Dash said he was "close by." Gage groaned, his fingers flying: "Dumb As Shit." Dash fired back a smiley face and assured him Layla was "fine." Gage looked up from his phone, still worried. He saw a tiny stuffed animal dangling from the driver's rearview mirror.

His heart stopped. He wasn't sure why he didn't think of it before. His godfather was looking in the wrong place. It wasn't a person Layla was close to. It was the exact opposite. *The one person who knew the terrible things in her past. The person who did them to her.* And now her half-brother was making her life worse, probably pissed his stepfather turned on him, pissed he didn't inherit anything, now leaking things to settle the score. The guy may even be stalking Layla. Gage wondered if he'd been in Atlanta—or maybe he was in Savannah now. *He's a dead man.*

Gage couldn't bear if anything happened to her. It would be his fault. His indecision put her at risk. It kept the coverage alive, allowing her half-brother to do his work. He hated being so indecisive. He took a few deep breaths. Dash said Layla was "fine." And they'd soon be on their honeymoon. Layla would be out of harm's way then. His godfather could use the time to have his people find her half-brother—

maybe put the guy on a private plane and crash it. *If the wedding wasn't in three days, I'd kill him myself.* It would be nice to hear during the honeymoon that he was dead. That would be a perfect wedding present.

The driver pulled to the curb, and Gage handed him a wad of cash. He jumped out and saw Dash leaning against a light post in front of a dance club. "What are you doing?"

"I've got it under control," Dash said.

"She's inside?"

"Yeah. They're dancing. It's been quiet. No reporters. No creeps."

"How do you know if you're not in there?" Gage barged inside, with Dash following behind. He scanned the crowd for Layla. She was dancing with Emerson and Poppy, a group of men gyrating all around them. Gage winced and cursed under his breath. He took some comfort that Layla wasn't doing what Poppy was, grinding her ass against some buff guy in a muscle shirt.

"I'm taking that asshole down," Dash said.

"Let me go in first," Gage said. "We shouldn't ambush them together."

Gage crossed the club, and the crowd parted for him. He pulled Layla into his arms, her body like a wet noodle. "Are you drunk?"

"No, just tipsy," she said. "But Emerson and Poppy are."

Gage gently pulled Emerson away. "For God's sake, you're a mother of three. Let's go."

"I can't!" Emerson said. "I haven't twerked yet!

"*What?*"

"It's on my sex bucket list!"

"Gage, don't be a party-pooper," Poppy said, laughing at her choice of words.

Gage looked around the club. There didn't seem to be any reporters around. Nobody had a camera or video. He didn't see Layla's half-brother. "OK, Emerson, do it quickly."

"Thank you, baby brother." Emerson got into a low squatting stance and dropped her hands to the floor. Then she began to thrust her hips rapidly, flapping her ass up and down, her glasses nearly flying off her face.

"You go, girl!" Poppy cried.

Dash lifted Poppy in his arms. "Come on, I'm getting you out of here."

Poppy kicked her arms and legs, demanding to be put down. The muscle shirt guy stepped up. "That's not how you treat a woman."

Dash put her down. "Neither is rubbing your cock against my lady on the dance floor."

"We were just dancing," Layla said.

"I just worry about you," Gage said. "I worry about all of you. I mean, the reporters, cameras. . . ."

"I'm fine." She kissed him on the cheek. "We're all fine. Well. . . ."

They looked down at Emerson, her face down and ass up, still twerking away. Gage lifted her by the back of her shirt.

Emerson popped up, straightened her clothes, and adjusted her glasses. "What are you guys doing here? This is a girl party."

"Lot of dudes around for a *girl party*," Dash said. "There's no girls here besides you three."

"That's because this is a gay bar, you idiots!" Poppy said.

Gage and Dash exchanged a confused look then started laughing.

"They were rescuing us!" Layla mocked.

"They are both so dumb," Emerson said. "To think Dash flies planes and my brother runs a national airline and may even be governor one day. God help us all."

Poppy grabbed the muscle shirt guy. "Boys, this is Joey. He comes to my book club every week."

Joey looked Gage and Dash up and down. "You two aren't a couple?"

GAGE CARRIED LAYLA to her bedroom as she kissed his neck. He put her down on the bed, but she kept her arms around him, her breasts pushing against him. She was tipsy and cute as hell. He didn't want to take advantage, but she hadn't stopped kissing and touching him since they left the nightclub. He'd been worried and pissed an hour ago, but now he just wanted to bury himself deep inside her. *Funny how a hard*

dick forgets so easily. Gage peeled her arms away.

"I want to be your naughty angel," she said. "I want to show you what heaven's really like."

He ran his fingers down her neck. "You want to be naughty?"

"Very naughty," Layla said and pushed him down on the bed. "Wait here. I'll be right back." She turned on some music and disappeared to her closet. She came out wearing a white silk satin corset with matching panties and towering black stiletto heels. She gave a little spin, and his eyes slid over her body. "This was for the honeymoon, but I thought you might want a sneak peek."

Gage watched her start to sway to the music, gracefully, naturally, sexy. If she could stay upright in heels—the highest ones he'd ever seen—he figured she knew what she was doing, and he wouldn't be taking advantage. She started a little striptease, and his dick grew even harder, poking out of his pants. Layla continued to surprise him. She shed her corset and pressed her ass against his lap.

He put his hands on her hips, and she leaned back on his chest, wrapping an arm around his neck, allowing him a perfect view of her round breasts. She pulsed her ass against his dick to the beat of the music, then she turned around, facing him. Gage looked in her eyes, and Layla flashed a sweet, subtle grin. She straddled his lap, one knee on each side, and he looked at her grinding against him, seeing her panties were crotchless. She tilted his chin so he'd look at her face then leaned forward, nuzzling his face to her breasts.

He could taste the lavender. He slipped a finger inside, and she moaned. "You're so wet for me," he said. "I have to have you."

"What do you want?" She reached over to the nightstand and held up a condom. "You can have anything you want."

"I need to taste you," he said, sliding down so she was on top of his face. He gave her booty a little swat. "What a sweet little ass."

His warm tongue outlined her, and she melted into his mouth. "Fuck."

"You are naughty, Angel." He stuck his tongue inside.

Layla pushed against it and arched her back. "Just like that."

"After you come like this, I'm going to fuck you while you wear nothing but those heels."

CHAPTER TWENTY-ONE

GAGE FLEW BACK to Atlanta in the morning. He had an office meeting with his godfather, then it was back to Savannah to prepare for the wedding. But first he had his sister to deal with—her eyes bloodshot, slurring her words ever so slightly.

"Have we got the press handled for the wedding?" Gage asked. "I don't want any reporters showing up."

"Right," Emerson said, fumbling through a file. "No one is expecting the wedding to happen so quick." She handed him a sheet of paper. "That's the press release I'll send out once you're on your honeymoon."

Gage glanced down at it. "Looks good."

"Speaking of the honeymoon," Emerson said, tilting her glasses down her nose, "where are you guys going?"

"You'd run and tell her."

"Just a hint?"

"No." Gage smiled. "It's nice you two are friends."

Emerson stood up slowly. "It is, so don't screw it up because I'd choose her over you." She stuck out her tongue and turned to leave. "Oh, one more thing—I was thinking about the negative coverage and. . . ."

"I don't want you involved."

"But I could help. . . ."

There was a knock at the door, and Governor Clements walked in. "Am I early?"

"Not at all," Gage said.

"Surprised to see you here," Emerson said, "I didn't think I'd see you until the wedding."

"I'm helping your brother. . . ."

"With my vows," Gage said and pushed Emerson out of his office. She flashed her brother a dirty look then shut the door behind her.

"I'm surprised you wanted to meet with me," his godfather said. "I figured you'd be knee-deep in wedding plans right now."

"I'm heading to Savannah after this. Layla and Emerson want me there a few days before the wedding for prep and whatever."

"Good luck with that."

"Thanks," Gage said. "I think I know who's behind the leaks to the press. I don't want Emerson to know anything. She and Layla are close. It might put her in an awkward spot."

"I understand."

"It's Layla's half-brother."

His godfather immediately shook his head. "He was the first person I considered."

"Why didn't you ever tell me that?"

"It wouldn't do you any good to think a pedophile is after your wife—when he's not."

"Are you sure?"

"I checked his financials. These rags pay big money for information. He's broke. There's no deposits in any of his accounts. To be extra careful, I had his cell phone records checked. He's had no communications with any media outlets. It's not him."

"I thought for sure it was him," Gage said, pinching the bridge of his nose. "It seems we're no closer to knowing anything."

"I can tell this is all eating at you. I'm sorry, boy." The old man patted his shoulder. "Look, I didn't want to say anything, but I have a lead. It's only a suspicion right now. I have some phone records, but they don't prove anything. I was waiting on confirmation before I said anything to you. Do you want to know?"

"Yes! I told you to keep me in the loop!"

"It's bad, Gage."

GAGE FLEW BACK to Savannah, his mind racing the entire flight. This was the last time he'd be making the commute. In two days, he'd be starting a new life with Layla. A small smile formed on his lips. *I'll have everything I wanted for 12 years.* He looked out at the sky surrounding him, wondering if his father was watching. He wished his father could be at the wedding. He hoped the man was proud of him.

He knew his father's dream for him was to seek public office, but then he remembered his father's words: "A real man thinks with his heart. . . ." His heart told him what he needed to do. It's what he should've figured out months ago. His job was to love Layla and be a good husband and father one day. It wasn't to run for governor. It wasn't to be in the public eye, with all the accompanying baggage.

He could see it clearly now. Nothing was more important than Layla—not even all the good work he thought he could do. Even his idiot friend Dash knew he was a "family man at heart." *Layla was right. Flying is my praying.* A weight lifted, he couldn't wait to get to Story Wings and tell her. He wanted her to be the first to know. He'd have Emerson issue a press release once Layla knew. It was a relief the coverage would stop and their time in the spotlight would end.

But there was another matter on his heart—his godfather's "suspicions" about who was leaking information. Gage wished his godfather had hard proof. But at the moment, the only evidence was a series of phone records showing a few brief calls with media outlets over the past few weeks. The significance of the calls was unknown. They could be nothing more than "no comments" or something much more sinister. His godfather was working on getting transcripts and financials.

Gage wondered whether to tell Layla. As much as she hated secrets, he decided not to. There was no proof. Her store was closing today. The wedding was in two days. She had enough going on. He didn't want to upset her unnecessarily. *I'll tell her when I get confirmation, when I know what I'm saying is true.*

HE WALKED INTO Story Wings, or what was left of it—empty shelves, boxes scattered around. He saw Poppy taking down some displays. "Last day, huh?"

"Sadly. What are you up to?"

"Wanted to see if you guys needed any help."

"I'm sure we can put you to work," Poppy said. "Layla's not here though."

"Is Dash with her?" he asked, checking his watch and phone.

"No, why would Dash be with her? He went to get me something to eat."

Gage called Layla's phone, but there was no answer. "Did she say where she was going?"

Poppy looked at him curiously. "Is there a problem?"

Dash walked in carrying a takeout bag. "Poppy, I've got dinner." He saw Gage, and the men locked eyes. "Oh, I was just about to call you, man."

"How long has she been gone?" Gage asked.

"A couple hours," Dash said. "She went down the street for a sandwich. She was there. I went and asked them, but she never came back here."

"She's not picking up her phone," Gage said.

"Gage, relax," Poppy said. "She had a few things to do before the wedding."

"What's she doing?" Gage asked.

"Private girl things. Why are you acting weird, Gage?"

Dash turned to Poppy. "You said you didn't know where she was."

"Why do *you* care where Layla is?" Poppy replied. Dash clammed up and looked at his friend for help.

Gage knew they were cornered. Dash had screwed this up so bad— such a simple task and he couldn't do it. "I asked Dash to keep an eye on Layla in Savannah."

"What?" Poppy cried and stared daggers at Dash. "This was a *job* for you? You've been hanging out here for weeks because Gage asked you to?"

"No, I wanted to be with you, too," Dash said.

Poppy's hand flew across his face, quick and hard, sending the takeout bag falling to the floor. "Was fucking me a bonus?"

The door opened, and Layla walked in. She looked around at everyone, wondering what she missed. Gage raced over and gave her a big hug. "Where have you been?"

"Pop?" Layla asked, looking over his shoulder.

"This was all just a game, a job!" Poppy said. "It was all about you, Layla!"

Layla tore herself from Gage and pulled Poppy into her arms. "What *job*? What *game*?"

"Dash is here to be some kind of protection for you. He's not here for me. He's just been using me, reporting back to Gage about you."

"I wasn't using you," Dash said and reached for Poppy. "I think you're great."

Poppy sniffled and pulled away. "All men are the same. They're replaceable."

"Gage, you've been spying on me?" Layla asked.

"It's not like that," he said.

"This is why you changed Dash's route?" Layla asked. "So when you weren't here, Dash was."

"I was protecting you!" Gage said.

"Dash gave you *reports* about me?"

"It wasn't like that," Gage said. "With all the coverage, I wanted to be careful. I wanted to make sure you were OK."

"Yeah," Dash said, "I was just checking for reporters, any strangers lurking around."

Layla winced. "And Poppy was what—collateral damage?"

"No, Dash likes Poppy," Gage said. "That's why this was perfect. They could be together, and he could keep an eye on you when I couldn't be here."

"You had things all figured out, huh? Pulling all the strings behind the scenes? You just might be the perfect politician."

"I don't think so," he said. "I've decided not to run. I came here to tell you. I'm going to have Emerson issue a press release tomorrow."

Layla shrugged. "I'm glad you finally made a decision."

He reached for her hand. "Can we go somewhere to talk alone and try to work this out?"

"Not now. I don't want to talk to you right now."

"I was trying to protect you."

"I can handle myself, Gage. I'm a big girl. I don't need you to invade my privacy."

"I'm sorry."

Layla looked past him to Poppy. "Are you going to be OK?" Her friend nodded and dried her eyes. "Good, because I'm leaving—alone." Layla glared at the men. "Don't you dare give Poppy any shit." She grabbed her purse, took a long wistful look at the shop, and walked out the door.

SHADOWED BY THE darkness, Layla walked home alone. For weeks, she knew this day would suck, the last day of Story Wings. She'd never set foot in the store again. Her lifelong dream was now bearing a "For Sale" sign. Sure, it was Poppy, and not her, that caused the store to close, but that didn't make her feel any better or ease the pain in any way. And now Layla had no clue where she'd work next, a bookstore or something else, or whether she'd ever have the courage to start another business.

On top of all that, Gage had suddenly screwed things up between them. It was infuriating he had someone watch her, invade her privacy, report back on her. *How dare he.* There was no excuse, but she knew why he did it. It was the same thing as always. It was the thing she couldn't run from, the thing she could never escape, the thing that never went away. It was the thing she hated the most. Her past was always lurking, always haunting, like the ghosts roaming the streets of Savannah.

And she hated the way Gage treated her because of it—like she was helpless, like she was some lost child in need of a guardian. He probably decided not to run for governor because he thought she was too fragile. *He has no idea.* She wasn't lost. She wasn't a child. She'd been through hell and come out the other side. She'd fought battles—alone—that he could never even dream of. She was capable. She was tested. She could handle an occasional crazy or a bimbo reporter with a microphone.

She took a deep breath and tried to see it from his perspective. Gage was just trying to protect her, to look out for her. He probably felt guilty for allowing the media circus to continue and wanted to make sure she didn't fall victim to it. He'd always looked out for her, ever since the first day they met on the beach. The man didn't know any better. He couldn't help himself. Maybe she should be grateful he wanted to care for her and keep her safe—especially since no one else ever bothered to.

All that sounded good, but she couldn't shake that Gage should've trusted her—to live her life and take care of herself. And if he had any questions or concerns, he could've talked to her about them or at least told her what he was up to. The fact that he didn't—and apparently didn't trust her—made her worry. She didn't want to marry too quickly. *Am I rushing into things? Is he?* Maybe Gage had Dash watch her out of fear, to make sure she didn't run off again. He recently said he was worried she might. Fear is no reason to get married.

Her phone dinged with a text. *I'm sorry. Where R U? We need to work this out.*

Layla stopped under a light post and looked down at her engagement ring. She slipped it off. She'd only taken it off to shower, move boxes, and let Ava try it on. This time was different. She placed it in a side pocket of her purse and studied her empty finger, a few tears running down her cheek. The ring had only been on her finger a month, but she'd grown used to seeing it there, feeling its beautiful weight, knowing the love behind it, a symbol of her life and future with Gage.

Gage texted again. *No running, right?*

She leaned against the post and wept. She'd closed her store. She'd sold her house. Her whole life was in boxes ready to move to Atlanta. She wondered if they should postpone the wedding. But the thought of shifting gears now, running away again, was too much. And she knew it would crush him. She hated the thought of him in pain. It might crush her, too. And she'd promised not to run again. She looked down into her purse pocket, the ring glistening in the moonlight. She slipped it back on.

Another text from Gage. *Can I talk to you for two minutes?*

A light flashed, and she jumped. She scanned the darkness for some photographer or cameraman. She tried to see who was out there, who was watching her. The photographer, the cameraman, could be anywhere. But maybe it wasn't a media person—but someone worse. Her body shivered. She wasn't sure whether to run or walk, whether that would attract more attention, or just stay put against the light post.

A group of tourists turned the corner, led by a tour guide with a flashlight, and she exhaled. She was losing her mind. She could use a light of her own, something to point her in the right direction. She started to walk again, realizing this was the first time she'd been alone in weeks. Gage had orchestrated things so well she hadn't even noticed. His heart was in the right place. But she was still pissed. Her heart ached. She needed time to think, to clear her mind. Some meditation would help when she got home. She turned the block to her street.

It didn't take long for his eyes to find her in the darkness. Of course, he could find her in the darkness. He'd guided her through it enough times before. She stepped up through her front gate and onto the porch, keeping her eyes on the ground.

"Can we talk?" Gage asked, his eyes puffy and scared.

"Now you want to talk? After keeping secrets from me?"

"I'm sorry. I think we can work this out if we talk."

"Not tonight. I need some time."

"Can you just tell me where you were? I was worried."

"I went to get some things done before the wedding."

"Like? I've got your passport and clothes already packed for you."

"Like getting a wax!"

He hung his head. "Damn. I'm sorry."

"Happy now? I didn't feel like broadcasting that to Dash," she said and disappeared inside.

LAYLA SPENT THE next day—her last as a single girl—fending off his calls and texts. She even shooed him away from her house a time or two. She still didn't know what to think. Meditation hadn't helped. She still needed time, but she didn't have much of it. Her head hurt. Her heart hurt.

When the night came, she and Poppy ordered pizza and watched chick flicks at her house, a couple of moving boxes serving as chairs and dinner trays. It seemed the perfect thing to do—something quiet, simple, with her best friend. They might not have the chance to do this again soon.

"I really liked Dash," Poppy said, playing with her new jet black extensions. "He made me smile and laugh until my cheeks hurt."

"You two were perfect together."

"No, you and Gage are perfect together," Poppy said. "How long are you going to make him suffer?"

"How long are you going to make *Dash* suffer?" Layla replied.

"It's not the same. Gage loves you. Dash just loves my pussy."

"Pop," Layla said, "Dash looked pretty upset to me."

"Why do I always do this? In a room full of good guys, I pick the one that will hurt me every time."

"I think you're wrong about Dash," Layla said.

"I know you're wrong about Gage."

"I can't be mad he had me *watched* for weeks?"

"*Protected* for weeks," Poppy corrected.

"You're supposed to be on my side."

"I am," Poppy said. "But Gage is a good guy—misguided and quite possibly a total idiot—but a good guy. I really don't know how he runs such a successful company. You two belong together. You've known that since you were a teenager. So, how long are you going to torture him?"

There was a knock on the front door. "Layla?" Gage called out.

"Go let him in," Poppy said.

"Layla, please open the door," Gage said.

Poppy frowned. "Either you go open the door, or I will."

"Don't you dare, Pop."

"I hope I don't wake up your neighbors," Gage said.

A few guitar chords vibrated through the door. "Oh my God, Layla!" Poppy said. "He's going to play for you!"

Layla took a deep breath, her heart melting just a little. She slowly walked to the front door then rested her head against it, listening to the man, her future husband, singing the hell out of Aerosmith's "Angel," his sweet Southern accent shining through. She put her hands over her chest, and her eyes began to water. Part of her wanted to take the guitar and hit him over the head with it. He could be so dense. But another part wanted to run to his arms and kiss him. He could be so sweet.

"I love Aerosmith," Poppy said, talking to herself. "I would so have sex with Steven Tyler. I don't care he's like 100 years old now."

Layla put her hand to the door knob, a few tears falling. Gage knew how to get to her. She'd loved the man her whole life. She couldn't help herself. She opened the door, finding him leaning against her porch railing, strumming his guitar. He looked like hell, unshaven, bloodshot eyes.

"I'm sorry," he said and took a huge step towards her. "I made a mistake. It was out of love."

"Don't," Layla said, wiping her face.

"I swear that Dash likes Poppy and. . . ."

"Stop," Layla said. "Poppy's a mess. She's been abusing her hair again. It's jet black and hanging down to her waist. She doesn't deserve this."

Gage pinched the bridge of his nose. "I know I need to apologize to her, too."

"You can't just put a bodyguard on me without telling me."

"I was worried about everything going on. I wanted to keep the press and any creeps away from you. And I didn't want your abuse to become public."

"At this point, if it comes out, then it comes out," Layla said. "I'm not going to be ashamed of something someone else did to me. But you can't hide things from me, even if you convince yourself it's for my protection. I mean, do you trust me? Can you be honest with me?"

"Of course."

"How am I supposed to trust you after something like this?"

"The same way I trusted you after you ran off and hurt me," Gage said, holding her eyes. "You believed you were doing the right thing, and so did I. You weren't trying to hurt me, and I wasn't trying to hurt you. You had reasons for not telling me certain things, and so did I."

Layla looked towards the dark Savannah sky. "You know how I feel about secrets."

"Yes, and you know how I feel about you." He reached for her hand. "How much I love you, how much I want you, need you. I'll do anything to protect you—anything."

She took his hand and squeezed it. "I wasn't leaving you. But I need you to tell me the truth. Is the press coverage the reason you're not running for governor?"

"It's not that simple," he said, wrapping his arms around her. "Here's the thing, Layla. You're the reason I do *everything*." She pulled back and looked into his deep blue eyes. "You're the reason for every good and bad decision I've made since I threw that football and broke that prick's nose." Layla smiled, her dimples coming out. "*You* are my reason." His eyes focused on her mouth, and he leaned in close. "Say you'll marry me?"

"Not today."

"Tomorrow?"

"Yes, tomorrow."

CHAPTER TWENTY-TWO

THE WEDDING SHOULD'VE started 10 minutes ago. Gage wasn't sure what was going on, but apparently Layla and Poppy were late arriving to his mother's house. He didn't care. He'd been waiting for 12 years; a few extra minutes was nothing. The string quartet started up, and Gage took his place next to the priest and Dash, underneath the gazebo and roses gracing the backyard.

He scanned the small crowd, no more than 50 people or so, all seated in white chairs. He saw his mother was already crying. And he saw Governor Clements, Helen from Hope Cottage, his secretary Mary, and other familiar faces. Then there was Jacob silently, anxiously, going over his reading part.

Gage looked down the aisle, along a white carpet runner cascaded in white rose petals, hoping to catch a glimpse of his bride. Instead, he saw Emerson dusting some dirt off Connor's tux. The boy was bouncing up and down like he was on a pogo stick, anxious to come down the aisle and officially start the ceremony.

Then it was time. Connor held up his pilot man like the Statue of Liberty. He looked straight ahead at the gazebo, and Gage gave him a little wave forward. The boy began his march, measuring each step, smiling and waving to the crowd. Connor made it to Gage and said, "Touchdown!" The crowd laughed, and Gage pulled the boy to his side, patting his head.

Gage looked down the aisle again, doing a double take when he saw Ava. Maybe it was the heels and strapless dress, but she looked like a young lady, not a young teenager. He wondered how Ava convinced her mother. It must've been quite a sales job. He was going to have to work hard to keep horny teenage boys away from her. Emerson followed her daughter down the aisle.

The music changed, and the crowd stood up. Gage cocked his head to see around them. But he couldn't see anything. Layla hadn't rounded the corner yet. He saw the back of Poppy, her hair back to its pixie length and blonde color. She was standing in front of Layla, talking. Poppy stepped aside, turned to face the gazebo, and took Layla by the hand.

They took a step towards the gazebo, towards him, and the entire world stopped spinning. He was sure he stopped breathing. Everyone, everything fell away. Everything fell quiet.

Layla walked down the aisle, bouquet in hand and barefoot, her chocolate brown hair flowing down her shoulders and back, the white gown hanging loosely from her body, making her appear she was floating. *Angel.* And when she moved just the right way, the dress clung to her curves, giving a peek at the sexy woman underneath.

They reached the gazebo, and Poppy stepped to the side. He intertwined her fingers with his. "Beautiful," he whispered in her ear.

"Sorry, I was late," she said. "Poppy had a hair crisis." Gage flashed a look to Poppy, who gave a little shrug before offering an evil eye to Dash.

The priest said a few words to the crowd, and Jacob headed to the front. He looked to Layla and Gage, who both nodded encouragingly. They could see the paper shaking in his hands. The boy swallowed hard: "Love is patient; love is kind." He paused a few times throughout the reading but never stumbled. When he reached the end—"But the greatest of these is love"—Jacob gave Layla a huge hug, with Gage patting him on the back. Connor marched his pilot man to Layla and Gage, and she handed her bouquet to Ava.

The priest spoke to the crowd. "Gage would like to say a few words before he and Layla exchange vows." Layla looked at Gage with wide eyes.

He smiled down at her then turned to the crowd. "4,524 days ago, I saw the most beautiful girl I'd ever seen. Then I lost her. 70 days ago, I found her again. And when I did, she was the most beautiful woman I'd ever seen. I wasn't going to risk losing her again. So I moved quickly this time. 30 days ago, she agreed to marry me. And today, she'll be my wife, the greatest blessing of my life."

Gage took her hands. "Layla, Angel, I never told you this. Remember the first time I kissed you under that old tree?" She smiled and nodded. "Remember how I backed away looking shocked? I'm sure you thought it was because the kiss was so hot." The crowd laughed, and Layla's dimples popped. "And it *was*. But the reason I was shocked was because the first time my lips touched yours, I felt the rest of my life." He wiped a few tears from her cheeks. "I love you, Angel."

She closed her eyes and shook her head, trying in vain to contain her emotions. She leaned in close to him. "I've been practicing my 'I do' for 4,524 days," she whispered. "I'm ready for the vows."

THE PRIVATE JET took off, and Layla guessed a hundred places they could be going. It could be anywhere. She wasn't even sure which direction they were flying. One place she never imagined was Lake Como, Italy. And she never imagined a historic villa overlooking the water, with a private staff and enough bedrooms for a small village, a library, a private boat dock with a yacht and speedboat, badminton, pool tables, and waterfront restaurants on the beach. It would be an understatement to say they were spoiled all of September, or Sextember, as Poppy came to call it.

Gage arranged side trips from Lake Como to Milan and Switzerland since both were just a short train ride away. He didn't want them to miss out on da Vinci's "The Last Supper" or the Swiss Alps. And then, on a whim during the third week, Gage thought it would be cool to see France, so he chartered a plane, and they spent several days in a legendary hotel overlooking the Eiffel Tower. When they got back to Lake Como, they spent their last few days out on the private boat dock, dancing on the balcony, wrapped in the moonlight.

It was like something out of a movie. It was all a beautiful dream—just like their summer 12 years ago. But the dream was coming to an end. Layla could feel reality creeping in. Gage was spending a little more time each day on emails and phone calls. She understood. Running Southern Wings wasn't easy. It was hard to be gone a month. She could tell he felt a pull to get back. And as wonderful as the honeymoon was, she felt a pull to get back, too—to settle into a life with her husband. Their flight to Atlanta was leaving in a few hours.

Layla stepped out of the bathroom and heard Gage's voice from the balcony. He was on the phone again. She threw on a robe and opened the balcony doors, shivering, and watched him for a few moments.

"So you got confirmation," Gage said. "I want to fly there right now!" He listened a bit more then gripped his hair. "You want me to let it go? I'm not sure I can do that. I'll talk to her." He saw Layla in the doorway. "I need to go."

She gave him a small smile and pulled him back inside as he tried to end the call. But his godfather kept talking. She pushed him down on the bed, pulled off her robe, and slid down his shorts. He closed his eyes, trying to keep focused on the conversation, but his sex brain was taking over. All he could give were short, one-word answers—"yes, um, hmm"—as Layla ran her tongue across his dick. He gripped the phone, hard.

"Am I distracting you?" she whispered, sliding up his body and kissing his neck. She put him inside her and tightened.

"Oh," Gage groaned. "No, I'm good. Very good."

Layla rolled her hips into him, pushing him deeper. "Just *good?*"

"I'll be back in the office tomorrow," he said quickly. "Thanks for letting me know." He hung up and tossed the phone on the floor. He grabbed her ass and sat up to face her, their hips rocking together, their eyes locked together. He slid his hands up her back, and his tongue lingered at her neck.

"Don't stop," she whispered, clenching him, her whole body tingling.

Gage smiled. He wouldn't stop if the villa was on fire. He loved watching her finish, more than he loved coming inside her. He pushed a little deeper, rolling into her, and felt her body quiver in his arms. She lowered her head on his shoulder and clung to him, tightening her legs around him, their bodies as close as could be.

And then she came. Usually it was loud, screaming his name, but other times it was quiet, like this. He wasn't sure why, but he didn't care. Her eyes always looked the same, her body always blushing. It never got old. He took her down on the bed and pulled her leg to his hip. He grabbed her ass and moved in and out of her. "That's right, baby," he said. "You feel better every time."

"I'm close again," she said and dug her fingers in his back.

"Get there, Angel," he begged, ramming into her, each thrust hard and quick, unsure how the hell she wasn't breaking in two.

"Oh, God! Gage!"

Gage let go, holding her tightly to his chest. He kissed her hair and lifted his head, looking down at her, fair skin, chocolate brown hair. He slowly rubbed her arm. "I can't believe you're mine."

"You're stuck with me now," Layla teased, yawning.

"Maybe I should sell the airline, and we could spend every day making love."

Layla moaned, liking the idea.

"Maybe we should think about getting a new place," he said, "a place that's ours, for our family."

Layla moaned again.

"Angel," Gage said, feeling her body go limp, falling asleep in his arms. "I'll tell you tomorrow." He tucked a lock of hair behind her ear, the moonlight casting a gentle glow on her skin. He never tired of seeing her like this—naked, peaceful. He'd waited so long to have her. And now she was his wife—his to protect, to love, to come home to each night.

It hit him. *I'm really married.*

CHAPTER TWENTY-THREE

THEY WALKED INSIDE Southern Wings headquarters together. Layla didn't know why he wanted her with him on his first day back. She could see the weight on his shoulders. He was clearly stressed, pinching the bridge of his nose, with so much work to catch up on, his desk most certainly a mess. But Gage insisted she come along, a slight twinkle in his eye.

"Nice not having reporters out front," she said.

Gage squeezed her hand. "Nothing to report now that I'm not running."

Layla gave him a small smile. She knew he wasn't running because of her. She didn't like being the reason. She'd told him more than once she could handle herself, the press. But it was time she let it go and respect his decision. It was time to focus on their life together and not look back.

They headed through the lobby, and employees stopped them every few seconds, welcoming them back from their honeymoon, congratulating their boss and the new "Mrs. Montgomery." His mother was right. It was strange. Layla gently corrected them each time, asking them to please use her first name. With all the small talk, it took Gage and Layla forever to get to the elevator to go up.

The elevator door closed, and Gage asked, "What's wrong with my name?"

"Nothing," she said. "But I want your employees to like me, not think of me as the boss' wife. Don't get all intense just cause you're back at work." She kissed him tenderly on the lips as the door opened on the executive floor.

"No PDA at work, please!"

Layla darted her eyes from Gage and found her best friend coming towards her, smothering her in a hug. "Poppy, what are you doing here?"

Poppy flashed Gage a look. "You can *really* keep a secret." Layla looked at them both, confused. "I work here now, Layla!"

Layla's jaw dropped. "You're *working* here?"

"Yep!" Poppy said.

"Wow! When did this happen? How did this happen? Are you living in Atlanta now?"

Poppy nodded excitedly. "Got an apartment here. I've been busy while you were gone!"

"I can't believe this!" Layla said and hugged Gage. "What's your job?"

Emerson approached them. "Poppy's my assistant." She pulled Layla and Gage into a hug. "Poppy and I got along so well planning the wedding that I offered her a job."

"I'm handling more of the marketing stuff," Poppy said. "Frees up Emerson to deal with the PR stuff."

Layla looked up at Gage. "This is wonderful. Thank you."

"It's the least I could do," Gage said.

"So, was the honeymoon hot?" Poppy asked. "Do you guys have a sex ache?"

Layla paused for a moment. "I'd say we're almost crippled."

"I'm going to my office," Gage said, not wanting to hear this. "Layla, please come see me after you all catch up."

POPPY BROUGHT LAYLA and Emerson down the hall to her office. The ladies spent a good while catching up on the past month—the wedding, the honeymoon, Poppy's new job and apartment. Layla noticed Poppy didn't mention one thing. "What about Dash?"

"I've been really busy moving and starting the new job."

"So you two are over?" Layla asked.

"I can't afford to fall in love with the wrong guy again."

"How's he handling it?"

"He's trying to convince me I can trust him."

"At least your hair is surviving."

"It has to," Emerson said. "Gage wrote it into her contract."

"You're kidding."

"Nope," Poppy said. "It actually says no colors other than blonde, red, or brown, and they can't be crazy shades of those colors, either. They have to be pre-approved by Gage personally." They all had a good laugh.

"How are my nephews and niece?" Layla asked.

"Everyone is good," Emerson said. "They are dying to see you and Gage—especially Connor. He asks me all the time."

"That's so sweet. We missed them, too. Maybe this weekend?"

"That would be perfect. I was actually hoping you and Gage might watch them for me," Emerson said. "Lately I've been having to work more here in Atlanta, and the commute is killing me. I need to get caught up on some things here at the office."

"I'll talk to Gage," Layla said. "I'm sure it's fine. And you can stay at the penthouse for the weekend."

PILES AND PILES were all over his desk: FAA reports to review, stacks of financials to approve, business correspondence to answer, employee 401(k) plans to consider, and thousands of other things. It looked like he'd been gone a year. But all of it was going to have to wait. The only thing that mattered was a brown envelope marked "confidential"—and the documents inside he was pouring over.

There were media reports on Layla and Gage, the publication date of each highlighted in yellow. There were bank statements showing various deposits, each dated a day or two before a report. There were stacks of checks and wire transfers from assorted media outlets, the amounts corresponding to the deposits on the bank statements. It was all confirmation of what his godfather suspected. He ran a hand along the cross she made for him. *I have to tell her.*

Gage looked up from his desk, catching Layla spying on him from the doorway. He held out his hand for her to come to him. "You got to catch up with Poppy and Emerson?"

"Yeah, I still can't believe you hired Poppy."

Mary walked in and handed Layla a folder. "I added you to Mr. Montgomery's accounts. There are credit cards and checks in here with your new name and address. And I arranged for your passport to be changed and for a new driver's license, too."

"Don't I have to go to the DMV or something?"

"I handled it, honey."

"Thank you," Layla said.

Mary turned to leave. "Please shut the door behind you," Gage said.

"Is something wrong?" Layla asked.

Gage came around his desk, and they sat down together on the sofa. "All the stories in the press were leaked. It wasn't just the press digging around."

"Really? Why would someone do that?"

"Money," he said and took her hand. "I found out for sure yesterday who was doing it. I don't have to tell you if you don't want to know. The press is gone. No one cares anymore. There won't be any more stories. The person no longer has a customer to sell to since I'm not running."

"Is it someone I know?"

"Yes, and I'm going to see that they pay."

"Tell me who it is."

"You sure?"

"Tell me."

"Your mother."

A sharp pain shot through her heart, and she began to cry. It didn't seem possible her mother could hurt her again—and Gage, too. "Are you sure?"

Gage handed her the envelope. "It's all in here—phone records, bank deposits. She was probably pissed about your father's will, your happiness. And this was payback."

Layla looked in the envelope—all the papers inside—then her eyes shot up. "My half-brother?"

"He's not involved," Gage said and wrapped his arms around her. "We ruled him out months ago. There's no recent activity on him. I'd never let him get close to you."

"What do we do now?"

Her tears hit his hand. "I'm going to fly over there. Your mother is going to hurt for this, for your childhood, for not protecting you, for everything."

Layla considered his words. It was tempting to think about her mother in pain. Layla fantasized many times about just that. But she learned a long time ago that holding onto anger only hurt her. It didn't hurt the ones she was angry with. They didn't care. She wasn't going to let that poison destroy her new life, everything she worked so hard for. *It's always better to forgive.* "No, Gage, let it go."

"The hell I will! She screwed up your life for weeks! More than that, really!"

"Everything she did only made me stronger. Everything that happened led me to where I am today—led me to you."

Gage about threw up. *Is this more hybrid Catholic-hippie shit?* "I'll think about it, but I can't make any promises right now."

"No, I want you to. . . ."

The door flew open. Emerson waltzed in with a tall, muscular man with deep brown eyes. Gage and Layla hopped up from the sofa, and Emerson flashed her a little wink. "Layla, this is Mateo."

The man stepped forward and extended a hand to Layla, his angular features softening, his lips curving up in the slightest hint of a smile. Gage greeted the man instead. "Hi, Mateo. I'm Gage Montgomery. Could you wait outside a minute?"

"Yes, sir."

Gage shut the door. "Really, Emerson? Is this some kind of joke?"

"I just thought if Layla has to have a guard, then he should be nice to look at."

"Get rid of him."

"He's the best. He comes," Emerson said, pausing for effect, "highly recommended."

"He's got a hard-on for my wife."

"Wait!" Layla cried. "Why do I need a guard?"

"You didn't tell her, Gage?" Emerson asked.

"You barged in before I could," Gage said and sat back down with Layla. "Angel, we've got no idea what your mother is capable of. I can't imagine a mother doing what yours has done to you."

"But all the stories stopped," Layla said. "Don't you think she's given up?"

"I'd like to go to Houston and make sure of that," he said.

"You'll only make it worse," Emerson said.

Layla squeezed his hand. "Gage, I'd rather you stay here with me." If it kept him out of harm's way, she wasn't above playing the damsel in distress card. She saw his blue eyes soften a little and knew she was winning.

"You'll keep the guard?" Gage asked his wife.

"I think you should, Layla," Emerson said. "He's great eye candy."

Layla giggled. "You think it's necessary?"

"I think it's best for a little while," Gage said. "Just a week or so. Just to be on the safe side."

"OK," Layla said. "Just have him be discreet. I don't want to feel like he's there. And I don't want him giving any reports to you, Gage. I need to feel like I have some power."

"I told you she'd be sensible," Emerson said. "Don't know what you were so worried about, baby brother."

"How long have you guys been planning this?" Layla asked, and Emerson looked at her brother. "Gage, how long have you known my mother was behind all this?"

"I just got the envelope this morning," he said. "It was here when I got back in the office."

Layla shook her head. "How long have you suspected?"

"I didn't want to say anything until I knew for sure."

Layla got to her feet. "How long? Don't make me ask again."

"Can we not do this in front of my sister?" Gage asked.

"I'll go," Emerson said, opening up his office door. "I'll be right outside—with Mateo."

When the door closed, Layla started up again. "How long have you suspected my mother?"

"A couple days before we got married," Gage said. "But I didn't have any real proof. I didn't want to upset you for no reason. I didn't want to dampen our wedding or honeymoon."

"You must think I'm so weak."

"You know I don't think that."

"You must," Layla said. "Am I destroyed? Did this news break me? Am I falling to pieces? You don't give me enough credit."

"Angel," Gage said, reaching for her.

Layla stepped back. "Let me tell you something about angels you obviously don't know. Angels aren't little winged fairies flying around granting wishes. They are warriors, fighters, protectors. You know who they fight? Demons and the evil in the world." She stiffened her spine. "You like to call me 'Angel' because you think it's cute and sweet. But I like it because I think it makes me a bad ass."

"I know you're a fighter. But it was two days before the wedding when I first suspected it was her. I had no real proof."

Layla waited a moment as clarity sunk in. "This is why you decided not to run, huh?" Gage opened his mouth, but Layla held up her hand. "You let my mother scare you off. Don't you realize what you did? You let her win." She shook her head and grabbed her purse. "I need some air." She walked out of the office, and Mateo fell in line behind her.

GAGE STAYED LATE to clear his desk and got home around eight. He felt the freeze as soon as he walked in. He pushed open the bedroom door, seeing the lights out and Layla on her side facing away. *Literally, the cold shoulder. The honeymoon is over.* The covers were up to her neck, and Pippa was curled up on his pillow. She never went to bed this early. She was obviously still pissed. He sighed as he got ready for bed.

He slid under the sheets and gently pushed Pippa aside. He went to hold his wife, to touch her skin, then recoiled as if burned by an iron.

She'd put on pajamas, and not just any pajamas—flannel ones—when it was still 90 degrees outside. She could be pissed all she wanted, but that was taking things too far. It crossed the line.

"You know what's the best thing about having a wife?" Gage whispered, his warm breath on her neck, sliding a hand under her shirt.

Layla swatted him away. "I'm tired."

"No, you're not," Gage said.

She rolled over. "I'm not?"

"No, you're not. You're mad." Gage leaned up on his elbow and stroked her cheek, waiting.

"I'm hurt," she whispered.

"We waited so long to be together, to get married. I didn't want your mother to steal one ounce of joy from that."

Layla flipped all the way over to face him, their heads resting on their pillows. "But you let her steal your dream to become governor."

"That's not true. And it wasn't my dream."

"I hate that my past, my family, robbed that from you. I hate it."

"Layla, I can promise you I don't want to hold public office. It doesn't have anything to do with your past, your family. It has everything to do with our future, our family." He ran his fingers through her hair. "Remember our first date a few months ago? You asked me to tell you what I wanted the next 5 years to look like. I never mentioned being governor. The only thing I could think about was our kids, a house, you waddling around pregnant." Layla nuzzled in closer to him. "Maybe I should've told you about your mother sooner, but I didn't want you to worry. It's my job as your husband to protect you and keep you happy and safe."

Layla wanted to scream at him for his old-fashioned notion, to stand up for feminism and equal rights. But she just couldn't manage it, at least not right now. His heart was in the right place. "I miss our honeymoon," she whispered.

Gage led her to the balcony and wrapped his arms around her. "It's not quite Italy, but the stars are the same."

CHAPTER TWENTY-FOUR

AFTER SPENDING A few days unpacking, Layla tried to settle into her new life in Atlanta. She loved being married but sitting around waiting for Gage to come home, luring him home for lunch and a quick roll in the sheets, exploring slivers of grass with Pippa along busy downtown streets, wasn't a long term plan. It wasn't exactly what she envisioned for her life. She felt like she needed a plan.

It seemed like years since she read to a child or stocked a shelf. There were no orders to fill. There were no bills to pay. And there was no laundry to do, either. Gage sent that out. She hadn't even found a yoga or meditation class she liked. They were all indoors, the noisy city streets of Atlanta making an outdoor class impossible. She needed to figure out what she was going to do with herself.

She didn't go to college, start a business, just to hang out at home alone. She knew she'd figure it out—maybe a part-time job, maybe some volunteer work. The possibilities were endless. And she actually looked forward to figuring it out. But until she did, she was going to try not to go stir crazy and do her best to enjoy herself. She was going to spend time with her friends, take it easy, without a press corps following her around—even if Mateo was.

POPPY KNOCKED OFF work a little early. She wanted Layla to see her new apartment. Layla jumped at the chance to get out and came straight over. Poppy immediately took a liking to Mateo.

"Do you mind him following you around?" Poppy asked, sizing

him up from another room, staring at the muscles in his arms.

"I'm getting used to it."

"I'd like some security from him. I know I'd feel real secure if he was bending me over a desk, either here at home or at work."

"Gage just better be thankful I love him so much. Did you know Mateo's company actually sends Gage a log sheet each night? I told Gage I didn't want that, but then I walk into the bedroom last night, and Gage slams down the laptop like I caught him looking at porn."

"Oh, the ole porn slam," Poppy said. "Hate that."

"Yeah, but it wasn't porn. It was the log sheet. I'd rather porn."

"My log sheet would have just one entry—'Bent Poppy over a desk.'"

When the tour was over, Poppy wanted to see Layla's place, or, as she put it, to "snoop around where the boss lives." She wanted to borrow some shoes, too. So, with Mateo in tow, the ladies headed over to the penthouse. Poppy was as crazy as ever, talking a mile a minute, making up words, blurting out any random thing that came into her head. A new city, a new job, hadn't changed that. But Layla could tell, despite her friend's silliness and brave face, something was a little off.

They rode up the elevator together. "You don't have to try to cheer me up," Poppy said. "I'm really OK. I actually have a date later."

"You're dating other people?" Layla stepped out on her floor, thanking Mateo and telling him she'd be in for the evening.

"Well, tonight will be a first date, but it counts. That's why I wanted to borrow your sexy black stilettos. I need to get my 'date face' on."

Layla opened up her door. "You know you can borrow them, but I really think you should think about Dash first."

Dash stepped out of the kitchen with a beer. "Think what about me?"

"Dash!" Layla said, throwing a look to Gage on the sofa. "I didn't know you were coming by."

"We're watching the game," Gage said.

"Poppy, I had no idea," Layla whispered. "Sorry."

"Can I get the shoes?" Poppy asked. "Quickly?" Layla hustled to her bedroom.

Dash offered the beer to Poppy, but she shook her head and gingerly walked towards a leather chair and took a seat on the arm, looking like she wanted to be anywhere else. Layla came out with the heels, almost tripping on Gage's briefcase in the den. She moved it off the floor and handed Poppy the heels.

"She's borrowing *those*?" Gage wondered.

"Is that a problem?" Layla asked.

"Well, you know. . . ." he said, a twinkle in his eye.

Poppy wrinkled her nose. "You fucked in these? Gross!" She tossed the shoes at them. "I'll get my own stripper heels."

"Come look in my closet," Layla said. "I've got other shoes."

"Virgin shoes, I hope?"

"All my other shoes are virgins."

"I don't understand women and their shoes," Dash said.

"You don't understand a lot," Poppy replied.

Gage threw a look to Dash not to engage. The guys turned their attention back to the game.

"I don't understand men and their sports," Layla teased.

"It's about the only action I'm seeing lately," Dash said.

"I believe that as much as I believe you were in the store everyday because you liked me."

Dash slugged the rest of his beer. "You want to do this *here*? In front of our friends?"

"Why not?" Poppy snapped.

"I'm sick of groveling," Dash said. "I don't know how many more times I can say 'I'm sorry.' I don't know what you want me to do. I even ripped up my TBF list to show you how serious I am."

Layla bit her lip, confused, and looked at Gage. "His 'To Be Fucked' list," he whispered to her.

"I mean that list is sacred, and I ripped mine up! That shows commitment!" Dash said. "What else do you want me to do?" Poppy shrugged her shoulders. "You are the most frustrating female. I don't know how much longer I can take this. I mean, I haven't had sex in over a month, waiting on you to calm the hell down."

Poppy raised an eyebrow. "Your dick has too big an appetite to fast for a month."

"You used to have quite an appetite for my dick," Dash said.

"You did *not* just say that to me!" Poppy cried and made an angry move towards him. Layla stepped in front of her.

"Hell yeah, I did. You called me a liar. You called my *dick* a liar!"

"Maybe now's not the best time to do this," Layla said.

"You're right," Poppy said. "I have a date anyway."

"Pop!" Layla gasped.

"I'm sure you'll find a reason to ditch him, too," Dash said. "You know why? You know what you're problem is, Poppy? You don't know how great you are. You don't know how beautiful and sexy you are. You can't believe that I was truly crazy about you—that any real man could be crazy about you!"

Poppy looked away, as Dash stood silent for a moment, his big brown eyes revealing his pain. "Sorry about all this," he said to Gage and Layla and gave them both a nod before heading towards the door, closing it softly behind him.

Gage and Layla stared at each other then heard a little whimper. Layla turned just in time to see Poppy cover her mouth, trying to hold in her cries and tears. Layla wrapped her arms around her friend. "What did I just do?" Poppy cried.

"You just acted like a raging bitch," Layla said.

"I did, didn't I? And in front of my new boss?"

"It's OK," Gage said.

"I think I love him," Poppy said. "That's why this hurts so much."

"Then go get him," Layla said.

Poppy drew a deep breath and walked to the door. She opened it and screamed. Dash was leaning up against the wall in the hallway, looking calm and cocky as hell. "Took you long enough," he said.

"I thought you left," Poppy said, smiling and leaping into his arms.

"I thought you had a date," Dash said.

"I did!"

CHAPTER TWENTY-FIVE

EMERSON PREPARED FIVE pages of notes about bedtimes, what the kids could and couldn't eat, appropriate TV shows, homework, how much time they could spend on the computer, directions to the nearest hospital, and the names of the kids' pediatrician and dentist and ENT and dermatologist. Layla paid close attention to each instruction, while Gage rolled his eyes behind his sister's back.

They were just watching the kids in Savannah for the weekend. It's not as if Emerson would be gone a year. They didn't need a dissertation of instructions. It was frustrating how much his sister was like his parents—so over-protective, always worried that something bad might happen. He caught himself for a moment and looked at Layla, knowing full well the same could be said of him.

Before Emerson headed out, she pulled Gage to a separate room. She'd been getting some disturbing calls lately from other parents. And they were all saying the same thing, all equally upset. Jacob apparently had blabbed to his friends at school about his "aunt and uncle going at it in the garden a few weeks back," and that his "Uncle G had given him a C-note to keep it on the down low."

"I don't think I ever said 'down low' or "C-note," Gage said. "I wouldn't use those words."

"That's not the point!" Emerson said through gritted teeth. "So when you're around my kids this time, keep your hands off Layla's tits and your dick in your pants."

"Can you write that down with the other instructions? I'd hate to forget and get in trouble again."

Of course, Gage didn't listen to his sister. He jumped Layla as soon as the kids were asleep. And he planned on starting the morning the same way, but Connor leapt into their bed around dawn and kneed him in the nuts, waking him up for good and ending any hope of morning sex.

After breakfast, they headed out to his mother's house. The noise in the car was deafening, Jacob and Ava asking constant questions while Connor carried on a conversation with Petey. Gage kept one hand on the bridge of his nose and the other on the wheel.

But the chatter didn't seem to bother Layla. She managed to talk to each of the kids, with Pippa curled on her lap. Gage put the car in park, and the three kids hopped, running up the path to their grandmother's house with Pippa.

Gage just sat for a moment. "You're right. Only two kids for us."

"Come on, only 24 hours left." She reached for the door handle.

"Stay in," he said. "I got my mom to watch the kids today. We have the day to ourselves."

"That's so nice of her." They saw the kids and dog go inside, and his mother give a little wave.

"I think she's hoping to get more grandkids soon," he said.

LAYLA LOOKED UP at what was once Story Wings. "I hope it's not going to be a Starbucks," she said, still able to make out the sign behind some scaffolding. "I miss it."

"I know," Gage said, taking her hand and walking down the street to her old house. "Have you decided what you want to do?"

"Well, I was thinking about. . . ."

He shook her hand a little. "Angel, you know I can help you. I mean, if you want another store or. . . ."

"It's not that. Story Wings was my dream. No other store would ever be the same."

Gage pulled her into a little kiss in the middle of the sidewalk, relishing they didn't have to worry about it ending up in the paper, and that Jacob wasn't around to tell his friends. "Tell me."

"I don't know," she said. "I've been thinking about the crosses I make—maybe trying to sell them in a few boutique stores. Donating the profits to charity, since we don't need the money. I know some artists donate prints to different organizations and schools for them to auction, like I do for Hope Cottage. I was kind of thinking about expanding that."

Gage looked down at her, still in his arms. Even now that she had money, she had no interest in shopping, spas, travel. She still wanted to do for others. And the way she spoke about her plans, with a quiet confidence, like she always carried herself, even as a teen, he knew she'd be successful. "You can turn the spare bedroom into your workspace."

"So you like the idea?"

"I love it." Gage kissed the side of her head, and they continued down the street. He saw her taking in the sights and sounds of the city she loved, the vintage houses, the quaint porches, the old oaks. And he saw the wheels spinning in her head, seemingly excited about finally having a plan, a new adventure.

Her smile faded at the sight of her house, a "Sold" sign in the front yard. "I can't believe it's not mine anymore," she said softly. "I was so proud the day I bought it."

He saw her eyes start to water. He wondered if she recognized her life. In the past three months, her entire life had changed. His had, too, but nothing compared to what she'd gone through. "I'm proud of you. I mean, you put yourself through school, started your own business, bought your own house. And now you've got this new project brewing. Makes me proud you're my wife."

She elbowed him gently. "That means a lot, Mr. CEO."

"My success is mostly on the shoulders of my dad."

"Don't be modest. You launched the whole company into orbit."

"Maybe a little," he said. "But what you've done is different, better. You are totally self-made, Angel. Not many people can say that."

"That's sweet of you to say." She looked back at the house and sighed. "At least I got a full price offer on it. The buyer is some LLC or closely-held company or something. They didn't even want an inspection. I sign the papers this week."

"I know," Gage said, smiling.

"How do you know?"

"I'm the buyer." He dangled a house key in front of her face. "A wedding gift."

"You bought my *house*?"

Gage couldn't tell if she was pissed or pleased. "You love this house. It's a part of you, and you've given up so much for my career, my life. I just thought we could use it when we come into town to visit. But if you. . . ."

She crashed her lips into his, and Gage picked her up. She wrapped her legs around his waist. He carried her to the door, fumbling to get the key in the lock. They both started laughing. "They make this look easier in the movies," he said, finally getting the door open. He pushed her against a wall and dropped to his knees, forcing her legs apart, letting her sundress drape over his head.

"Gage," she whispered, embarrassed.

He took her panties in his teeth, his breath making her legs tremble. He slid his fingers along the side of her panties and lightly stroked her. "No more panties," he said, pulling them down and swatting her naked butt. He gently outlined her with his tongue, and she melted into his mouth. He slid his hands to her ass, squeezing her gently. "Fuck my mouth, baby," he said, placing his tongue at her entrance and pushing her ass, encouraging her. "God, you're so sweet."

Layla was sure she was all shades of red as she moved her hips against his mouth, clenching her muscles around his tongue. "Oh," she moaned, losing self-control, totally greedy, wanting nothing more than to finish. Her nails gripped his shoulders as her body began to quake, coming hard against his mouth. "Yes!" she screamed.

He slapped her ass then squeezed it. "Give me all of it."

"Please!"

Gage sucked down hard and stuck his tongue deep inside. He continued to lick her as she came down from her orgasm, trembling. Layla panted and looked down at Gage, still on his knees. He came out from under her dress, grinning. No matter where they were, no matter what position they were in, he always made it about pleasing her. It seemed nothing was more important to him.

His dark blue eyes stared up at her, warming her body all over again. She reached for him and ripped at his clothes. Within seconds, their clothes were spread on the floor. Layla instinctively started up the stairs to her bedroom. Gage caught her from behind, one arm around her waist, the other between her legs, rubbing her gently. "Kneel," he whispered and kissed her neck.

Layla did as he wanted, and he kneeled one stair below. He ran his fingers down her spine and watched her body roll. His hard dick pulsed at her entrance, her slick wetness surrounding him, begging him. He looked back at his shorts on the floor, the condom in his wallet in the pocket. He wasn't about to stop and get it, hating them anyway, especially with Layla. He slipped himself inside.

Layla leaned forward, her hand gripping the banister. "God," she moaned.

"You like that, Angel?" he grunted, moving her chocolate hair to see her profile.

Layla nodded and pushed her ass against him. "Yes, oh. . . ." Her body started to tremble, meeting him thrust for thrust. Her head flew back as her orgasm ripped through her, her muscles convulsing and pulling his orgasm from him.

"Christ!" he groaned, finishing, holding her ass to steady himself. He lowered his head down on her back to catch his breath. "Your body is incredible. *You* are incredible." Then in one smooth move, he took her in his arms and carried her down the stairs.

THEY DROVE OFF through the Historic District. "Do you ever wonder where we'd be if you hadn't left the island?" he asked.

"I try not to," she said, checking out the passing mansions. "You think we would've stayed together?"

"Of course."

"We were so young. I don't think the odds were in our favor."

"Screw the odds!" he said. "By now, we'd have been married at least 10 years."

"That means I would've married you at 18."

"That sounds about right," Gage said, slipping his hand in hers.

"I hope I'd still have met Poppy in college."

"You would've. And you would've still opened Story Wings with her. And run it in between having kids." He patted her belly, and she rolled her eyes. "I'd still be ruggedly handsome, and you'd still be sexy as hell."

"Of course," she said, twisting her torso slightly.

Gage tilted his head. "You OK?"

"Yeah."

Gage placed his hand on her hip. "Christ, Angel, if I hurt you. . . ."

"I'm fine," she said.

He pulled in front of Hope Cottage. "We're breaking ground on the new building next month. Sarah wants us there." He pointed to a sign. Gage watched her eyes as she read, seeing her stop breathing for a moment, her hands flying over her mouth.

"I don't know what to say," Layla said.

"I wanted the building to have your name, but I didn't want you to feel vulnerable. Is it OK?"

Layla rolled down her window to get a better look. *Coming Next Summer—The Angel Wing of Hope Cottage.* She unbuckled her seatbelt and slid into his lap, wrapping her arms around his neck, a few tears rolling on his skin. "I love it."

THEY GOT BACK to his mother's house in the late afternoon. It was time to scoop up the kids and play house back at Emerson's. Layla fed the kids pizza and got them bathed, while Gage handled a little work at the kitchen table.

"Hurry up, Uncle G!" Jacob yelled from the family room.

Layla put down a bowl of popcorn and hushed him, pointing to Connor asleep on the floor, exhausted after throwing up twice, an apparent by-product of feasting on every kind of sugar imaginable at his grandmother's house. Gage walked in, and Layla motioned for him to pick up Connor and take him to bed. Gage scooped him up and headed upstairs.

Jacob picked up Pippa and patted her sweetly. "I wish we could get a dog," the boy said. "But my mom says she doesn't need something else to take care of."

"Well, you can visit Pippa anytime," Layla said.

"Really?" Jacob said. "Could I come stay with you guys in Atlanta one weekend?"

"Sure, buddy," Gage said, coming back down. "We can go to a baseball game or a football game. What movie did you pick?"

"I haven't decided yet," Jacob said.

"Aunt Layla?" Ava called out softly, holding her stomach, her face pale.

Layla felt the the girl's forehead, then they whispered to each other. "Gage, Ava doesn't feel well. Do you know where Emerson keeps the heating pad?"

"No," Gage said. "Ava, did Grandma give you a bunch of junk, too?"

"Ava, sweetie, go lay down in your room," Layla said, kissing her on the forehead. "I'll be right there."

Ava headed upstairs, and Layla whispered to Gage, "She got her period."

"What? She's a little girl."

Layla smiled. "She's 14."

"I'm calling Emerson to come back home."

"Relax, she's just emotional and cramping. It's only the second one she's gotten."

"This wasn't in Emerson's notes," Gage said.

"Just help me find a heating pad and some aspirin."

ABOUT HALFWAY THROUGH zombies invading the world, Jacob feel asleep on the couch. Gage threw a blanket over him and let Pippa out for the night. Then he headed upstairs, hearing his wife's voice in Ava's bedroom. He stopped outside the door.

"Thanks for hanging out with me," Ava said. "I didn't want to be around the boys."

"Sure thing, sweetie."

"It's so unfair. Nothing happens to boys."

"Yes, it does," Layla said, pulling the covers over Ava and tucking her in. "They get a whole lot stupider as teenagers." Gage heard them giggle, and he tried not to laugh.

"Didn't you meet Uncle G when you were a teenager?"

"Yeah," Layla said dreamily.

"Can I tell you something?" Ava asked. "I haven't even told Mom, but I just have to tell somebody. I had my first kiss Friday."

Gage gnashed his teeth, considering what kind of weapon to use on the boy.

"Wow, tell me all about it."

"You won't tell Mom?"

"I won't tell her, but you might want to. I bet she'd surprise you with her reaction."

"Maybe," Ava said. "It was Justin and. . . ."

Gage leaned in closer, listening intently, considering whether to use more than one weapon, or perhaps just turn the matter over to Mateo.

"How do I get him to kiss me with tongue next time?"

Gage nearly choked and walked in the room. "Time for bed, kiddo." He kissed Ava on top of the head and took Layla's hand. Layla patted Ava on the leg, shut off the lamp, and turned towards the door with Gage.

"Aunt Layla?" Ava called out, and Layla and Gage turned around. "I'm glad you married Uncle G."

Layla smiled. "Me, too."

CHAPTER TWENTY-SIX

THEY FELL INTO bed when they got back to Atlanta. Playing house was exhausting, but it was a nice glimpse into their future. Despite the sick kids, periods, and teen angst, Gage loved every second of it. And he loved seeing the way Layla handled the kids, how she listened to Ava without judgment, excited for his niece, giving solid advice. It was a good sneak peek at Layla as a mom.

A few hours before the sun, Gage woke up to the sound of loud coughing. He scanned the dark bedroom. The bed was empty, except for Pippa snoring softly without a care in the world. He flicked on a lamp and heard more coughing. It was more of a gagging sound this time – horrible and violent—coming from the bathroom. "Angel?" He hopped out of bed and threw on some shorts, stepping over his briefcase.

"Don't come in!" Layla said.

But Gage was already inside, finding his wife hunched over the toilet, naked, holding back her hair with one hand and gripping the seat with the other. "Are you OK?" Layla reached for some toilet paper and wiped her mouth. Then she heaved again, a rush of bile hitting the water, a putrid odor filling the bathroom. He made a move towards her, but Layla held up a hand.

"Don't come too close," she said. "I don't want to get you sick."

He sat down beside her and touched her forehead. "You don't feel warm. How many times have you thrown up?"

Layla closed her eyes and rested her head on the edge of seat. "I don't know. I lost count."

Gage ran his hand down to her belly. "Maybe you're pregnant?

Maybe this is morning sickness?"

Her head shot up. "I'm not pregnant. I'm sure I just have a touch of what Connor had."

Gage handed her a towel. "Do you think you're done?"

"For now," she said and wiped her mouth.

He helped her to her feet. "Maybe wash your face and hands, then go lay back down. I'll make you some toast. There's some ginger ale in the refrigerator. I'll get you some."

"I'm sure I'll be better when. . . ." She quickly dropped to her knees and threw up again.

LAYLA WOKE UP late morning with Pippa nuzzled at her side. She looked over at the nightstand, set up with a glass of ginger ale, saltine crackers, and a pregnancy test. She almost threw up again. *The man is impossible.* She picked up the test and went in search of her husband, finding him in his office on the phone. She put the test on his desk, forced a smile, and headed back to bed. Gage ended his call and, box in hand, followed her to the bedroom. "Can you take the test and find out?"

"I'm not pregnant," she said and slipped under the covers. "Plus, you have to miss your period for those things to work and. . . ."

"No, you don't. I talked to the pharmacist." He pointed to the box. "This one works six days before a missed period."

Layla threw a pillow over her head. "Of course."

"You could be pregnant," Gage said. "We haven't always been careful."

"I'm sick," she said, throwing the pillow at him, "and you're not helping me feel better with all this."

Gage stroked her cheek and felt her forehead. "Maybe you should see a doctor?"

"If I don't feel better soon, I will. I just want to sleep."

"Can you take the test first? I need to know."

"I just peed before getting back to bed, so no." She yawned and turned on her side. "Good night."

Gage tucked her in and sat on the edge of the bed. He heard her breathing slow and knew she was already asleep. He thought about the baby—hopefully—in her belly and reached for the wings around his neck, knowing one day he'd pass them down. He couldn't wait to be a father, to teach their child to fly, like his dad taught him. He missed his dad. The man always had sound fatherly advice, whether solicited or not. He wished his dad was still around to see his child.

Lord knows, Mrs. Baxter was never going to see his child. The mere thought of the woman made him physically ill.

GAGE SPENT THE next few days working from home, taking care of Layla in between calls and video conferences. He was around so much he didn't require Mateo any longer. But he told Mateo he'd keep his number handy. There was a good chance he'd need the man down the road, to look out for Layla again or kneecap one of Ava's boyfriends. Mateo said he was just a phone call away and would welcome the chance to rough up a teenager. Gage was pleased to hear it. The world needed more men like Mateo.

Unfortunately, Layla wasn't getting any better. A steady diet of ginger ale and toast wasn't doing much good. When the nausea turned to abdominal pain, she made a doctor's appointment. And she wanted to go alone. Gage didn't like the idea but didn't want to argue. He knew she was used to doing these things alone and wanted to respect that. Or maybe she needed some space to adjust to the idea of being a mother, though she still hadn't taken the pregnancy test. And he'd stopped asking her days ago.

He arranged for a driver to take her to the doctor and took the chance to go to corporate headquarters, to visit with his management team, to clear his desk again. He looked at the clock on his office wall. The hands were moving slowly. She'd been gone over an hour and hadn't called. He kicked himself for not going with her. Hopefully she wasn't doubled-over somewhere. Surely the driver would call if she got sick in the car or something was terribly wrong. Hopefully everything was fine, and she'd soon call with good news.

"Mr. Montgomery," Mary said over the speaker. "There's someone here to see you."

"Layla?"

"No, sir. She says she's Layla's mother."

CHAPTER TWENTY-SEVEN

GAGE TOSSED HIS briefcase in the living room and started to pace, a massive headache attacking him. The bitch had some nerve, flying all the way to Atlanta, showing up to his office unannounced, admitting she sold the stories to the press – and then demanding money. *Unbelievable.*

The gall she had to sell out her own daughter and then, when the cash well ran dry, come to him seeking out more. The whole thing was actually a little scary—and not for himself. He was scared for Layla—for her health, their possible baby, and what this new information would do to her.

He never had the urge to kill someone before, to look someone in the eye and watch the life drain out. He was tempted, and if anything could push him over the edge, it was someone hurting Layla. Surely no one would miss Mrs. Baxter. It took every ounce of self-control not to wrap his hands around her neck and snap it—like her sociopathic pervert son had done to Layla's dog. He picked up Pippa, and his stomach turned at the thought, at the inhumanity of it. The creep deserved to die, too. It was long overdue. His time was coming.

If ever there was a time to fly, it was now—to escape to the skies and look down on the world and gain some perspective. But there was no time for that now, not with Layla wherever the hell she was. He hadn't heard from her all afternoon, and his calls were rolling over to voicemail. He had no idea what was going on, what tests were being done. For all he knew, his wife could be vomiting on the side of the road or having emergency surgery at some unknown hospital. His excitement about being a father was now a flurry of nerves.

He thought to scream from his balcony. But instead he gave Pippa a kiss. He had to calm down. Whenever she got back, Layla was going to need him—whether she was pregnant, or to deal with her mother.

He replayed the conversation with Mrs. Baxter in his mind, the reason she needed money, the reason she needed it so urgently. He had no idea if it was true. The woman was a calculated cunt, but no one could possibly make up what she said. There'd be no easy way out of this mess, and the decision wasn't really his to make. Sure, it was his money, but it was Layla's family. He'd tell Layla about it when she got home, provided she was feeling better.

The house phone rang. "Could I please speak with Layla Tanner?" a female voice asked.

"Layla Montgomery?"

"Oh, yes, I see that now. Yes, Mrs. Montgomery."

"She's not in. This is her husband."

"This is the nurse. I have her test results. Could you please have her call us when she gets home?"

"I figured she was still there."

"No, she left about 30 minutes ago."

"OK. You can give me the results."

"I'm sorry, Mr. Montgomery. You're not listed as someone we can release records to."

"We got married last month."

"I'm not at liberty to disclose any medical information with you. Please have your wife call us when she gets home, and the doctor will speak with her about her ultrasound and test results."

Gage hung up, grinning from ear to ear. *An ultrasound!* That meant only one thing. He calculated her due date in his head. It would be late May or early June, which would be perfect, just before the oppressive Georgia heat set in. He looked around the penthouse. They'd need to convert a room into a nursery, or maybe just go ahead and get a new place – a place of their own. They'd already talked about doing that. Now was as good a time as any.

He heard the front door and raced towards it. Layla was as white as a ghost. Gage took her hands and led her to the sofa. "Sit down! Rest!

260 | PRESCOTT LANE

Put your feet up!"

"What's going on?" she asked.

"The nurse called a few minutes ago," Gage said, smiling.

"What did she say?"

"She wouldn't tell me anything. But I know you had an ultrasound and a pregnancy test."

"Gage. . . ."

"I can't believe it. I know I said I thought you were pregnant, but for it to actually happen so soon." He kissed her hard on the mouth. "I'm so happy." He pulled back, seeing a few tears in her eyes. "You're not happy."

"I'm not. . . ."

"Angel, I know it's unexpected," he said, rubbing her belly, "but this is a blessing."

"Gage. . . ."

"I really hope we have a girl first. I know everyone always wants a boy first, but. . . ."

"I'm *not* having a baby," she whispered, a tear falling down.

Her words like a kick to the gut, Gage staggered a little and felt like an idiot. He pulled her to his chest. "It's OK, Angel. We can have a baby whenever you want."

Layla pushed him away. "No, we can't," she said, the tears coming quicker. "I might not ever be able to get pregnant."

"*What?* Of course, you can."

"No, the doctor said. . . ."

"I wish you would've let me come with you. Can you tell me what the doctor said?"

"He thinks the vomiting was from Connor, but he's concerned about the abdominal pain."

"What does he think is wrong?"

"Endometriosis, maybe." Gage gave a confused look. "It's the leading cause of infertility in women."

"You said *maybe*. So he doesn't know for sure, right? Let's call and get your results."

Layla trembled at the thought. The results could bring more pain, both for her and him. And she'd already put him through so much—leaving him like she did, the news coverage, now this. "I've always had bad cramping. I never thought. . . ."

"There's no reason to assume the worst."

"What if I can't have your babies? I know you've been happy thinking I was pregnant."

He kneeled at her feet. "I'm happy with you. We'll work something out. In sickness and in health, right?"

THEY SPENT 15 minutes on the phone with the doctor. They learned a laparoscopy, a type of out-patient surgery, was the only way to diagnose endometriosis. The ultrasound and the rest of her test results looked normal, but they needed to schedule the surgery. Gage wanted it done soon—today, if possible. He had to know what was going on. Layla wasn't eager to go under the knife, but she wanted to get to the bottom of things, too. And she was tired of feeling terrible.

The doctor connected them to his scheduling assistant, who informed them the next opening was in three weeks. The assistant assured them that was the soonest possible date. Layla threw up her hands at the thought of three weeks, walked to the bedroom, and left her husband to deal with scheduling. Gage gnashed his teeth. He couldn't bear the unknown, or seeing his wife in physical and emotional pain. And the woman on the phone didn't really seem to care.

With Layla out of earshot, Gage took the phone off speaker and held it to his ear. He told the assistant who he was. He couldn't remember the last time he did that, but he didn't mind playing the card now—not when his wife's health was at stake. He told her three weeks wasn't going to work. He promised her family free flights on Southern Wings for the next year if she could do better. A moment of silence followed. Gage considered upping his offer to two years of free flights. If the assistant was going to play hardball, he was ready.

The assistant finally spoke up. "I'm looking over the schedule again. It appears we can work in Mrs. Montgomery later this week."

Gage breathed again and thanked the assistant profusely, praising her customer service, even offering to write a letter to the doctor about how great she was, what an asset she must be for the doctor's practice. He knew it was all bullshit—the assistant certainly knew it, too—but he didn't care. Layla was going to get the best care, and if he had to butter up the assistant—or bribe her—so be it.

He hung up and took a look at the closed bedroom door. He couldn't tell Layla her mother had showed up today, making threats, wanting money. There were too many balls in the air now, too much happening at once, too many changes of direction. He needed to resolve one issue once and for all. He fired up his laptop, logged into his accounts, and wired $50,000 to Mrs. Baxter. It was a drop in the bucket, but he hated to do it. He'd rather throw the money from his balcony. But there was no other option now. He printed the wire transfer and put it in his briefcase.

He headed to the bedroom, finding Layla's head buried deep in Pippa's fur. "I got it scheduled for the end of the week. Can I get you anything?"

"No," she whispered.

He brushed back her hair. "We'll be fine, either way. We promised we'd stick it out no matter what. No running."

"I don't want to be the reason you don't have kids," Layla said, raising her eyes to him. "If anyone should be a dad, it's you. If anyone should have mini-versions of themselves, it's you."

Gage tilted his head slightly, feeling his heart swell. "We don't even know if it's endometriosis or not. Hopefully it's not. But if it is, we can get you treatment anywhere in the world. And if that doesn't work, there are lots of other options."

"But I want to get big and waddle around and feel our baby in my belly. I want you to feel our baby moving in my stomach. I want you to hold my hand when I push our baby out."

"I want those things, too. But if that can't happen, then we'll try other options. The goal is a baby, right?"

Layla gave an unconvincing nod and lay down on the bed, crying silently. Gage cuddled in behind her. He hated when she cried. He felt so helpless. He just wanted to fix things, to make her pain, the uncertainty, go away. *At least I made her mother go away.*

The phone rang, and Gage looked at the caller ID. "It's Poppy."

"I don't want to talk to anyone," Layla said. "I don't want anyone to know."

"But you might feel better if. . . ."

"Please, Gage. I feel so. . . . I just feel like I'm letting everyone down."

"That's ridiculous. You're sick. Angel, you aren't alone anymore. You've got a family now. Don't deny them the chance to love you."

IT WAS ANOTHER day of the same, another day closer to surgery. Layla stretched out on the sofa in the living room, a heating pad on her stomach. She said a prayer for peace, asking her angels to intervene. She hadn't asked for much lately. This would be a good time for them to help. She was, after all, named after the angel of childbirth and conception.

She asked for a sign. Her mind had been so cluttered lately. She wondered if she'd been missing signs all over the place. She reached for the remote, flipping through some channels. She landed on an episode of "Teen Mom." *Surely this isn't a sign.* Her blood boiling, she strangled the remote with her hand.

"It's not fair!" she cried. "These little girls can get pregnant!" She had a mind to hurl the remote at the flatscreen but instead made Gage's briefcase her target. She'd asked him days ago to move it to his office, but it was still everywhere but there. She fired the remote at it just as Gage came in with a bowl of chicken broth.

"I'll get it out of here," he said, handing her the bowl and scooping up the briefcase, tossing it on the floor in the bedroom.

"Not in there!" she snapped. "Put it in your office!"

"OK, I'll move it later." He flipped off the television and rubbed her leg.

"I'm sorry," she said. "That was hateful."

"You can feel hateful right now if you want."

"I shouldn't take it out on your briefcase. And I shouldn't be jealous of the teen moms."

There was a knock at the door, and Gage got up to answer. Layla saw him talking to someone and could tell by the way he was standing, acting, that he was surprised by whoever was there. Gage shut the door and walked back, pinching the bridge of his nose.

"Who's at the door?"

"My mom," he said sheepishly.

"What's she doing here?"

"I told her you weren't feeling well, and she hopped on a plane from Savannah."

"I said I don't want to anyone to know."

"She dragged it out of me. I didn't think she'd show up at our door!"

"You are such a 'momma's boy,'" she said, smiling.

"Do you want me to tell her to leave?"

"That would be real good for my relationship with her."

"How about I tell her *I* want her to go?"

"She won't believe that." Layla wiped her eyes and patted her hair. "I'm sure I look like hell."

"No, you don't."

"Liar. Let her in."

"I'll make sure she just stays a few minutes." He hustled to the door and got his mother.

Helen handed him her purse, shooed him to his office, and greeted Layla. "You poor thing! Gage told me you didn't really want anyone to know or to see anybody. But I just had to come."

"I don't want anyone to worry."

"I'm a mother. I'm supposed to worry. That way I can blame my wrinkles on my children."

Layla smiled. "Did you bring any of those little bottles of whiskey? I could use a few of those right now."

"Let me tell you what helps in these situations—family. We are a close family. We're here for you. Better to be honest with family. My husband wasn't about his illness. Really had an effect on Gage."

"I know. I'm just feeling so. . . ."

"Worthless, incapable, insecure, sad, angry, depressed."

Layla's eye's bulged. "Exactly."

"I've been there, honey. You think Emerson and Gage being 10 years apart was planned? His father and I struggled for years to get pregnant again. Back then, they didn't have all these fancy procedures to help. We'd given up on having another child and then. . . ." She snapped her fingers. "There he was."

"He's a good guy," Layla said, holding back tears. "I know he wants kids."

"Gage wants you more than anything, even kids. His life only makes sense with you. Don't give up hope."

"Mom," Gage said, coming out of his office, "Layla really should rest."

Helen kissed her son on the head and headed to the door with him. "She's in a fragile place right now, Gage. You have to stay strong for her. You must do whatever it takes to take care of her."

Gage nodded and looked over at his laptop. *I already did.*

GAGE WAS NERVOUS. He knew Layla was, too. He couldn't wait to get to sleep, for the morning to come, for the surgery to be over, for some good results. He crawled into bed beside her.

"I need you to promise me something," Layla said. "Promise me that when I'm in surgery, you won't let them take anything out. I don't care how bad it is. Don't let them take out my ovaries or my uterus."

"Come on, Angel. I mean, the doctor. . . ."

"No matter what, Gage."

"But if the doctor says he needs to remove something to help you feel better. . . ."

"I need to know you won't let him. I already told the doctor, but I need you to promise, too."

"I can't promise that."

"Then we have no chance," she said and turned away from him. "There's no hope."

He wrapped his arms around her. "Quiet, Angel. I know in my heart you're going to be fine, perfect."

"LAYLA," A WHISPER called out. "Layla, wake up."

She shot up and looked around. She could barely hear the voice and didn't recognize it. Gage wasn't saying her name. He was fast asleep, exhausted. He'd worried himself into a coma. A hurricane couldn't wake him right now. She looked at Pippa, sitting up and staring at the ceiling. The dog was the only other soul in the world awake right now.

She thought she must be dreaming. She looked at the clock—three hours until the alarm, until they went off to the hospital. She felt her stomach twinge. The surgery needed to go OK. And Gage needed to do as she asked. She didn't want to give up hope. His mother told her not to. But it was hard not to fear the worst.

"Layla," the voice said again, a bit louder, a bit more clearly.

Layla's heart skipped a beat. She knew the voice this time. It had been so long. She hadn't heard it since she was a child. *Aria.* Her body warm and tingling, she threw off the covers. Pippa was still staring at the ceiling, transfixed by it. Layla looked up, but there was nothing. At least she couldn't see anything—not a sparkle, not a shred of light.

It didn't make sense. Aria would always come with a flicker, but there was nothing but darkness now. Maybe Aria was coming in a different way this time. Maybe Aria had changed her *modus operandi* over the past 20 years. Or maybe, and more likely, Layla was just going crazy, hearing things, finally losing her mind. That's probably what was happening.

She ran her fingers through Gage's sandy blond hair then traced her fingers down his chest, along the path of the leather rope cord holding her wings. She loved he always wore them. She was thankful he was in her life, that he'd be with her before and after the surgery. She reached for the clock and turned off the alarm. There was no way she was going back to sleep now.

"Layla!"

She stood up and glanced towards the bedroom window, faint shades of red, blue, and yellow coming through the curtains. She rubbed her eyes and stepped closer to the window, pulling the curtains to the side, finding a lunar rainbow flying across downtown Atlanta. She threw her hands over her mouth, and her eyes welled up with tears. *I'm going to be OK.*

She had to get a better look out on the balcony. But she didn't want to wake up Gage. So she headed there through the living room, her once-wobbly legs now moving with a spring. She couldn't wait to get outside, so anxious to see what Aria had left her, but tripped over Gage's briefcase and fell forward, barely keeping herself upright. *How many times do I have to tell him?* She reached down to pick it up and felt an array of papers littering the floor.

She shuffled the papers into a pile and put them and the briefcase on a living room table. Then she stepped out onto the balcony, the cold cement on her feet giving her goosebumps, and looked up into the night sky. The arc of Aria's rainbow was sweeping high across the moon, painting the sky with bright full colors. She'd never seen anything like this. She'd asked for a sign, and Aria delivered big time.

She had to tell Gage. She slipped back into the living room and walked past the table, flicking on a lamp. One word leaped off a page. *Baxter.* She sat down to steady herself, her blood pressure skyrocketing, her hands shaking, a thin layer of sweat covering her body. She scanned the papers. It didn't make sense he'd send money to her mother, the woman who never believed her, never protected her, and sold her out to the world.

She'd told Gage so many times she hated secrets. He never listened. And this was more than just a secret. This was betrayal. She put the papers back in the briefcase and looked out towards the balcony. The rainbow was gone. The time for rainbows was over.

GAGE OPENED HIS eyes and stared at the clock. They were going to be late to the hospital. The alarm hadn't gone off. He reached for Layla to shake her awake, but she wasn't there. He called out for her. She didn't answer. He looked around the house. She wasn't there.

He came back to the bedroom and looked at the alarm clock. He'd double-checked he set it last night. Now he saw it was turned off. *Why would she turn it off?* He stared down at the cold, empty sheets and began to panic.

His hands shaking, this was the nightmare he'd had so many times, waking up to her gone, vanishing in the middle of the night, leaving him scared, confused, lathered in a sweat. He was back to being 18.

He looked around the house again and made dozens of calls. No one knew anything. He tried Poppy, but no answer. She was probably sleeping. He thought to call the police but knew they wouldn't do anything, not at this point, except maybe be suspicious of him.

She promised she'd never run again, but he always feared she would. It was always in the back of his mind. It made no sense for her to run now, just because she was scared of surgery, scared of maybe not having children.

He was pissed she'd do this again. She wasn't a teenager on a faraway island anymore. She had a lot going for her. She had a home, a dog, a husband. She should be able to face her fears, to rely on him for help.

Instead, she left him behind again, without a note or the courtesy of a phone call, without any regard for his feelings. She had no idea how humiliating and horrible it was to call friends and neighbors asking if they'd seen his wife.

He reached for the leather cord around his neck, hoping it didn't take another 12 years to find her. He tried Poppy again. Hopefully Layla was at her apartment, just needing a girlfriend's perspective before surgery. *Please be there.*

Poppy answered this time. She knew nothing. He believed her. She sounded as scared as he was. She said she was coming right over. She showed up with Dash within minutes. "Have you heard from her?" Gage asked frantically.

"No," Poppy said.

"Where the hell is she? Why would she just leave me in the middle of the damn night *again*?"

"I don't know."

Dash rubbed Poppy's shoulders and whispered, "What's he talking about 'again'?"

Poppy waved him off. "Don't worry about it now."

"Maybe you should call her?" Gage asked. "Maybe she'll pick up for you?"

"I tried on the way over. No answer. Did you guys get in a fight?"

"No," he said. "She was supposed to have surgery this morning."

"What?"

"Endometriosis—maybe."

"Jesus! I haven't talked to her in a few days," she said. "I had no idea."

"She didn't want anyone to know," Gage said. "She didn't want anyone to worry."

Poppy rolled her eyes and dialed Layla again.

"What is endo. . . .?" Dash wondered but couldn't remember the rest of the word.

"I'm thinking maybe she got scared," Gage said. "Maybe she went back to Savannah."

"No answer," Poppy said. "I'll try again."

Dash patted Gage's shoulder. "We'll find her. You're the boss man. Call Southern Wings and have them check if her name comes up on any flights. Or they can get in touch with the FAA."

Gage dialed his company and demanded a quick check of passenger names. "Layla Montgomery. . . .Yes, my wife." He lowered his head and waited a few moments, seeing Poppy hit redial over and over again. "Nobody by that name? Are you sure?"

"Try Tanner," Poppy said.

Gage looked at her like she had three heads. "Why would she do that?"

"I don't know. Maybe she's still using her old license. Just check, dammit!"

Gage groaned, pissed Layla could've reverted to her maiden name.

"Try Layla Tanner."

"Layla!" Poppy cried, waving her hands in the air.

"Check the name and text me," Gage ordered and hung up. "Poppy, put her on speaker!"

"Layla, where are you?" Poppy asked, holding up a finger to Gage, then hitting the speaker button.

"Just out doing some thinking," Layla said, clutching her stomach.

"In the middle of the night? You don't sound so good. Gage told me about the surgery. I wish you would've told me."

"I'm glad Gage talks to you because he doesn't tell me shit!"

Poppy shot Gage a death look. The man shrugged his shoulders. "Are you OK? What's going on?"

Layla wiped her forehead. "I might have fever. I don't know. My stomach really hurts."

"You're supposed to be in surgery."

"I know."

"Why aren't you? You need to figure out what's wrong"

"Gage is a liar! That's what's wrong."

Poppy shot Gage another death look and mouthed, "What did you do?"

"Angel!" he cried. "Tell me where you are. I'm coming to get you." There was silence, except for a faint background noise, an unmistakable hustle and bustle he knew all his life. "Angel?"

"Yes," she said quietly.

"What airport are you in?"

"Don't come after me."

"Surgery isn't a reason to disappear, to run away."

Layla laughed. "How about you giving my mother money? Is *that* a good enough reason?"

Gage took the phone off speaker and put it to his ear. "How did you. . . .?"

"Does it matter? I know."

"Layla, give me a chance to explain."

"Your chance to explain is over."

"For fuck's sake, listen to me."

"No, you listen to me! I can't believe you'd betray me like this. Does this have something to do with you not running for office?"

"I'm not running because I want to focus on you and our family."

"I can't give you a family!" Layla barked then broke down.

"Jesus Christ! Where are you?" Gage heard a ding on his phone. "Let me come get you."

"I'm going to find out the truth," Layla said. "I've got to do it myself because I can't trust my husband to tell me. Don't come after me."

"Layla? Layla?" There was only silence. She was gone. His phone dinged again, and he rushed to read the text.

Poppy stared daggers at her boss. "What the hell is going on? What the hell did you do?"

"I'll tell you on the plane," Gage said.

"Plane? Where?"

"Houston."

CHAPTER TWENTY-EIGHT

LAYLA BARELY MADE it to Houston in one piece. She felt like shit, and her stomach pulsed from the pain. She stumbled out of the elevator on the sixth floor of the hospital. She hadn't gone for herself, though she was supposed to be in a different one 800 miles away. She was going to this hospital because her mother's maid said that's where her mother was. The maid wouldn't say anything more.

Layla headed to the nurses' station. "I'm looking for my mother, Mrs. Baxter?" A young nurse told her the room number, and Layla walked down the corridor, unsure what she was going to find. She'd been so focused on getting to Houston without passing out that she hadn't developed a plan for what to do once she got here. And now she was in a strange hospital, going to see her mother.

Her mind began to race. Her mother probably had a hangnail and, so dramatic, was making a big deal out of it, looking for sympathy from health care professionals. She'd get none from Layla—even if it was something serious. She didn't deserve it. She'd committed the worst sin a parent could ever commit—not protecting her own child, then selling out her child for money. She even managed to get a huge amount from Gage.

Layla reached the room and drew a deep breath. She pushed open the door, slowly. As the scene came into view, her body started to tremble, and she let out a little cry. Like so much of her life, it wasn't anything she expected.

"Quiet."

THIRTY THOUSAND FEET in the air, Gage paced the aisle of the corporate jet. Dash and Poppy were getting dizzy watching him go back and forth.

"What's going on with Layla's mother?" Poppy asked.

"It's complicated," Gage said.

"No, it's not," she said. "Layla's mother is a raging bitch. You know that, right?"

Gage nodded. "Mrs. Baxter was selling stories about Layla to the press."

"That bitch! Does Layla know this?"

"Yes. I told her when we got back from our honeymoon."

"Why would her mother do that?" Dash asked.

"She needed the money," Gage said. "She saw our engagement in the papers, on the news, and figured that was the answer."

"I need money, too!" Poppy said. "But I don't screw over my family to get it! What does this have to do with Layla going to Houston?"

"Her mother came to see me about a week ago. I never told Layla. I was going to, but she got sick. She must've found out somehow."

"Why'd her mother come to you?"

"Because her son is dying."

"Good. I hope that asshole is in terrible, blinding pain."

"So you know what he did to Layla?"

"Of course," Poppy said and flashed a look to Dash not to ask questions.

"Her son is broke. No health insurance. The money Mrs. Baxter got from the media outlets helped with some medical bills, but there's tons more. She can't afford to pay them."

Poppy shrugged. "I hope the hospital stops treatment for non-payment or something. I hope he dies—the sooner, the better. I actually hope he's already dead." Then it clicked in her mind, what Layla had said about money, just before Gage took the phone off speaker. Poppy sprung out of her seat like a wild animal, her arms flailing. "Tell me you aren't paying for his care!" Dash jumped up and held Poppy back. "Tell me you're not doing that! Tell me you're not doing that, Gage!"

Gage held her stare. "I am."

Poppy wiggled an arm free and fired a right cross to Gage's jaw. "That bastard raped her over and over again! And you're fucking taking care of him!" She went for a left jab, but Dash pulled her back before she landed it.

"Layla's brother did that to her?" Dash asked.

"Her half-brother," Poppy corrected, pulling at the ends of her hair. "Gage, how could you do this? How could you take care of him?"

"You think I don't want to kill him with my own two hands? You think I don't want him to burn in hell? Of course I do!" Gage rubbed his jaw. "But I had to think about Layla, too."

"What the hell are you talking about?" Poppy asked. "You think Layla would want to pay his bills?"

"I don't think she'd *want* to," Gage said, "but I think she'd be real conflicted about it. She's a good person. She puts others before herself. She's all about forgiveness. I think it would be a painful decision for her. Can you imagine having to decide if the man who abused you—part of your own family—should live or die, suffer or not?"

"You should've let Layla make it!"

"I was going to, but then she got sick! I didn't want her having to make that kind of decision when she can barely stand up! It would be hard enough if she was healthy!"

"It would be an easy decision for me," Poppy said.

"But not for Layla. And her mother knew that," he said. "That's why Mrs. Baxter came to me. She wasn't sure if Layla would give her the money, but she knew I would—that I'd want to protect Layla, to keep the woman away from her. Mrs. Baxter said if I didn't pay, she'd go straight to Layla."

"This is disgusting," Poppy said. "You let her play you."

"I don't care. I couldn't have her talking to Layla when she's so sick and so upset about maybe not being a mother herself. She's going through enough." Gage lowered his head and pulled at his hair. "Things are so screwed up."

"They sure are," Poppy said. "So if Layla were well, you would've told her?"

"I think so. I think I would. This should've been her decision to make. I just wanted to keep her mother away from her."

"And now Layla is going to see her?"

"Apparently so."

"And maybe her half-brother, too! Layla will be totally blindsided. How long until we're there?"

"About an hour."

Poppy looked away and exhaled. "You own the damn plane, don't you? Tell them to go faster!"

OUT IN THE hallway, Mrs. Baxter told Layla about her son's illness, his coming death, why she sold the stories, how she blackmailed Gage into paying the bills. The woman was especially proud of the last part, how easy it was to get money from the head of Southern Wings, how happy she was when she received the wire. "Your husband had no business even thinking about running for office," her mother said before going back in the room. "I wouldn't trust him with the public's money."

Layla brushed off her mother's bullshit and thought about her half-brother behind the wall, just a few feet away—dying. She'd prayed so hard for this moment as a young girl. But now she couldn't bring herself to watch it. And she wasn't giddy about it, either—which was strange because she used to wish him dead every day, especially on those haunting nights when she could hear him creeping to her room, his footsteps getting closer and closer, wishing he'd die before getting in her bed, before breathing on her, before touching her skin. And if he didn't die on the way in, she'd take it if he died on the way out. At least it'd be the last time he touched her.

Years later, when she left the house and was out of reach, she sometimes still wished him dead, but not as often. She came to believe there was something unseemly about wishing a person dead—even a piece of shit. No good karma could come from that. There was no reason to dwell on the man anyway when she'd made such good progress recovering. She'd done her best to move on. She wasn't going to let her half-brother have any more power over her life. She wanted nothing to do with him or her mother.

She figured that's why Gage paid the money—to keep them out of her life, to keep her from a life and death decision. *Especially in my condition. He always wants to protect me.*

But the time for protection was over. Now she was here, in the thick of things in a Houston hospital. She hadn't come all this way to be shoved in the hallway by her mother. She hadn't come all this way to be "quiet," as her half-brother always told her. The time for that was over, too. She wanted him to see her before he died. She wanted him to take her vision to the grave. No one could stop her from doing that—not even her husband. If her half-brother was going to die, she was going to be there when he fell quiet.

She gathered the last bit of energy she had and pushed open the door to the hospital room. She stared down at her half-brother, laying on his back in the bed, his body pale and skin and bones, his eyes yellow, tubes criss-crossing through his nose and arm, just a few strands of hair left on his head, an oxygen mask over his face. Her mother was holding vigil at his side, their hands intertwined. Layla held back a twinge of vomit. "Get out, Mother."

"Excuse me?"

"Get out. I want to talk to him alone."

Her mother got to her feet. "You don't order me around. You owe me respect. I'm your mother."

"I don't owe you a damn thing."

"It's always about *you*, isn't it?"

"No, Mother, it's not. You've always made that very clear."

"I don't know what you're talking about. You're crazy."

"If I'm crazy, you should just get out."

"Did you ever think about what all this was like for *me*? To have to choose between your children?"

"You chose wrong, Mother."

"You know, I have feelings, too! Do you know how disappointing it is to have to find out your only daughter is engaged, married, in the media? I raised you better than that."

"You raised me in hell."

"You have such a chip on your shoulder."

"Yeah, I do. That's what happens when your mother doesn't protect you."

Mrs. Baxter scowled. "Just get over it already."

"He molested me for years, Mother. You don't get over that."

"You must stop blaming him for your problems. We did everything we could for you. You had the best treatment, years of therapy. Now you have a handsome husband with a ton of money. I really don't know what you're complaining about. I must've done something right."

"You get no credit for my marriage or the success in my life."

"Really? Because I could've taken it all away." Her mother stepped closer. "I could've told the papers about how the next Georgia governor is married to a girl who stabs homeless people."

"Go tell them," Layla said. "I don't care anymore."

"I don't like all this talk in front of your brother. He shouldn't have to hear this in his condition."

"I've got a right to be here. Just like you said he had a right to be at my father's funeral. Remember that, Mother? Remember me having to stand at the coffin, across from the man who molested me?"

Mrs. Baxter patted her son's leg. "I'll just be gone a minute, honey. You rest. I'm going to get someone to remove her. I'll be right back."

"Yes, probably best to let the pedophile die in peace."

Her mother gone, Layla stood at the bottom of his bed, running her eyes over his frail body. He could barely keep his eyes open. And he seemed to be struggling to breathe, to get a hint of air, even with the oxygen mask. There was nothing she could or needed to do to make him suffer. Nature was taking care of that. He was getting what he deserved.

For a moment, she wasn't sure what to do, what she was waiting for, hoping for—maybe a deathbed apology or confession, some kind of "come to Jesus" moment. She'd seen it on TV before. She wondered if her half-brother was even capable of being sorry, and, if so, whether that would make a difference, whether she'd feel any differently, whether she'd forgive him.

278 | PRESCOTT LANE

She began to speak but stopped when he suddenly began to move, straining, his whole mind and body seemingly focused on lifting his thin arm. He labored for several moments then finally got it up and brushed the mask off his face. Then he gasped for air and managed a few awkward breaths to try to steady himself. "Still a little bitch," he muttered through raspy breath, beginning to cough and gag, his face turning blue.

All sorts of beeps and bells began to cry out from the machines in the room. Her half-brother's eyes popped. She could see the panic, the fear, in them. He struggled to move his arm to the mask, fighting to put it back on, his arms and hands shaking. Layla held her ground, watching, waiting. There was no need to say a thing. It was fine to be quiet now. He got the mask back on but couldn't breathe.

Her mother came in with a nurse, the weight of death heavy in the room. "What is going on?" she cried.

Layla kept her eyes fixed on her half-brother, struggling, his body clenching, turning a deeper shade of blue. The nurse hustled to the machines and hurriedly called for a doctor.

"What the hell did you do, Layla?"

Still quiet, Layla gripped the bottom of the bed and held the man's eyes with her own. She would've stood there for hours, days if she had to. The sick fuck was going to look at her face when he breathed his last breath. The beeps and bells grew louder, and his eyes grew huge. She started to tremble, the bed frame shaking slightly.

He seemed to be fighting the inevitable, her mother weeping at his side, begging him to stay alive. Then suddenly a long, extended beep filled the room, as his body went still, his eyes open, straight on Layla. His mother fell on his chest, sobbing. Layla stood frozen, numb, the dead coldness of his eyes so familiar. A doctor rushed in, but there was nothing to do. The nurse shut off the machines and closed his eyes.

A heavy weight lifted, Layla felt a blinding pain in her body. Her feet gave way beneath her, and she fell to the floor.

AFTER TOUCHING DOWN, they took turns texting and calling, but Layla never answered. Still, Gage knew where she'd go. He knew what she'd be facing. He blew through the hospital entrance, his eyes darting for an information desk, needing a room number for the half-brother. He saw a receptionist area and headed straight there. He tapped his fingers on the desk, as Poppy and Dash waited behind him.

The young receptionist lifted her head, her eyes soft. "I'm sorry to have to tell you, but he died less than an hour ago."

Gage smiled inside. He hoped the asshole died before Layla saw him, before he had the chance to hurt her again. He tried not to grin, not to celebrate. The only thing keeping him from fist-pumping Poppy and Dash was that he now had no idea where Layla could be.

"Now what?" Poppy asked.

Gage pinched the bridge of his nose and scanned the hospital lobby, his eyes locking on Mrs. Baxter stepping out of an elevator, dabbing her eyes with a tissue. "Dash, Poppy, wait here." He marched towards the woman. "Where's Layla?"

"My son is dead," she said.

"I heard. I hope he suffered."

"You're a bastard. You and Layla deserve each other."

"Where's my wife?"

"She fainted when her brother died."

"What?" he barked and yelled to Poppy and Dash. "See if Layla's been admitted!" He glared down at Mrs. Baxter. "What did you do? What the hell happened?"

"She just collapsed. She always was a weak little thing." Mrs. Baxter shook her head. "That's all I know."

Poppy hurried over to Gage. "Layla's been admitted. They won't tell me anything. Just that she's in surgery."

Gage turned back to Mrs. Baxter. "Your daughter is in surgery, and you're just *leaving*?"

"I have a funeral to plan. Layla won't care if I'm not here."

Poppy stepped up. "Mrs. Baxter?"

"Yes."

"You're a pervert-loving cunt!"

CHAPTER TWENTY-NINE

POPPY LOOKED INTO the hospital room from the hallway. The surgery had been successful, but Layla still lay motionless in bed. She'd been this way—asleep, breathing peacefully—for almost 24 hours. It didn't make sense she'd still be like this. There was no medical reason for it.

Gage stayed by her side for every nerve-wracking minute. He never ate, changed clothes, or washed his face. He barely went to the bathroom. Every hour or so, Poppy and Dash told him to get something to eat or take a walk or get some fresh air. But he never did. He had no intention of leaving his wife. He was going to be by her side. And he'd need his family beside him for whatever happened, whether good or bad.

Helen and Emerson hopped on the first flight they could. Poppy brought them up to speed. "Layla had 'walking appendicitis.'"

"Not endometriosis?" Helen asked.

"The laparoscopy ruled that out right away," Poppy said.

"What is 'walking appendicitis'?" Emerson asked.

"It's when the toxins leak out slowly rather than a full-on burst," Poppy said. "Luckily, Layla developed an abscess of some kind that walled off the toxins from the rest of her body. If not for that, she could've developed septic shock and died."

"Oh my!" Helen said. "Were they able to get the toxins out?"

"Yes, and they set up a drain to take care of the rest," Poppy said. "She has IV antibiotics to kill off any infection."

"Why hasn't she woken up?" Emerson asked.

"They don't really know. They say she's in perfect health. They ordered a CAT scan, and it came back clean—no stroke, no blood clots, nothing."

"Poor dear," Helen said. "Can we see her?"

"You'd have to get your son out," Poppy said. "Only one visitor at a time. Pretty strict policy around here."

"Whatever," Helen said. "I'm going to see my daughter-in-law." She walked past Poppy and pushed open the door.

"I'm coming, too," Emerson said.

"No, let me visit with my son first."

GAGE LOOKED DOWN at his wife, her hands folded across her chest, her lips full and red, her skin soft and luminous. She didn't look sick anymore. She didn't look like she needed to be in the hospital—except she wouldn't wake up. And the doctors and nurses were at a loss for what to do. They'd never seen anything like it. Gage was on the verge of madness, pulling at his hair, squeezing the bridge of his nose into oblivion.

He thought back to when they were teenagers, when all he wanted was to see her like this in bed, asleep, next to him. And now he'd give anything for her to wake up. He picked up her hand and caressed her fingers, brushing her wedding ring. "Please wake up," he begged, touching the wings around his neck. "I love you." He suddenly felt a familiar hand on his shoulder. "*Mom?*" He quickly dried his eyes.

"Emerson and I came as soon as we could."

"I don't know what's going on, why she won't wake up."

Helen touched Layla's hand. "Her body and soul are just in shock, honey. She's been through a surgery and a terrible ordeal. I heard a little about her childhood. Poppy told me some. Is this why she left that summer?" Her son nodded. "She's going to be OK. This is her way of healing, taking the rest she needs."

"I can't lose her."

"You won't, Gage." She kissed him on the forehead. "She'll be fine. In the meantime, you need to take care of yourself—eat, change clothes, wash up."

"Poppy put you up to this?"

"I don't take cues from her. This is coming from me. You look terrible."

He felt the stubble on this face. "I'm fine, Mom. I really don't. . . ."

"Son, you look *terrible*."

He exhaled. "Fine, Mom. I'm not going out to get any food, but Poppy can bring me some if she wants. Please have Dash get me some clothes and stuff. I'll change in here."

"Good boy."

The heart rate monitor beeped a little quicker. "Why's it doing that?"

"She's probably dreaming."

"Do you think she can hear me?"

"I'm sure she can," his mother said. "Now, you have to keep hope. Your father is watching out for her. Layla will wake up when she's ready. Our minds, our bodies, are designed to protect us."

A BEAUTIFUL LIGHT all around, Layla didn't feel any pain. And better than that, she'd never have to see her half-brother again. This was the best dream ever, blanketed in Aria's soft feathers, a soft hum of music raining down like a lullaby, the sweet scent of lavender all around. Nothing could be better than this. To be wrapped in Aria's love, something she hadn't felt in years, was even better than she remembered.

She wanted to stay this time, to never wake up. But off in the distance, she could hear a series of voices begging her to.

"You're my best friend. I miss you."

"Sweet Layla, come back to us."

"Wake up, Angel, wake up."

Layla felt her fingers start to tingle, and she looked down at them, the bright light making her skin glow. She could feel her lips now tingling, too. Then she heard Gage begging.

"Kiss me back," he said. "Wake up and kiss me back."

GAGE CRAWLED IN beside her amidst the tubes and wires, thankful his friends and family had gone to eat. He needed to be alone with his wife. He cradled her in his arms. He couldn't imagine not hearing her laugh again, not seeing her dimples pop out again. He'd only just found her again. He couldn't lose her now. This had to be a nightmare or some evil joke, or perhaps payback for not always being upfront with her. He ran his fingers through her chocolate brown hair and, his lips quivering, planted kisses all over her face. He buried his head in her hair, breathing in her lavender. His mother said not to give up hope. He never had—not even in the years they were apart. Deep inside, he always felt he'd find her again. He wasn't going to give up now. He looked down at Layla's peaceful face. "Remember when we first met on the beach. . . ."

LAYLA HEARD HIS voice, their story, their beautiful life together so far. She listened to him talk about how they watched the sunset together during their summer, how nervous he was to hold her hand the first time, how lucky he was the first time they made love, how they danced together in the Italian moonlight, how she was a better high than flying.

"The story of my life begins and ends with you," he said. "And it's not finished. We only just started."

His voice grew stronger, closer, as he went on about all the things they still had to do together—to find a home of their own, to build out the Angel Wing of Hope Cottage, to get her charity cross business off the ground, to finally get her up in the glider, to make lots of babies. Her body started to tingle at the thought, a warm sensation blanketing every inch of her.

He finished their past, their future, and the room fell quiet. He had no idea where to go from here. *Help me, Dad.*

A small white feather no bigger than a penny floated down and landed in her chocolate hair. He picked it up and rubbed it gently between his fingers. He looked up at the ceiling. There was nothing but tiles and an air vent. And there was nothing but wires and machines all around. He felt the bed pillow; it was solid and full of foam, not punctured, either.

Her voice echoed in his head, her words by the fountain in Forsyth Park. *A feather means an angel is near.*

He reached for the leather cord under his shirt, lifting it over his head. He stared at the wings in his hand. He'd never taken them off before. But he knew Layla needed them now. She needed them back. He slid the cord over her head, lifting her up to place it around her neck. "You're going to wake up," he said and fixed her hair around the wings.

LAYLA FELT HER feet land on sand. She breathed in the salty air and looked out to the ocean. There wasn't a soul in sight, and everything was perfectly still, even the water, except for a few gentle waves lapping her feet. She called out to Aria, and a blinding white light appeared in front of her. She reached towards the light, but it burned out as quickly as it came, making way for the angel's sweet face and white wings.

Hovering in the sky, Aria looked down at Layla like a proud mother, one whose child had managed the world's worst and thrived and survived, one who knew her work was nearly done and it was time to let go. Layla whispered a few words to Aria. The angel gave a tiny smile and nodded her head. The ugly chapters were over. It was time for peace, time for quiet. Layla's time was just beginning. The angel closed her eyes and disappeared over the horizon.

Layla opened her eyes and blinked a few times, not sure where she was. Things were blurry. There were strange beeps all around. The scene began to come into focus—the hospital room, the machines, the IV drip. She felt a medical band on her arm and saw the words "State of Texas." She saw her husband sitting in a chair beside her. He looked like hell. His eyes were heavy, closed. "Hey," she said. "Babies?"

Gage burst from the chair, kissing her. "You're awake! Thank God!

Thank you, Dad!"

"Babies?"

He nodded, tears in his eyes. "The doctor said you have a 'beautiful uterus.' Those were his exact words."

Layla smiled and threw a hand over her mouth. She felt a pain in her abdomen.

"Take it easy," he said. "You have a few stitches. Took out your appendix. You'll be fine."

She touched the wings around her neck. "Things must have been pretty bad."

"They're good now," he said. "But probably best you wear them for a little while."

"He's dead," she whispered.

"I know."

She looked in his eyes, her lip quivering. "I left you in the middle of the night—again. I'm so sorry. I wasn't thinking clearly. I won't run again. I was worried about. . . ."

"It's OK." His lips landed softly on hers. "I'm sorry, too. I won't keep stuff from you, even if you're sick or I think I'm protecting you."

"I know why you kept it from me." She took in her husband. "How long have I been here? How long have *you* been here?"

"However long you needed."

Layla smiled. "Aria came to me."

"I thought so," he said, tilting his head to the side. "She saved you again."

"No, you saved me. I was with her, but I kept hearing you. I said 'goodbye' to her. I don't need her anymore. Your love saved me when I was 16. Your love saves me each day of my life."

"Angel. . . ."

"That's where you're wrong," Layla said, reaching for his face. "You were always *my* angel."

EPILOGUE

18 MONTHS LATER

THE ANGEL WING of Hope Cottage was billed as the most modern and innovative sexual abuse treatment center in the United States. And Gage spared no expense in the design. When Layla had an idea for a butterfly garden in a courtyard area, a place where survivors and angels could spend some quiet time together, it happened—no questions asked.

And they incorporated whatever Sarah wanted, too. The only thing Gage asked was that each survivor who was interested in learning to fly be allowed to take lessons. He thought it might give a sense of perspective and control. And of course, he'd provide the instructors and the planes free of charge.

After a year and half, the Angel Wing was opening its doors today. Layla peeked out from a window inside. The spring sun was shining down. Media was getting ready for the dedication ceremony, and people were taking their seats. She saw everyone she loved: Poppy, Dash, Emerson, Helen, even Ava. At 16, she was old enough and wanted to support her aunt and uncle.

Layla caught a glimpse of Gage shaking a few hands, his eyes searching the crowd, no doubt for her. She'd told him she was coming out early. She hadn't told him she was speaking today. He would've had a heart attack. As it was, she promised she'd sit during the whole ceremony. But she hadn't really sat all day. There was too much to do.

She looked at her sundress and rubbed her hands across her huge belly, now two days overdue. "Stay in there a few more hours, or I'll never hear the end of it from Daddy." Gage had been almost impossible to live with since she told him she was pregnant, threatening to call Mateo, paying her OB to be on call every day. She figured an ambulance was parked around the corner.

Sarah patted Layla on the shoulder, and Layla gave a little nod she was ready. They came out of the building together and stepped onto a little stage to a round of applause. Gage smiled and shook his head at his wife, subtly biting his bottom lip. She could see his eyes moisten and could tell he was proud of her.

"Thank you for coming. This has been a great team effort. I'll keep this brief," Layla said and patted her belly. "Time is short for me these days, and if I stay on my feet too long, my protective husband may storm the stage." The crowd chuckled, and Layla took the chance to take a deep breath. "I'm Layla Montgomery, Gage's wife. I'm a wife, soon-to-be mother, friend, daughter, former bookstore owner, artist, yogi. I love sundresses and first edition books. And I'm a child sexual abuse survivor." She twirled the wings around her neck.

"Let me say that one more time. *I'm a sexual abuse survivor.* I never thought in a million years I'd make that public. I once told Gage I didn't want to be the face of child sexual abuse. That was a mistake. Of all the things I am in my life, all the things I represent, being a survivor is one of those things. And even though it's not anyone's business, I refuse to hide from it anymore. As you know, a couple years ago the media had a field day analyzing my choices, wondering what the heck I was doing as a teenager. I'm not saying every choice I made was the right one, but every choice I made was to survive—to survive to marry the most wonderful man, to survive to talk to you here today, to survive to have a daughter of my own."

She looked down at her belly. "This is the reason I'm finally speaking publicly. My daughter gave me the courage. I wasn't brave enough to talk before. I just let the media and others wonder about my life. But I don't want that for my daughter. I don't want people wondering about her. I want my daughter to be brave and fearless, and I can't ask her to be those things if I'm not myself." She pointed to the Angel Wing behind her. "Enough about me. This new building is beautiful, amazing, special—as you will see in a few minutes. It is a refuge when the world has become too much, when you are silenced, or when you aren't believed. It is a place of quiet and peace amidst the chaos. And the girls—they're coming later today—will be able to get the help they so desperately need from the minute they walk in the door. I'm grateful for that." She paused for a moment.

"But you know, I'm sad, too, because *every room, every bed*, is reserved. That means there are at least 100 separate incidents of sexual abuse Hope Cottage needs to deal with, that the girls need to deal with. And those are just the ones we know about. How many more survivors are out there? How many survivors are lurking in the shadows, keeping quiet—because they were told to or feel they have to—without anyone or anything to turn to?" She let the question hang in the air. "I don't want any more survivors. I don't want Hope Cottage to have to build another building. The abuse of children has *got to stop*, and it has to stop *now*." The crowd applauded.

"Underneath each seat, you should have a box." Layla waited while the crowd pulled out leather cords with angel wing pendants. She held up hers. "I've had this for as long as I can remember. It was a gift from my father. He told me to always wear it and not to take it off unless you give it to someone you love. A long time ago, I gave it to my husband, Gage. A while back when I was sick, he placed it back around my neck, and when our little one is born, we'll give it to her together. Every girl who comes to Hope Cottage will receive one, to remind them that she has her own angel, that she is an angel, that there are angels looking out for all of us. Go ahead and put yours on. Share it with someone you love. We all need a little help. We all need a little hope."

Layla stepped back to a standing ovation, and Gage met her on-stage, tears in his eyes. She rested her head on his chest, his heartbeat the only noise she could hear. Everything else was quiet. Being quiet was no longer the enemy, the thing her half-brother demanded, the thing that kept her imprisoned. It was now her friend, her peace, the thing she wanted more than anything else in the world. To rest quietly in a man's arms was home.

ACKNOWLEDGEMENTS

Many thanks to the makers of Jack Daniel's because this book would not have seen the light of day without it. More importantly, many thanks to my dear husband for his tireless support and encouragement. Also thanks to my children for their patience and good listening when I told them not to read over my shoulder. A huge shout out to my sister, Kathy, and childhood friend, Dani Lee, for their helpful feedback and encouraging words. Thank you to Laura Hidalgo at Book Fabulous Designs for my wonderful cover, which I just love. Thank you to Scandalicious Book Reviews for their support since the beginning. Lastly, thank you to everyone who read my first two books, *First Position* and *Perfectly Broken*. I am very grateful and moved by the response both books have received. Thank you!

ABOUT THE AUTHOR

PRESCOTT LANE is originally from Little Rock, Arkansas, and graduated from Centenary College in 1997 with a degree in sociology. She went on to Tulane University to receive her MSW in 1998, after which she worked with developmentally delayed and disabled children. She currently lives in New Orleans with her husband, two children, and two dogs. She is also the author of *First Position* and *Perfectly Broken*. Contact her at any of the following:

www.authorprescottlane.com
facebook.com/PrescottLane1
twitter.com/prescottlane1
instagram.com/prescottlane1
pinterest.com/PrescottLane1

47633488R00164

Made in the USA
Lexington, KY
10 December 2015